PRAISE FOR MINA AND THE SLAYERS:

'Mina is back with bite in this action-packed romp of a sequel.
It was absolute, murderous fun to travel with her through the
gothic atmosphere of vampire-loving 90s New Orleans.'
KENDARE BLAKE

'*Buffy* meets *Scream* in this high-stakes rush through
a darkly atmospheric 90s New Orleans.'
M.A. KUZNIAR

'I couldn't wait to sink my fangs into this book
and I wasn't disappointed. It leaves you gasping
for more and never knowing who to trust.'
CYNTHIA MURPHY

'A fiendishly good sequel, brimming with 90s pop culture,
smooth Southern vampires and a body count to rival *Buffy*.'
KAT ELLIS

'Amy McCaw's much-anticipated sequel is
everything a discerning h
With added 90s US
SUE WA

*For the booksellers and online book community
who made this sequel possible*

Mina and the Slayers is a uclanpublishing book

First published in Great Britain in 2022 by
uclanpublishing
University of Central Lancashire
Preston, PR1 2HE, UK

978-1-912979-91-2

1 3 5 7 9 10 8 6 4 2

Set in 10/16pt Kingfisher by Becky Chilcott.

A CIP catalogue record for this book is available from the British Library.

Printed and bound in Great Britain by Clays Ltd, Elcograf S.p.A.

Amy McCaw

MINA

and the Slayers

uclanpublishing

Chapter 1

Halloween has always been my favourite time of year. I'd spent my childhood in Whitby running around dressed as a tiny vampire and only bit one boy who really deserved it. Knowing vampires were real now gave those fanged, caped kids roaming New Orleans a whole new slant.

My first Halloween in the city was a few days away, but for now I was stuck in school. My English teacher, Ms. Kimble, was dutifully setting homework, her eyes magnified behind tortoiseshell glasses. I wasn't the only one clock watching. In a few minutes, fall break would begin: a whole week to appreciate spooky season and, in my case, to squeeze in some work experience with the police.

I'd had such high hopes for Fang Fest when I arrived in New Orleans this summer, and that had ended in blood and death. I slid the brown leather cuff down over the faded bite marks on my wrist. After the stares at school, I'd taken to wearing it and blaming my non-existent dog. Halloween would be different. I was so engrossed in memories that the bell caught me off guard.

My classmates scrambled for the door, voices raised in excited conversations. Nat appeared, her shoulder-length brown waves and black skull dress immaculate after a long day. A roll of toilet paper arced across our path, unravelling like a crisp new bandage.

"Let's get out of here!" she said.

She hooked her arm into mine and dragged me into the corridor, my backpack weighing down one shoulder. We'd already emptied our lockers, and I was glad of Nat's foresight. The corridor was chaos. Silly string shot into the air, landing on heads with accompanying squeals. More toilet roll arced through the air, getting tangled in a 'Go Vipers' banner.

A bloody-mouthed vampire lunged in front of me, fangs bared and clawed hands raised. I flinched back, pressing against the nearest locker as my arm fell away from Nat's. For a second, the bustling hallway blurred with the cell where John Carter had trapped me and Libby, using his frightening vampire abilities to control our actions. John was dead now, his murder spree ending with his life. His ruthless accomplice, Veronica, was unfortunately still undead – location unknown.

A girl with short, curly hair peeled back the rubbery vampire mask and grinned. "Happy Halloween!"

"Back off!" Nat said to the girl. She looped her arm through mine again and pulled us into the flow of people. I tried to ground myself in the loud conversations and clamour to escape. On the other side of the corridor, someone shook up a bottle of coke and unleashed the foam.

"Are you all right?" Nat asked, leaning close enough for me to hear.

"I'll manage," I said. "I think I'm still jumpy … after this summer."

"Let me know if you want to talk about what happened," she said, as someone jostled her against me.

"I will – thanks." Nat knew Libby had been arrested and that we'd been through a hard time, but that was all. Even though she was the best friend I'd made at school, I wasn't planning to unload the truth on her, especially not in a crowded hallway.

It was hard not to get carried away by the shared elation around me. Principal Cutter glared disapprovingly by the exit, unmoved by his students' excitement. He caught me looking and the glare intensified, along with extreme *Demon Headmaster* vibes. He took off after a short, skinny guy blasting 'Bad Reputation' from a Boombox.

The fresh air outside lifted the sleepy stuffiness of the classroom. Brown leaves crunched underfoot as we jogged down the front steps, but the obnoxious growl of a motorbike drowned everything out. I guessed who we'd see from Nat's descriptions. We'd fallen hard and fast into friendship over the past few weeks after we discovered a shared love of scary movies, so I hadn't met Nat's elusive half-brother yet. He was on break from college, so this had to be him.

Nat sighed as the motorbike pulled up in front of us. "One day he'll listen to me."

Will had the same colouring as Nat: golden brown skin

and glossy brown hair that hung over one eye and brushed his collarbone. He was slimmer and shorter than my boyfriend, Jared, with a sharp jawline and cheekbones. There was no helmet in sight, but he was wearing a long black jacket. It probably looked very cool flying out behind him when he rode, without the same safety benefits. "You must be Mina," he said, pushing his hair behind one ear. A cigarette was tucked there – his deadly habits were stacking up.

"Hi Will," I said. "Nice to finally meet you."

"I only got back from college a few days ago." He raised an already arched eyebrow at me. "Nice accent. Nats didn't mention you were British." He frowned at the back of his bike, brows sinking low. "I don't think there's room for two of you. Hop on – Nats can walk."

"I'm confused – I'm getting a ride because I'm British?" I asked, drawing a laugh from him.

"*Nats* told you she didn't need a ride today," she cut in. "I'm headin' to Fanged Friends with Mina."

Will shrugged, unconcerned. He flipped up the collar of his coat, touching an index finger to his eyebrow in a quick salute. "I'll see if Sammyboy wants a ride then."

Nat checked her watch. "He'll be another hour at AV club. Plenty of time for you to remember he hates when you call him that."

"Guess I'll go for a ride 'til then. Catch you later." He released the kickstand with one clompy boot and peeled off.

We watched him go. Nat's other brother, Sam, was quiet and bookish. Even though he was almost a year younger, we were all in the same year at school. He and I were a lot alike, particularly in contrast with our fun but spiky sisters. Will was an unknown entity.

Nat folded her arms as we set off walking. Expressive eyebrows must have been a family trait. One of hers was raised in an accusing V. "Not you too!"

"Not me what?"

"Don't give me that innocent face. As my friend and possessor of your own cute guy, you're supposed to be immune to my brother."

"Sorry – I'm only human. You know I'm dating Jared, anyway." Human was a word that no longer applied to him. I could never tell Nat that John Carter had kidnapped Jared and turned him, forever changing our relationship. "I'm not the one with a crush on a police officer almost ten years older than me."

I closed my eyes against Nat's outrage for a moment, letting the sunshine warm my face. It was much more bearable without the mugginess of summer. "Excuse me," Nat said, "but he's a *detective.*"

"And that makes a difference?" I teased. We paused by a window with a display of Halloween lollipops: witches' hats, spiders and pumpkins. Bat fairy lights blinked among the tangle of plants in the spiral-patterned balcony above us.

"It's all about the suits," she said. "Maybe 'cause I saw him on TV too, talking about that case . . ." She trailed off, her gaze flashing to me. Cafferty and Boudreaux had both got a lot of screen time over the Fang Fest Fiend, and Nat had heard about the case before we were even friends. She returned to less distressing subjects. "Detective Cafferty can investigate me any day. Anyhow, you're the one givin' up your fall break to work with him."

We advanced into the French Quarter, passing a home with a red door that contrasted against the pale turquoise of its battered shutters. Lanterns hung under the balcony cast an orange glow against loops of thin, black fabric with fuzzy spiders nestled among them.

"Not because I have a crush on the hot police detective," I said. "I choose to use my powers for good instead of evil."

"But you admit that he's hot. Interesting . . ."

I laughed without much feeling. My opinion of Cafferty was complicated. He'd agreed to let me do work experience with him, but he was also one of the detectives who'd falsely accused my sister of the murders John Carter had committed. It wasn't Cafferty's fault. John had gone to great lengths to set Libby up, wrongly assuming our mum would find out and come running back to him. "We've got less than a year left at school, and I need to figure out what to do with my life," I said. "This feels sort of . . . right."

"Then who am I to mock? You follow those dreams, girl."

"I'm working on it – one unpaid job at a time," I said.

I'd never dreamed of being a police officer, but I wasn't going to sit back and let my life fall apart again. Learning self-defence with Della was a good start, but I wanted to help people put their lives back together. I'd convinced Cafferty to let me do work experience, and he'd got his superiors to sign off on it. He thought I had potential after the work I'd done to prove Libby's innocence.

Nat bumped her shoulder against me, smiling. Things were so easy between us. I'd gravitated to her because she had the same giving-zero-craps attitude as Libby, minus the sister angst. Her family was as dysfunctional as ours, with a side of tragedy. Her older sister, Louisa, had died not long ago, my worst nightmare made real, and her dad had left when she was little. We had that in common. Will was his son, but he'd left him behind with his stepmum – Nat, Sam and Louisa's mum. When it turned out her family had a killer VHS collection, it cemented the friendship.

"I heard something that sucks today," Nat said.

"And you feel the need to share it?"

Nat shrugged, her smile wicked. "I know you. Now I've said that, you want me to tell you."

She was right – she'd woken the inquisitiveness that had landed me in trouble on occasion.

"You got me."

"So this girl Laurel Jenkins, who graduated last year? She was found dead on her street two nights ago."

Chapter 2

"**S**eriously?" I asked. The story of a murdered girl once would've filled me with a dark, guilty need to know more. But I'd faced a real killer and narrowly survived joining the ranks of his victims.

If Nat was disappointed at my lacklustre response, she kept it to herself. "Someone stabbed her over and over again – I hear it was pretty gnarly. They didn't find the guy yet."

"Well, I hope they do."

We arrived at Fanged Friends, bringing a welcome end to the discussion. The shop had a hand-carved sign that displayed its name between an open pair of fangs. A sticker on the door advertised the Halloween sale, and the shop was getting busy.

The red velvet walls were crammed with Gothic clothing and vampire toys. They had everything from a vampire Mickey Mouse and Countess Barbie to a furry lilac unicorn, its fangs dripping fluffy red blood. 'Gangsta's Paradise' was playing over the hum of chatting voices.

For Halloween, the shop had continued the fanged theme. A white paper chain of vampire fangs was strung from corner to corner. A Halloween tree stood in the corner: a black branch decorated with figurines of movie vampires. The owner, Emmeline, had set up a stand of spooky sweets where you could help yourself to pick-and-mix. We scooped gummy worms, pink fangs and jelly spiders into white paper bags and left a dollar apiece in a dish shaped like a staring eyeball.

Emmeline smiled approvingly from behind the counter. Her grey afro looked especially voluminous, and she'd dyed one curl at the front a vibrant green. "I wish everyone that came in here was like you two." Other customers swirled around us, but none seemed particularly offended.

"See?" Nat said. "I told you we were her favourites."

"You do spend your wages here every week," I said. Nat's weekend job at the mall paid well, but the money never lasted.

"Mina has you there," Emmeline said.

Nat was drawn to a rack of Gothic dresses, and I approached the counter. "How are you?" I asked. I'd met Emmeline at Thandie's beautifully chaotic jazz funeral. We'd bonded over our lost friend and got talking about Emmeline's shop. It'd become clear that Emmeline knew Thandie was a vampire and that John Carter and Veronica had ended her life.

Emmeline's smile was pained. "I'm OK. Being without my best friend . . . It's hard. I couldn't see her all that often, but she was always at the end of the phone. How's that sister of yours doin'?"

"Keeping busy," I said. Though that was Libby's way of dealing, it couldn't last. Thandie had left her business, the Mansion of the Macabre, to Libby in her will. We'd both already worked there doing the greatest job on Earth – scaring people in a horror movie experience. "She's pretty stressed about the mansion. Did Thandie ever talk to you about struggling with the business?"

"Not in person," Emmeline said, casting her gaze upwards while she thought it over, "but I might have somethin' for you. I'll be right back."

I'd only scanned one shelf of jewelled earrings when Emmeline was back with a black leather folder. A pile of letters was tucked inside, the paper yellowing and old. I recognised the spidery handwriting before Emmeline explained, "Thandie sent me these. She didn't always get out much." Emmeline paused with a sad smile. We both knew the Carter brothers had frightened her into staying at home. "We often communicated by letter. I've picked some out from around the time Thandie was setting up the business. She'd want to help you girls."

"Thank you," I said, putting the folder in my bag. Business had declined ever since Thandie had died. The mansion wasn't the same without her, but hopefully these would help.

"Best not to flash those around," Emmeline said, glancing at Nat and the other customers. "She mentions . . . private things."

"Understood," I said. Thandie had kept her vampire identity secret. I wouldn't expose what she was after her death, and potentially the rest of them along with her.

"What do you two think of this?" Nat reappeared, holding up a black dress with a round, white collar. "Is it too Wednesday Addams?"

"It's expensive, so I'm all for you buyin' it," Emmeline said. "But also? It's real cute."

"I'm with Emmeline – I think it's just Wednesday Addams enough," I said. "But are you sure you can wear it in the heat?"

"We do get winter, you know," she said, draping it over her arm. Her idea of winter was probably very different from mine. October here felt more like summer in Whitby.

I checked the price tag on a black leather jacket. My meagre salary from the mansion would never cover it. I'd have to work on my Buffy wardrobe elsewhere.

Vampire costumes were hung alongside a shelf of accessories. They had wax fangs that moulded to your teeth, fake blood and white face paint. A shelf of rubber masks featured vampire greats from Christopher Lee to the *Sesame Street* puppet Count von Count. I ran my hand down a plastic cape. Jared wouldn't be caught dead in it.

"You should convince Libby to make the cape part of Jared's costume," Nat said. "I'd pay extra to see that."

I abandoned the vampire gear, glad Nat didn't know why I was drawn to it. "He'd kill me," I said – poor choice of words.

"So when am I going to meet the elusive Jared?"

"You've met him," I said, pretending to examine the nearest rack of clothing. I'd not been intentionally keeping them apart, but I may have been doing it subconsciously. How was I supposed to explain my lurking, increasingly pale boyfriend who was reluctant to kiss me?

In the two minutes that my back was turned, Nat had filled her arms with clothes. I joined her in the fitting room queue. "I'm waiting for you to set me up with one of his hot friends," she said.

"If I find one, I'll let you know." I answered easily enough, but the truth was a snarled mess. His clever, artistic and entirely deceitful best friend was dead. Thinking of Lucas brought a fresh swell of grief.

Reaching the front of the queue, Nat ducked into the fitting room, swishing the black velvet curtain shut. "You'd better," she called.

Minutes later, Nat pushed the curtain back. She was wearing shredded black jeans held together with safety pins and a grey vest top with a sparkly black raven on it. "Survey says?"

"You look ace!"

We chatted over creamy pumpkin pastries and then parted ways. I headed to the start of Jared's first ever haunted city tour. The temperature had dipped with the fading light, and I curved my hands around my to-go cup of tea. I paused by a window featuring a beige squash carved with the *Jaws* shark's gaping mouth, the cut edges painted red.

It was a pretty macabre sight to remind me of my dad, but he'd always been into Halloween. Being American, he gave us the best of both traditions: homemade costumes, bowls overflowing with candycorn, an obstacle course of ghoulish decorations and trick-or-treating. Dad had a lot of shortcomings, but we were able to forget about them for one night.

Despite the vampire obsession, Mum had no interest in plastic fangs and fake blood. For her, vampires were tied to the scar on her neck and everything that represented. She'd got her wish since then and become one of them.

I passed Jared's apartment building not far from where his tour group would be waiting. He'd got the new place because living around humans wasn't an option yet. He'd been seriously down about having to put his nursing degree on hold – he wanted nothing more than to heal people. Instead, he'd settled for his second love of the macabre and set up a tour to fit around his mansion job. Jared was a master at telling creepy stories, but I was nervous for him. I wanted it to go well.

I was a few minutes early, so I found a bench and took out one of Thandie's letters. The fragile paper was covered with Thandie's dense, scrawling handwriting.

Dear Emm,

Thank you for your latest package of tea. I'm sorry I haven't been able to visit the store. Lately, I've felt the prickle that suggests the brothers are near, and I can't risk it.

I've finally decided what to do with this place. It's much too big for just me, and my idea will allow me to use my power and generate an income. I think Mother would have liked that. Do you recall when you dragged me to the movie theatre, assuring me that the Carter brothers would be unlikely to show up there? I had such fun toying with the audience's emotions, amplifying their joy at the humour and shaping their terror into exhilaration.

I've decided to use that ability to create a tourist attraction like New Orleans has never seen. I plan to create an experience where people can face their fears in immersive scenes from horror movies, giving them a rush they'll never forget. I've designed sets for some favourites: *The Exorcist*, *The Amityville Horror*, *Carrie* and *Halloween*. *Salem's Lot* is a little too close to home, and I've yet to finalise how I could create an *Alien* room. I hope you'll visit when it's completed.

I think I'll also display my collection of gruesome local artefacts in an exhibition of sorts. I'm sure some people will enjoy them as much as I do. You can't blame me for the fascination — I am part of one of those legends, after all.

I must go. The Exorcist vomit is causing me some difficulty. Perhaps you can suggest a natural dye to give it that distinctive pea-green shade?

Yours,
Thandie

This changed everything. We weren't failing Thandie – we were pulling in fewer customers without her power.

Chapter 3

I put Thandie's letter back into the folder, unsure of how Libby would respond to facing Thandie's memory head-on.

Libby and Della were coming from the opposite direction, their hands clasped and swinging between them. It was a rare opportunity to observe them: my small, slight sister with wild brown hair as big as her personality and olive skin like mine. Della was tall and athletically built, her skin a velvety dark brown and thin braids of hair falling over her beaming face.

I walked over to join them by a cluster of black-clad teens. They were waiting by the cast-iron lamp post on the corner. Libby hugged me and inhaled deeply. She gasped. "You pumpkin spiced without me!"

"It was just a pastry! I only did it once," I said, holding my hands up.

She couldn't keep up the outrage, and her eyes were gleaming. "That's once too often!"

"There's a fine line between cute and annoyin'," Della said, "and you two just about make it over."

"Aww," Libby rested her head on Della's shoulder. "Wait – which side of the line?"

Della shrugged, her expression playful.

While the mood was light, I decided to broach the subject of Thandie. "Emmeline at Fanged Friends found some of Thandie's letters – I thought . . ."

I stopped talking at the shake of Libby's head. "Can we not do this now? Jared's tour will be starting any minute."

Lately, I'd been trying not to let her get away with her old avoidance tricks, but I wasn't about to make a scene before Jared's first tour.

Under the streetlight, he was talking to a lean white man with neat brown hair and nervous body language: his gaze never settling and hands constantly on the move. I wished I could hear what they were saying.

Jared was wearing one of the T-shirts Lucas had made before he died: a hand-painted Christian Slater from *Pump up the Volume*, with the slogan 'Talk hard' written in neat block print. My stomach twisted at the thought of Lucas. Even after his betrayal, helping John Carter torment and nearly kill us, I was broken up that he'd died.

The man finished whatever he had to say to Jared, retreating to stand behind the other guests. He had a notepad and pen in his hand as if he was planning to make notes about the tour.

Jared gave me a small smile, pushing back his dark curls. They sprang back into place, more dishevelled than before. I remembered the first night I met him at the mansion: the Lestat costume with its gaping neckline, tight leather trousers and his lips painted red. Their sticky softness had brushed my neck when he pretended to bite me. That was before he became a vampire and bit me for real. "Later," he mouthed, and I liked to think that meant I'd get the full story about the mystery tour guest.

We stayed back so the paying customers wouldn't think Jared's groupies were tagging along.

Apart from the man with the notebook who'd approached Jared, the rest were young women, most of whom were eying Jared with interest. If they wanted to admire him while getting their ghost stories fix, it was fine with me. I was about to do the same thing. Fortunately, I wasn't the jealous type. The thought of Jared feeding on strangers to get the blood he needed was a different story.

He did a head count, and I tried to see him how the tour group did, beyond his height and lean muscle. The obvious things hadn't changed, but he was different. He once would've been fiddling with the leather cord at his wrist or spinning the chunky silver ring around his thumb. Instead of energy crackling off him, he was still and composed, with everything turned inwards. The streetlight accentuated the slightly pallid appearance of his bronze skin, but the fangs that would've revealed him were tucked away in his gums.

"Thank you all for coming," he called, so clear and assured that he didn't have to be loud. That deep, Hawaiian-tinged voice still sent a thrill through me. "Tonight, I'm gonna take you on a tour of the darker side of New Orleans. We'll talk ghosts, voodoo, witches and, of course, vampires."

Libby coughed loudly, and Della jabbed an elbow into her ribs.

Excited whispers rippled through the crowd, and I was there with them. He was made for this – even better at storytelling than before. He'd always been mesmerising as Lestat, but with no costume it was all him: more confidence and allure, plus a hint of darkness. "Follow me to our first location."

We trailed after Jared with the tour group. Only the man remained apart, scribbling in his notebook.

"Jared's good at this," Della said grudgingly.

"Shh, they'll hear you," I said, gesturing at the giddy group ahead of us.

"Sorry. I mean, he's great!" she said louder, all fake cheer and brittle grin. I couldn't blame her. Della's mum had been murdered years before, the injuries suggesting a vampire was responsible. Since we found out vampires were real, Della's hatred extended to all of them. Her friendship with Jared had disintegrated into mistrust and distaste for what he was, even though it hadn't been his choice.

After walking for a few minutes, Jared stopped us on the corner of Bourbon and St. Philip Street, gesturing at a business across the road. "This is Lafitte's Blacksmith Shop, but it's actually a bar if you wanna come back later – one of the oldest in the country."

It was an unusual building: red bricks with a sloping grey roof that had two shuttered windows cut into it. The windows were covered in wire mesh, and the wooden doors were open to let out the bar noise of voices and live rock music. Plastic skeletons were set up in the windows, beer bottles taped to their hands. Tourists milled around us, drinks in hands and smiles on their faces.

Jared raised his voice to be heard over them. "There are some good stories about this bar. In the late 1700s, it was allegedly used by the infamous pirate brothers, Pierre and Jean Lafitte, as a front for their smuggling operation." Some bones in Thandie's museum at the mansion had allegedly come from Jean Lafitte's trigger finger. "People claim to have seen the ghost of Jean Lafitte roaming his bar, unwinding there after death. Some believe the brothers buried their treasure under a fireplace in the basement, but I wouldn't recommend trying to steal it. If you dare to gaze into the fireplace, legend has it that a pair of angry red eyes appears." He paused for the ripple of whispers and nervous laughter. "Let's head to the next spot."

Jared talked as we walked, pointing out a shop once owned by a voodoo priestess and a hotel where Civil War ghosts were meant to have lingered. I let Jared's familiar stories of the Axeman and Madame LaLaurie wash over me. I tuned back in when we reached a new location.

"An eccentric billionaire called Jacques Saint Germain lived there a century ago," Jared said, pointing out a tall brick house on the corner, its balconies threaded with gnarled broomsticks and strewn with crumpled black witches' hats. Lacy black arches made a repeating pattern around the first floor, and a hanging basket of ferns left a splash of green in each archway.

"Saint Germain was known for staying up all night and throwing amazing parties, offering fine food and *plenty* of entertainment." Jared paused, catching my eye as he waggled his eyebrows. It was comforting to get reminders that he was still Jared.

"Saint Germain's guests found him more entertaining than any show. He told them stories of his escapades all over the world, from Egypt to his homeland of France. But how could he have lived through world events centuries apart?"

Jared let the question hang, his tour group's whispers filling the space. A lot of the girls were mesmerised – I'd been the same when I'd first heard Jared's stories. The man observing the tour was writing furiously, flipping pages as he scrawled.

Jared went on, oblivious. "His stories only became more outlandish. One night, he confessed that he was a descendent of the Comte de Saint Germain, a friend of King Louis during the 18th century. His party guests noted that he did look rather like portraits of the comte . . . They didn't put together that in paintings, the comte was never painted to be any older than forty, the same age as Jacques Saint Germain.

Rumours spread that they were one and the same person. After all, Jacques never ate the lavish foods at his parties, only sipping from a metal goblet. There were ways of living forever, if you were prepared to drink blood like a cursed thing." Jared's mouth formed a wry smile that brought a dark gleam to his eyes.

"A woman hurried into the police station one night. She'd leaped from Saint Germain's balcony after he tried to bite her neck. They went to question him, but he was gone. Inside his famed goblet, the police found traces of blood. His large collection of wine bottles contained the expensive wine you'd expect, mixed with large quantities of human blood.

If the story ended there, that would've been good enough, right? There's more. A musician in the 70s called Richard Chanfray claimed to be the infamous count, and that he'd lain low all that time. Not a lot of people believed him. But isn't that exactly what a vampire would want you to think?"

Jared's grin exposed a lot of very white, even teeth. "Come with me to the last location."

Chapter 4

The rest of the tour group ambled behind Jared as the man with a notebook scuttled up to him, talking earnestly.

I followed closely, trying to listen to them instead of Libby and Della. I could hardly pick anything out, beyond 'party' and 'stories'. The man handed some ivory envelopes to Jared and rushed away.

I pounced on Jared. "Who was that?"

Jared looked down at the envelopes. "He works for a guy called Claude Sejour. They're looking for a tour guide, and he liked what he heard. I just got us invited to an awesome event. All I have to do is tell some New Orleans ghost stories there."

"Like a party?" Libby asked, she and Della coming up beside us. It only took a hint at fun to summon my sister.

"The Orchard Estate ball," he said, "and I scored four extra tickets."

"Yes!" Libby said, grabbing the envelopes and fanning them out greedily in front of her face.

"Orchard Estate?" I asked. "Why does that sound familiar?"

"It's only the most exclusive Halloween celebration in the city," Libby said.

Della picked up her explanation. "People say if you even make it onto the waiting list, it's your grandchildren that get to go." Her eyes were bright with excitement.

"They've also filmed a bunch of movies there," Jared said.

I wanted to learn more, but then I recognised the last tour location. Jared had warned us about this, and Libby tucked into my side in preparation, hanging onto my arm. He'd included this story on the tour as a way of exorcising his demons, but I wouldn't want to talk about the mythical vampire who had turned out to be a real-life serial killer. The vampire who made Jared like him.

The area around John and Wayne Carter's old apartment was quiet and dark. This community had no Halloween decorations – only the ghosts of traumatic memories waiting to ensnare us. There was a sinister hush and no signs of the living. The nightmarish events that happened here had seeped into the place.

Jared led us into a circle of light from the single working street lamp. The apartment building was in as bad a state of repair as when we'd been inside, thinking we were having a great time on the Horror Quest. Instead, we'd wandered into John Carter's game. One of his minions had stabbed Lucas as part of his plan to set

Libby up for murder, in the same apartment where John and his brother had once kept the victims they fed on in the 1930s.

While I'd replayed those devastating events, Jared had almost finished the story. His relaxed, jovial air had gone as he rattled through what the brothers did back then and how the police captured them because one brave girl escaped: Thandie. He was too close to this story for his usual charming, relaxed manner of telling his tales.

With the magic of Jared's storytelling lost, the tour group were growing restless, whispering over him. They didn't know the part Thandie had played in our lives, or that John Carter had found her in the 1970s and left her for dead as punishment for turning them in to the police. Wayne had taken pity, changing her into a vampire, but she'd lived in constant paranoia that they'd come back to finish her. Thandie's only joy had come from the Mansion of the Macabre where John and Veronica had eventually murdered her on the last night of Fang Fest. We'd found Veronica standing over Thandie, a stake driven deep into her chest. Veronica's blonde hair had been spattered with blood, and she would've used her mallet to kill us if John hadn't wanted us alive for more mind games.

Libby wrapped her arm around my waist, grieving alongside me. The vanilla and hairspray scent of her was comforting, reminding me we had to go on. I was finally with my sister, and the only direction we had left was forward.

Jared went on, finding his groove with the story. "The brothers were entombed in St. Louis Cemetery No. 1. Their tomb was opened a year and a day after their execution to inter another family member. But their bodies were gone." Jared's charm had returned, and the tour group were mesmerised again. I fixed on his handsome face, the strong lines of his jaw and brow bone and eyes that usually shifted from hazel to green, depending on the light. Right now, they were shadowed and dark. "Many people have seen the brothers since. If you look up on a balcony or down an alley, you might catch a glimpse. Just don't approach them, unless you want to become a part of their story . . . or their dinner."

The tour group's laughter broke the spell of his words, and he grinned. "Thank you all for coming. I—"

A shriek cut him off as someone came running towards the tour group, their silhouette wild haired in the darkness.

Jared's audience let out delighted shrieks as the figure burst among them, illuminated by the streetlamp's pool of light. They couldn't have known that this wasn't part of the tour.

It was a vampire, bloody mouthed and eyes full of animalistic blood lust. Her black hair was a tangle around her face, and she was dressed in layers of black. She let out a raucous laugh, snapping her crimson teeth towards some of the girls. They shrieked, clinging to one another.

The horrible moment stretched on, filled with potential bloodshed. The vampire hesitated, her glistening black eyes scanning the group and wet tongue flicking between bloody lips. The girls clung to each other, squealing and laughing. They should've been running, putting as much distance between themselves and the vampire as possible.

Libby, Della and Jared were frozen on one side of the crowd, and I'd ended up on the other. We knew what we were facing, but that didn't make it clear what to do, surrounded as we were by onlookers and possible victims.

The vampire moved so fast that I took a beat to realise she was coming towards me, the easy target on the fringe of the crowd. She grabbed my coat and yanked me towards her open, bloody mouth.

I fought and twisted, but the vampire held on. Della had taught me moves to counter a grab, but nothing worked. I even gripped the root of the vampire's thumb, and she kept pulling on my jacket. That red mouth strained closer, breathing the metallic stink of decay into my face. More motivated than ever, I tried twisting under the vampire's arm, and she let go with a tearing sound.

The tour group weren't making it easy, cheering and jostling to get a better look, still believing this was part of the act. Jared and Della finally made it round to me. Perhaps sensing she was outnumbered, the vampire took off across the deserted road. Jared and Della gave chase. I was about to follow, when Libby put a hand on my arm. "Show's over!" she called out to the group. "Be sure to tell your friends!"

They drifted away, some looking disappointed that they weren't about to get more Jared time. They had no idea that death had stepped among them and decided today wasn't their day.

Jared took off down a shadowed space between two boarded-up restaurants. Della hesitated in the mouth of the alleyway as Libby and I caught up. She'd proven herself capable of taking down a badass vampire, but she wouldn't leave me and Libby with a creature like that running loose.

Metal fire-escape stairs snaked up the sides of the buildings, but the street level was pitch black. There was an eye-watering stench of rotting food. I heard Jared's running feet and nothing else.

"Do you see anything?" Della asked, angling herself in front of me and Libby.

"Nope," Libby said, the sleeve of her shirt muffling her speech as she pressed it over her nose. "But the smell makes up for it."

Jared could take care of himself, but I hated the thought of him running straight into trouble. That vampire had got way too close, and it hadn't mattered that I'd been surrounded by people. I'd always felt protected by crowds, safe in the belief that vampires wanted to keep their secret.

That was when Jared's anguished yell tore through the night.

Chapter 5

"That's enough," Della said, launching herself into the alleyway. Apparently, she didn't hate what Jared was enough to let him die.

I tried to go after her, and again Libby stopped me. "Please," she said, squeezing my arm. "Don't leave me out here."

Resentful, I stayed. Della had Jared's back, and I had my sister's. The basic self-defence moves we'd been learning from Della wouldn't get us very far. I cycled through scenarios while we waited – the creature grabbing a shard of wood and taking its chances, Jared bleeding out on the ground . . . Jared was stronger as a vampire but not invincible. If he didn't come out soon, I was going in there, rotten stench and monsters be damned.

The entrance to the alleyway gaped in front of us, black and menacing. Anything could have waited in the shadows, ready to leap out and latch onto our throats. Or reach out a clawed hand and drag us into the darkness.

Della's footsteps had fallen silent. I stepped backwards, pulling Libby with me – not that it would've made much difference to a vampire in pursuit.

"He's OK," Della called.

The sound of jogging feet accompanied the dizzying pace of my pulse. Then they emerged from the alleyway.

"Little shit bit me and ran off." Jared held up his bleeding forearm for us to see.

"Vampires bite vampires? Now I've heard everything." That was as much sympathy as he'd get from Libby.

I reached for him but let my hand fall. The wound had closed in a jagged bite mark, surrounded by a fringe of clotting, but I couldn't risk touching vampire blood. I wasn't sure how much it would take to turn, and I wasn't prepared to find out.

"It looked like that . . . *thing* had bitten someone before it got to us. How do we help them?" Della asked.

Jared shook his head, acting like he'd missed her wording choices. "They could be anywhere, and there's no blood trail." That wasn't the encouraging statement he thought it was.

"Let's take a look around," I said, and we set off down the empty road, checking down a side street.

"What was it doing running round like that?" Della asked.

"I don't know," I said. "Isn't the whole point that no one knows about vampires? That wasn't normal."

"I think we left normal behind a while back," Jared said.

"We're never going to find the person that got attacked," Libby said. "Let's get to the movies. I don't think we should be out on the streets tonight."

"Fine with me," I said. It was one thing to hang out with Jared, who had some control. With her snarling mouth and wildness, the vampire had seemed more animal than human.

Jared raised his bloody arm. "I should clean this up. Mind if we stop by my apartment on the way to the movie theatre?"

I answered into the uneasy silence. "Sure."

Libby pointed at me. "It murdered your coat."

I needed that Buffy jacket from Fanged Friends more than ever. The thin denim along my left shoulder had come apart at the seam. More unsettling were the frayed holes left by brutally sharp fingernails. How close had the vampire come to hitting flesh? In a way, it was lucky she'd grabbed me rather than one of the unsuspecting tour guests. At least Della had given me some training. Della and Libby went off, talking about our near miss.

Left with my vampire, I assessed the clues. He was smiling, not too pale and there was no edgy agitation that meant he needed to feed. We were outside, so he wasn't confined with my tasty blood smell.

He let me make the first move. I advanced slowly, and he laughed. "I'm not going to bite."

I smiled at him without real warmth. I trusted him – of course I did or I wouldn't have been here. But there was a hint of doubt. He'd bitten me before, and I wanted to avoid repeating that for both of our sakes.

After the vampire encounter, I wanted to press against Jared with his arms closed around me and kiss him until I forgot about her. But he was a vampire – a step away from being like her if I pushed him too hard.

We moved at the same time, meeting in a quick, awkward hug. He was so tall that his head cleared mine easily. I buried my face in his chest, breathing him in. He smelled of salt and metal instead of fresh, green things like he once did.

Jared pulled away. "I don't want to get my crusty blood all over you." He spoke casually enough, but his mournful expression told the truth. We needed each other, craving the intimacy we'd once shared, but we couldn't have it.

We set off side by side, close but not touching. "I know new vampires have no impulse control," I said. The memory of Jared's face loomed in my mind, red-eyed and remorseless as he'd latched onto my arm. "But that seemed . . . weird. Have you ever heard of a vampire taking on a crowd of humans? Or attacking another vampire?"

"Not as a rule," he said. "Usually, a vampire's sire is on hand for a while to keep them in check. There's a fail-safe to keep them close. Remember Thandie told us the new vampire gets excruciating headaches if their sire leaves town? Anyway, it's in both of their interests to make sure vampires don't get exposed."

Jared never had a sire's support. John turned him and dumped him in a hole for us to find. I had no response to that.

After a while, Jared started humming 'Come as You Are'. He noticed me watching him. "What's up?"

"I just heard you humming the second greatest Nirvana song."

As the streets became busier and less seedy around us, we debated the pros and cons of our favourite songs. I was obviously on the right side with 'Smells like Teen Spirit'.

In the bustling street outside Jared's apartment, Armand stood out, even though he'd prefer otherwise. His height and build were pretty average, and his hair was a medium brown now the black was growing out. But there was a quality about him that demanded notice, much like his brother, John Carter. I couldn't think of Armand as Wayne Carter, and he seemed happy about that. He looked different enough from his brother that I could pretend, except for the brilliant blue eyes.

Libby slowed down to ask loudly, "What's *he* doing at your apartment?"

Armand approached slowly, eying all of us with caution – particularly Libby. "Are you free tonight?"

"I can be," Jared said.

"Are you all well?" Armand asked, his eyes passing over us and landing on me.

"We're fine," I said, which was true on the new scale we lived by. The vampire had left without biting or turning any of us, so that was a win.

"Good," he said, nodding thoughtfully. It was unnerving to be around him knowing his abilities were real, if unreliable. Could he read what I was thinking, or see into my past or future? From how he'd explained it, close proximity made it easier to use his power. When we first met, he'd accurately predicted that I'd encounter tragedy in an attic. He'd also warned Jared about death and healing, though I wasn't sure if that referred to him ending up as a vampire or his desire to become a nurse.

"See you later." Jared kissed me, a fleeting graze of his lips across my cheekbone. Then he walked off with Armand, leaving his injured arm as it was.

"Shall we try the cinema tomorrow?" Libby asked. "I still haven't met Nat's brothers – why not invite the three of them along?"

"And how about pyjamas and a movie at home for tonight? Mina?" Della asked, always the one to check with me.

"Yes to both."

We stopped at Blockbuster Video. I'd always loved wandering video shops with Dad, when he wasn't away working on some crucial project. This was where my fascination with horror movies had started. I'd always been drawn to the cases of horror movies like *Critters* and *Child's Play*, before my dad redirected me to *The NeverEnding Story* and *An American Tail*.

Libby and Della left me to choose the movie. I went for *Kalifornia*, even though the serial killer storyline might be hard to swallow. It was tough to find one that ticked off Della's thirst for action and Libby's preference for drama.

On the walk home, our vampire encounter was on my mind. It wasn't far to our place, but the vampire was in the city somewhere. And if she wasn't causing havoc in our lives, she was probably doing it to someone else. Armand and Jared were the only vampires I saw day to day, and they blended in with humans most of the time. She was a different creature entirely. How many vampires were more like her?

Chapter 6

Our housemate, Tessa, was on her way out when we got in. She had a thick college textbook and a clear pencil case hugged against her chest. I'd never seen such an array of biros, in every colour from crimson to sparkly yellow. Tessa had been at home in LA all summer, so when she came back I'd almost forgotten that the room I'd been using was actually hers. Tessa of the long, silky black hair and even longer legs, who dated Jared last year and everyone forgot to tell me.

"Have fun on Jared's tour?" she asked, looping a floaty, multi-coloured scarf around her neck. She dropped his name into every conversation – a not-so-subtle reminder that she'd got there first.

"He did great – you should've come," Libby said, an edge to her voice.

Tessa's smile showed no trace of angst. "I'm glad he's having fun with it. I've hardly seen him since I got back – we need to catch up."

Probably because he was avoiding her. He hadn't told me that, but I knew the signs. I grew up in a house full of avoiders. There was no easy way to tell her what had been done to him.

"What happened to your jacket?" Tessa asked.

"I snagged it on a doorframe."

She frowned but let it go. "I should go – I'm late for study group. Have a good night!" Tessa left with a jangle of keys and a cloud of white musk perfume.

I threw the jacket into the washing machine with lots of detergent, then went to my room to get comfy for the movie. I had to remind myself to call it mine. When Tessa came back in September, I'd had to choose between Jared and Lucas's rooms. We hadn't told the landlord that Jared had moved out, but he'd notice that most of his things were gone if he ever checked. Libby was covering the extra room from the mansion's earnings. We weren't ready for a stranger to move in or to close the door on Jared coming back. Staying in Lucas's space was a painful reminder of him, but I didn't want to be the reason Jared couldn't pick up his life when he was ready.

We'd taken down Lucas's artwork, exposing darker grey rectangles where the paint hadn't faded. He'd been so talented, using paint, pencil and pastels with the same confident strokes that brought every subject to life. Libby screwed up every piece and stuffed them in a bin bag. Lucas's parents had collected most of his things by then. They were a tearful older couple that were nothing like the hard-faced pair from Lucas's stories. They hadn't approved of his art, so they'd left it behind. I never found the unfinished painting of his mum, so perhaps they took that one.

Libby and Della had helped me to paint the room turquoise, and it was quite cathartic. We were covering over the past, even if we couldn't erase it. With my *Gremlins*, *Leon* and *The Usual Suspects* posters up, it felt more like my room.

I grabbed my comfy flannel pyjamas, revealing Thandie's box on the floor when I closed my drawer. A life that spanned almost a hundred years and all that was left were possessions.

Libby appeared in my doorway, wearing a *21 Jump Street* T-shirt that she'd chopped the top off so it hung low on her shoulders. "How long does it take to . . .?" She saw Thandie's box and trailed off.

"We should sort through her things," I said. Libby hadn't let us touch Thandie's bedroom or office at the mansion, but me and Della had started sifting through the other rooms. This was mostly the kitchen junk drawer.

"Do what you want," Libby said, her face defiant as her arms closed around her waist like she was hugging herself. "It won't bring her back."

I would've once let Libby's moods steer us, but since moving to New Orleans, I'd learned to stand my ground. "At least read her letter. I think it'll help you."

Libby scowled, the refusal as plain as if she'd spoken. Then she relented. "Fine."

She dropped down onto the bed, and I scrambled to get the letter before she changed her mind. The stony set of her features softened as she read. "Thandie had a power," she said, clutching the letter. "She never told us."

"We're doing great at the mansion," I said. "You're doing great. It was never going to be easy, and it turns out we're working without a huge advantage."

"You're right," she said, sniffing. "Thank you for making me wear my big-girl pants."

"You're welcome."

She took the letter with her, and I thought Emmeline would understand.

We settled down in Libby's room with a packet of Twizzlers and put *Kalifornia* on. Della and Libby were immediately engrossed. David Duchovny and Michelle Forbes were travelling the country researching serial killers. Michelle snapped photos of the locations of famous murders, while David recorded the gory tales on his Dictaphone. To save gas money, they accidentally picked up a hitchhiking serial killer and his girlfriend. Brad Pitt was killing it as usual, pun intended, but I was rooting for David Duchovny to get the better of him.

The movie was fast-paced and bloody, and I was mostly able to sever the killings from recent events. My blinks were very long by the time the end credits rolled. "I should get to bed."

"You do that," Libby said sleepily, snuggling closer to Della. It looked like she'd be asleep before I was.

"So, it's your first day tomorrow," Della says. "How you feelin'?"

I'd managed to forget my work-experience nerves, but they

piled on again. "Good, I think."

"I can't believe you volunteered to work on a Saturday," Libby murmured. "I don't know where that go-getter gene came from." It wasn't our mum and dad. Mum had lost every decent job to researching her vampire obsession, staying up late and forgetting to go when she thought she was close to a breakthrough. My dad always had wads of money stashed around the house but never had a job that we knew of. Libby and I guessed everything from politician to cult leader or bank robber.

All of the parent thoughts had put me in a mood, and getting ready only made me feel more awake. I almost got into bed to read, but my attention fell on Thandie's things. Libby had made a good step in facing up to her loss by reading Thandie's letter, and I'd never shied away from difficult tasks.

I set the box on my bed and prepared to sort through the remnants of Thandie's life. I sat cross-legged, breathing in her scent of cigarettes and incense. Choked up, I started making three piles: one to keep, one to throw away and one to run past Libby when she was up to it.

It wasn't as hard as I'd expected, if I focused on the motions of what I was doing and not what the objects meant. Keys in the keep pile, a screwed-up list in the disposal pile. I tried not to think about the fact that Thandie could never tell us what the keys opened or tick off items on her list.

The last objects near the bottom of the box felt dusty, and I checked inside it. Feeling a smushed spider wasn't how I wanted this to go.

There were a couple of nondescript things, like pen lids and the loose metal spiral from the top of a notebook. There was also a grey Dictaphone.

I picked it up, turning it over in my hands. The dust made my palms dry, and I almost put the Dictaphone into Libby's pile. That was when I read the date on the cassette through the clear window. It said 7/17/95 – the night John Carter ended Thandie's life and then kidnapped us with Veronica's help. Thandie must have recorded it the day she died.

Immediately invested, I replaced the batteries and hit 'play'. Most of the buttons were stuck down, and I couldn't get the tape to eject. Frustrated, I left it with the other items to keep and then put the rubbish pile in the bin.

After the disappointment of not hearing Thandie's voice, I picked up her letters. They were the next best thing. I flicked through them, not looking for anything in particular. She really had spent most of her vampire life worrying about the Carter brothers. I enjoyed reading extracts about the mansion and her delight in testing new ways to frighten customers without the use of her powers. She'd tried sound effects, illusions and different sensory touches. I set those letters aside for Libby and put the rest back into the folder.

I needed to unwind, and soon I was engrossed in *The Forbidden Game*. This was in the running to become a new favourite book: a game of life or death, a group of friends banding together and a handsome, mysterious boy running the show.

Getting sleepy, I went to refill my glass. I stared out into the darkness behind the window while the tap ran. It was refreshing to look out into the night without fearing for my life.

A long creak came from the hallway. I clocked the distance to the knife block – two long strides should do the trick. Apparently, I wasn't as chilled as I'd thought. I listened again, trying to convince myself that the front door was locked. Hearing nothing, I edged closer to the knives.

Della stuck her head through the kitchen door. I jumped, sloshing water over my hand. "You can't sleep either?" she asked.

"I haven't tried yet – I've been reading."

"I've been thinking about that vampire." Her nose wrinkled. "I hate that she's hunting in our city." Her speech was guarded, as if there was more that she couldn't trust me with. We both knew she'd prefer it if there were no vampires in the city at all. But in that universe, Jared would be dead.

Anger towards her flared, quick and hot. I reined myself in before I said something I couldn't take back. "Have you been at work?" I asked, noticing Della's outdoor clothes and shoes. She couldn't have been trying to sleep as she'd claimed.

Glancing down, Della frowned. "Oh . . . yeah. Armand called me in at the last minute."

That was plausible, except the bar closed ages ago. Despite our different stances on vampires, Della was one of the few people I trusted. If I wanted to keep it that way, I had to let this go.

The next morning, I was so wired about starting work experience with Detective Cafferty that I jolted awake before my alarm, convinced I'd overslept. Since I was up early, I put on my running gear. I pounded the pavement faster than normal, running off some excess energy. Whenever I ran, my brain was quiet. All I thought about was that next step, one after the other. It was also handy to know I had a chance of escaping if I was being chased.

The Times-Picayune newspaper had arrived by the time I'd got ready, so I took it to the table to read over breakfast. I poured some cardboard cereal, missing Jared's endless varieties of eggs.

Flipping past the usual articles about local events and minor crimes, I paused on a piece a few pages in. The headline read 'Animal attacks on the rise'. I ended up so enrapt in the article that I dripped milk onto the page. Hospitals all over New Orleans had reported people coming in with torn skin and blood loss. Some of them could describe their attacker and swore it was a person. A lot of the attacks happened at night and the victims had been drinking, so their stories were confused. Some had reported a shadowy shape, and others had a blank space where the memory of the incident should've been. Some victims hadn't made it at all.

A police statement said they couldn't comment on an ongoing investigation but that they were investigating alongside animal control.

Last night, we'd narrowly missed getting attacked by a feral vampire. That obviously wasn't a one-off incident – multiple people had been attacked lately. Unless there was a herd of predatory animals going undetected, I had a theory about what was hunting people. Vampires were running wild in the city.

Chapter 7

The police believed animals were responsible for the attacks, but they were looking for a threat they didn't even know existed.

Tessa breezed in as I sat there stirring my cereal to mush. "Mornin', sunshine," she said. Even though she was wearing an oversized tie-dyed T-Shirt and cycling shorts, her tangled hair spilling over one shoulder, she made me feel underdressed. I'd picked a white shirt and black trousers, which in hindsight looked a lot like my school uniform from back in Whitby.

"Morning," I said. "Did you sleep well?"

"Not really," she said. "I got in late, and I'd had too much caffeine. My own stupid fault. Anything interestin' in the news?"

"Just a piece about animal attacks," I said, standing and tipping my cereal into the bin. "There've been loads of them recently."

Tessa paused with the kettle under the tap, and water flowed over her hand. "What kind of animals?"

"They don't know," I said, wishing I'd not brought it up.

"Huh," Tessa said, noticing what she'd done and turning off the tap. "Hey, isn't this your big day?"

It took me a second to realise she'd moved on the conversation. I had no memory of telling her about my work experience, but I nodded politely.

"I couldn't work for the police, but it's great that you want to!" I wasn't sure if there was an insult hidden within the enthusiasm.

"Thanks," I said. "I should go – I don't want to be late on my first day."

"Don't let me stop you. Good luck!"

I packed my backpack, grabbing Thandie's Dictaphone. I'd arranged to meet Nat after her shift before we hit the cinema. Someone at the mall might be able to mend it. As I set it snugly into my bag, the record button got stuck down. I jabbed it with my finger, trying to stop what might be Thandie's last words from getting erased. The tape wasn't spinning, so the contents were safe.

The sunlight chased away the irritation caused by my chat with Tessa. Tiptoeing around the animal attacks with her had made me realise something. Could I face Cafferty, knowing I had a possible insight that I couldn't share with him? If he was on that case, my knowledge could be valuable, even if he was missing parts of the story.

By the time I pushed through the doors of the police station, I was optimistic. I'd had ideas about joining the cadets straight after high school. If my work experience went well, it might make the decision for me. Cold air blasted down as I approached the counter.

"I'm here to see Detective Cafferty," I said.

"One moment." The young officer behind the desk smiled, picking up his phone. "Detective Cafferty? Mina's here."

Cafferty hurried into the reception area minutes later. I should've spotted that he was a cop when I saw him on an undercover investigation on my first day at the mansion. He'd had the disguise of normal clothes, but keenness and authority radiated off him. He was one of those people with an entirely uncomplicated smile, like his moral compass pointed dead north with not a quiver of ambiguity. He'd been one of the tallest people in the tour group, and he stood out with his golden hair and angular jaw. He was in his late twenties but didn't look that much older than us.

"Hey, you're early. That's a good start. You might not be smilin' when it comes to your first task – paperwork."

I followed Detective Cafferty into a busy room of people wearing suits or uniforms. Some were filling in paperwork and sipping coffee, while several were talking on the phone and typing on computers. There was a real sense of purpose, which was exactly what I wanted. "Where's Detective Boudreaux?" I asked.

"She got promoted," he said, all proud. "She's the one who approved you to do this."

They'd both rooted for me, so I needed to make sure I did them proud. "That's great – she deserves it." Boudreaux had been Cafferty's partner when they'd wrongly arrested Libby. Despite that serious misstep, she was a smart, dedicated cop.

No one paid us much attention as I followed Cafferty to a desk in the corner. There was only a computer and a neat stationery organiser on it. He pulled up a chair for me. Sitting next to him was an improvement on sitting across an interview table.

"I'm gonna be straight with you. We've had work experience kids before, and usually we have them doing copies and buyin' coffee. I'm guessin' that's not gonna fly with you. You did good work on your sister's case, and I know you've handled more than your share of tragedy with a level head."

I nodded, sensing this wasn't the time to plead my case.

"I've been given clearance to have you work cases alongside me. Not everything – no active crime scenes, and I'll judge the rest as we go. Plus I reserve the right to pull you off a case at any time."

"That's great!" I said, not able to contain myself for any longer.

"Don't thank me yet," he warned. "The department has a few active cases – some violent crimes. You OK with that?"

"With people committing violent crimes? Not really."

"Good point – let me rephrase that. Do you think it will bother you?"

"I've probably seen worse than a lot of things," I said, considering what he knew. He'd interviewed me about finding Heather's body but was oblivious to everything vampire-related that happened in the basement at John Carter's bar, Empire of the Dead. John had tried to turn us against each other, making us believe our loved ones were dead. We'd almost died, and Cafferty didn't even know we'd been there.

"Fair enough," he said, and I appreciated how he took me at my word. "Then I just have one more question. Why do you want to do this?"

My first instinct was to pull a Libby and skirt around the deeper issues, but in truth I'd given this some thought. "I've never known what to do with my life, but after seeing you and Detective Boudreaux working on Libby's case, I want in on that. I've been through bad things . . . You were there for some of them." His expression was intense, but the softness in his eyes told me he understood. "I know there are bad people out there, and I want to help anyone who has to face them." I was including vampires in that, even if I was the only one who knew it.

"Good answer," Cafferty said. "Do you have any questions before we do the paperwork?"

"Just one," I said. "Are you working on the animal attack case?"

Cafferty's grin was strained. "You've done your homework. It's not my case, but it's provin' to be quite a headache for the department. The victims' reports don't line up, and nobody can figure out who or what's behind the attacks. It's happened before, in the 70s I think, and it stopped eventually. Could be the same will happen this time."

"That sounds rough," I said neutrally.

"It is, but I have enough to think about with my own caseload."

"That's fair," I said. "So what's your case?"

"I've just been handed this one." Cafferty unlocked his top drawer and took out a grey cardboard file. "We've had two stabbings in as many days with a very similar M.O." I must have looked blank. "That means a lot of the facts match . . . I'm not showing you the crime scene photos, but here's what we know. The female victim, Laurel Jenkins, was nineteen and the male, Carl Landry, was twenty one. Both were found in front of their homes and each had been stabbed a total of nine times in the chest, throat and upper body, probably with a sizeable knife. The victims also had defensive wounds on their hands and forearms. They were probably killed late at night or in the early hours of the morning." He explained everything in a long list, light on emotion.

"They were stabbed nine times?" I asked, letting the horror of that sink in.

"Yeah, it's very specific, right?" Cafferty said. "They both bled out at the scene."

"Do you have any leads?" I asked, seeing why he stayed to the facts. My imagination was circling what had been done to them: a lifeless body discarded by the victim's own house, their blood spreading over the pavement from punctures in their flesh . . . A person only a little older than me coming home from a fun night with friends, having no sense that it would be their last. A murderer waiting in the darkness, knife at their side . . . .

I pushed all of that away and kept the victims' names in my mind – Laurel and Carl. They were the reason we were here.

"My friend told me about Laurel," I said. "She used to go to my school."

"Is that right? I'm sorry to hear that. We're at the early stages of the investigation. I've taken the photos out of the case file so you can take a look at what we have so far. Before that, we have to fill out your work experience forms. Let's see if you wanna stick around after your first taste of paperwork."

Cafferty gave me a form, and he worked on his computer while

I filled it in. It was mostly standard work experience stuff. Then I got to the non-disclosure agreement and the part about signing away liability should anything unfortunate happen on a case. You know, like my untimely death. I bet he'd have to fill in a lot of forms for that.

I signed and dated the last page as Cafferty's phone rang. "Yeah?" he said. "OK, got it. I'll be right over there." He put down the phone and stood up. "You ready for your first witness interview? Someone might have seen a figure leaving the area around the time of the attack."

Chapter 8

afferty's sleek grey Crown Victoria was parked outside. "Am I dressed right for interviewing someone?" I asked.

"You're dressed fine for listening and not scaring off my witness. If you behave, I'll let you record the interview while I take notes."

"I can do that."

He unlocked the car without telling me where to sit, so I went for the front. Cafferty pulled out from the space, checking around him as we exited the car park.

His concentration gave me time to take a breather. Being here with him felt so right, but I hadn't expected the vampire stuff right out of the gate. I couldn't get away from them. Now that I wasn't on the animal-attack case, I could admit that it was a load off my mind. It wouldn't have been right to work alongside Cafferty when I knew what he was up against and he didn't. I had to console myself that the police were doing fine not knowing about vampires long before I came along.

"During training, my drill sergeant used to quiz us about cases to make sure we had the facts," Cafferty said, checking his mirror as we pulled off Royal Street. "You game for that?"

"Sure," I said, running through what he'd told me. I wanted to impress him.

"The animal attacks?"

"Not your case. The department is looking into the rise in suspected animal attacks alongside animal control."

"Very good. And my case?" he asked.

I took a moment to get this right. "Two people in their late teens and early twenties have been found by their homes with multiple . . . nine stab wounds. You hope the witness might have seen something."

"Excellent. The first day can be overwhelming, especially with multiple cases, but you got it in one."

Before Cafferty could go on, a voice crackled over his radio. "Detective Cafferty, we have a DB code 44, possible 10-78 to the north-west of City Park."

The string of numbers and letters meant nothing to me, but it affected Cafferty. He sighed, running his hands up and down the steering wheel with quick, agitated motions. "On my way. Can you postpone my witness interview?"

When the person on the other end agreed, Cafferty addressed

me. "Change of plan." He kept one hand on the wheel and pressed a button on his dashboard. The siren wailed to life over us and blue lights flashed at the top of the windscreen. He did a U-turn so fast that my head knocked against the side window.

"That's so cool!" I said, rubbing my head and trying to see where the bulbs were hidden. It hadn't occurred to me that this car would have all the good stuff. It looked so normal from the outside, which was probably the point. "Where are we going?"

"I'm respondin' to a call. I don't have time to drop you back at the station, so here's what we're gonna do. I'm going onto an active crime scene, and I can't take you with me. So you need to stay in the car, and I'll update you after I've assessed the scene."

"What happened?" I asked.

"They found another stabbing victim."

Cafferty brooded for the rest of the journey. At first, I observed him as if I could pick up some morsel of what he knew. When he gave me nothing, I watched New Orleans passing by. The pastel-coloured houses round here were mostly in the shotgun style like ours, which were deceptively deep despite their narrow fronts. Most had a pumpkin either nestled in the window or sitting on the step outside. The traffic slowed us down by a symmetrical mint-green house, its steps leading up to a door on each side. Realistic black cats had their tails curved up the railings, and rubber bats were strung along them.

After a short drive, we pulled up outside City Park. This was my first visit, and it had the most intriguing trees I'd ever seen. Some clung to their summery green shades, but many had succumbed to the burnt rust and gold of autumn. They had thick, almost black trunks, their gnarled branches obscured by fluffy grey plants trailing down. "What's that on the trees?" I asked.

"Spanish moss," he said curtly. The crime scene must be bad.

Across the park, yellow tape was threaded around two trees. Police in dark uniforms and CSIs in white hurried around. "Good luck," I said.

Cafferty nodded absently, already lost to the incident across the park. He left the car with a murmured goodbye and marched across the expanse of grass.

With the engine and air conditioning off, the car heated up almost immediately. Cafferty had said to stay in the car, but he'd presumably prefer it if I didn't melt into a sweaty puddle.

I got out and leaned against the bonnet. That lasted all of five seconds, until the hot metal became unbearable.

Cafferty reached the line of tape and ducked underneath. There were passersby standing along it, but beyond them police officers were building a white tent. Whatever had happened, they were hiding it from onlookers. People who had stumbled upon the scene had a better view than me.

Technically, a park was a public place. If I hadn't been there with Cafferty, I could've gone up to the tape to see what was happening.

Before I had time to think it through, I was walking. Outside the suffocating car, the sun felt good on my skin. Some people were getting active, tossing balls or Frisbees around, while others soaked up the sunshine on blankets. The park smelled earthy and green. It was too bright a day for whatever was behind the tape. I wasn't supposed to be doing this, but I had to know more.

One police officer was shooing away onlookers, but I found a spot by the closest tree. From here, I could see into the tent.

Three months ago, I'd witnessed some terrible things. I'd found

Heather's body, someone I'd never met before she was murdered and put on display in the attic at the mansion. Then there was Elvira, the girl whose body shared a cell with me and Libby when John locked us up under Empire. He'd danced around with her lifeless body right in front of us. Here was another dead person, and this time I'd brought the sight on myself.

The police officer wrestling with the tent got the opening sealed, but it was too late. I'd seen everything.

The victim was lying on their back. I couldn't make out much from this distance, but the body looked wrong. Too flat, as if it had deflated. And the colour . . . It had the dark tinge of dried blood from top to toe. The facial features were almost unrecognisable, with the skin shrunken like a mummy over exposed teeth that were broken down with decay. A CSI in a pristine white overall leaned over the body as the tent zip came down, swatting something away. Flies.

A sour taste filled my mouth. The body was decomposing.

I'd lost track of Cafferty, and he popped up in front of me. "Didn't I tell you to stay in the car?"

"Did you want me to boil in my own skin?" I tried to quip, but the lingering sight from the tent turned it too dark. "What happened?"

"Wait in the parking lot. I'll talk to you there." Cafferty looked over his shoulder. He'd warned me that bringing the work experience kid to an active crime scene was a big no no. He and Boudreaux had pulled a lot of strings to get me this experience. I hoped it wasn't about to end.

I crossed the park with less purpose than before, feeling the presence of the scene behind me. The happy people enjoying their day took on a new meaning. I'd come here by choice and seen someone whose life was over. Worse than that, Cafferty said they'd been stabbed, so the killer had left their remains to rot. It would be easier to stay oblivious like the people chasing around the park, but did I want to be?

I thought about that until Cafferty came back. "In future, you have to follow my instructions. If what you pulled today gets back to Boudreaux, you're done."

I wanted to fight my corner, but I kept my mouth shut. I was lucky to have a future with the police, but I couldn't hold in my questions for long. "Do you mind telling me what happened?"

"In the car. Now." At least I knew where I stood with strict Cafferty.

We got in, and he turned on the engine.

He didn't talk or start driving. Cold air drifted from the vents as I waited impatiently. Anger was rolling off him, alongside other emotions.

We hadn't put a time frame on my work experience beyond this week off school, but I didn't want this to be my last day. As disturbing as the scene was, it'd lit a fire inside me. It was too late for the person who'd died, but there was a crime to solve and a killer to catch. Unlike the other problems in my life, this one could be fixed.

"Did you see inside the tent?" Cafferty was looking at his hands where they gripped the steering wheel.

"The body? Yeah, I saw it." I hated that a person had been reduced to that. I'd seen someone dead once again, adding another macabre tableau to the list that I'd never forget.

He looked at me, hopelessness turning his features downwards.

Was he worried about me rather than angry? "Are you OK?" he asked.

"Honestly? I think I'm in shock," I said. If I kept talking, I could outrun the thought of death a little longer. "But I'm not going to fall apart. You said they were murdered?"

He was eying me cautiously. "They were stabbed in the heart. Only once, but that's all it took."

"Had they been there a long time?" I asked.

"Perceptive. How did you know that?"

I was in no rush to say it. Emotions were eroding the protective numbness. "The flies," I said, remembering them swarming over decomposing flesh even though I tried to block it out.

Cafferty bit the inside of one cheek. "It's a busy park, so you'd think someone would've found the body before decomposition set in. Still, in this climate it's possible – I've seen it before."

I put together what I'd seen and Cafferty's description: a stab wound to the chest, a suspicious amount of decomposition . . . They'd got a dead vampire on their hands.

Chapter 9

The police would try to investigate the vampire's murder, but they'd be working with huge chunks of the truth missing.

Cafferty said, "Boudreaux wants me to concentrate on the original stabbing case, so I'll open a new file and pass it to another detective. This one has a completely different M.O."

"Different how?"

"You really want to hear this?" he asked.

"I'm still here, not throwing up in your car. That has to count for something, right?"

"Guess so," he said. "All right . . . This was one round wound to the chest, compared to multiple stab wounds with a medium-sized bladed weapon. The victim was left out in the open, unlike those found by their homes not long after they died."

"And the killer isn't likely to change what they do when they've killed two people in the same way?"

"Right. You're catching on quickly."

It'd probably be healthier if my mind didn't wrap itself around these ideas so easily, but I was working with the tools I had. "Thanks."

Cafferty turned off the engine. "I need food, and we're right by one of my favourite places. You want anythin'?"

"Whatever you're having is fine," I said.

While he was gone, I reassured myself that Jared and the other vampires who deserved their privacy weren't about to be exposed. When Thandie's body was found by the police, Armand had explained that vampires decompose too fast to be identifiable as anything other than human. Even their fangs crumble. How did Armand put it? Their lives had been unnaturally prolonged, and their bodies returned to the earth quickly. It would've helped if he'd not talked in riddles, but that was the way his mind worked.

Cafferty came back with two brown paper bags that smelled of fragrant seafood and said 'Deanie's' on the side. "I got you a shrimp po' boy – hope that's all right. We'd better eat them here – the other detectives would give me grief that I didn't bring more back to the station."

He accepted my thanks but refused payment. We found a bench by the park. The sandwiches tasted as good as they smelled: huge, juicy shrimp in crunchy batter, tangy sauce and fresh salad.

We chatted while we ate. Cafferty asked me about school

and then got onto the fun stuff. "Do you have any plans over Halloween?"

"Plenty," I said. "The mansion is relaunching tomorrow after updating some rooms. We've got a costume ball, the carnival . . . Are you going to the Mask Parade on Halloween?"

"Partying's not my thing," he said. "I'm happier with a beer and my Playstation."

"That sounds fun too – except the beer part."

I went to throw away our rubbish and got a good view of the road running alongside the park. A car I'd ridden in many times was speeding away from the scene – Della's. Before it turned the corner, I'd confirmed that Della was driving, and an unfamiliar girl was in the passenger seat.

I spent a good part of the journey to the police station fretting about Della. First she'd lied about where she'd been last night, and now I'd seen her out with a girl when she was supposed to be at work. I decided to give her the benefit of the doubt. She could've been running an errand from her job at Empire of the Dead. I should ask her about it later, then I'd be able to let it go.

The afternoon at the station wasn't quite so eventful, but I appreciated the time to decompress. The sight of the dead vampire had left a sickly residue clinging to me, a sense of wrongness that I'd seen another terrible thing. And yet, like when I saw Heather and Elvira's bodies, I was coping. Cafferty and his colleagues had to handle things like this every day. It wasn't getting any easier, but maybe I could be like them.

Cafferty talked me through the paperwork to set up a case file and then gave me some photocopying and filing while he filled it in.

There was some satisfaction in the repetitive motion of laying the paper on the screen, waiting for the light to slide across and then putting the warm copies to one side. Mostly, he had me copying boring forms, but halfway through the stack I came across a photocopy he'd put a sticky note on: 'For the new evidence file'.

Cafferty had told me about this evidence. The victim from the park, a male vampire as it turned out, hadn't carried any ID, but he'd had a wad of cinema tickets in his pocket. For the past two weeks, he'd been to the cinema almost every day. Someone had laid out the tickets to make a copy, and that got my mind churning over what might take a vampire to the same cinema every day. Perhaps he worked there, or it was a vampire hangout. This wasn't Cafferty's case, but the dead vampire had me curious to know more. We'd moved last night's movie plans to tonight but hadn't settled on a cinema. This would be as good a place as any. I'd technically be dragging my friends along on an unofficial investigation, but they'd be safe enough in a crowded cinema.

In my break, I went to the phone booth outside the police station to phone Libby at the mansion. "How do you feel about Crescent Screens for tonight?" I asked. "Cafferty and I just drove past, and it looks amazing."

"Sure," she said.

"Great – I'll let Nat and her brothers know later," I said, stirring up some guilt that I'd stretched the truth about how I'd discovered the cinema.

Back in the police station, I did more administrative jobs for Cafferty, getting excited about my outing. I'd get to have a night with my friends and do some amateur detective work at the same time.

"Mina?"

I took the papers back to Cafferty, putting neat stacks on his desk. "Hey, thanks for those."

"I just have a few more to do," I said.

"Leave them. Take a look at this package that just arrived."

Cafferty handed me a copy of *Interview with the Vampire* with a gold cover and cream lettering edged in red. 'Vampire' was written in black.

"No way . . ." I said.

"It's a first edition," he said proudly. "Signed too. I got it for my little sister's 21st."

I gently opened the cover to reveal elegant, looping handwriting:

For Carly,

All blessings,

Anne Rice
1995

Anne Rice had held this book, keeping Cafferty's sister's name in her mind while her pen flowed over the page. I gave it back to him. "You're going to win some serious points with that."

"Sure – if I could figure out where to take her. She wants to do something fun before she hits the club with her friends tomorrow night."

I looked at him, waiting for the solution to sink in. He stared back blankly. "What about a trip to the mansion? You know . . . The *Interview with the Vampire* room, Jared's costume . . . We work in there together."

He laughed. "Good thing I'm not needed for my deductive skills."

"We're trialling a new room, so it's good timing. If Carly's anything like me, she'll love it."

"She is – thank you. I'm pretty sure she's never been, so that'll be perfect. I've worked you hard enough for today. Can I drop you off somewhere? I can finish this up at home."

"Do you mind taking me to Clearview Mall?" I asked.

"Sure thing," he said. "I used to take Carly there all the time."

Cafferty packed up his paperwork, and we went out into the grey of twilight. As he pulled out of the car park, I took in the city. Halloween made New Orleans even more magical, with ringed hands reaching out of windows to light stubs of candles or switch on fairy lights. Glowing pumpkins grinned from steps, and cobwebs stretched across doorways. A strange, elongated skeleton swayed in front of a shop window, even though there was no breeze.

We pulled up at a set of traffic lights, and a group of teens wearing vampire capes sauntered in front of the car. A skinny guy drummed on Cafferty's bonnet with flat palms, giving a devilish grin that suggested he knew a cop was behind the wheel. Cafferty rolled his eyes at me. "They're not worth the paperwork."

"And here I was thinking you loved it."

A woman came in the opposite direction. Thin braids at the top of her hair gave way to spiralling curls over her shoulders. She had huge, expressive eyes that gleamed almost black as she peered into the car. When she flashed me a grin, a neat pair of fangs flicked down. She wove past the teenagers and stalked off down the street.

Cafferty tapped his steering wheel irritably, clueless. If he'd seen the vampire, he would've come to a reasonable explanation, from costume fangs to questionable dentistry. He drove on without knowing how in the dark he was.

Chapter 10

Night had fallen by the time Cafferty pulled up outside the mall. "You did good today – aside from that stunt you pulled in the park," he said. "It's not an easy thing you saw, but you handled it . . . And you had some great insights."

"Thanks," I said. "It's been tough, but I'm trying to stay focused on what we can do about it."

"How is it that you already know what it took me a year to figure out?" Cafferty asked.

"Familiarity with trauma?" What started as a joke ended up uncomfortably close to the truth.

"Well if that's the case, I'm real sorry about it."

"Don't be," I said. "Thanks for today. I'll see you on Monday." Cafferty wasn't working tomorrow, so that meant I got the day off too. I'd rather have gone to work – we'd just got started.

Cafferty only drove away once I was inside.

The Clearview Mall had two floors crammed with shops. It wasn't quite the dazzling mall of my movie dreams, but it had its charm. The ground-floor ceilings were low, and amber lamps cast a welcoming light over the tiled floor and potted plants between the shops. Orange and purple Halloween decorations drooped from the ceilings, and some shops had mannequins of skeletons, werewolves and other Halloween monsters outside.

A toy shop was handing out sweets to passing children, the staff dressed as witches with convincing rubber masks. They had a seasonal display of *Ghostbusters* and *Scooby Doo* toys in the window. On a whim, I bought one to add to Jared's collection.

I had some time to kill, so I went straight to the independent bookshop. I was pleasantly surprised to bump into Nat's younger brother, Sam. He must have decided to browse too. We'd never had a proper conversation, but I wasn't too nervous like with Will. Libby and Nat were fun but volatile. Sam had a more even temperament like me.

"Hi Sam," I said. "I didn't expect to see you here."

"Hi!" he said a touch too enthusiastically. He winced as if he'd realised the moment it came out. "I was early to meet Will and Nat."

"Me too," I said.

He gave me a shy smile. Sam had the same shiny brown hair as his siblings, but his features were more exaggerated: full lips, large eyes and pronounced cheekbones. Also like them, he was nice to look at, though with less confidence.

The tiny Gothic bookshop had my name all over it. In a way it did, because there were more copies of *Dracula* than any one shop needed.

It was dimly lit by countless electric candles crammed onto every shelf. Swathes of floaty white fabric were pinned from corner to corner so they hung down in loops. This was how it looked all year round, not just for Halloween.

"Are you looking for anything in particular?" I asked Sam, scanning the shelves. They had everything I liked, from Gothic classics to urban fantasy. I picked up *The Last Vampire* by Christopher Pike.

"I read a lot of different things. I've been pretty into epic poetry and classic literature lately, and I really like Point Horror," Sam said tentatively, looking down at me under his blunt fringe.

"Me too!" I said. "I'm reading *The Forbidden Game* at the moment, and it's great."

"Yeah, that was a good one," Sam said. "Will makes fun of me for reading them." He looked mortified at the confession.

"Not everyone has good taste," I said, joining him by the Point Horror shelf. "Have you read this one?" I pulled out *The Mall*.

"I'm usually an RL Stine guy, but I'll give it a go. Maybe I'll convince Will to read it and get him all freaked about working here."

"I'd like to see that."

We split up outside the bookshop as Sam had some errands to

run. I wanted to find the Radio Shack where Will worked when he was back from college. Someone there might be able to help with Thandie's Dictaphone.

Glass lifts led up to an impressive second floor, the glass roof exposing the dark sky. I'd found the food court, and there were a lot of vendors I wanted to tick off on a future visit, especially Cinnabon and Dairy Queen. Groups of kids rested against the railings and sat at tables with food and milkshakes. Radio Shack was tucked into the far corner of this floor.

After spending time around Sam's anxious energy, the differences from his half-brother were more obvious. Will was leaning on the counter, the picture of cool and boredom. Every wall around him was covered with electrical devices, batteries and coils of wires. "And here I was thinking you'd go straight down to Nat. Unless it's new speakers and not me you want."

I grabbed the Dictaphone from my backpack and set it on the counter. "Any suggestions how I might get this to work?"

Will took the device and turned it over, examining the battery compartment underneath. His hair fell over his face, which had taken on a look of intense concentration. "Our tech guy can check it out. It might take a few days – we have a backlog right now."

"Thanks. How much?"

He smiled, looping the wire around one hand and securing it with a cable tie. "You tolerate my brother and sister – that's payment enough."

"Thank you. Do you mind . . . It's not mine – is it OK not to listen to it?"

"Our technicians are discreet – no creeps here."

"I should go to meet Nat. See you in a bit."

He saluted me and then resumed his bored slouching over the counter.

The mall was closing soon, so I ambled past JC Penney and Sears before landing at the shop where Nat worked.

Movies 'N Stuff was an entertainment store that sold merchandise from every franchise I could think of. They had *Star Wars*, *Star Trek* and other big budget sci-fi, but I lingered at the 80s movie section. A *Near Dark* vampire T-shirt with a bright sunset at its centre was calling to me.

I browsed the tall cases until I almost fell over Nat.

"Hey you," she said from the floor, ripping open a box. Her purple dress was spread out around her, the black lace hem trailing. "Did you find the shop OK?"

"Yeah. I ran into Sam in the bookshop on the way," I said.

"No surprise there," she said. "How was your day with Cafferty?" She started pulling out boxed *He-Man* and *Thundercats* figures and stuffing them onto shelves.

"It was OK," I said, hesitating over how much to tell her. One of the joys of my relationship with Nat was that it wasn't built on drama. "We ended up at a crime scene."

"Ooh, spill," she said, pausing with a large Cheetara figure in her hands.

"I signed something that said I'm not supposed to talk about it," I said. Dead vampires were definitely off the menu of topics with Nat.

"Seriously, that would kill me!" Nat said, returning to the action figures. "What's the point of knowing stuff if you can't share?"

"I did find out that the girl you told me about, Laurel, isn't the only person who's been murdered lately," I said. Surely Cafferty wouldn't mind me talking about that – he'd said the newspapers had already got hold of the story.

"Seriously? Didn't we just have a serial killer? You know ... The guy who used to own that Empire of the Dead bar?"

I knew that far too well. "Yeah, but I don't think we can call this one a serial killer at two victims."

"Did you find out who did it?" she asked, stacking more boxes.

"Not yet."

Nat stood up, brushing off her dusty knees. "Where did Sam get to, by the way?"

"He went off to buy a few things. I think he mentioned stationery?"

Nat groaned. "Lucky the mall closes soon – we could've lost him for hours. I'm about done here. Help me grab the shutters so no one sneaks in. That's always the kind of person who never leaves."

I helped Nat yank down the metal shutters until they were a foot off the ground. "Lemme cash up, and then we can go find Will and Sam."

Outside the shutters was a Halloween display that I'd rushed past on my way in. Some evil genius had made a miniature cornfield, complete with life-sized stalks and a scarecrow with a pumpkin head. It was wearing a clown suit, a red wig pulled over its head and toothy grin cut into its face. The mall was deathly quiet, until a shadow skittered across my peripheral vision. It was gone when I looked. Anyone, or anything, could be beyond the flimsy metal barrier. Even vampires needed no invitation into a public place, especially now it was dark.

Trying to brush off the jittery feeling, I hurried back to the checkout where Nat was counting the money in the till. I'd held it together around Cafferty, but the sight of that dead vampire had shaken me more than I'd thought.

I hoped it wasn't a mistake inviting my friends to the cinema the vampire had visited regularly. After seeing Jared and Della in action at the end of his tour, I knew they'd keep us safe if needed.

"And I'm done," Nat said, closing the till and grabbing her keys. "That was almost too easy – we might even get to the car before the boys." She flicked off the light by the till and plunged us into darkness.

"Thanks for the warning," I said.

We followed the light coming in from the mall towards the front of the shop. Without gaudy fluorescent lights, the shop turned sinister. We passed a case of movie villains, and Chuckie's tiny knife cast my thoughts to the stabbing cases Cafferty was investigating. Our faces were shifting ghosts in the glass as we made our cautious way among the cabinets.

We made it to the shutters and crouched to open them. They dropped down, leaving only a couple of clear inches above the floor.

"Holy balls," Nat said. "Stupid piece of junk." Nat reached out to push the shutter up, and it trembled. She let her hand fall at the sound of a repetitive tap, tap, tap of metal on metal. An object being dragged along the shutters.

"Someone's out there," I said, catching myself before I said 'something'.

"Back door," Nat said.

We shuffled away from the shutters, eyes on the empty mall.

We had to move, but I couldn't look away. While no one was in sight, we were safe.

The moment I turned my back, someone slammed into the shutter in an angry crash of metal.

Chapter 11

Nat and I spun round, clutching each other, to see Will laughing. He was leaning against the shutters, his fingers looped through the metal.

"Your faces," he said, his voice shaking. "Classic!"

"That is so *not funny*," Nat seethed. She yanked up the shutters and punched him in the arm. "You're lucky I didn't call 911."

"Have to say, I expected better," Will said, rubbing his arm. "You should be more on your guard, Nats."

"Sure, next time a fake attacker comes for me I'll get right on that."

Sam wandered back then, carrying a bag from somewhere called Paper Tree.

"More stationery?" Nat said. "Let's get to the movies. Which movie theatre did we decide on?"

"Crescent Screens," I said.

Only a few cars were left in the car park by the time we got outside. Their mum's car was a pale blue AMC Pacer with chrome bumpers.

Nat let me climb in first. I managed to catch my foot on the doorframe and fell into the back seat, which Nat found deeply entertaining. Sam got into the front with Will. His head immediately tilted forward in the reading stance, so he wasn't likely to join a conversation.

The car smelled of too-strong pine air freshener and cigarettes, both of which I suspected were to do with Will. It took me a moment to figure out where I recognised the car from. Will slid a cassette into the player and the opening harmony of 'Bohemian Rhapsody' blared.

"Wait," I said, as Will pulled out of the space. "You're playing the *Wayne's World* song in a car exactly like the *Wayne's World* one?"

Will raised his eyebrows at me in the mirror. "I play that song in here all the time, and you're the first one to get it. You definitely *are* worthy."

"Why thank you," I said, settling down in the broken-in leather seat to listen.

"What are you two talking about?" Nat asked.

"My point exactly," Will said, and I laughed.

Nat narrowed her eyes at me. "Don't encourage him."

Will stayed in his seat when we pulled up outside the cinema. "Stay put, bud," Will said, patting Sam on the shoulder. His head jerked up, and his eyes were disoriented in the rear-view mirror. He must have been really into that book.

"Will," Nat warned. "Get out of the car. I'm not climbin' out of the tailgate again."

"Come on – we're late," Will said, grinning and gesturing for her to hurry.

Nat sighed. "Whatever. Follow my lead," she said to me.

She used the latch to open the rear window over the boot and wriggled out over the parcel shelf, her legs jerking around so much that I had to move back.

"Just another minute," Will murmured, grinning ever wider. "I'm not going to make you do that, by the way."

He waited until Nat was clear of the back window before getting out of the car. He tilted his seat forward to let me out and offered a hand to me. "Don't mistake this for chivalry," he said. "I saw you almost face plant as you got in. I don't wanna peel you off the sidewalk." I took his hand and let him help me out.

"Jerk," Nat said, straightening out her purple dress.

Sam clambered out of the passenger side, book clutched against him. He needed to loosen up or Libby would eat him for breakfast.

Jared was waiting in the entrance of the cinema with Libby and Della, though he was the only one who looked like he wanted to kill Will for holding my hand.

"Hey guys," Nat said. "These are my brothers, Will and Sam."

Will nodded as the others greeted him. Sam's silence was more likely down to nerves than thinking he was too cool for school. Jared managed a smile, though he was definitely brooding.

I shook off my annoyance. He'd never cared about me talking to other guys before – being undead was no excuse. Instead, I took in the white board over the entrance with the movies' names spelled out on it. An actual ticket booth sat at the front of the building. If that vampire had come here to enjoy movies with no sinister motive, I could guess why he picked this place.

Nat gave me hard side eyes. "You have been to a movie theatre before, right?"

"I've been to cinema chains. This is an experience!" I said.

Will shrugged. "Can't argue with that enthusiasm."

Libby got us back on track. "What are we going to see again?"

I scanned the options: *How to Make an American Quilt*, *Mallrats*, *Vampire in Brooklyn* and *Halloween: The Curse of Michael Myers*.

"I think we're missing out by not seeing my girl Winona . . . making a quilt, for some reason," Jared said.

"Your girl's right here," Della said, gesturing at me, "and you were outvoted." Funnily enough, no one had opted for the vampire movie.

"What about my vote?" Will asked good naturedly. "I'm a film student – doesn't it carry some weight?"

"New guy doesn't get one," Nat said, her grin bright and victorious. "We're watching *Mallrats*."

"Not the slasher? You do know it's almost Halloween, right?" Will asked.

"How long is *Mallrats*?" Sam asked, peering at the board. "I'm meeting some friends in an AOL online chat room for book club later."

"Bro, we're in a real-life chat room right now," Will said.

"I don't know – isn't chatting frowned on in a movie theatre?" Libby asked.

74

It was so great to see the rapport between my old friends and new. This could become a regular arrangement. Libby had been so stressed juggling college and the mansion lately that it was good to see her cutting loose. She'd promised in the run-up to Halloween that we'd spend lots of time together in the evenings, so I predicted a fun but tiring week.

We paid at the booth, and the boy who handed over our tickets didn't share my excitement.

The foyer was crowded with cinemagoers and an array of life-sized Hammer horror monster statues. A blank-faced mummy, axe raised, was snuggled up to a masked Phantom of the Opera, complete with a bad wig and grey silk cravat. Frankenstein's monster, his wax face melting, leered between a very hairy werewolf and an accurate wax model of Christopher Lee's Dracula.

While the others examined the monsters, I took a quick look around the room for vampires. Apart from Jared, I clocked one other possibility: a bored looking guy with a mass of curly hair and milk-white skin behind the counter. A long queue snaked away from him, but perhaps I could make sure he served me when we got snacks to see if he was on team human or vampire.

I joined Nat and the others by the werewolf statue. "God I love this place," she said. "Although that grungy werewolf guy looks a lot like my ex."

"Huh," Libby said. "You finally got a friend that I like."

"My life's mission realised," I said, reaching for Jared's hand automatically.

I'd managed to forget not only that he was sulking but that it was possibly too much for him. The feel of his cold skin against mine was a huge reassurance as he threaded our fingers together. He smiled down at me, and I took in his lightly flushed complexion. Had he fed today? The blood must have come from a living person. Even though Armand was helping him adjust, the thought of them out there feeding on people was hard to face. I pushed all of that down, where it'd probably start festering later.

Jared stayed with the Hammer monsters while we joined the snack queue. Choosing snacks was no fun when you couldn't eat them.

Will was chatting to Libby like they'd always known each other, but Sam was hanging on quietly to one side. "How's *The Mall*?" I asked.

"Pretty cool," he said. A receipt was slotted into the book. He'd read a decent amount in the car. "Have you . . . Did you like this one?"

"Yeah, I read it in one go." We moved slowly towards the guy behind the counter. There was no way to tell if he was a vampire or just not into tanning.

When it was finally our turn, we bought armfuls of stuff, from Milk Duds to doughy pretzels that smelled of garlic bread and leaked oil through the paper bags. Libby got rainbow-coloured popcorn that tasted like sherbet, and Will picked a luminous-green apple slushie and a fully loaded hotdog. "I'll pay," I said, accepting their cash and waiting to hand it over with growing anticipation. My little investigation had come down to this moment.

"$22.50," he said in a monotone, hand out.

I put the money into it, making sure I brushed against his skin. He grabbed some change and handed it over, but I'd learned what I needed to know. His skin was cold, firmer than normal and pallid. He was a vampire.

I followed the others, not sure what to do with that information. Even the screening rooms were more fun than cinemas back home. The decor was pure haunted house, with wooden-panelled walls adorned with portraits of stony-faced men and women. Delicate spiders' webs were strewn all over them, and ragged sheaths of cloth swooped down from the high ceiling.

Jared stood aside to let the rest of us pass and then took the aisle seat – convenient for stretching out his long legs and keeping a distance from his friends' tasty blood. Sam ended up on the opposite end of the row by the wall. Even though Will hardly knew us, he slouched down between Nat and Della, seeming entirely at ease. I was glad he'd not mentioned Thandie's Dictaphone to the others. I wasn't ready to tell them until I found out what was on the tape, if anything.

I settled down between Jared and Libby with my lap full of snacks. Cramming a sticky, chewy Milk Dud in my mouth, I felt bad for him that he couldn't eat. He cooked for me sometimes but without his previous enthusiasm. For now, Jared was staring straight at the screen, so I couldn't tell whether it bothered him or not.

I leaned right up to his ear, whispering more quietly than any human could decipher, to update him about the body of the vampire we'd found in the park. Knowing my proximity would be difficult, I kept it brief, adding that the murdered vampire had been here and I'd decided to look around.

Since he became a vampire, Jared had become difficult to read. With the screen light flickering on his face in the darkness, it was impossible. "So you came here to investigate a vampire's death?" he whispered back. His face was impassive, but the hostile tone was unmistakeable. "There's another one feeding on a girl in the back row."

Chapter 12

"I was about to head back there," he said, his breath moving my hair. "Let me talk to him – I'll do some digging."

Jared stood up, marched down the aisle and inched along the back row towards the pair. They were entangled in an embrace, and I couldn't see where the vampire ended and the human began. The feeding relationship looked so uncomplicated compared to what I had with Jared. I spared a glance at Libby, but she was shovelling popcorn into her mouth with no apparent interest in us. One seat along, Will was cast in shadow, his gaze on the screen.

Jared crouched down, talking to the couple. The biter pulled back – a young, thin man. I couldn't make out his features in the dark, apart from the gleam of a blood-stained, fanged grin. Another real vampire. Whoever he was feeding on sagged back in their seat.

The two of them stood, and the vampire stalked out without looking back. A tall girl followed, stumbling but smiling. She was wearing a chunky scarf and had it pressed against one side of her throat.

Jared slid back into his seat, his face a mask of fury.

I leaned close to him. "What do we do? It's not like we can explain it to the police."

Jared murmured into my ear, his expression troubled. "Nothing we can do. It was consensual. I've got some stuff to tell you after."

I looked down the row, and the others were intent on the screen. I wanted some of us to have a normal night.

While the adverts played, I thought about what Jared had said. Was what they were doing acceptable if the girl wanted it? Surely public biting wasn't usually the done thing, or everyone would know about vampires. I was unbearably curious about what Jared had found out, but that would have to wait.

When *Mallrats* started, it hooked me right in. A day of normal, low-stakes fun sounded pretty good, especially if it was with Jeremy London and Jason Lee. And then there was Jay and Silent Bob – the *Star Wars* referencing, haphazard pair that would improve any movie.

By the time the credits rolled, I was working on letting go of the scene with the girl. No one made her do anything she didn't want to, as far as I could tell. If she wasn't concerned for herself, I shouldn't take on that burden. Besides, I was hoping my vampire had some information for me that would make dragging everyone to this cinema worthwhile, aside from the fun we'd had.

"Well *Mallrats* is awesome, and I'm never shaking anyone's hand ever again," Nat said.

"What's the matter – don't wanna risk the stink palm?" Jared stuck his hand out, almost touching her face. She laughed and batted it away.

"I preferred *Clerks*, but that wasn't half bad," Will said.

Although Will wasn't the most easy-going person, I was glad he seemed comfortable with us. "I haven't seen that. I'll have to rent it."

His smile infused his grey eyes with warmth and showed the gap between his front teeth. "You should. Thanks for letting us tag along. You two coming?"

"I guess. See you tomorrow?" Nat asked me.

"Sure," I said.

The three of them said goodbye, waving on their way out.

"Snack for the road?" Jared asked, tilting his head towards the skinny, curly-headed vampire behind the counter.

"I could eat," I said.

Everyone else was on their way out, so we didn't have to wait. Jared went in hard, leaning on the counter with an intimidating growl to his voice. "So, your buddy told me you guys have an arrangement. He said you let your *friends* in for free to do what they want under the cover of darkness. I guess I want to know what you get in exchange for that." So the vampire who died had been friends with this guy – more vampires who had no regard for their secrecy.

The vampire's bloodshot eyes darted to a grizzled guy at the other end of the counter who looked very human – probably his manager. "They just bring me weed . . . and chicks sometimes."

Chicks – did he become a vampire before my parents were born?

"I think you mean they *did*, because you're not going to pull such a dumbass move again, right?" Jared's suggestion was entirely friendly on the surface, but the meaning beneath it was like an alligator lurking in the swamp, its teeth promising death. I'd never heard him speak like that and had to force myself to stand my ground instead of shrinking away.

"Sure thing, man," the vampire said quickly, holding both hands up. "No problem."

Jared stalked away, and I followed empty handed. I would've taken the excuse for a snack, but I wasn't hungry anymore.

Jared had his humanity back in place by the time we joined Libby and Della. "Gotta say I like your new friends," he said to me, "as long as you're not thinking of replacin' us."

"That depends – which one of them do you think you are?" I asked him, struggling to shake off my unease no matter how charming he was being.

"I'm Nat," Libby said, "You're basically the girl version of Sam, and Jared's obviously Will. I kinda like him. Does anyone else think he smells like cigarettes and danger?"

"What does danger smell like?" Della asked.

"Take a whiff of him next time – you'll see. Anyway, I think he could be fun."

"He's all right," Jared says. "His taste in movies sucks though."

"I don't think you can say 'sucks' anymore," Libby said.

Before they launched into never-ending banter, I got onto the important issue. "Has anyone else noticed the lively *vampires* lately?" I whispered the key word, then described the pair in the cinema to Della and Libby as we set off for home.

"It's getting worse, isn't it?" Libby said, pausing to bite a loose thread of skin by one thumbnail. "I had no idea that vamps were real the first year I was here. Now they're everywhere."

"Seems so," Della said, quiet and thoughtful. She directed a question at Jared, her tone turning hostile, "What do *you* make of it?"

We all looked at him. He squirmed at the scrutiny, fiddling with the collar of his T-shirt. "There's no club where we hold hands and talk. Or if there is, I'm not a member."

"So what do we do about it?" I asked.

None of them answered – not the resounding range of options I was hoping for.

"I don't know, but it can't be good for secrecy. I'll mention it to Armand," Jared said, checking both ways before we crossed a pot-holed stretch of road.

What made Wayne Carter the boss of all things vampire?

Libby squinted at me. "You're making a face. Wait . . . let me try something. Armaaaand. There it is again!"

"No face," I said. "OK, maybe a little one. I could just do without the daily Carter brother mentions, that's all." Jared was very quick to offer up his trust, but Armand had to work a bit harder to earn mine. Helping Jared was a very selfless act for the brother of a serial killer. What was Armand getting out of it?

"Not a problem," Jared said, brushing his lips against the top of my head. The rare intimacy loosened me up, letting some air out of the ball of anger inside me. "Sorry . . . I know I've been spending a lot of time with him, but hopefully it won't be for much longer."

"It's fine," I said. "And there's something else." The one

downside of my friendship with Nat was that I had to hold in key information until she was gone.

"Isn't there always?" Libby asked.

"What is it?" Della asked, ignoring Libby.

"I went to a crime scene with Cafferty today . . . Someone had been murdered." Libby let out an angry sound of protest, and I went on before she got going. "It was a vampire . . . with a hole in his chest."

Chapter 13

" S o there's a lot of vampires running around and someone's killing them?" Libby asked. She looked from me to Della. "I can figure things out too!"

"The vampire who was killed used to come here," I said. "Turns out a guy who works there was letting other vampires come to feed on people in the dark."

"Hang on . . . You took us there under false pretences? To investigate a murder?" Libby stopped walking.

We fanned out around her, but Della was uncharacteristically silent. I could've done with her level head. "It's not Cafferty's case, so I wasn't stepping on his toes. I was curious, and I was right to be. Something was going on, but Jared put a stop to it."

"Just for the record," Jared said, quieter than Libby but equally hostile, "the vampire at the movies wasn't a bad guy. He was just a dumbass for lettin' people feed in public."

"Maybe the problem is that they were feeding at all," Della said.

If this went on much longer, our group was at risk of disintegrating. "Cafferty is working a case where people around our age are being stabbed to death in the middle of the night. There have been two already! So can we put this to one side for now and think about what's actually important?"

"Fine with me," Jared said neutrally. "Let's go."

Libby dragged Della off ahead. It must have been bad if Libby was diffusing the situation.

"You're not like that vampire," I said. "Vampires have choices like humans, and you're making the right ones."

Jared's laugh was hollow. "I don't know that it's all about choice."

He was usually so reluctant to discuss being a vampire, but I sensed a sliver of openness. "What do you mean?"

"You know who made me. When I saw you with Will earlier, you don't wanna know the violent things that came into my head. I know I didn't act on them, but I'm scared that one day I might snap and turn out just like John Carter."

"Look at where I came from. Shall we start with the mum who ditched us to become a vampire or the dad who collected a group of adoring groupies and then split? As far as I know, he's on the same continent as us and I don't even know where. I hope I'm not like either of them."

"You make a good point," Jared said, some warmth showing

through. "But John was pure evil. Those vampires feeding in public might not be bad like him, but they don't care if they expose us. What if it's only a matter of time before I give up and become like them?"

"You won't," I said, grabbing his hand. We stopped walking, and he felt impossibly far away even though I was holding onto him. "Just because you dress like Lestat doesn't mean you can't be a Louis. Actually, I think even stressing about becoming Lestat automatically puts you on the side with Louis and Stefan."

"Was that a reference to those *Vampire Diaries* books?" Jared asked, grinning. "I thought Damon was the cool brother."

"If homicide is cool, then sure," I said.

His laugh was genuine, filling me with very real and fragile hope. "Let's catch up with the others."

"Wait – I have something for you." I swung my backpack round to my front and pulled out the *Ghostbusters* toy I'd bought at the mall.

Jared flipped the box over in his hands. "How did you know I love Slimer?" The little green ghost's mouth was open, its tongue lolling out.

"I took a stab in the dark. Maybe he can be a reminder that you're still you – whatever or whoever you eat."

He gripped the box, complicated emotions passing over his face. "Thank you."

Jared kept looking at Slimer as we set off. When we reached his apartment building, I leaned in to hug him. We connected for only a moment before he was pulling back, still clutching Slimer. I could have given him any amount of reassurance, but it wouldn't bring back the closeness we'd once had.

Della and Libby approached when he left. "So, you saw a dead vampire today," Della said. They were holding hands and both considered me seriously.

"And you're working on a freaking murder case after what we've been through. Are you OK with all that?" Libby added.

"Actually . . . yeah. It was from a distance, and the police are dealing with it. I think I want to be like them – solving crimes and stuff."

"That's great," Della said. "You could really make a difference."

"I don't know," Libby said, snuggling up to my arm. "It sounds kind of dangerous."

"What isn't?" I asked.

I waited until Libby was in the bathroom later to tie up the last loose thread of the day. "Did I see you in your car with a girl by City Park earlier?"

I'd wanted Della to tell me that she'd just gone on an errand for Armand because he couldn't leave the bar during daylight hours. "Nope," she said, something secretive and defiant behind her dark eyes. "Sorry – wasn't me."

She ducked into Libby's room, and I wondered when this would become a subject I'd have to raise with my sister.

I wasn't sure if the sound woke me or if I was still processing what I'd learned today when I heard it. Either way, someone was definitely in the hallway.

I pushed back my quilt, listening. They were moving back and forth as if they were looking for something. Or someone. I lowered my feet gently, creeping across my room. The front door made its distinctive creak. The person was leaving. Since uninvited fanged visitors couldn't be inside, I decided to see what was what and settle my sense of disquiet.

The hallway was dark, the corners shadowy enough if something needed to hide. The front door closed, and I made a quick decision. My trainers were there, and my pyjamas could pass as workout wear if anyone saw me. I could stick my head out of the front door to see who was sneaking around and go to bed with my curiosity satisfied.

I hurried down the hallway, the air heavy with the heat of the day. When I opened the front door, the temperature had fallen.

Della was halfway down the street, braids swinging. There was no one else around.

I could've gone back to bed, but Della had first lied to me about being out last night and then about being near the park with a girl today. I needed to know what she was up to, especially if it could hurt Libby.

Stealth wasn't my strong suit, and I made no attempt to duck into shadows or down alleyways. New Orleans was creepy enough without putting myself in those dark places.

Even though some parts of the city never really went to bed, near our house it was unnervingly quiet. I listened hard, thinking about the stabbing victims and the people who went home confused and missing quantities of blood. Why did I decide to follow Della again?

She was walking quick and purposefully, but I managed to

keep up without getting too close. I thought I was doing a good job when Della called, "I can hear you, you know."

She never broke stride, so I jogged to catch up with her. Our workout sessions were doing the trick, because I didn't end up gasping for air.

"How come you're following me?" she asked, a note of disquiet behind the tease.

"How come you're out for a stroll in the middle of the night?"

Della ran a hand through her braids. She glanced sideways at me. "I should lie to you, right? Say I couldn't sleep and needed some air. I don't wanna lie anymore."

"So tell me the truth," I said.

"It's easier to show you."

Chapter 14

Della led me around the back of a restaurant to a low, warped door. The smell of fresh seafood was underlaid with old grease, curdling with the nerves in my stomach.

"Don't tell me you have another job," I said.

"Nah. One seedy workplace is enough for me." Della inserted a black key into the lock. After a lot of coaxing, she got the door open.

I followed her through an empty room that smelled faintly of cleaning products and down a concrete stairwell. The walls pressed in on me and I kept close to Della. This might have been an occasion where I would've been better off asleep and unknowing.

We came out into a low-ceilinged room like nowhere I'd been before. It was full of punching bags, weights benches and racks of weights being used by very fit looking men and women around Della's age. There was a boxing ring in the centre of the room.

A gym wasn't my most natural of habitats, but that wasn't what had grabbed my interest. The walls and ceiling were covered with rough, jagged stalactites the colour of grey clay. Roughly hewn pillars supported the ceiling. "Is this your gym?"

"Not quite," Della said. "Give me a minute."

Della strode off towards a girl in the corner with short, choppy brown hair and amazing muscle definition. She was pummelling a round punching bag like she meant it.

I tried to figure out what they were saying. The girl was looking at me with some kind of interest. She wasn't alone – scrutiny was coming from all sides.

As Della and the girl approached me, a redhead broke away from a nearby group and got there first. "Who the hell are you?"

"*Paige*." The girl with Della had arrived, and she communicated endless strength in the single name.

"Are we letting people in off the street now?" Paige's red hair was scraped back to reveal a flawless, bone-white face. Her rosebud lips were slicked with red and quirked in a sneer.

"Della's vouched for her, and she's given her some defence training," the girl said. I'd watched enough TV to recognise her Spanish-tinged accent as Mexican. "Mina, is it?" Sweat glowed on her golden brown skin and made small ringlets in her hair. "I'm Rosario. Della tells me you tagged along? I like that – shows initiative. She tell you what we do?"

"No," I admitted.

"Paige needs an attitude adjustment, but she's on the right lines. We don't let just anybody in. But right now, we need all the help we can get."

Paige huffed beside her. "Whatever. Can we get started? Della's already put us behind coming late."

Ouch. I was hard to ruffle after growing up with Libby, but Paige's barbs could pierce the thickest of skins. Della was more patient than me. She kept her level gaze on Rosario, even as angry colour bloomed across Paige's pale cheeks.

"Gather round, everyone," Rosario called. The others ditched their equipment and ducked into the ring, giving me interested eyes as they passed. Paige and Della followed suit, though Rosario waited to speak to me. "I'm sure it goes without saying that you mustn't speak about what you see tonight. Listen, then decide if you want to come back. We need good people on our side. Take a seat."

She gestured to a stack of thick mats by the ring. Baffled, I sat cross legged on them as Rosario slid under the ropes and joined the circle.

With them all in one place, it was easier to take their measure. They were dressed in black, either short haired or wearing long hair tied back. They looked seriously fit, with lean bodies and muscle in all the right places. There was roughly an even number of guys and girls, and they looked ready for action. I just didn't know what kind yet.

"Team leaders – give your reports," Rosario said.

Paige spoke up. "We took down a biter in the park not long before dawn." Her upbeat tone made me apprehensive given the context. I started forming theories, though none of them seemed quite right.

"And left the body for the rest of us to clear up?" Rosario asked coldly. The vampire in the park – that was Paige and her cronies.

"We were interrupted," Paige said petulantly. "We got away before anyone saw us."

"What's done is done," Rosario said, waving a dismissive hand. "But plan your locations better next time. I had to send Taz and Della in on retrieval, but the police got there first."

Paige did a jerky little shrug, even though her cheeks had scarlet patches in the middle of them.

"I take it you followed the code," Rosario continued, "despite screwing up at the end. How'd you do it?"

"A stake – my favourite." Paige flashed a victorious grin, too delighted for the death she'd doled out and the body she'd left for the police to find.

My half-baked assumptions about Della being unfaithful had been way off. She and her buddies were killing vampires.

After that, they discussed quadrants of the city for patrolling, rotas and practical things that had nothing to do with blood and murder. While they talked, I kept looking at the deadly skewers of rock overhead. Della was hunting down people . . . vampires like Jared, and she'd kept it from us. He didn't deserve to die for trying to survive. She was watching me through the ropes of the ring, anxiety sparking off her.

"Before I let tonight's rotation go hunting, we have some special visitors," Rosario said.

Energy rippled through the slayers, alongside whispers and whoops. A group of three women and two men walked in. They looked like a rock band, adorned in leather, tattoos and swagger that's impossible to fake.

"Guys – meet your predecessors. They were slaying vamps around the time of the last surge, and they're going to share some wisdom with y'all tonight."

The young slayers showed a range of excited reactions, from bouncing where they sat to brilliant grins. Della had her arms wrapped around her knees and a look somewhere between shock and sadness.

"Good to meet y'all." A black woman with long, thick braids stepped forwards. She had a full mouth that fell into an easy smile, deepening the lines around her mouth and eyes. "My name's Monique. I was the leader of the slayers in the late 70s and early 80s. I remember bein' in your place when our elders came to visit, so I'll try not to keep y'all too long. Your task is hard. You do day jobs and then walk the city at night, defendin' people who don't even know you're there. But it's important, and y'all are smack bang in the middle of a surge. It's up to you to bring the vampires under control. That doesn't mean killing them indiscriminately – stick to the code. But there've been a hell of a lot of new vampires lately, and some of them aren't playin' by the rules. We've passed on some locations to your team leaders that we patrolled during the last surge.

Just one word of warnin' . . . You wanna be careful around the police. If you have a run-in with them, at best you'll be branded a vigilante. At worst, they'll see you as a murderer. The police deal with humans and we tackle vampires – that's how it's worked for centuries. I only know of one cop we've trusted with our secret in the past, and we need to keep it that way. Anythin' you wanna add, Jacklean?"

Another black woman stepped forwards. Her hair was cut

short, emphasising her strong bone structure and large eyes. She was a lot more serious than Monique. "We've been followin' the news and readin' Rosario's reports. You never stop bein' a slayer. We reduced the numbers back in the day, but many of our friends died for it. As Monique said, the police don't know shit about vampires. They put it down to migratin' animals and leave it to animal control. There isn't always a reason why there are surges in vampire activity. But if you can find out the cause, it may help us prevent the next one."

Monique took over with a smile. "Usually I'd remind y'all that older vamps are the ones to watch out for. They only get stronger and more ruthless. It's a real blessin' that one of the worst, John Carter, was taken down recently. We've reason to believe his brother has fled, and he was never a significant player. But often when numbers surge, it's newer vampires who haven't been properly guided by their sires. They're inexperienced fighters, but they have numbers on their side, and they're wild from being left unchecked."

Rosario stepped up. "Thanks Jacklean and Monique. Your team leader will hand out locations from the 70s surge for y'all to start searchin'."

A scattering of applause went round the room as Rosario started passing around lists. The younger slayers jumped up to mingle with the originals, and Della headed straight for one of them. I clambered off my mat, stiff-legged.

She reached Jacklean as I got to her side. "Auntie Jackie? I can't believe it's you!"

"Hey De-De. It's been a long time. You grew up."

"Yeah, and you left before you got to see that." I'd never seen Della look so wounded.

"I'm sorry, kiddo." Jacklean's expression softened. "It was too hard after your mom . . . She'd be proud that you became a slayer like her."

Chapter 15

"**M**om was a slayer?" Della's eyes filled up.

"It's in our blood," Jacklean said.

"So a vampire really killed her." Della wiped both eyes with her fingers, blinking hard. "I could never prove it."

"Honey, that's a much longer conversation." Jacklean fidgeted, looking at the door.

"Just tell me. Do you know what happened?"

Jacklean sighed. "We'd had a few close calls with vampires the week she passed. My car wouldn't start this one night, so I set off jogging to meet your mom on our patrol route. Then I found her... You sure you wanna hear this?"

Della nodded, her certainty coming through loud and clear.

"She'd ripped her throat out. One bite and it was all over." Sorrow took over Jacklean's features. "I'd lost my sister and my best friend."

"And then you split, leaving me and Dad with no clue what happened to her . . . or you."

Jacklean was unflinching in the face of Della's anger. "And I'd do it again. You lost your mother. I wasn't about to steal your youth. I knew if you were meant to be a slayer, your blood would call you to us when you were ready. I really have to be going—"

"You're leaving again?"

"It's not like that. Here . . ." Jacklean grabbed a biro and a scrap of paper from her pocket, leaning on her hand to write. "This is my number. If you'd like to meet, give me a call."

Della accepted it. "Why'd you say *she* ripped her throat out if you didn't see the vampire?"

"I don't know for certain – prob'ly never will. But the fang marks were narrower – consistent with a female bite."

Della nodded. The tight line of her mouth looked like it was holding back a sob. "Thank you for tellin' me. It was good to see you."

"You too, baby."

Jacklean strode out, and Della said, "I have to see Rosario. Then can we talk?"

"Yeah."

As soon as I was alone, Paige sidled up. "Don't take this the wrong way," she said, her voice syrupy with fake concern, "but I give you a week. We've seen girls like you before. They either die or quit." She smoothed her red ponytail over one shoulder, a satisfied smile on her glossy lips.

Another girl approached me – the one I'd seen in Della's car near the park. Her hair was shaved to a fine fuzz over her head, exposing delicate features on an open, friendly face. "Ignore Paige. She pulls that tough act with everyone. I'm Taz. Are you joinin' us?"

"I don't know yet," I said. I had too much to absorb and plenty to ask Della.

"Let me know if y'all have any questions. The first meetin's a lot to take."

"Thank you," I said. Taz's kindness felt disconnected from the brutality of what the slayers did.

"Don't feel bad if you can't handle it," Paige said sympathetically.

"Hi Paige." Della came up to us. Paige looked like she'd eaten something that disagreed with her. "Hasslin' the new recruits?"

"Just checking for weak links," Paige said with a predatory smile.

"Sure you are," Della said. "Come on, Mina."

"Nice to meet you, Taz," I said, ignoring Paige.

Taz smirked, glancing at the death-ray eyes Paige was giving me. "Feelin's mutual."

"I'm gonna skip my shift on patrols," Della said. "We need to talk."

She had that right. We headed up the stairs and onto the dark street. Della locked the door behind us, pushing against it to check that it held.

The usual night crowd mingled around us, and a woman was singing a sultry jazz song about how easy it was in the summertime. She hadn't lived our lives this past July.

"I'm sorry about your mom," I said. Della had kept secrets,

but she'd lost a lot too. "It must've been hard to hear what really happened to her."

"Thanks, it was . . . but it was kind of . . . good to finally know. Seein' Auntie Jackie though . . . That's the part I'm gettin' my head around. I'm so sorry I didn't tell you what I was doin'. What do you think?"

"I think," I said, quiet and full of intent, "that you're killing vampires, and Jared is a vampire."

Della twined a braid around her finger, tugging on it. "It's not like that. We don't kill vampires who feed consensually. We have a code."

"Oh really?" I stopped and almost collided with a tourist cradling a plastic bowl of gumbo.

Della took my arm and led me into an all-night coffee shop. "We can talk in here."

She queued to buy hot chocolates, while I simmered at a corner table. 'Creep' by Radiohead was playing, and the place was deserted. If I hadn't been busy trying to figure out what I was feeling, I would've appreciated the decor more. They'd gone for an undead rock god vibe. Motorcycle parts and guitars covered the brick walls in dazzling disarray. The staff wore band T-shirts with slashes cut into them and knots along the hems. They were also wearing brilliant vampire make-up, their eyes turned into deep hollows and subtle fangs pressing into their lower lips.

"You like?" Della asked, casting her eyes around.

"Yes, but don't try to distract me – I'm deciding whether or not to be mad at you," I said, sipping my hot chocolate. It was melted chocolate mixed with cream, and the thick, sugary sweetness usually would've put me in a favourable mood.

"Let me explain how it works," she pleaded. "We patrol the city in quadrants, focusing on areas of reported vampire activity. If we see someone getting attacked, we stop it. If there's no consent, we kill the vampire."

She made it sound so straightforward. "So they need to kill someone for you to kill them? Or hurt them really badly? Where's the line?"

"We don't have the backing of the law like the police or jails if vampires do wrong. If they kill, we kill. It's pretty simple."

God, she really just said that. "And you get to decide who lives or dies."

Della leaned forward, an overzealous look on her face. "I know you care for Jared – I get it. He's one of the good guys."

"But if he made a mistake, you'd kill him," I said. Her hesitation was all the answer I needed. "Have you killed anyone?"

"Not yet." Her face fell. "Except Lucas."

I wasn't going to hold that against her. He'd betrayed us in exchange for becoming a vampire, and he would've killed us if she hadn't got there first.

Della went on, a little shaken. "I've only been patrolling a couple months, but I've managed to stop the vamps before they killed anyone."

I'd heard all I could take. "Thanks for explaining all that. It's just . . . a lot. Do you mind if we go?"

"Not at all."

Once we'd transferred the delicious hot chocolates into to-go cups, we set off.

"What's the deal with Paige?" I asked, moving onto less morally grey areas. Surely we'd agree that she was awful.

"That's just how she is. She loathes me more than most people after I floored her ass."

"Tell me everything," I said, picturing Paige getting slammed down, red hair splayed out around her.

"Long story, but it starts with Armand." A crowd separated us as we waited to cross a road. I got back to her outside a packed venue blasting *The Addams Family* theme song, where everyone was clicking and singing. Della picked up the story. "Where was I? OK, so after Armand took over Empire, he kept giving me strange looks. Stranger than usual, anyway. After two shifts like that, I cornered him and asked what was what. He said he'd had a vision about me with a bunch of slayers in Lafayette Cemetery. You know what he's like. He said he saw a moon swollen and full overhead – all that stuff. He thought I might have found them already, but I hadn't. So I hung out there each full moon until they showed up. Luckily I only had to wait until the second month. I talked Rosario into taking me on, and here we are."

Armand had steered our actions again, plunging Della into a life that could get her killed. Jared and I had dressed up as Lestat and Claudia and chased down a lead after one of his visions, ending up in John Carter's sights. How often did he get visions about us and keep them to himself, toying with our lives? "What did Rosario think of a vampire's vision telling you about the slayers?"

"I skipped that part. I told them I'd killed Lucas and that John was dead. I said Wayne had split. I figured we owed Armand a solid for killing his brother to save us."

"And they let you join after that?"

"Not exactly. That was how I ended up laying Paige out in the ring. Nobody knew me, so they made me fight her to prove myself, but I've vouched for you."

"How do other people join?" I asked.

"They don't usually turn up off the street. The slayers recruit suitable candidates, especially during surges, but often it's passed through families and close friendships. Previous slayers don't go out on patrol or anything, but they help out with other things. There's a network all over the world. Wherever there's a lot of vamp activity, we got slayers."

"Really?" I asked, trying to wrap my mind around that. I hadn't given much thought to the whole world having a vampire problem. "So how come you didn't tell us about it?"

"It's not Libby's thing, and I knew she'd be scared for me. And you're with Jared . . . I wanted to figure out if it's right for me before tellin' the two of you."

I understood that. "And is it?"

Della sipped her drink, wrapping her hands around the cardboard cup. "I think so. Knowing what happened to my mom only makes it clearer. I couldn't save her, but I can save someone else."

"And Jacklean thinks it was a female vampire," I said.

"As soon as we have this surge under control, I'm going to see if Rosario will put the slayers on it," Della said. That was a typically measured response for Della, but with a deep undercurrent of rage that could easily pull her under and make her impulsive.

With the streets getting busy, we couldn't talk much. That gave me time to digest what Della had told me. The slayers had a moral code, so they had that in their favour. They were only killing vampires who killed humans.

When we got back, Della snuck into Libby's room. My mum used to say a stampeding herd of elephants couldn't wake Libby, so that worked out for Della.

With the night running out, I tried to sleep while slayers and murders blurred together. The slayers were helping people, but they were doing it by killing vampires. Rosario wanted me to be one of them, and what bothered me the most was that I didn't hate the idea.

Chapter 16

fter getting in past midnight, I slept in too late. I woke feeling fuzzy headed, glad I had only minimal plans. Hanging out with Nat and then the mansion reopening later wouldn't take too much out of me. That gave me the first touch of nerves, so I dragged myself up to make tea. Then I retreated to bed with some cupcakes Libby had picked up yesterday. They had pecan praline chunks in them, and soon me and my book were sticky. The light horror and seductively dark world of *The Forbidden Game* were engrossing, and I raced through the pages until I could get my next fix of Julian, the morally ambiguous antagonist who was also fiendishly gorgeous.

I wasn't aware of Libby and Della in my doorway until Libby spoke. Della was in her black bar uniform, and Libby had her smart-casual work clothes on. "Morning, sleepyhead. I thought you were never getting up."

"Leave her be," Della said with a smile. She'd obviously found a way to be at peace with Libby not knowing about the slayers. For now, I was too afraid of Libby seeing right through us to look her in the eye. "We're goin' to work. You need anythin'?"

"I have everything I need, thanks," I said.

"Including my cupcakes," Libby said. "See you later."

"Wait!" I said, scrambling out of bed. "I've got more of Thandie's letters. She talks about effects she used at the mansion and stuff like that."

Libby's hand trembled as she took them. "Thanks – I'll read them at the mansion later." I liked the thought of Libby sitting at Thandie's old desk to read her letters. When I'd first got to New Orleans, Libby would've done anything to escape from difficult subjects. We'd both come a long way.

Nat arrived about an hour later, unexpectedly laden down with bags and accompanied by Will. He looked uncomfortable in the unseasonable sunshine with that black coat glued to him. She was pristine in the Wednesday Addams dress from Fanged Friends.

"Morning," I said. "What's in the bags?"

"Gwyneth Paltrow's head," Will said.

I laughed. "I think that was a box. Now are you going to tell me what you've brought, or should I start rummaging?"

The red plastic bags were bulging with scraps of white fabric, glimpses of orange and lots of black.

"Spoil my fun," Nat grumbled, but she was grinning. "Your house was looking sad, so I brought Halloween and snacks. Libby said I could."

I was impressed. Libby was like a steel trap when it came to feelings, but give her a secret and she was usually begging to let it out.

"So . . . we're decorating the house for Halloween." A giddy feeling bubbled up inside me. I preferred Halloween to Christmas. Between school for me, college for Libby, the mansion and money being tight, decorating had slipped through the cracks. I wasn't used to having a thoughtful friend, and Nat caught me off guard every time. Only having Jared here would make this better. He missed so much sleeping away the day.

I stashed that in the stack of things I could do nothing about and concentrated on Nat. She'd got an impressive spread: fragile spiders' webs that tangled the second we touched them, rubber bats, plastic candles, vinyl window stickers of hands clawing from graves, tiny plastic pumpkins and a huge real one.

"Did Sam not want to join us?" I asked.

"He's just discovered this new website where you can buy and sell stuff called Ebuy . . . no Ebay! That was it. Besides, this is not really his thing," Nat said.

Will laughed. "And you think it's mine?"

"Hush," Nat said. "It's not long 'til you go back to college, and I want to spend as much time with you as I can, however annoying you are. Let's get some decorations up then break for lunch."

"I thought you said this would be fun," Will said.

"Organised fun," Nat said. "You guys put the spider's web up in the hallway – it's a two-person job."

Will muttered about where she could shove her two-person job, but he took the opposite corners to mine and helped me carry the webs.

"Halloween really brings out the dictator in her," I said, crouching to spread out the web.

"I heard that!" Nat said. A tub of pins bounced into the hallway. She'd thought of everything.

"Let's get this over with," Will said, opening the pins. "Do you think the web will reach all the way across the hall?"

"Only one way to find out," I said, threading a few pins along one side to start us off. "So, you're into Brad Pitt movies?"

"You don't have to," Will said, poking some pins through the other side of the web.

"Pin this? I don't know how we'll get it to stay up without them."

He raised his eyebrows at me, making sharp arches. "Make an effort with me for Nat's sake."

"Can't it be for mine? Or yours?" I asked, standing up. "Let's give this a go."

We stretched out the web, both standing on our tiptoes to pin along the top of the wall. It looked pretty good when we stepped back. "Let's add a few more pins and do the other sides," Will said.

"I thought you were too cool to care," I teased.

"Definitely not," he said. "And I do . . . like Brad Pitt films, I mean. Love some *Thelma and Louise* and *True Romance*."

We started on the other two sides. However much of a lone wolf Will wanted to be, we made a good team.

"Have you seen *Kalifornia*? We rented it the other day, and it was great," I said, crouching down to retrieve an escaped pin.

"Not seen that one," he said. "What's it about?"

"David Duchovny researching serial killers. Brad Pitt plays one that he accidentally picks up in his car."

"Huh," he said, "Sounds like something I have to see. I'm done with my side."

"Me too."

We stood underneath the web. It bowed down in the middle, with the edges forming even loops. "Ever considered a job in interior decorating?" I asked.

"I've always felt there was something missing from my life," Will said.

"You're done?" Nat said. "Excellent! You can add the spiders now."

Will and I exchanged the kind of knowing glance that usually takes years to refine. Even though this was the most fun I'd had in a while, it was touched with sadness. It'd been too long since I'd had light-hearted time like this with Jared, just being together without agonising about what it would do to him. I wanted to believe that we'd be like this again.

By the time Nat deemed us worthy of a break, we were ravenous. Nat had picked up Sicilian sandwiches called *muffulettas*, which were stuffed with thin layers of meat, cheese and spicy olive salad. We took our time over lunch and then got back to decorating.

"Let's do the pumpkin," Nat said, appearing in the doorway as I applied the last vinyl sticker to Libby's window.

"I have to get to Radio Shack," Will said. "I'll see if your Dictaphone is ready, but it'll probably be a few more days."

By the time I reached the hallway, he was at the front door. "Thanks for helping," I said, "and for the movie chat."

"Any time," he said, low on his usual swagger.

As soon as Will left, Nat and I lugged the huge pumpkin onto the kitchen table. She started drawing a face on it that looked like Jack Skellington. "Will likes you," she said, her voice distorted by the pen lid clamped between her side teeth, "and he doesn't like anyone."

"Good," I said. "The feeling's mutual."

Nat sat back to look at her handiwork, putting the cap back on the pen. "He's a bit of a loner, so it's great to see him having actual conversations. Losing Louisa . . . It's been worse since then."

Nat hardly mentioned her sister, so I was undecided if she wanted me to ask about her. She seemed almost too focused on the pumpkin, so I glossed over it. "He can hang out with us any time." I'd never had a group that felt like mine until I came here.

Nat and I had grabbed a knife each when Libby breezed into the kitchen, freezing in the doorway. "Don't do that to me! You two are scary enough without being armed."

"What, this?" Nat stabbed the knife into the pumpkin. She left the blade stuck in there, handle trembling.

"You're a bad influence," Libby said, grabbing a coke from the fridge. She pressed it against her forehead, then cracked it open. "Are you two still helping at the mansion later?"

"We'll be there with bats on," Nat said.

"Your enthusiasm is appreciated," Libby said. "I'll grab some paperwork and get out of your way."

Once Libby left, Nat carved the pumpkin with disturbing glee, orange flesh and gloopy seeds flying. Jack Skellington had morphed into Jack Nicholson's joker, his eyebrows arched like Will's. I kept that to myself – Nat was holding the knife after all.

After polishing off the leftover sandwiches and putting up the final decorations, we headed off to meet Libby.

I rummaged for the key in my backpack as we approached the Mansion of the Macabre: a tall, thin building that was deceptively large inside.

The grey front was black and charred, and Libby had fitted green lights that created a ghoulish, almost mouldy appearance. Black bars made decisive slashes across each window, as if we were trying to keep something inside. The round attic window peered down as I located my key, dredging up memories of the night I'd found Heather up there in a pool of blood. John had arranged her body to set Libby up for murder, in a failed attempt to bring our mum out of hiding.

That took the brightness out of my mood, right before I opened the door to find my sister crouching down in a nest of bear traps.

Chapter 17

"Libby," I said carefully, so as not to startle her. "What are you doing?"

"What does it look like?" Libby asked, wiping a streak of dust from her cheek with the back of her hand. "It's filthy!"

Libby had one foot inside the bear trap chandelier, her slim ankle bared to the tangle of jagged teeth and light bulbs as she wiped them with a duster.

"Those things aren't active, right?" Nat asked.

"Of course not," Libby said, her mocking tone not entirely certain.

I couldn't trust myself to speak again until she'd stepped free of the deadly web of metal. Nat helped her to pull on the long chain that raised the bear traps back over our heads. Libby wrapped it around a pair of hooks on the wall. It was unsettling that two thin pieces of metal were all that stood between us and bloody death. Thandie's eye for aesthetics had been impeccable.

"We need to check the *Candyman* room and brief Jason," Libby said, retrieving her clipboard from the bottom step. "Della has to work, so you two are all I've got. Everything has to be perfect."

"It will be," I said. It'd be fun to spend time with Jason. We'd clicked when he'd scared the crap out of me as Leatherface on my first night working here. Since Libby had moved me to Jared's room, I'd not had chance to hang out with Jason.

"Come on then!" Libby hurried upstairs. After being bossed around by Nat all day, it was Libby's turn.

"She seems more . . . Libby than usual," Nat said. Her *Addams Family* dress blended in with the mansion's Gothic decor. Libby hadn't touched the hallway, so it was all Thandie. The chair shaped like a contorted skeleton was still to one side, still freaking me out. Behind Nat, grey wallpaper shimmered with the ghostly imprints of children's hands. They shifted as I approached the stairs, fading and reappearing. The carpet was a plush black and the lighting was weak, creating a funereal air.

"She's stressed," I said. "Sales have been down since Thandie . . . since what happened here." Since she was murdered in her own museum. "Libby's trying to give it a boost." Thandie's power of infusing visitors with fear had gone when she'd passed away. Even though we knew that, Libby was trying to make up for it.

"I get that," Nat said. "Let's go before she implodes."

We went up to the changing room to ditch my backpack before

joining Libby in the new *Candyman* room. Libby hated clowns, so she'd replaced the *IT* experience at the first opportunity.

The room hadn't taken much updating. We'd left the yellowed tiles, but the bath had been replaced by a line of toilet cubicles covered in graffiti. Extra sinks created the illusion of a public bathroom. I'd talked Libby out of using smell effects.

There was a full-length mirror by the sinks. In the movie, the main character had climbed over a sink through a hole behind the mirror, but we'd decided it was best if the tour goers didn't fall on their faces.

"Scour every inch of this room. We can't leave tripping hazards or anything that kills the illusion. Then we'll do the walk through."

"So nothing that kills the fun or the guests – got it," Nat said.

"Let's hope you help better than you make jokes." Libby had started a lap of the room, her eyes on the ground. We all did a pass, and everything was in order apart from some screws and wood shavings.

"OK, let's do this." Libby said, closing her eyes. When she opened them, a malicious curve tweaked her lips and a devious look made her eyes shifty. "Welcome to your portal to the mansion," she announced, standing in the middle of the bathroom with her arms outstretched.

"Play along," I murmured to Nat, trying to get in the headspace of someone doing the tour.

"Simply stand in front of the mirror and repeat one word to gain entry. Who will be brave enough?" She'd got the concept for the *Candyman* room from me. On my first visit as a tourist, I'd seen the *IT* bathroom and had initially guessed the wrong movie.

"The word . . ." She paused, her expression eerily blank as she let her eyes land on me and then Nat. ". . . is Candyman."

We all knew Candyman wasn't real. But anyone with an imagination would surely have some doubt. He was supposed to appear and use a hook to kill anyone who dared to speak his name five times in front of a mirror. And this was no ordinary mirror.

Libby faced the glossy surface. "Anyone curious to see if he's real? *Candyman.*"

We missed her first cue. Her lips pinched in irritation, but we joined in the second time. "Candyman."

The high ceiling tiles sent an echo back to us. We said it twice more, our voices synchronised.

One more time left. Even though this wasn't a real tour, the atmosphere was electric.

"Candyman!" Libby called, arms flung in the air.

A buzzing noise began, so subtle that you could almost miss it. It soon crescendoed to an impatient growl. The lights flickered, and a draft swirled around our feet.

The mirror melted away, the taut reflective plastic on a timed release.

Nat pressed against me, and the buzzing grew louder. A dark space waited where the mirror had once been.

"This is—" Nat began.

Libby put a finger to her lips. "Follow me."

The buzzing intensified along with my doubts. What if this was too much for the tour group and Libby's redesign flopped?

We inched through a cramped, dark space where the buzzing reached a fever pitch. Projectors cast crawling swarms of bees all over the ceiling.

"Look behind you," Libby said, her voice so convincingly frightened that it infected me.

The wall behind us came into brilliant illumination as we followed her instruction. Red spots danced over my vision, but everything soon came into focus. A mural of Candyman's face was painted around the hole where we'd entered. We'd walked out through his open mouth, his unhinged eyes staring daggers at us. His dark brown skin looked almost too real. Beside the mural was a bag spilling out possessions and bright sweet wrappers, minus the razor blades from the movie. A bed was tucked into the corner, its headboard replaced with a crumbling gravestone.

"Turn around," a low, resonant voice boomed behind us.

We obeyed, and a large, shadowed figure had appeared. It slowly raised one hand into the air, the hook shining in the darkness. Then, he stepped into the light.

Jason was wearing a matted fur coat with a thick white collar at his throat. His chest was covered with a red, writhing mass of bees, an effective trick of the projector.

He scooped up a mannequin. In a darkened room full of unsuspecting tour guests, it'd be easy to pretend one had been taken. He secured the doll with an arm around the throat. "I will let most of you go, but there has to be a sacrifice."

Jason raised the hook and slashed it down into the mannequin with a sickening crunch. "Tell those you love to fear me. Now go!"

"And cut," Libby said, and the lights came up.

"Thanks *a lot* for inviting me here to ruin a perfectly good pair of underwear," Nat said.

"She means that was brilliant!" I said. "The effects were impeccable, and I don't know how you manage to be the nicest person and yet so terrifying." I directed the last part to Jason. His dimpled smile was as friendly as when we'd first met, but the tight curls of his hair were shorter.

"Thanks so much," he said, humble and almost shy after shedding the role. He seemed to have lost about a foot in height, and his dark brown skin gleamed after the exertion. "I used to love swinging my chainsaw around, but I do have fun with that hook."

"You're a natural," Nat said. "Definite serial killer material, if you ever want a career change."

Jason chuckled, his eyes lingering on the hook. "My dad showed me how to use a knife when he taught me to fish. I never figured on using my gutting skills here. Hey, do you know if Tessa's coming tonight?"

"No, you're fine," Libby said. "She has other plans."

"Good," he said, smiling on his way out.

"Did *anything* not come off right?" Libby asked.

"The guests will love it," I said.

"You know I'd tell you the truth," Nat said, "and she's right. I should get going before the crowds come."

"I'll let you out," I said. Guests had a tendency of snooping if we left the door unlocked.

With Jason gone, I asked Libby, "Did Tessa used to date Jason too?"

"Yeah – after Jared. It was earlier this year. She spent the whole summer at home because of their break-up, and they mostly try to stay clear of each other now," Libby said.

I walked Nat out, and a few customers were hovering along the street. You could spot them a mile off, usually wearing something Gothic or movie-themed and gesturing excitedly in this direction. Cafferty and his sister were coming down the street, and I waved.

"Well he looks just as good in real life, even without the suit," Nat said, "but I really have to leave. My mom . . ."

"Go," I said. "I'll catch up with you later." Like Della, Nat's only parent was protective. It was understandable. Della's dad had lost his wife, and Nat's mum had lost her eldest daughter.

Nat hurried away, and I crossed the road. "Hi! You must be Carly."

"So that makes you Mina, the work experience girl," Carly said, "and not some criminal he's arrested. I like to check these things out."

Carly was blonde like Cafferty. She had the same defined jaw and easy, genuine smile, but the similarities ended there. He was wearing a red and blue plaid shirt – very Clark Kent. She was more like the Kryptonian villains in black leather trousers and a black mesh top with red underneath it. Her eyes were surrounded by heavy black eyeliner and red eyeshadow that made them especially blue.

"Jesus Carly," he muttered. "Hey, Mina. How you doin'?"

"Pretty good."

"Sorry," Carly said. "I wasn't tryin' to say you look like a criminal. I'm just glad to see Matt havin' an actual conversation. He's all do-gooding and no play usually."

'Matt' blushed and nudged a shoulder into his sister. "Sorry about her. I'd say she's usually nicer but . . ."

Carly nudged him back, laughing. So Cafferty and I had annoying siblings in common.

"I take it you're not interested in being a cop?" I asked Carly.

"Hell no. Matt took me on a ride along this one time, and that was enough."

"I should get back inside, but it was really nice to meet you," I said to Carly. "See you on the tour."

Chapter 18

I was running late after my chat with Cafferty, so I hurried into the busy changing room. I wriggled into my blue-silk Claudia dress with everyone chatting around me. Libby appeared for long enough to zip me in. She was in her tuxedo jacket dress and grey horror make-up that made her look dead. Frantic energy poured off her, and I gave her a quick hug before she disappeared again.

I dusted my skin white, applying red lip gloss and a dot of black eyeliner for a beauty spot. Finally, I pinned myself into the blonde, curly wig, my fingers quick with practice. My reflection looked younger and more innocent than me.

I knocked on the door of the *Interview with the Vampire* room.

Jared opened it, leaning seductively against the frame in front of the backdrop of lush red and gold furnishings.

Jared had always made my brain stop working in his Lestat costume. As an actual vampire, he was even more alluring, because the danger was real. He still used the pale make-up, even though the healthy bronze of his skin had dulled without sun exposure. With eyeliner and a sticky red mouth, not to mention those sprayed-on leather trousers, he looked like someone else entirely. "My lady," he said, taking my hand and leaning down for a cautious kiss.

I tugged it free. "Behave! I don't have anything to wipe off the syrup."

Jared's eyes strayed to my mouth, the look loaded with Lestat's charisma. I took in the open neckline of his frilly white shirt, the sliver of chest I wanted so badly to touch. I couldn't remember the last time we'd really kissed. I hadn't known then that I should've captured the moment for when I needed it.

"How's your arm?" I asked, concentrating on a safer part of the body.

He pushed the floaty sleeve up to his elbow. "Good as new." The skin the vampire had bitten was unmarked. "One of the perks, I guess."

"Speaking of those . . . A friend of Thandie's gave me some of her letters, and I found out what power she had."

Jared tensed. "Oh yeah?"

"She could manipulate emotions, which she mainly used to give the mansion's guests a boost of fear on their way around."

"Woah . . . That'd be scary if the wrong person had it. I hope . . ." He swallowed hard. "I'd rather not have a power if I get one like John's."

I wanted to offer support, but he was right. A power would

only make us more different, especially one as sinister as John's mind control. Thandie had told us over the summer that powers often stemmed from someone's personality traits, so John must have been almost as awful as a human. Before I could reply, Jared was moving on. "Can we talk about somethin' else? Or try . . . not talking?"

We'd been light on the not talking lately. My nerves were shifty, spiky things, no longer the light, excited bubbles from when we first met. "What did you have in mind?" I asked, standing my ground even though every instinct was telling me to back away.

He smiled wickedly. He was so much . . . *more* since he became a vampire. Everything about him was amped up, shaping his clumsy charm into predatory magnetism and his wholesome handsomeness into something darker and more compelling.

I inched towards him, conscious of all the places my pulse throbbed, how he must be able to hear it. My chest was the obvious one, but my wrists and throat ached with the heat of the blood coursing through them. I wanted him to kiss me – not just the fleeting brushes of his mouth on my skin that he'd offered lately. It wasn't the first time I'd wondered what it would be like for him to drink my blood on my terms, even though the feeling was wrapped up in doubt.

We edged closer, our gazes intense as we weighed each other's responses. I kept my breathing steady, willing my pulse to slow.

He was close enough to touch. I held his cheeks, looking into his eyes. The blend of brown to hazel and green was unchanged, but there was something cold and distant in them.

The muscles along his jaw flexed under my hands. We'd got into a pattern of rushed intimacy: a quick brush of his lips against my forehead or tucking myself under his arm and then veering away. We had to move past it. "Is this OK?" I whispered.

He gave the tiniest nod, licking his lips – not the most reassuring motion. If we hadn't been this close, I might have missed the signs. The skin around his eyes was pink, and a faint sheen of sweat coated his skin. Thin red capillaries threaded his eyes.

"When did you last feed?" I asked, keeping my voice even and my hands in place, though it might have been time to run.

"Yesterday," he said, his gaze flicking down to my wrist, so close to his mouth where I was holding his face. "I shouldn't need more yet. I'm fine."

I lowered my hands slowly. "I don't think you are. You don't have to hide from me – I understand."

He laughed bitterly, backing away. "How can you?"

"The tour group will be here soon. Do you need to feed?" Anxiety pulsed through me, hot and potent as the blood I was offering.

Jared moved back. "Please don't say what I think you're going to. I can get through the tour."

"Are you sure?" I asked, pressing the issue even as my fear grew more concentrated.

"You're trembling," he said, "and I can hear your heartbeat. Neither of us want this, so can we drop it?" Jared's gaze travelled from my chest to my throat, lingering there.

"I only want to help you. If you need blood, we should talk about it." That was true, but I was scared about how this could change things. The scar on my wrist was a warning about what happened last time.

"It's not that simple. I don't bite people for pleasure. If I bite you, it'll blur the lines. I don't want you to be that to me."

And I'd backed him into a corner about it. "Sorry . . . I get it."

"I know." His smile was tight. "You don't have to apologise. We should take our places."

Burning with shame, I sat at the piano and Jared hopped onto the coffin at the end of the bed. "Mina," he said, gentler now that we weren't so close. "Don't agonise over this. I know you're trying to help."

"Thank you," I said, the guilt fading.

I forced myself into character, sitting up straighter and reaching for Claudia's confidence and sense of entitlement. I inserted my plastic fangs, running my tongue over them. Jared no longer needed the fake ones.

Since I have no musical talent, I idly tapped the piano keys as the tour group entered. "Hello," I said, making my voice high and petulant. "What do you want?"

"Claudia," Jared chastised, capturing Lestat's silky tones. "These are our guests."

"Oh goody." I slammed the piano lid, sending jumps through the group. Cafferty's sister laughed and pressed against him, while he looked like he was fantasising about being anywhere else. "I like it when you order room service. How many can I have?"

"Don't be greedy, child," Jared said. "One will suffice."

Banging started from inside the coffin where he sat. Jason had rigged up a motorised mallet, and it was working a treat. Jared scowled down at it as the knocking intensified. "Quiet!" he yelled, and the noises stopped.

Jared's look was especially mischievous, and I was glad he appeared to have let our conversation go. Impulsively, I decided to have some fun.

"Fine," I said, sticking out my bottom lip. "I want . . . him."

The crowd parted for Cafferty. Carly was grinning broadly as he sloped over, hands in pockets.

Jared's face was a mask of impatience and disapproval, though I couldn't tell where Lestat ended and he began. "Now now," he said. "It's not nice to play with your food."

"I won't," I said sullenly, returning to Cafferty. "Please sit." I clambered on top of the piano, vacating the stool.

Cafferty did as he was told, wiping his hands down his jeans and looking up at me.

"Come along, everyone," Libby said in a bright, sing-song voice, despite the murder in her eyes. "You don't need to see this."

"But I do love an audience," I said, leaning down towards Cafferty's throat, tilting my head as if I was inspecting the best place to bite.

I timed my lunge as the lights cut out. Strobes flashed as water sprayed down, dyeing the droplets red.

Gratifying squeals cut through the darkness. We were scaring people, even without Thandie's power. I drew back and stayed put on the piano. Falling on top of Cafferty would be the worst possible finale.

The door closed on the tour group and the lights came on. "Thanks for playing along," I said, sliding off the side of the piano. That was harder than it looked in a corset.

"Thanks for givin' my sister somethin' new to torment me about," Cafferty said, impressively good natured. "Can I go, or is this where I get bitten?"

"I know I want to bite you," Jared said, giving a wolfish grin. The red skin around his eyes had flared up, an indication that he was close to losing control. He must have really needed to feed.

"And on that note, I'll let you out," I said.

Carly and a less-than-enthused Libby were on the other side of the door.

"I've never seen you look so uncomfortable. Best birthday present ever!" Carly said.

"I don't know about that – you've not opened your actual present yet," Cafferty said, tapping the bag strapped across his body and grinning at me. "See you tomorrow."

Libby glowered at us as we listened to the two of them jogging downstairs, Carly ribbing her brother.

As soon as we heard the front door close, Libby laid into me. "It's bad enough that you're doing work experience with the cop who arrested me, but you had to pull him out too?"

"It was just a bit of fun," I said. "It's not like we're breaking any laws."

"Let's keep it that way," Libby said, stomping off.

I retreated to the *Interview with the Vampire* room. Usually I loved embodying Claudia, but tonight I had to work at it as the next few tour groups came through. Jared and I chatted between visits, but he stayed on his coffin and I sat by the piano. There was no obvious tension, but not a lot of affection either.

When we were done, I headed for the changing room. Jason was on his way out. "How did the new *Candyman* room go?" I asked.

He smiled shyly. "Not too bad. When I get the crowd in front of me, it makes performin' so much better, you know?"

"Yeah, I do. Don't tell Jared, but I miss the rush of doing the *Texas Chainsaw Massacre* room with you." It'd been so exciting when he'd chased me, the kind of safe scare that got my heart pumping.

"It was fun – you did great in there." His expression was unusually closed off. Could he have been remembering what had happened later that night? I'd found Heather in the attic, dead and covered in blood. Jason and a few others had run up when I screamed, the terrible sight leaving us forever changed and bound together.

As I peeled off my Claudia dress amidst the scramble of girls getting ready, I thought about Jared on the boys' side and all the blood-filled bodies around him.

I grabbed my clothes from my backpack, and a folded sheet of white paper came out with them. Sickly dread pooled in my stomach as I read the note. It was written in red biro scratched hard into the paper. For a few words, they packed a punch.

HAVE YOU FORGOTTEN FANG FEST?

I HAVEN'T.

Chapter 19

stuffed the page into the bottom of my bag and retrieved my clothes, heart pounding. Loads of people worked at the mansion, and some had questionable ideas about humour. It was likely just a sick joke – maybe not even intended for me. Whoever did it was probably watching to get a kick out of my reaction. I'd worked on my blank ignoring face growing up with Libby, and I put it to good use. But why did they have to bring up the scariest few days of my life?

After receiving the note and the awkward feeding conversation with Jared earlier, I felt unnerved as I got dressed. Libby and I headed down together, her face pink where she'd scrubbed off the horror make-up. "Do you really think we pulled it off?" Libby asked. She looked tired, the dark circles under her eyes standing out against unusually pale skin.

"It was a hit," I said as we reached the bottom of the stairs. "Thandie would be seriously proud."

Guardedness slammed down over Libby's features. "Thanks…" she said. "I have a tonne of work to do. Can you ask Jared to walk you home?"

She looked so worn out that I tried not to let my disappointment show. "Sure," I said. I'd expected a chance to celebrate and spend some time together. At least we had plenty of plans over Halloween. We only had a day to wait until the legendary Orchard Estate ball, and she wouldn't miss that.

Jason stampeded downstairs, all long legs and awkwardness. "So," he said shyly, much more self-contained when he wasn't in costume. "Did I pull it off, boss?"

"As good as the real Candyman guy," Libby said.

"Tony Todd," Jared called, coming down behind Jason.

"You took the words right out of my mouth," I said.

"Glad I didn't let you down. Night y'all," Jason said, before heading out of the front door.

"Did you say you need me?" Jared asked. "I have an errand, but I can drop you off on the way." That sounded like he was going to feed, so soon after he'd refused my blood. It was getting harder not to be offended about him going off to share that intimate act with someone else: his mouth on their bare skin, blood pulsing beneath the surface …

Libby spoke before I could spiral any further. "What have I told you about listening in on conversations?"

Jared shrugged. "Not like I can help it. Are you ready?"

The night air cut through my thin cotton jacket, and I rubbed my arms. Jared set a quick pace, and I soon warmed up. I was working on an apology when he got there first. "I'm sorry. I shouldn't have gone off on you."

"It was my fault," I said. "I shouldn't have pushed."

He held out his hand, and I accepted it. I wanted to bury my face in his chest like I once would've done, but instead I'd have to make do with the way his fingers interlaced with mine.

Jared was quiet on the way back, and the evidence that he needed to feed was intensifying. His hand was even colder than usual, and his bronze skin was dull. The red capillaries in his eyes were pronounced, and the skin around them was raw. His grip tightened, and I flexed my fingers. My senses of sight and hearing sharpened, preparing me in case I needed to escape. Jared was more in control than when he'd bitten me, but we were still figuring out his threshold.

Another vampire with questionable willpower was waiting by our door. Mum hadn't changed since the day she left us in Whitby over a year ago. We'd inherited her unmanageable dark brown hair and darker eyes but not the secretive way she surveyed everything, deciding whether it was worth sticking around for. "Hey you two," she said.

"Evenin', ma'am," Jared said politely.

"Hi Mum," I said.

"Sorry for just stopping by like this. Is it a bad time?" She assessed Jared and answered for us. "Never mind – I can see that it is. I'll go."

Instead of letting her leave, I made one last-ditch attempt at a connection. "Can we try this again soon?"

Her smile was unconvincing. "Of course. It may not seem like it now, but I promise you we'll fix things. See you soon." Then she was gone all over again, the latest in a series of failed meetings and empty promises. Last time she'd left me and Libby waiting outside a cinema for her. We gave up once the film was too far in to make any sense. The best she'd managed was a rushed cup of coffee when she spent the whole time watching the door.

Jared's cough brought me back to him. "I really should get going," he said, looking truly awful.

"Thanks for walking me back. See you tomorrow," I said.

"Night Mina," he said, a deep frown telling me there was more he wanted to say.

I walked into the empty house, failing to shrug off the sense of rejection. I was used to feeling abandoned by Mum, but the difference was that it wasn't Jared's fault. Still, it was wearing on me more every day. He wasn't ready to talk about feeding on humans, but I knew someone who had been a vampire for a lot longer. Though I'd had my reservations about Armand, I understood why the others leaned on him. There was no one else who could answer my questions.

Armand picked up the phone on the first ring. "Hello?"

"It's Mina," I said. "I hope you don't mind me phoning, but I have a question about vampires. How come it hurt when Jared bit me, but people line up for it at The Underground?"

Armand sighed. "I'm very well – thank you for asking. Wouldn't you prefer to discuss this with Jared?"

"It's all so new, and he doesn't want to talk about it. Can't you tell me?"

Another sigh. "You're putting me in rather a difficult position, but I can see where this is going. I'll be there in ten minutes."

Armand hung up. He was true to his word, and I only had ten minutes of pacing. "You could've told me on the phone," I said through the open door, very pointedly not inviting him inside. He might have been about to help me, but I wasn't giving the remaining Carter brother access to our house.

"I'd rather take you to The Underground so you can see for yourself. You're planning something, and it'd be better for everyone if you know all of the information."

"Did you just use your powers on me?" A chill rippled over my skin as I replayed what he'd said. He was taking me to a place where vampires and people role playing as vampires went to drink blood.

Armand continued, oblivious to my thoughts. Luckily his powers didn't work like that. "I know you."

"OK . . . Let me grab my coat."

A strange blankness came over Armand's face, and his eyes seemed unseeing. Was I supposed to snap him out of it? What was the rule with sleepwalkers again?

His eyes swivelled onto me, and it was frightening how inhuman he looked. His face appeared utterly blank, almost dead. "It's you," he said.

"It's me what?" I asked, going for a light tone even though a lump of fear had lodged in my throat.

He blinked hard, recovering. "I saw something. I go into a trance when I have a vision."

"Anything interesting?"

He eyed me as we set off. "I saw you wearing a stripy red and green sweater – a rather ratty one. You were in a steamy room, and I sensed a lot of fear. You held something sharp, and you were waiting."

"Sounds like Libby's finally going to let me play a villain at the mansion," I said, thinking of the *Nightmare on Elm Street* room with its billows of dry ice and Freddy Krueger's iconic costume.

Armand frowned. "It was unclear if I'd seen your past or future, but I'm glad it seems to be nothing sinister. Let's go."

We set off together, and it was strange to walk down the street with him. I'd never spent much time with Armand, if you didn't count him appearing unannounced to give ambiguous warnings.

The streets were packed with people drinking and wandering in and out of bars. Different songs competed to be heard, and there was a real party atmosphere. Armand looked like anyone else, brooding and dressed all in black. Yet around us, there was a radius of quiet, as if intuition told people to stay away from a predator.

My mind strayed to one of other vampires in my life. "What if Jared's feeding at The Underground?" I was going there to figure things out, not run into him.

"Not tonight," Armand said, more certain of Jared's whereabouts than I ever was.

"Oh, OK." I said. I had an audience with a vampire, and I was wasting time angsting about Jared. "Do you know why there are more vampires in New Orleans than there used to be?"

He scrutinised me. "How do you know that?"

"Animal attacks have been all over the news. It can't be very good for your secrecy."

Armand veered around a girl who had stumbled into our

path. "No, it isn't. There have been a lot of us recently. There are fluctuations in vampire numbers from time to time and forces that bring them in line."

"Like the slayers?"

"I saw you with them," he said. "The clearest picture I've had of late. Are you joining their ranks . . . or thinking of becoming a police officer even?"

It felt weird to talk slayers with him, especially when I hadn't mentioned it to Jared. I'd been too wrapped up in our personal drama. "I don't know yet. I haven't told Jared . . ."

"Your secret's safe with me. I don't interfere with things I see in visions unless I have to."

I wasn't used to Armand being so open or letting me benefit from the wealth of his knowledge. I wished I'd had the opportunity to get to know Thandie better. Her letters, and hopefully the Dictaphone, would have to do to give me some insights into her life. Last time I'd come to The Underground, I'd seen her feeding consensually, and it had undone everything I thought I knew about vampires. This time, I'd be arriving with a vampire.

Chapter 20

We reached the unmarked front of The Underground. It was entirely mundane apart from the burly bodyguard on the door.

We walked through the dreary club, with its wilted people drained of their spirit along with their blood. The red ribbons trailing from pockets and tied around throats and wrists meant these people were willing to let someone drink their blood. I was curious about being one of them, but only with Jared. It frightened me too, and I automatically touched the raised skin on my scarred wrist.

The only thing The Underground got right was the music. Last time, it was The Smiths. Tonight, they were playing my favourite Shakespears Sister song. 'Stay' was at the part where the second singer warns someone to pray they make it back safely. I knew how that felt.

A well-muscled female bouncer at the back of the room was the most alert-looking person in the place. Everyone else was drooped over tables or downing shots at the bar.

My hands were clammy by the time we reached the bouncer. Without Armand, I wouldn't make it through the door. We'd succeeded in the summer because Jared knew what to say, getting us in without medical clearance by presenting Lucas's red token.

"Armand." The bouncer nodded to us, raising a clipboard with a thick wad of papers attached. "Name?"

"Mina Sheppard," I said, my voice even despite my reservations. Was this when I'd get thrown out?

The woman flicked through the papers, smiling when she found my name. "Mina – one of Elvira's clients. Your last visit was . . . in July. It's her night off, but she'll be back tomorrow. We can set you up if you'd like to see someone else."

Dazed, I struggled to ask, "Isn't . . . Didn't she . . . pass away?"

"She did," the woman said, "but another girl took on her role and client list. She was popular, and so far our clients like the new Elvira too."

They'd replaced Elvira as if her death was meaningless. Regret made it hard to find the words, and Armand stepped in. "Is there a problem?"

"Mina's missing medical clearance," she replied. I'd not been tested for communicable diseases like everyone else.

"That's not an issue," Armand said. "The only person feeding from her tonight will be me, and I've had her tested privately."

"Fine," the woman said, moving back to let us pass.

I'd asked Armand to help me understand feeding. He'd never said how he was going to teach that lesson.

The stairs were bare stone worn smooth in the middle from the passage of countless feet. I'd previously had a red ribbon tied around my throat and a vague lead in our quest to prove Libby's innocence. I was here to find answers again.

After the stone walls and exposed bulbs of the stairwell, the room below was a stark contrast. Red velvet curtains covered each booth, hiding real vampires feeding on humans and lifestylers – humans who enjoyed a vampire lifestyle on either side of the feeding relationship. The plush carpet was the exact shade of blood. A bouncer stood to one side of the room, glowering at a blank spot on the wall.

"What now?" I whispered.

"You wanted to see why people let vampires bite them. This booth is for observation, so let's observe."

We slipped into the centre booth and sat by the curtain. Being this close to Armand was uncomfortable, like balancing on the edge of a shark tank with my blood dripping into the water.

The booth was round like where we'd met Elvira. My stomach clenched at the thought of her, ending up dead in one of John Carter's cells under Empire as punishment for sharing information with us.

I forced myself to focus. A leather-clad vampire was feeding on someone across the booth. He had glossy, dark brown skin and was huge in height and musculature, though he seemed to be handling the human with care. He had his mouth pressed against the inner elbow of a slender guy with tightly curled hair and walnut-brown skin. The vampire was real, pulling blood too rhythmically and efficiently for a human and sealing his mouth around the flow.

The human was lolling back in the booth, so I had to sit up straight to see his face. There was pleasure, but the strain of agony underneath. He shifted around, moaning, his eyelids lowered.

"I've seen enough," I whispered. The guy was biting his lip, a pained crease forming across his forehead, but he let the vampire continue.

"Stay," Armand murmured. He had no power of compulsion like his brother, but I obeyed. Watching was hypnotic, and a dark part of me wanted to see how this would end.

The vampire flung back his head, delicately swiping a thumb under his lips to erase the smear of blood. His fangs retracted smoothly. He licked the blood off his thumb, acknowledging us for the first time. He had a full, serious mouth. "We don't usually get a human in the audience. Did you want to participate?"

"No, thank you," I said.

The human sat up, moving slowly and fluidly. Everything about him was dreamy bliss, despite the bleeding puncture marks in his arm. "Why did you stop?" he asked, his voice raw and pleading.

"I've taken enough." The vampire reached over the table and grabbed a large plaster, pressing it over the wound. The human boy flinched, hugging his arm. "Let's go," the vampire said, sliding out of the booth. His long, black leather jacket creaked when he moved.

The human staggered after him. I didn't know what to call his role in their relationship. Boyfriend? Client? Victim?

Armand called between the curtains, "We don't wish to be disturbed."

Then he closed the narrow gap. Excellent – no witnesses.

He sat across the table from me, like Christian Slater questioning Brad Pitt in *Interview with the Vampire*. "Well? Are you ready to rush off and feed Jared?"

"I was never planning to do that."

"Right." Armand picked up a bandage from the table and ran it through his fingers. "You're evaluating whether you're ready . . . Perhaps you feel it will support him, or you're trying to ease your jealousy about him feeding on others."

In one swoop, he'd exposed the conflict I'd been wrestling with. He was right. I hadn't decided if I wanted to feed Jared, and he certainly didn't want it right now. But I hated the thought of others feeding him.

"Let's move on – tell me what you observed," Armand said, correctly reading my hesitation. He often said his power was unreliable, but it was spot on tonight.

"The guy was in pain, but he liked it and wanted more."

Armand leaned forward, stretching the bandage taut. "Exactly. What I've experienced from those who consent is that they fall in love with the pain. It's a small step from pleasure, and if they let themselves go, the pain becomes bliss and erases everything else."

The chance to step out of my own head sounded appealing . . . and terrifying. I wasn't any closer to figuring out how Jared and I could move forward, but I understood what Armand was saying. Letting someone feed on me would be as intoxicating as it was dangerous, and there'd be no going back. Mum had started off like that and ended up losing her family and becoming a vampire. Lucas's path had ended in his death.

"So why did Jared's bite hurt me? The consent thing?"

"That's part of it. Consider the fight or flight mechanism that has kept your species alive for millennia. If your survival is under threat, the nervous system will do everything in its power to fight. Once you accept and no longer fear it, the body no longer begs for help. But a newly turned vampire or attacker won't take care. They'll tear through flesh and capillaries to reach the blood. That was Jared once, though things are different now."

"Can we go? I get it."

"Do you?" Armand let the bandage flutter down to the table. "Very well. I'll walk you home."

"Thanks." I was probably safer with him than fending for myself. There were more vampires roaming the city than ever before and a human murderer that Cafferty was yet to track down. Although it occurred to me that he hadn't fed while we were here – where did Armand get his blood?

Picturing the boy's blissed-out and anguished face, I stepped through the curtains and almost ran straight into Cafferty's little sister coming out of the next booth.

Chapter 21

wasn't sure who was more shocked. Carly had changed from the outfit she'd worn at the mansion into an equally cute white vest with a long, beaded cross necklace over it and black shorts over tights. She shrugged into a plum-coloured leather jacket that matched her lipstick, but not before I saw the compress taped to her wrist. "What are you doing here?" Carly asked.

A girl stepped out of her booth, trailing the velvet curtain through her fingers. She had hair in tight, blonde curls like Claudia's, but we didn't have a real vampire on our hands. Her skin was tanned, and a neat tray of scalpels lay on the table behind her. Carly was possibly only aware of lifestylers, so we'd need to tread carefully.

"Shall we talk outside?" Armand asked me and Carly, setting off towards the stairway.

"I don't know who you are, but sure," Carly said, frowning.

Armand led us out, and I walked up the stairs between him and Carly. I couldn't have picked two less likely people to put together.

The club looked as dead as before but with another excellent song choice. 'Two Princes' by the Spin Doctors was way too perky and optimistic for the gloomy environment.

We walked down the street from The Underground to a shadowed spot without streetlights. We stood under a balcony cascading with greenery, which made the darkness even more oppressive.

"I won't tell Matt I saw you if you don't tell him about me," Carly said, arms crossed tightly.

Cafferty was the least of her problems. I pushed my hair back to expose my neck, holding out my bare wrists and elbows for her to inspect. "No bite marks. No new ones anyway."

Carly zeroed in on my scarred wrist. "But you've been fed on – you get it."

"It wasn't consensual."

Her hard edges softened. "Oh man . . . I'm sorry. Look – I just come here to let off steam. People like playing at being a vampire, and I like letting them, so it's a win win. You don't have to tell Matt."

Carly was older than me, but I felt more like an adult. "No, I don't – it's none of my business. And I'm not going to tell you what to do, but I think you should stop going. I knew someone who used to go there, and it didn't end well for him." I couldn't explain that Lucas used to frequent The Underground, and he'd become so obsessed with becoming a vampire that it got him killed.

Her gaze slid onto Armand. "Where does he fit in? Aren't you dating that hot guy who dressed as Lestat?"

"I'm not important," Armand said, "but Mina's advice is. Believe me when I say that Matt will find out. I have a sense for these things. And anyone who keeps going to that place eventually gets dragged down by it. Do you want to be like them?"

"I just wanna have fun," Carly said. "I know you're tryin' to help me, but I don't need it."

"We should walk you home," I said.

"I've listened to your advice. Don't push it." She walked off. Soon only the red tip of a cigarette glowed against her silhouette.

"I don't think she's a fan of ours," Armand said.

"She doesn't have to like us," I said, "but let's hope she listens."

We set off, and I had to swerve around a guy chugging from a metre-long tube of blue liquid. "I have another question."

"I would've been surprised if you didn't."

"What happens if someone like Carly doesn't know about vampires and they get one at The Underground?" I asked.

"Good question," Armand said, "and one the owners take very seriously. People are screened rigorously. Human lifestylers and vampires with a taste for blood are encouraged to keep extensive notes on their clients. If you aren't on a vampire's list and you don't arrive with a vampire, you'll only know of and see lifestylers who drink blood for fun."

A lot of effort went into keeping vampires a secret. How many of them deserved it?

The crowds thinned, and the Halloween decorations around here were strange. A long white chain was looped under a balcony. Huge, yellowing teeth were strung along it. A disembodied hand clung to the door knocker of the next house, the wrist ragged and bloody.

"Do you mind . . . Can I ask you about what happened during Fang Fest?" I rarely got Armand alone and never in a sharing mood. As much as I'd tried to bury those events, hearing the bouncer discuss Elvira had brought it all to the surface.

"Are you sure you want to know?" he asked.

"Can you tell me what you did?" John had mentioned that Armand had played a part in his plan. How could I trust him to help Jared without the full story?

Armand sighed. "I knew we'd have this conversation at some point. And not because I had a vision," he added before I could ask.

We'd slowed right down as Armand retreated into his memories. "You know my brother had power over me. On this occasion, he ordered me to do things I can live with. He told me to read your fortune. He let me give you a true reading . . . He just wanted to know what it was in case your mom appeared in it."

That betrayal made me equal parts embarrassed and annoyed. Armand shouldn't have given his brother that insight, though he was right that John wouldn't have left him much choice. "Anything else?" I asked.

"He had me follow you, and I fed information to the press. He was hoping they would run a story that would draw out your mother. I also helped him to dig the hole . . . where we left Jared." Of all the things he'd done, the pained look on Armand's face suggested that had given him the most guilt.

John had been willing to ruin our lives, even kill us, to have another go at dating our mum. I wanted to believe that wrongness inside him was nothing to do with being a vampire. Jared was good, and he'd stay that way.

"Did you kill anyone?" I said, very aware of the risk in what I was asking.

"Not for John," he said, wording that too selectively for comfort. "I regret to say that I helped him stage the bodies, but that was all." That was enough – putting his hands on dead flesh, knowing what happened to John's victims while their families grieved . . . He'd been under his brother's influence, but it was hard to take. Armand was finally being open, and I'd never given him a chance. I'd let John's actions colour how I'd seen Armand and questioned how he could be helping Jared. But I was starting to see it.

The curtains of the nearest house had been replaced by trailing rolls of bloody bandages, reminding me of blood-tinged blonde hair. "What did Veronica do during Fang Fest?" I asked. She'd herded us through the city, taking great pleasure in threatening us with her mallet, but there had to be more.

"She had quite the to-do list," he said gravely. "She skewered the note about Jared's location to your door and was quite put out at the loss of her dagger. That was the least of her crimes. She stabbed two people to make it seem like a human killer: Lucas and the Elvira girl you were unfortunate enough to find in the cell at Empire. She was gentle with Lucas because John had plans for him, but not that poor girl . . ." Her lifeless face was scorched into my memory, gore crusting her throat and chest. "Veronica only does things in exchange for a favour, so God knows what my brother promised her."

"The bloodiest things were Veronica," I said. Even though I was with Armand, the deserted street felt ominous. "Have you seen her lately?"

His head whipped up, and I thought he might not answer. Finally, he said, "We move in the same circles, but I avoid her like the proverbial plague. Why do you ask?"

Armand had described the note on my door as the least of her crimes, but that was the part that bothered me most. "I got a note about remembering what happened at Fang Fest. It could be a prank or a threat, and Veronica's the only one I can think of on the threat side."

"Giving veiled threats doesn't sound like her, but it's best to be on your guard. Travel with your friends and lock your doors, but don't let it consume you."

I wished he'd dismissed my fears. What he'd said had only fed them. John had started with notes and worked his way up to murder. What if Veronica was modelling herself on him?

As I dwelled on that, I heard footsteps. Someone was following us. This part of the city was a peaceful community, and usually we walked the street at night without seeing anyone. But Cafferty was investigating a killer who stabbed their victims during these quiet hours.

"I hear them," Armand murmured. "Two humans drawing near."

"Hey!" I knew that voice. By the time I'd turned around, Libby's angry striding had brought her to us, leaving Della trailing behind.

"What are you doing here?" Libby asked.

"I think it's time for me to say good night," Armand began to walk away, as he tended to do.

"You're not going anywhere. Why did I think my kid sister was safe at home when she was out with you?" Libby asked.

"Mina had questions about Fang Fest," Armand said, quiet and controlled. "I answered them and brought her back here." I was impressed – there was just enough truth in his story. He'd had the insight to know Della and Libby wouldn't approve of our trip to The Underground.

"Fine," Libby said reluctantly. "Thank you for bringing her home."

"You're welcome," he said. "I hope you'll stop by John's . . . *my* new restaurant soon. You can have your meals on the house. Good night," he said again more firmly, taking off with long, quick strides.

"Why dredge up that stuff again?" Libby asked.

"You know we deal with things in different ways," I said, trying to stay calm through the niggle of old resentment.

"I hope he made you feel really good about everything. I'm going to bed."

"Wait," I said. "Mum was here when I got home tonight."

"Oh yeah? What did she want?" Libby had always been the first to defend Mum, but even her patience was wearing thin.

"Just to hang out, but she decided it was a bad time and went off."

"I suppose that's progress from not turning up at all. Come on – let's go inside."

Libby went into her room, but Della hung back in the hallway. "You wanna talk about it?" she asked.

"Which vampire?" I asked, trying to smile. "The parent or the one who just dropped me off?"

"Either," she said, almost following Libby but pausing in her doorway. "I know I can't tell you what to do, but I'd rather you stayed away from Armand." So Della could work for him but I couldn't hang out with him? Was she going to ban me from seeing my mum and boyfriend while she was at it?

After we said goodnight, Della closed the door of Libby's room. I was glad I hadn't snapped at Della. She had her own issues with vampires to work through.

Tessa was in the kitchen, so I decided to make an effort with her. She was throwing ingredients into a bowl that smelled of sugary vanilla deliciousness. "I'm making cookies. Give me two minutes and you can taste the dough if you want." She sprinkled in a handful of chocolate chips, then threw in the whole bag. I was warming to her more all the time.

"Things seem to be goin' good with Jared," she said.

Either she was antagonising me or she'd missed Jared keeping me at arm's length. She'd never seen us together when things were good, before he was forced to become a vampire. "It's going great," I lied. Since she'd brought him up, I decided to be bold. "Do you mind me asking . . . what went wrong with the two of you?"

"I screwed up. I can be kinda . . . all over the place. I got busy studying and didn't make time for him. He's a good guy – I'm the disaster."

I appreciated her honesty but not the implication that she wasn't over him. I asked, so that was on me. "He really is. So you dated Jason after him?"

She didn't seem to mind that I'd got personal. "Wow, that doesn't make me look good, does it? It was a whole lot worse with Jason. Think explosion rather than fizzling out, and I'll leave it there."

"Sorry to hear that."

She shrugged, kneading the cookie dough. "It happens."

I couldn't imagine Jason exploding at anyone, but I'd been nosy enough. "I should get ready for bed – good night."

Tessa raised the gloopy spoon. "Want me to bring you some cookies when they're done?"

"I'll try them in the morning if there are any left."

There was a piece of folded paper on the mat when I got back into the hallway. Either we'd walked over it when we came in or it had just been delivered.

After discussing Veronica and my note with Armand, I was instantly uneasy. I walked over there slowly, prolonging the inevitable. Already, the red biro was visible. I picked the note up with my sleeve. Not long ago, Libby's fingerprints had been used against her.

TICK TOCK.
READY TO COME
CLEAN?

Chapter 22

Was this note referring to Fang Fest like the last one? What was I supposed to have done? We'd all been there when John tormented us, but I was being singled out. Nobody knew what had happened, except my closest friends and family. John Carter would've been my prime suspect – he was the one who'd enjoyed mind games. But I'd seen a crossbow bolt lodge in his skull . . . and felt the rotten splash of his blood on my face.

A patch of darkness shifted behind the front door. It was a figure disguised by the patterned glass and shadows. Was it the person who sent the note?

Part of me wanted to fling the door open and challenge them, but fear pinned me in place. Scary, fanged things lurked at night, in addition to the human killers who stalked people outside their homes.

The shadowy figure and I looked at each other. Their scrutiny raked over me like razor-edged claws. My fingernails dug into my palm, and the pain brought me out of the paralysis of terror. I wanted to help the police and the slayers, and yet I was cowering behind a door. I reached for the handle, instantly questioning myself. Anyone, or anything, could be out there. The shadow slipped out of sight, making the decision for me. I was safer inside and not knowing.

"Everything all right?" Tessa appeared in the kitchen doorway. I stuffed the note in my bag. She followed the motion with her eyes, but I appreciated her not mentioning it.

I shut myself in my bedroom and smoothed out both notes on the bed. Each was written in bold, red capital letters scored deep into lined paper. I'd wanted to assume it was a nondescript nobody pranking me, but the suspicion I'd shared with Armand seemed more and more likely to be right. Only one not-person might have held onto their anger after Fang Fest: Veronica. John was her friend, and he'd died trying to kill us.

Tomorrow, I'd have to tell the others. It could be nothing, but I shouldn't keep them in the dark.

I was taking my time to get ready for bed when there was a knock on my door. Della was there, all dressed in black. "Libby's in bed. Are you comin' with me on patrol?"

I thought about what Jared would say, knowing the hurt he'd feel if he found out I was hunting down vampires like him. And yet, could I let Della go without me? If I really wanted to help people and know if this was for me, there was only one way to find out. "Give me two minutes."

We walked quickly, and I couldn't think of anything to say. I tried not to think at all, in case I talked myself out of it.

When we got to the slayers' hangout, Paige was kicking the crap out of a punching bag, her red ponytail slashing around her like a whip. Rosario was with Monique, the leader of the original slayers, and the others were talking or exercising.

The room was equally impressive the second time around. Della spotted me examining the countless spikes of rock overhead and lining the walls. "They're fake. This place used to be a club called The Cave. Word on the street is it got torn down, but here we are."

"You came back!" Taz appeared. She'd tied a thin, polka-dotted bandana around her shaved head, and the delight on her dainty face was undisguised.

"I did."

"I'm glad Paige didn't put you off," she said, glancing at the angry redhead. "We're not all like her."

Rosario came up alongside Taz. "Paige has her strengths," she said. "Tact isn't one of them. Great to see you."

"I'm glad to be here," I said, grateful that she wasn't giving me a hard time.

"We need good people right now." Rosario assessed me with eyes of a deep, glossy brown and a scary amount of intelligence.

"She's only just turned 18," Della said. "Can we ease her into it?"

"Vamps wouldn't care how old she is if they drank her dry. When the sun goes down, this city becomes an all-you-can-eat buffet. And don't think the daylight makes her safe. They could drag her into an alleyway or abandoned building. A sun-scorched hand heals pretty quickly with young victims' blood pumping around their veins. Don't you think we'll prepare her? You've started her training. We can finish it."

"Can she come out with me?" Della asked.

"We can go together," Rosario said. "You're still in training."

With no further ado, she addressed the room. "Listen up!"

The slayers' reactions were instantaneous. They stopped what they were doing and faced us. A lot of them looked serious or expectant, while Taz was grinning. Paige's folded arms and surliness were textbook hostility.

"I won't keep y'all long," Rosario said, not needing to raise her voice. "Tonight, I want you to keep a low profile on patrol. Intervene if you must, but don't go looking for trouble. If you've been assigned a potential hotspot by the legacy slayers, report back any vampire activity tonight. We're looking for locations where large numbers are holing up or chatter about vamps mobilising. If you find any, question them if it's safe but don't engage unless required by the code. That's all."

Paige's expression was sourer than before. Rosario's instructions had sounded rational to me. Were they not bloodthirsty enough for Paige?

The others went out into the night. We stayed back to go over some basics of attack and defence. Then Rosario and Della set off too, and I stumbled to keep up. "Don't we need stakes?"

Rosario looked over her shoulder, grinning. "We have ours, newbie. You have to earn it."

The two of them chatted until we hit the street. Their focus renewed my sense of foreboding. Hunting vampires looked fun when Buffy did it, but what would happen if we found one?

The happy buzz of the French Quarter soothed some of my anxiety. Halloween costumes were out in full force. Some were generic, like plastic-caped vampires and witches with floppy black hats. Some people had gone all out even though Halloween was days away. My favourite was Regan from *The Exorcist*. She wore full white horror make-up, thick gashes in the nose and cheeks and grey contact lenses. The girl's grin showed sludge-stained teeth, and she'd even gone for the nightgown drenched in pea soup.

"Thoughts on demon-possessed kids?" I asked Rosario.

She smirked, scanning the street. "Not our problem."

Della was almost as poised as Rosario, though she kept patting the waistline of her black leggings where I presumed she'd stashed the stake. "You OK?" she asked.

"Yeah, I'm fine."

That feeling trickled away as we left civilisation behind. Laughing partygoers and live music gave way to empty streets. Halloween decorations hung limp as corpses, and curtains twitched when we passed. If this went sideways, no one would leap to our defence.

"How long have you been doing this?" I asked Rosario.

She cast me a despairing look. "Three years. But vampire activity these last few months has gone off the scale."

Since I arrived in New Orleans – lucky me. "How long have you been in charge?"

"Probably not as long as you've been this inquisitive."

When the conversation fizzled out, apprehension crept over my skin. The area grew more intimidating the further we walked. Houses in pastel colours with cute Halloween decorations were replaced by boarded windows and patches of darkness where streetlights had blown. The pavement was bumpier and more cracked than usual, while rubbish and broken glass were strewn in the gutters.

"We're almost at our first stop," Rosario said. I'd guessed as much. Across the road, a cemetery stretched out in either direction behind an iron fence. The gate had a name spelled out in crooked metal letters: 'Moss Hollow Cemetery'. "The legacy slayers' intel said there's an abandoned church behind it with a crypt underneath. A bunch of vampires set up here in the 70s."

"What if we find some?" I asked.

"If they don't engage in combat, neither do we. I'll question them if the mood is right. Remember vampires aren't automatically bad – just those who put humans at risk. If we come across any like that, Della and I will give them hell and you stay back. You're here for observation only."

I wanted to be offended, but honestly I was relieved. I needed to build up to taking on a vampire.

"Fine with me," Della said, setting off across the road with her hand poised at her side.

"Let's go then, rookie." Rosario took off after Della, and I scurried to keep up.

I was about to go on my first vampire hunt with no weapons and no clue what I was doing. That sounded like a disaster waiting to happen.

Being in a graveyard at night was a new experience. I'd visited St. Louis Cemetery No. 1 while the sun was burning hot, the neat brick and stone tombs all around us.

This was more like a cemetery in England, with gravestones

and people buried underground. Crooked oak trees grew all over the cemetery, casting us in unsettling darkness as we stepped under the canopy. Spanish moss trailed down, drifting back and forth in the breeze. There was no apparent organisation to the graves, and most had weeds tangled over them.

Weak light from the streetlamps touched the edge of the graveyard, but it got darker the further we advanced. My eyes slowly adjusted to the encroaching blackness, but we had to pick our way through the tombstones. Some lay in broken pieces in the grass and others leaned at angles like crooked teeth.

"Why are people buried underground?" I whispered, stepping over a fallen stone with a pang of regret for its owner. "Isn't it too swampy?"

"It's not used any more, but a lot of people were buried here. Don't come after a storm – it's like bone soup."

"Thanks for that image," I said.

"Any time." Rosario brushed back a loop of Spanish moss, and it got me in the face as it fell. Its scratchy softness tickled, and I batted it away.

The church was a bleak skeleton. Its roof was gone, and black openings remained instead of stained glass. One rotten door hung open, the wood misshapen and splintered.

Without any speech or ceremony, Rosario led us inside.

There was no light, and the sensation of stepping into nothingness was disquieting. I had an urge to grab Rosario or Della, but I couldn't see where they were even if I'd dared.

I began to pick out shapes: the outlines of pews and lumps of crumbling stone. We advanced slowly, and the stench of damp and rotting wood was so pungent that I could almost taste it.

"The crypt's here." Rosario led us to a gap in the wall that descended down to pitch blackness.

"Why don't we come back in the day?" I whispered.

"We only hunt during the day if it's a confirmed killer and we need the advantage."

Rosario tossed a lump of rock down the stairs. We heard it thudding down, a bang and then nothing.

We let the silence draw out until Della said, "I think we're good." She slipped her hand into mine, squeezing it before letting go.

Rosario approached the stairs. "There's a stone rail. Hold tight and follow me."

There was no light in the stairway, and only the quiet fall of Rosario's feet and the rough stone rail in my hand to lead the way. I felt charged with fear that verged on excitement. The blackness was an oppressive thing, taking on a life of its own. It wrapped around us, pressing on my chest and cutting off my sight. I listened out, but I could hear only three sets of footsteps. Of course, Jared was able to sneak up on me without stirring the air, and not all vampires were as friendly as him.

The stairway spiralled downwards, and the stone under my hand guided me. I placed each foot at a steady pace, slowing my breathing by matching the repetitive movement.

"Stop," Rosario ordered in a whisper.

I waited in the darkness, feeling Della's comforting presence behind me.

Brilliant light flooded the space, and I squeezed my eyes shut. "A little warning next time!"

"Not likely," Rosario said.

I cautiously opened one eye and then the other. Red spots

bloomed over my vision, soon settling to reveal a striking space lit by Rosario's torch.

The crypt had arched ceilings of grey stone that met in crosses overhead. The structure was supported by smooth pillars carved with intricate vines, like nature was destined to reclaim this place.

Four tombs against the walls were carved to look like their inhabitants were sleeping on their caskets. I was about to inspect the nearest one when a more important detail occurred to me. Someone was living here.

Since this wasn't *Interview with the Vampire*, there were no coffins, and luckily we weren't in a *Lost Boys* situation of vampires hanging from the ceiling like bats. But there were sleeping bags and other signs of inhabitants. A battery-powered stereo was in the corner with a stack of tapes. An open magazine was spread out on one of the sleeping bags, and in another corner was a heap of clothes.

"Humans or vamps?" Della asked, scanning the evidence.

"Vamps," Rosario said.

"How do you know?" I asked.

"Close your eyes, and breathe through your nose." Rosario was a natural leader, because I followed her bizarre orders without question. I knew what she meant and opened my eyes. There were undertones of rotting meat and old blood, the coppery stench bitter and musty.

"You get that?" Rosario asked.

"It smells like death," Della said, wrinkling her nose. "We need to get out of here."

A low, nasal voice caught me off guard. "What's your hurry?"

Chapter 23

'd expected Rosario to launch herself at him or start asking questions, but she moved towards the exit. "Sorry to bust in on you. We'll go."

She trained her torch on the vampire, illuminating his stringy, unwashed hair and dirty skin. He had an appraising look on his thin face.

"Why not stay a while?" A female vampire stepped into the pool of torchlight. She looked unkempt like the male and was a thousand times more frightening. He might have been hungry, but her expression was vicious.

Rosario lifted one side of her T-shirt, exposing the butt of a wooden stake. "Because you have a choice. You can make it through the night . . . or not. Either way, me and my friends are walking out of here unbitten."

"Why did you come if you don't want to be bitten?" The female vampire's body language was more predator than human, her body poised to leap.

Rosario raised her hands in the universal peaceful gesture. "We want to know why there's been a surge in the numbers of new vampires and where they're hiding out. If you can tell us, there'll be no trouble. You've not attacked us."

The female sprang forward. She was smart, aiming for Della rather than Rosario. Another vampire strolled down the stairs as Della and Rosario tackled the other two. Three of them and three of us.

The new male's black hair was slicked back off his face, and the wide collar of his shirt was straight out of the 1970s. "Nice of you to come to us."

Adrenaline pumped hard, and I was convinced that I wouldn't survive my second vampire bite. The vampire went for me at the same time that Rosario moved. She swept her leg behind the knees of her vampire, then got mine with a graceful roundhouse kick.

The vampire clutched his face. "You goddamn bitch."

Rosario grabbed the stake from her waistband. "I really don't like that word."

She slashed towards his chest, but the female vampire smashed into Rosario and threw her off course.

Della reclaimed the female's attention. Rosario spared a glance for me, yanking another stake from an ankle holster. "Here!"

She flung the stake at me, and I reached out my hand. Buffy

would've snatched it out of the air and staked the vamp in one smooth motion. My fingers grazed the stake, sending it clattering to the ground.

My vampire recovered from Rosario's foot to the face. As he advanced on me, I was dimly aware of the others. Rosario plunged her stake into her vampire's chest, and Della was getting the better of the female.

That left me scrambling towards my stake while the hungry vampire took his time to come over, licking his lips.

He let out an enraged roar at what Rosario had done to his friend. With no idea what I was doing, I surged forward and jabbed the stake as hard as I could into his chest. It turned out that stabbing someone with a piece of wood was really difficult. The force juddered up my arm, and the vampire clamoured to pull out the stake from where it'd lodged in his chest. I must have got it nowhere near the heart with the way he was writhing around.

Rosario and Della were there at the same time, leaving bodies behind. Yanking my stake out, Rosario jammed it back in where it counted. The vampire's hands closed around it, and the life left him. His eyes were vacant and his mouth slack as he slumped onto his side.

Rosario grabbed the stake and stood beside Della. They were about as impressive as two people could possibly look.

"You were both incredible," I said, exhilarated by what we'd done. I understood the code – it had been us or them. I'd stumbled through my first slaying venture, but it wouldn't be the last.

"You didn't do so bad yourself," Rosario said. "Now, I count four sleeping bags and three dead vamps. What do you say we get out of here?"

"What about the . . . bodies?" I asked, keeping it together until the last part.

"No time," she said. "Their friend can deal with it."

The last traces of adrenaline carried me onwards. I'd staked a vampire. OK, I'd missed the heart and could've ended up as dinner, but I'd done it. After my moral quandaries, I was a slayer. And it felt good.

We powered through the graveyard by the light of Rosario's torch, and I must have bumped my shins on every gravestone. I scraped my side along one of them, feeling the sting of drawn blood. I managed not to faceplant – I didn't need to be an easier target if the fourth vampire was lurking. Civilisation was right ahead, with the lit street tantalisingly close.

The torch's beam flared white as the light caught on something. Rosario stopped, fending off the darkness as she swept the beam back and forth. "Your friends are dead. Care to join them? Or perhaps you have some information for us?"

There was another blur in the light. We froze in place, listening to the uneven inhale and exhale of the three living people in the graveyard. The vampire was chillingly silent. They could be anywhere, sneaking closer and ready to sink their fangs into one of our throats. One bite was all it would take to end up bleeding out among the long dead of the graveyard. I would've already died tonight without Della and Rosario.

The air moved behind me and I spun around, clutching the bloodstained stake. The vampire was armed with fangs and seeing us with eyes unhindered by the darkness.

"I smell blood," an agitated voice said from way too close. I held a hand over the throbbing place where I'd nicked my side on a gravestone.

"Want it to be yours?" Rosario asked, swinging the torch around and bathing me in light that burned my eyes.

Disoriented, I lost track of Della. I hated the thought of her out there with the vampire. Rosario moved the beam of light away, leaving me in the dark. There was a grunt of pain. What would I tell Libby if Della got hurt? She'd never forgive me, and I wouldn't forgive myself.

The torchlight fell on Della with her arm around a blonde vampire's throat, stringy blonde hair falling down over her face. Veronica?

Her long hair fell back, revealing a gaunt face nothing like Veronica's. I had little time for relief before the vampire girl threw her head back, trying to hit Della. She hung on, adjusting the stake pointed at the vampire's heart.

"Don't fight it," Rosario said. "Right now, you have a chance to get out of this. You haven't hurt us. You can walk away."

"My friends won't," the vampire girl said, sorrow overcoming her last bit of fight. "I can smell their blood. Did you kill them all?"

"I'm sorry," Della said. "They attacked us."

The vampire's lips trembled. Blood-tinged tears leaked from her eyes.

"There were four of you?" Rosario asked. "You're not part of a larger gang?"

"Why would I tell you? They took care of me and now I'm all alone. What am I supposed to do now?"

"Can't help you there," Rosario said.

"I'm sorry about your friends," I said, trying a different tactic. "What were their names?"

"Jack, Lucinda and Khalid," she said.

"And yours?" I asked.

"Fiona."

"There's a bar called Empire of the Dead. If you go there and ask for Armand, he'll help you," I said. I wouldn't send every lone vampire to Armand, but we were responsible for this one.

"OK . . . Thanks," she said, sniffing.

Taking my lead, Rosario asked kindly, "Can I ask again how many of y'all there were?"

"OK, I'll talk," she said, "but only because *she* was nice to me. It was just us . . . Just me now. The guy who turned us wanted something. It seemed like there was this big plan, but we didn't stick around to find out what."

So people were getting turned into vampires for a reason.

Chapter 24

"When were you turned?" Rosario asked.

"This past June." Not long before I arrived in the city. She'd been a young girl like me and now had the same burden as Jared. I squirmed with guilt at the thought of him. Would he be able to forgive me for this?

"I have somethin' else to ask," Rosario said, kind now. I appreciated that. We knew nothing of the vampire's story except that we'd killed her friends. We had to presume she was good unless she proved otherwise. "You say your sire wanted you for something. Who turned you?"

"I don't know his name," she said. "It's not like he asked what

I thought about this."

Though Della kept her arm around the girl's throat, she lowered the one holding the stake. With my energy levels low, more complex emotions were surfacing: regret, doubt, empathy . . .

"Can you describe him?" Rosario asked.

"It was just this short guy with a really bad haircut. I can't think . . . He had a gang with him – I thought they were gonna kill me." She shuddered, hugging herself.

"Is there anything else?" Rosario asked.

The girl shook her head, fresh tears falling. Rosario's pause felt endless. The vampire had done nothing wrong, but would Rosario let her go?

"Release her." Rosario said, tucking her stake away.

Della did, and I expected the girl to flee. Instead, she trudged towards the church – in the direction of her dead friends.

"I've never thought about what happens to them afterwards," Rosario said. "That was a good thing you did, Mina."

We scrambled out of the graveyard, torchlight swinging. Rosario cleaned one of the bloodstained stakes with a cloth from her pocket. "You did good, girl. This one's yours." I accepted it, less excited than I'd thought for it to be official. I was a slayer, but three vampires had died. If the police ever found their bodies, they'd be searching for another murderer.

Della and I followed her at a jog, not slowing until we were among tourists. Della looked shaken up. It was the first time she'd had to kill since Lucas.

Rosario threw an arm around my shoulder. I wasn't used to strangers being casual with affection, but after tonight we were friends. "It'd be great to have you on the team, if you want to be."

Doubt crept in as the giddiness faded. If that fourth vampire had returned sooner, we would've been outnumbered. Not to mention that I'd staked a vampire. Even though I didn't kill him, what would Jared think? "I don't know yet," I said.

"I'd like you on board," Rosario said. "You've got fighting potential, and you managed to get her to open up."

"Thanks. I'll think about it." Actually going out and staking vampires was much more complicated than the idea of it.

"So who's Armand?" Rosario asked, our collective mood subdued despite the Halloween merriment going on around us. A group of girls were bouncing up and down in the open front of a bar, singing along to 'Heaven is a Place on Earth' with their arms around each other.

"The owner of the bar where I work," Della said. "He's not a threat."

"He's a good guy," I added.

"If there were more good vampires than bad and that put me out of a job, I'm all for it," Rosario said. "Shame she couldn't tell us more about her sire, but we did learn the vamps are changing people for a purpose. So our next step has to be figurin' out what that is. You two did good tonight – make sure y'all get some rest."

Rosario went off with a casual wave, and Della homed in on me. "You handled yourself great down there. How you feelin'?"

"I don't know," I said. "If we hadn't gone looking for them, they'd be alive."

"Yeah, but other people might not be. They attacked us, and we fought them off. I know it's sometimes kind of . . . morally grey, but tonight we did the right thing. The last vamp didn't attack us, and she got to live."

I tried to take solace from that, though my mind wasn't made up.

Libby's door was shut, so it seemed like we'd got away with it. Della had reached out to close the front door when Tessa appeared in the doorway.

"What are you two doing up?" Tessa asked, too bright and alert for the middle of the night.

"I could say the same about you. We couldn't sleep, so we went for some air," Della said.

"Guess you didn't have as much fun as I did!" she said, grinning as her heels clacked on the wooden floor on the way to her room.

She lived in the same city as us, the same house even, but she was in the dark. Was it better to know or not? Jared was certainly safer without the world knowing what he was. Whichever was best, I liked to think that the slayers were protecting everyone.

I wasn't quite ready for sleep, so I got out Thandie's letters. Reading her words brought so much comfort. She'd had a rough time but was always strong and resilient through it.

I flicked through ones I'd read about the mansion until a word stood out: slayers.

Emm,

Tell me you know something of these latest fiends that would rob me of my freedom, and my life given half a chance. They call themselves slayers, but that's merely a pretty word for murderers.

I understand that people are more interested in my kind than ever before with the publication of that Anne Rice book. I've also noticed that our numbers *are rising — I'm not a fool. It appears that these 'slayers' have risen up to correct this imbalance. I've always feared the brothers would return for me, but this new threat is much more urgent. What kind of person goes out of their way to kill others who are merely trying to survive?*

I skimmed the rest of the letter and flicked through the others, but that was the only mention of the slayers. Would the Dictaphone teach me anything new if Will's colleague got it working? I could've asked Emmeline for more letters, but I'd learned all I needed to. I'd known that Thandie lived in fear of the Carter brothers, and now I'd discovered that the slayers had been another source. It seemed she'd been unaware of the code. Every time she'd left the mansion, she'd believed one of them could take her down.

There was no doubt in my mind that the slayers protected the city. But it was a sobering thought that they struck fear into vampires like Thandie and Jared who were trying to live their lives.

I woke up not looking forward to facing my sister. I had to act normal knowing we'd been out with the slayers last night, but first I needed to come clean about the notes. I had some time before I was due at the police station, so I grabbed them and followed the smell of cooking.

"Morning," Libby said as I came into the kitchen. "You excited about the ball tonight?"

"Absolutely," I said, even though I'd not had the headspace to think about it. Sitting down, I helped myself to some chocolate chip pancakes. "But I have something to show you."

Della sat down, grabbing two pancakes and swirling them with syrup. "Oh yeah?"

"Someone sent me these . . . Well, they put one in my bag and one through the door."

I put the notes on the table. Libby pressed both hands against her cheeks, sighing. "I thought we were done with vendettas against us. Are you all right?"

"I'm fine," I said. "They're just notes." In the morning light, I almost believed that.

"Mina's right – let's not get ahead of ourselves. Any ideas who sent them?" Della asked.

"Only one . . . Veronica." A mouthful of pancake lodged in my throat. It took a gulp of tea to force it down.

Libby's eyes widened, the pancakes abandoned in front of her. "Seriously? Armand said we were safe from her."

"I don't know. I didn't see who put it in my backpack, but someone was watching me through the door last night."

"Veronica seems more like the type who'd hit you with a sledgehammer if she had a grievance," Della said. "Let's not stress too much – there's nothing to suggest someone wants to hurt you." The worst of my worries eased. Della wouldn't have said that if she didn't believe it. "We can always go to the police if they make a threat."

"Until then, don't go anywhere alone. It may not be worth worrying about, but it's creepy as hell." Libby said. I opened my mouth to argue, and she added, "I mean it."

I let her have that one. If I got no more notes, we could move on. The police had bigger concerns – Cafferty was on the trail of a killer. The slayers had their hands full with vampires getting out of hand. I assumed Della and Libby were yet to have the slayer conversation, since Libby was eating contentedly now the subject of my needing a babysitter was decided.

After finishing breakfast and getting ready, Della offered to take the first shift. I made one last bid for freedom. "I can get myself to the police station alone, then I'll be with Cafferty all day. Anyway, aren't I safe during daylight hours?"

"From vampires," Libby said. "We don't know who sent the notes."

That shut me up. Libby wasn't trying to make life difficult – she wanted to protect me. I'd never had that from a parental direction, so it was no wonder that I'd missed it. "OK," I said, tucking into my pancakes.

Libby watched me, but if she was waiting for an argument it didn't come.

I grabbed the folder of Thandie's letters on the way out of my room. If I got any time to read, I needed to sort through to see if any more were relevant to Libby and then return them to Emmeline.

Della and I set off as Libby clattered around getting ready. She'd put the TV on, and we heard her singing all the wrong words to the *Fresh Prince of Bel-Air* theme song before Della closed the front door.

"You didn't tell Libby about the slayers," I said. I hated the idea of Della keeping secrets from Libby and that she was forcing me to do it by association. Then again, Libby was known for blowing up, so I understood waiting for the right moment.

"I will," Della said. "I wanted to get your thoughts first."

"I'll let you know when I figure them out," I said. I'd only been out on one hunt, and it hadn't been a resounding success.

"OK," Della said, subdued but understanding. "Take your time."

She dropped me outside the police station, and Cafferty was waiting inside the reception. "We're heading out," he said. "I'll explain on the way." He had deep circles around his eyes and a light scruff of stubble. Even his tanned skin looked washed out.

"What did you and Carly think of the tour?" I asked as we got to Cafferty's car.

He grinned. "It was great, except for one part. Thanks for the cameo."

"You're very welcome. Did Carly appreciate it?"

"That was the highlight of her night," Cafferty said, letting us into the car. "It's some consolation that Hannibal Lecter picked her out to be part of *The Silence of the Lambs*. She thought it was all fun and games until he sniffed her."

"Excellent," I laughed.

By the time we'd driven down several more blocks, his smile had vanished. "So . . . what's happened?" I asked.

"You really get to the point, don't you? There's been another victim on the stabbing case. I ended up workin' yesterday. I spent most of the day on the crime scene and talking to the medical examiner. Sorry I didn't mention it last night, but it didn't seem appropriate to bring it up at the mansion."

"I get it. So where are we going?"

"I need to interview the victim's mother and look around. It's not like being at an active crime scene, but it'll be difficult in its own way. You can observe the interview and give me a fresh pair of eyes. Are you up to that?"

"Definitely," I said, though it wasn't an easy answer. The stark finality of death might be easier to handle than facing the people left behind. "Who was the victim?"

"He was in his early 20s like some of the other victims," Cafferty said, the corners of his mouth turning down. "He was called Lawrence Broussard. He lived with his mother. She found him on the steps outside their home in the early hours of yesterday morning."

That must have been the worst thing a mother could imagine. Losing him had to be hard enough. Seeing his body after what the killer did to him was unthinkable.

Chapter 25

This was my first time in the Garden District, though I'd read about it in Wayne Carter's diary before I knew he and Armand were one and the same person. He'd written that scores of flowers were planted to disguise the stench of local slaughterhouses in the nineteenth century.

Despite that morbid nugget, the area was gorgeous. Flame-coloured trees lined the streets of sprawling mansions with lush green gardens, and a sprinkling of brown leaves covered the pavements. We pulled up outside the victim's house as the street car rattled by. It looked like a small tram, and its olive-green shade almost blended in with the surroundings.

The victim's property had black metal railings along a garden thick with ferns and mosses on the ground and shaded by trees heavy with light green pears. The house was painted a bright cream in contrast to the black shutters, pillars and a balcony that ran the width of the building.

"Wow," I said.

"They got nice houses round here, and Anne Rice lives right around the corner. But murders can happen anywhere."

On that unsettling note, we got out of the car. Cafferty grabbed a black case from the boot. "Here – you can ask Mrs. Broussard if she minds being recorded. It helps to make sure we don't miss anything."

I accepted the plastic case, pleased that he was trusting me. I unzipped it, and the device looked straightforward – a lot like Thandie's Dictaphone that I'd dropped off at Radio Shack.

Cafferty opened the black metal gate, pausing to let me go through first. There was no hint of what had happened, although a lighter patch of the grey stone path and stairs looked as if it'd been scrubbed recently.

A slim white woman opened the door. She had short grey hair brushed off her face and a regal quality that money can't buy. Her grey eyes were bloodshot, and there were tear tracks on her cheeks. "Thank you for coming, detective," she said, her voice hoarse.

"Mrs. Broussard." Cafferty dipped his head. "I'm Detective Cafferty. This is my colleague, Mina. Once again, I'm so sorry for your loss."

She pressed a hand against her mouth, giving a fragile smile once she'd steadied herself. "Thank you. Please do come in."

She continued talking as we stepped into a light, airy hallway. On nearly every piece of furniture, there was an abstract sculpture, most made from curved metal. "Can I fix either of you some sweet tea?"

"We're good, thank you," Cafferty said. "We have a few questions, and then I'd like to take a look around Lawrence's room, if that's all right."

"Of course, detective." Lawrence's mum was polite, but there was no life in her expression.

She led us into a room that had to be a parlour, though I'd never been in one. Everything was decorated in neutral tones, from the armchair and sofa patterned with a tan flower print to the cream furniture and fireplace.

Mrs. Broussard sat in the armchair, leaving me and Cafferty to take the sofa.

Cafferty drew out his notebook. "I won't keep you long. I've read the notes from your previous interview, but there are a few things I'd like to ask."

"Fine," she said, hands clasped tightly on her lap.

Cafferty glanced at me, and I asked, "Do you mind . . . Is it OK if we record you?"

"Go right ahead," she said.

I pressed the record button and checked the tape was whirring. Cafferty reeled off the date, location and names, before diving into the questions. "When did you last see your son?"

That was a harsh one to open with, but perhaps it was best to get it out of the way.

"The night before last. I made dinner, and then he went out."

"Do you know who with?" Cafferty asked.

"There are two boys he was close to," Mrs. Broussard said. "I can find you their contact information."

"Thank you – I'll need to get in touch with them," Cafferty said. "Did you hear him come home?"

She looked upwards, fidgeting anxiously with her ring. "I don't think so," she said. "He usually woke me when he came home late, as quiet as he tried to be." A smile flickered over her features, soon vanishing. If he'd never made it inside, the killer must have attacked him on the way home – so close to safety.

"How did he seem to you?" Cafferty jotted a few notes then went back to giving eye contact.

"Like my son," she said, defensiveness sharpening the angles of her body: arms tightly folded, cheeks sucked in to make harsh lines of her cheekbones. "I don't know what you want me to say, detective. Would you prefer it if I said he was angry or withdrawn? He was my Lawrence, and that's all I have to say on the matter."

"I'm sorry," Cafferty said, full of feeling. "This must be very difficult. I won't keep you much longer. Did your son's movements or activities change in recent weeks?"

"No," she said, icier now. "He worked shifts at a coffee bar called Bean in the French Quarter most days. He went to bars or movies with his friends most nights."

"Thank you, Mrs Broussard," Cafferty said, making more notes. "That's all very useful. Would you like to take us up to Lawrence's room or—"

"It's the first door at the top of the stairs." Mrs. Broussard remained in her seat, so Cafferty thanked her and led the way.

Photographs up the stairs showed Lawrence at different ages: a spiky-haired boy with gaps from lost teeth, a high school graduate with piercing green eyes and a natural, friendly smile. Near the top, there was a photograph of Lawrence how he might have looked around the time he died. He had his arm around his mum's shoulder, and happiness radiated from their smiling faces.

We stepped into his bedroom, and the ache of loss in my chest intensified. It was an ordinary enough room, with plain navy curtains and bedding. The carpet and walls were grey, and there was a television on a table at the end of the bed. Books, videos and magazines were stacked on his desk and the top of the television, and the quilt was flung back as if Lawrence had been so sure he'd get into his bed that night. A huge *Interview with the Vampire* poster took up one wall, Tom Cruise's face smouldering down at us.

"What are we looking for?" I asked.

"Usually, these things aren't sitting there in plain sight. I suggest checking pockets, drawers, under the mattress . . . Always look before you put your hand somewhere – trust me on that. If you see anything that seems interesting, out of place or that makes you pause over it, lemme know. We're lookin' for evidence of where he's spent time recently and who with: receipts, flyers – that kind of thing."

"Will do," I said.

I accepted a pair of white rubber gloves from Cafferty and put them on with a satisfying snap. He started checking bags and pockets in the wardrobe. I tried the drawers by Lawrence's bed. There was a glass pot of coins, loyalty cards, old concert tickets, elastic bands and other bits and pieces in the top drawer. I pulled out receipts and a cinema ticket for *Vampire in Brooklyn* from this week, and Cafferty bagged them.

The second drawer was crammed with documents. I flicked through, but there was nothing recent.

The obvious places weren't yielding much, so I tried to think like my family. They'd all had things to hide. Dad favoured novelty objects with secret compartments for paperwork: a wooden book, a clock with a sliding back and probably others that I'd never found. Mum had shoved things into carrier bags in the bottom of her wardrobe or old handbags. Libby went through a phase of taping things to the top of her wardrobe or drawers.

I checked every object in the room, but everything seemed solid and real. Mum's trick didn't work either. It was Libby's method that got results. I pulled out Lawrence's drawers and tilted my head to look at the smooth wood under the top.

"What are you doing?" Cafferty asked.

"Trying one of my sister's tricks. I've got something!"

A small, flat object was taped at the back of the drawer. I peeled the tape with my fingernails, which was difficult through gloves.

The object came away. It was a red token to gain entry to The Underground.

Chapter 26

"That looks familiar," Cafferty said, accepting the counter. He turned it over, inspecting both sides, before bagging and labelling it.

"It's from The Underground," I said, knowing what I was risking by telling him.

He raised his eyebrows. "And how do you know that?"

"My friend Lucas got mixed up there . . . the one Libby was wrongly accused of stabbing," I said. I hated lying to Cafferty, but I couldn't tell him I'd been there last night and run into his sister.

"Sorry to bring that up," he said, subdued. "We investigated

The Underground during the summer after your tip about people drinking blood there."

"Did you find anything?" I asked. The real vampires must have been nowhere near the place when the police were there.

"Just a bunch of people with strange pastimes – nothing illegal so long as it's consensual. People are tested rigorously, and everything's as clean as a hospital. It'd be better if they donated to a blood bank, but we can't police what people do with their time – or their blood. It's strange how it's turned up again. Obviously we don't know if he was there this week or last year, but it's worth looking into."

"What do you think it means?" I asked.

"Objects like this provide an insight into a victim's life. It may be that's all it does, but it could establish connections to other victims or speak to the killer's motive."

After another hour, we'd checked everywhere. Cafferty went through the evidence we'd collected, as I took a last look at Lawrence's room. He'd been murdered, and it'd opened his life up to scrutiny.

We said goodbye to Lawrence's mother. She was sitting where we'd left her in the living room and hardly acknowledged us as we let ourselves out.

"That was rough," I breathed, as we walked down the path towards Cafferty's car. The air was thick with the scent of flowers and greenery, the sunlight casting beams through the trees. Lawrence's mother was surrounded by beauty that she couldn't enjoy.

"You did well," Cafferty said, unlocking the car. He continued as we fastened our seatbelts. "A lot of experienced officers crumble when they're faced with bereavement."

"Thank you," I said. I'd had a lot of practice. "Where do we go from here?"

"Back to the station. I have to sign in the evidence, and I'd like to look over the case file. It feels like this case is going to be all about small steps and finding connections, but we don't have all the pieces yet. In any case, I think we need to check out The Underground."

A loud knock on the window left my ears ringing. My mind flashed to the silhouette outside our front door last night, when only a thin sheet of glass like this one had protected me.

An old man was standing at the window, lowering the walking stick he'd used to clobber it.

Cafferty got out of the car and I followed. Though I was shaken, Cafferty smiled politely. "Can we help you, sir?"

"Sorry officer . . . Or is it detective?" the man said in a low, rumbling voice. He was wearing hearing aids and thick glasses. A little Jack Russell on a lead was snuffling around his feet, its short tail wagging. "Are y'all here 'bout that poor boy? I got some information. Don't know why nobody came by my place."

"Sorry about that, sir. My notes say officers tried all the neighbours but they didn't get a reply from some addresses."

The man shrugged, adjusting his grip on his stick. "I'm always home, son. Anyhow, I can tell you."

I'd expected Cafferty to ask him to come down to the station, but he whipped out a notebook. "Go ahead."

"It was dark, and I couldn't see clearly, but when I was takin' out my dog into the backyard around midnight, you know – to do her business – I saw a fella in dark overalls come over from the Broussard yard. My dog chased him, but he went clean over my back fence and got away. She's only a little thing – my Bessie." He smiled down at her fondly.

"Did you identify anything distinguishing about the perpetrator?" Cafferty asked.

"Like I said, son – it was dark. But there was one thing. He was wearin' a mask. Didn't see any details beyond that, but it was a light-coloured thing that covered his face."

"You say *he* . . ." Cafferty began.

"Can't say for certain," the man said. "They were pretty average height and build, and a long way off. The way they jumped over that fence though . . . They must'a been a lot more sprightly than me." The man chuckled.

"Is there anythin' else?" Cafferty asked, pen poised.

"Not that I can think of."

Cafferty gave the man his card and took down his details, inviting him to call if he had any more information. "If it's all right with you, we'll send out a sketch artist so we can try to create a visual of the suspect."

"I don't know 'bout that," he said. "I wouldn't want to miss my shows."

I crouched down beside Bessie, taking a last stab at winning him over. "My Nana used to have Jack Russells," I said, offering a hand. She sniffed it with her little black nose, then swiped a rough tongue over my hand. "How old's Bessie?"

"She'll be six in May," he said, beaming. "She usually don't like strangers. But since she likes you, how 'bout you send that dang sketch artist? Not sure how much use I'll be."

"That would be very helpful, thank you," Cafferty said.

The man watched us drive away, leaning heavily on his stick as he raised a hand to wave. Bessie sat to watch us too.

"I could learn a thing or two from you," Cafferty said. "It's too easy to forget the human angle."

I thought about how that vampire last night had opened up when I showed her some kindness. It felt good that I had something to offer the police and the slayers.

As we drove down that gloriously green street, I went over what the witness had said. A lot of criminals probably wore masks to hide their identities, but in the context of a murderer, it had chilling associations. So many fictional serial killers hid behind masks to commit atrocities. Was that what we were dealing with?

Cafferty went to the evidence room, while I spent the rest of the day doing administrative tasks. This gave me time to sort through what we'd found out. The connection to The Underground made me uneasy. It was a treacherous place full of secrets, where real vampires and humans fed on blood. It would be better for Cafferty if his case stayed away from there, especially because his sister was a regular.

I was finishing off a stack of filing when Cafferty returned. "Thank you. I always end up covered in paper cuts when I do that."

I checked my watch. "Is it OK if I go? I'm supposed to get ready for the ball with Libby."

"Not the Orchard Estate ball?" he asked.

"Is that a bad thing?"

"Not at all. I've heard it's super exclusive – there are locals who'd wrestle those tickets off of you given the chance. Let me give you a ride."

We stood up, and the phone on Cafferty's desk rang. "And that's what I get for even thinking about clocking off on time," he said to me and then picked up the phone. "It's Cafferty. Carly? I can't hear you – slow down. Where are you?" He listened, his face grim. "I'll be right there."

Cafferty hung up the phone. "Carly needs a ride – do you mind if we pick her up on the way to your place?"

"Not at all," I said. "I like her. Plus, I understand sister drama."

"I guess you do. I didn't get the full story, but I think she's on a date with some new guy. Sounds like it's gone south."

We pulled up outside the Devil's Pool Hall as the last light was bleeding out of the day. The name was spelled out over the door in red neon, though it hadn't been switched on yet. The paint was peeling, and the windows were mostly boarded up. A mural on one side of the building featured a leering devil, its forked tongue hanging out with a pool ball rolling down it. Classy.

The car park was deserted except for a van with tinted windows right by the back door. Drifts of dead leaves and rubbish swirled around it. Even though the place screamed horror movie, Cafferty was getting out of the car. "I'll be right back," he said, tossing me the keys. "In case you need them. Lock yourself in."

Misgivings had me tied up in knots as I watched Cafferty rattling the door. The sign said 'Closed'. So what was Carly doing here?

Cafferty hammered on the door with his fist. "Carly?" he yelled, loud enough for me to hear him through the window. Something made him take off running. He disappeared down the side of the building.

Chapter 27

The moment Cafferty vanished, I regretted letting him run off alone. I got out of the car and locked it, hurrying across to the smeared window by the door of the pool hall. Carly was lying on a pool table, kicking her legs and bucking her body as her date tried to pin her down. Her date had his back to me, but his intentions were clear enough when he buried his mouth in her throat.

Cafferty burst through a door across the room, gun raised. His mouth was moving, but I heard only a jumble of sounds through the glass. His eyes were wide and disbelieving. He'd seen the vampire but couldn't know what to do. A bullet was more likely to kill Carly than the vampire.

I ran full pelt round the building, breath coming fast and feet skidding in the carpet of dead leaves. I burst into a dim, musty bar, the stench of stale beer and cigarettes invading my nose. Carly was on one of several pool tables with the vampire pinning her down. Cafferty was in front of me with his gun raised.

The vampire's mouth came free, his teeth gory and his body holding Carly down while she struggled. Carly's blood trickled down his chin as he grinned, showing his fangs. He had brown hair highlighted blonde like Zack from *Saved by the Bell*.

I could only see the back of Cafferty's head, but his shoulders were relaxed and his voice was measured. "Step away from her slowly with your hands raised."

The vampire's grin widened. Carly's struggling intensified. "You need a stake – like in the movies!" I yelled, checking around for weapons. Mine was at home – I couldn't take it to work with the police.

I grabbed a wooden chair by the bar and swung it at the wall. The chair bounced back and nearly hit me, not leaving a mark on it.

That was when the vampire moved. Cafferty did too, holstering his gun and grabbing a pool cue from the nearest table. Vampires were too fast: Cafferty would be dead before he armed himself. I failed to take Carly into account, attacked and bleeding but not helpless. With her legs freed, she jerked her knee upwards, getting the vampire right in the crotch. I knew I liked her. Carly slid off the table, hand against her bloody neck. The vampire doubled over, groaning.

Cafferty smashed the pool cue on the side of the table.

Unlike my effort, it snapped neatly, leaving a shard of wood attached to the rubber grip.

The vampire recovered fast. He sprang from the table and knocked Cafferty onto his back, snapping towards Cafferty's throat with his sister's blood on his fangs. I grabbed the half of the cue that Cafferty had discarded and approached where they were tussling on the floor.

Gripping the stake in slick hands, I waited for my opportunity. They were thrashing and rolling around too much. Though Cafferty had kept hold of his stake, I couldn't tell who was winning. Cafferty was taller and bigger, but that meant nothing against a vampire's strength.

Finally, the vampire presented its back to me. Cafferty got there first. He thrust upwards at one of the vampire's shoulders and flipped him over.

Cafferty slammed the broken cue into the vampire's chest. He knelt there with the shard of wood in his hand, his breathing harsh as the vampire died.

Carly slid down by the pool table, hand loose against her throat. I grabbed a roll of bandages from the first-aid kit behind the bar and ran to her side. I pressed them to Carly's throat. Cafferty appeared, taking over the pressure. The white wadding bloomed red. "Dammit Carly," he said. "You're gonna be OK."

"What do we do about him?" he asked me, and we both looked at the vampire's body. It was slowly collapsing, decomposition taking hold fast. He no longer looked like Zack Morris, unless *Saved by the Bell* went in a bold new direction.

"I'll call the slayers," I blurted out, knowing I was opening myself up to some serious explanations. "They can dispose of him."

"Slayers?" Deep lines furrowed Cafferty's forehead. "Never mind . . . fill me in later. I'm sure they'll have a phone behind the bar."

Worry for Carly made me clumsy, and I fumbled while I dialled Empire's number. Luck was on my side, because Della answered. I explained fast, and Della was typically efficient. "Leave it with me," she said. "Get her to the hospital."

Carly must have been all right, because Cafferty was chastising her as he applied a dressing to her wound. "What were you thinkin'?"

"I didn't realise he was the real deal. I didn't even know the real deal existed," she said, pale but defensive. "He was nice at first."

"Get in the car – both of you." Cafferty shared out the disapproval. "We're going to the hospital, and you're gonna tell me everything."

Cafferty set the sirens wailing and sped off down the quiet road. Carly glared sullenly out of the window, and Cafferty's frown was pensive in the rear-view mirror.

"You do know you could've been killed, right?" He sounded more tired than angry.

"I know, I know," Carly said. "I screwed up . . . Like I said, I didn't know he was a real vampire. I met him going into The Underground last night and thought he was cute. He asked me to meet him here today – just to hang. By the time I figured something was up, I called you. Just so you know, I saw Mina at The Underground too." She gave me a sheepish grin. Apparently we were going down together.

"Mina and I are gonna have a long chat once we get you seen to. I've got a lot of things to figure out, but I do know one thing –

you're done with it. A kid who'd been going there got stabbed to death yesterday. Me and Mina went to visit his mother today. And you almost got your throat ripped out."

"I know," she said, finally subdued. "Not the dead guy part, but the rest of it. You're right – no more Underground for me. Are you gonna call it in?"

"Sure. I'll tell them I staked a vampire right before Halloween. At best they'll laugh . . . at worst they'll take my badge." Cafferty pulled up at a set of traffic lights, taking a hand off the wheel to scrub over his eyes. "We need a story."

We decided on the dog bite narrative that the press had swallowed time and time again.

The only other patient in the waiting room was a boy cradling his arm, while a frazzled woman stroked his hair. When Carly was called to get stitches, Cafferty stood up. "Let's talk outside."

We walked past ambulances and patients smoking before finding a memorial garden. Cafferty led me to a stone bench by a pond spotted with pink lilies and surrounded by rushes.

Cafferty sat there patiently, waiting for me to open up. He must have been really good at interrogations, because I told him everything.

I started with the uncensored truth about what happened at Fang Fest, from John Carter's games to turning Jared and imprisoning us. I almost held back what happened to Jared, but Cafferty needed all the facts if he was going to be on our side.

I explained how I'd seen Thandie feeding at The Underground, and she'd given us the rundown on how to kill vampires.

He was a good listener, his expressions shifting between concentration and empathy. By all appearances, he was handling it, but his job must have equipped him for difficult truths. He let out a long whistle of breath when I finished. "Jesus. You went through all that and the police couldn't help you. *I* couldn't help you."

"You wouldn't have believed me. People always rationalise strange things, like the decomposing body in the park. You needed to see it."

He nodded, staring into the depths of the pond. A black fish grazed the surface. "You're right. You mentioned slayers earlier. What's that about?"

"That's a new one on me too," I said. "Vampire numbers are on the rise and the slayers get together to take them down when that happens. They only kill vampires that hurt humans. So the body in the park . . ."

"That was them?" He rested his head on one hand. "Am I supposed to be OK with this? Vigilantes running around and murdering people . . . vampires?"

"You can feel however you want," I said.

"What I need is time to think this through," he said.

"I've been there, and I'm here if you want to talk about it."

"Thanks. I need to wait for Carly – I'll radio a patrol officer to take you home. For now, I'm calling this one in as a dog attack. But if the slayers don't get this vampire problem under control and more people die, that's on us too. So if you hear the slayers have a lead on ending this, I want in."

"Understood," I said, not even sure that was a promise I could keep. "After the way you fought that vamp, I'm sure they'd want you on their side."

"I don't know about that." Cafferty smiled tiredly. "I hope you know this, but if you ever need me, call the police department and ask them to patch you right through."

"Thank you," I said. The pressure of the day was finally taking me down, because I felt the scratchy warning of tears.

As Cafferty went back into the hospital, I had doubts about not mentioning the notes. There was probably no point when he couldn't do anything, with no threat or clue who sent them. More important things had happened today. I was glad Cafferty knew about vampires. It was a burden, but we needed him.

Officer Dupres was a smiling teddy bear of a man, though he'd probably be offended by that comparison. He was big and friendly, but I could tell from the way he assessed the environment that he'd be good in a crisis. He chatted amicably about his kids and wife on the way home. Apparently his daughter was getting into RL Stine, so I promised to get her a few Fear Street books when we got back.

When our conversation ran dry, I took out Thandie's letters to do some more reading. A lot of them covered the same things, from concerns about the brothers to musings on the mansion. I paused over an extract at the bottom of a letter that set off all kinds of misgivings.

> You always have your finger on the pulse of this city, so perhaps you can help me. A strange man visited yesterday. He refused to give a name but insisted on prying first into my business and then into whether I have a power.

Yes — he knew I was a vampire, and it took little time to determine that he was like me. Might you help me figure out who he is? He was white, handsome and entitled. I suppose that doesn't really narrow it down. I sent him on his way with a healthy touch of self-doubt, though I'm sure it won't last.

I shouldn't commit any more words about him to paper — I'll call you. If he's as influential as I suspect, I don't know who could be reading this. I'll pluck up the courage to come see you myself, but until then please think through your contacts to consider who he might be. My intention is to stay as far from him as possible, so it would help to know who I'm dealing with. I got the impression that he would like to collect me, much like the macabre artefacts I store in glass cases. But you know me, and I will not be caged any more than I already am.

Thandie

Poor Thandie had never felt much peace, between the slayers, the Carter brothers and this new vampire sniffing around. Jared had shown little interest in developing powers. If having them made him a target, perhaps it'd be better if he never got them.

Jason was leaving the house when the police car pulled up. "Hey," he said, jangling the mansion's master key before tucking it into his pocket. "I'm having a night off from Candyman and keeping an eye on things for Libby at the mansion while you're at the ball." He patted his pocket, bringing his hand up to rake it through his short curls. "I've done it before, but still . . ."

"You'll be great. Everyone knows their part," I said.

"Yeah . . . but I feel more comfortable playing a monster than tellin' them what to do. Have fun tonight."

I took the RL Stine books out to Officer Dupres, and Della was waiting for me when I got back inside. "Did the slayers deal with that vampire?" I whispered.

"Yeah, we got him. Is Carly OK?"

"I think so. Cafferty . . ."

I stopped talking, because Libby came out of her room. "How was your day?" she asked.

"Good thanks. Shall we get ready to go out?" I said.

"Not yet. First you can tell me why you were talking about vampire slayers."

Chapter 28

"Can we explain in the kitchen?" Della asked, resting a hand on Libby's arm.

She shrugged it off. "No, you can tell me now why my sister and girlfriend are talking behind my back!" She was shrill by the end, her voice laced with hurt.

Della sighed. "I didn't want you to find out this way. For the past couple months, I've been hunting vampires. Mina just found out, and she came along last night."

Libby's laugh was ugly, and an angry flush spread across her cheeks. "You lied to me because you're killing people?"

"It's not like that," Della pleaded, and her desperation for Libby to understand was plain. I knew my sister, and the lie would bother her as much as our association with the slayers. Della explained the code and the rising numbers of vampires while Libby stood there with her arms folded.

"OK, I get all of that," Libby said, still agitated. "But why do you two need to be the ones to fight? Can't you leave it to someone else?"

"If not us, then who?" Della asked. "I found out that a vampire killed my mom – like I always suspected – and that she was a slayer too. But it isn't just about her. I want to do this."

"I'm sorry about your mom," Libby said, taking Della's hand. Her empathy didn't extend to me. "What about you? Does Jared know?" She left no space for me to speak. "Of course not. You're attacking people like him."

"Not like him," I said. "Just vampires who break the code." That rolled out so easily – Rosario's words from my mouth. But I actually believed them. What happened to Carly had decided for me. The slayers were holding vampires who hurt people to account. I would've been more useful to Carly and Cafferty if I'd been fully trained.

"Will he see that distinction?" she asked.

Tessa burst through the door, dress bag in one hand and a clinking carrier bag in the other. The tension sputtered out. "Oh good! You're not ready. I thought I was late."

"You're just in time," Libby said, her brightness fragile. "Let's get started!"

Libby was surly at first, but her excitement gradually became real as we got out our dresses. She put the radio on, and the haunting melody of 'Zombie' by the Cranberries built to a roar by the chorus.

I'd decided to go as Mina Harker from *Dracula*, and the dress took a lot of swearing and yanking from Libby until she got me into it. Piles of crimson silk swooped down from the tightly boned corset. It made me stand up straighter, shoulders back, as we helped Della into her dress.

She and Libby were perfect as Sarah and Jareth from *Labyrinth*. The beaded ivory dress was breathtaking against Della's dark brown skin, exposing her toned shoulders and back. Libby's punky mullet wig bordered on absurd, but she definitely pulled off Jareth's blue velvet suit and white ruffled shirt. Della helped Libby to fasten her jacket, taking her time as they smiled at each other. I'd never seen two people who fit together like they did.

I helped Tessa zip her Catwoman dress up the back. It was long black satin, with thick stitches zig-zagged all over the bodice. "This is amazing! Where did you get it?"

"I made it," she said. "The fabric was murder for my sewing machine. My mask will take like two minutes to put on – I'll make drinks."

By the time Tessa came back, Della and I had finished Libby's make-up: David Bowie's trademark eyeliner flicks and heavy white eyeshadow. Tessa set down four red drinks on Libby's drawers. "What are those?" I asked. The thick, red consistency and swirl of black were totally unappetising.

"Bloody Marys," Tessa said. "Not the horror story. Just tomato juice, vodka and some other stuff."

That sounded revolting. I picked one up, mixing it with the stick of celery that wasn't helping.

"Bloody Mary? Do I know that one?" Libby asked, taking a cautious sip. She winced.

"People used to tell it at school," I said. "You know . . . Say her name three times in front of the mirror and she appears. Like a vengeful female Candyman."

"I like her already," Libby said, drinking more and shuddering. "This tastes weird, and yet I can't stop drinking it."

"I don't know that one." Jared spoke quietly, but I leapt out of my skin and slopped my drink over my hand. Without us noticing, he'd arrived with the night.

"A myth you haven't heard?" I got the quip out before I looked at him.

I'd known he was going to dress as Gary Oldman's Dracula to my Mina, but not that he was going to look like that.

He was wearing a wig and stuck-on facial hair, which should have been ridiculous. Not on Jared. The straight, dark wig fell to his shoulders and the light moustache and goatee framed his full lips. He wore a black suit jacket and a gold, patterned shirt that came up to his throat. He looked enticing and dangerous.

"Jared!" Tessa chastised, gulping down her Bloody Mary. "You shouldn't sneak up on people."

"Sorry," he said, addressing me next. "You look gorgeous."

"Thank you. Want me to tell you that myth?"

"In your room?" Jared waggled his eyebrows.

"Keep the door open!" Libby sang. I slammed the door on our way in.

Jared stretched out on my bed. "Have you . . . ?" I asked.

"Drunk my fill of blood so I won't bite you? We're good."

I couldn't help laughing as I sat down. Even though it wouldn't last, it was nice to know we could get closer tonight. "Do you want to hear that myth or was this an excuse?"

"Both?" Jared grinned.

"It feels weird being on this side of the urban legend . . . OK, the story goes that if you turn out the lights and stand in front of a mirror with a candle, you say Bloody Mary three times to make her appear. Supposedly, blood runs down the mirror and Mary replaces your reflection. Some people say the ritual expels her from the afterlife to haunt you. I've also heard that a few people said it and disappeared."

"I'm guessin' the lesson here is not to say her name three times – got it," Jared said. "We've actually got a local voodoo priestess called Bloody Mary who runs a haunted museum in New Orleans – obviously not the same woman. I wonder if there's a local version of the legend that I can add to my tour."

"Are you enjoying it?" I asked.

"Yeah." He ran his hand down my red silk skirt, looking at that rather than me. "The plan to be a nurse is off for now. When I do tours, I'm in the moment. I don't have to think about myself."

That was the feeling I was chasing with the police and slayers. "I've got something to tell you."

"Oh yeah?" He was relaxed, so he couldn't have any idea what I was about to drop on him.

"Yeah. Della has been training to be a slayer, and I went out with them last night."

Chapter 29

He jumped up faster than a human could, blurring into a seated position. "You did what?"

"I've only been twice, but I think . . . I want to go back." I'd never seen Jared looking at me like that – as if he didn't know me. "I'm not explaining myself very well. Slayers have a code. If vampires take blood without consent, a slayer stops them. If the vampire murders someone, a slayer—"

"I understand what they do," Jared said, his tone cold and controlled. "Della's involved, so I'm sure it's all very moral and *good*." Venom leaked into the last word. "I don't understand why *you* want to do it. You're with me."

He made it sound simple, but there were other angles. Vampires were getting out of control, and who would stop them if not the slayers? My opinion was getting clearer, but that wasn't what this conversation was about. I needed to change that look on Jared's face. "Isn't it in every vampire's interests to take down the ones who are killing people . . . like putting murderers in prison? They're attacking people for their blood and killing some. You don't do that."

"How would you know?" he shot back.

"That's not fair. I've tried to have this conversation with you."

His rigid stance slackened, and he wrapped his arms around his knees. "I know. And you're right – I don't feed without consent. But what if I slip? John sired me – it might only be a matter of time. Would you go after me?"

"You won't," I said, leaning forward to rest my hands on his.

"I wasn't planning to, but it's not on the cards now." His laugh was bitter, crueller than I was used to. He slid his hands out from under mine. "Will you stop if I ask you to?"

"I can't do that," I said. "And I didn't think you'd ever try to stop me from doing something I believe in."

"Look – we're never going to agree about this," he said. "Let's come back to it later." He swooped forward to give me a quick kiss on the forehead, continuing the motion to get off the bed and away. He paused in the doorway. "We're about to go to the party of the year – we should make the most of it."

When he extended his hand, I took it. "You read my mind."

As we walked into the hallway, I thought back to the notes and their words scored angrily into the paper. I'd laid enough on Jared for tonight – they could wait. "I'll be right back," I said, popping back to my room. I put the stake into my handbag and snapped it shut, slinging it across my body. It symbolised the latest obstacle between me and Jared, but I couldn't risk being unarmed if I encountered one of the vampires causing mayhem.

Orchard Estate got its name from the spread of orange orchards that we saw as the taxi dropped us off. A long walkway of ancient oaks lined the path to the mansion. Jared had mentioned on the ride over here that the property was built less than 100 years ago, but the oaks had been there a lot longer.

The white mansion ahead blazed with light, but first we had to walk along the tunnel of trees. The air was muggy, leaving moisture clinging to my skin.

Jared asked, "Do you want to hear some ghost stories about the mansion? It may be less than a century old, but it's acquired a few. I could use some practice before they unleash me on the guests."

I was relieved to fall into my usual pattern with Jared – that I hadn't driven a wedge between us too deep to remove. "Why not?" A kernel of curiosity grew as we set off down the pathway of trees. Only a few other partygoers disturbed the stillness ahead.

"We'll leave you to your ghosts," Libby said, looping her arms into Tessa and Della's and urging them on under the blanket of branches.

"Libby's spoken!" Tessa called back, laughing. "See you at the party!"

In the day, the black branches and their sparse covering of

leaves would likely look striking against a bright sky. At night, their contorted, rustling shapes were menacing. The branches almost interlinked overhead. Some were bowed over and others had split near the base of the trunk, spraying outward like a layer of peeling skin. A red light nestled among the branches of each tree, casting an eerie glow over the scene.

Jared began as we progressed slowly. "After a private party, not unlike this one, the wait staff saw from outside the house that the study light was on. They all knew the lights were off before they'd set the alarm.

A woman appeared in the window of the lit room, resembling a painting of the original owner. The staff had spent enough time feeling her eyes on them as they waited tables at the dinner party.

The lights flickered, and the employees all rushed to their cars. They later reported that when they looked back, the house was dark again.

Other people have reported things like rocking chairs moving on their own, distant crying and the sound of a horse-drawn carriage trundling down this very driveway. The ghosts of Orchard Estate are gentle, but they're here."

The hairs along my arms lifted, and I rubbed the skin. I wasn't sure I believed in ghosts, but quiet ones shouldn't be underestimated. Poltergeists would rage and smash things up. Quiet ghosts would drift around where you least expected, watching and waiting.

"How'd I do – did I scare you?"

"You got me. Ghosts looking out of windows are my secret fear."

"I dunno, those chair rockers are pretty sneaky too."

I leaned against him and looked up into the trees, listening to the other three laughing ahead of us like the darkness had no power over them. "You did great – the guests will love it." I relished being close to him, though it was threaded through with sadness. Every moment like this brought us closer to the next time when he couldn't bear to be anywhere near me – when he'd need someone else's blood to be satisfied. And aligning myself with the slayers would only create more problems for us.

We broke free of the tree line and got our first proper look at the sprawling mansion. Pillars broke up the front and a metal balcony with a spiral pattern ran around the first floor. Small windows set into the grey roof reminded me of the attic windows of the Ursuline Convent, with its legendary vampires hiding behind shutters. Lights shone behind every window, and orchestral music drifted through them.

People milled around a red-tiled porch that extended around the mansion. Some wore variations on traditional costumes: ghosts in flimsy white gowns, witches in black cocktail dresses and stylised hats, and suited devils with horns and leering masks. Others were characters like us, from a werewolf in a basketball uniform to a group dressed as the cast of *Friends*.

The grand hallway had polished wooden floors and a cream-carpeted staircase. "Dare me to do a *Risky Business* sock slide?" Jared whispered. "I just need to take my shoes off . . ."

"If you do, you're on your own," I teased.

The walls were panelled in mahogany and covered in carvings of drooping trees. A skeletal black tree by the stairs was strung with red fairy lights.

The guy who gave us the tickets on Jared's tour hurried down the stairs, clipboard in hand and flustered. He paused halfway down, beckoning at Jared.

"I have to go – the ghosts need me," Jared said.

"I'll find the others."

Libby, Della and Tessa had grabbed glasses of champagne and found a great corner of the veranda where they could watch everyone arriving. I ordered a Coke that came with cherries and pink, cherry-flavoured sugar around the rim.

We whiled away an hour ranking costumes and eating Halloween canapés. My favourite was a puff pastry with an olive spider nestled inside, its legs made from olive slivers.

I was enjoying a spider puff when a waiter came to the open door of the mansion. "Would everyone please join us in the ballroom?"

Libby and Della merged into the crowd, but Tessa loomed in front of me. She was swaying slightly, and her dilated pupils couldn't quite land on me. "I've been wanting to ask you something," she said, her speech steady when she looked anything but. "What happened the night Lucas died?"

Chapter 30

Why would she bring up Lucas? "Wouldn't you rather talk to Libby or Della?" I asked, scanning the crowd for them. Looked like I was on my own.

"I tried, but they blew me off."

She looked so sad about her former housemate, but I couldn't tell her the unfiltered truth that she wanted. "I don't know what to say. We went on this horror tour as part of Fang Fest, and he got stabbed in a dark room. He seemed OK at first, but he died the next day in hospital."

"That's what they told me," Tessa said, her words slurring slightly. "But something about it doesn't add up."

Tessa was drunk and bereaved, but she was also massively intimidating.

"Is everything all right?" Most people had gone inside, but Jared was there when I needed him.

"Peachy," Tessa said, approaching the doors with an uneven gait. "Thanks Mina," she called over her shoulder.

"What was that about?" Jared asked.

"Lucas," I said, pushing on in the face of Jared's surprise. "She wanted answers, and I told her what I could. Let's go inside." I felt for Tessa, but anything to do with vampires was off limits for her own safety.

"If you insist." Jared offered me a hand, and we went in together.

The ballroom was like a scene from *Pride and Prejudice*. Everything was gilded in dull gold, from the intricate mouldings on the ceilings to the portrait frames. Most of the subjects were likely from the same family, judging by the high cheekbones and deep-set eyes. One could have been the woman from Jared's ghost story.

The small orchestra sat in the corner. A singer in a gold-beaded flapper dress sang her heart out to 'Moon River'.

People glided across the dance floor or lingered around a mahogany bar. Della and Libby were dancing, and Tessa had vanished.

Everything was so refined and elegant that I was out of my depth. "Care for a dance?" Jared asked. "Or a drink?"

"Let's check out the bar," I said.

We joined the queue, and Jared came up behind me. His lips brushed tantalisingly against my earlobe as he whispered, "I've heard the party gets wilder later."

I leaned into him, tilting my head back so he could hear me. "Is wild better?"

"Sometimes," Jared said, his breath cool on my neck. I was painfully aware of his body behind mine, so close but not touching. He moved away as longing rippled through me. I wanted so much more, even though I should have been grateful for what we had.

We grabbed two Cokes, and after the caffeinated sweetness, I'd worked up the courage to dance. This type of dancing was all about light feet and clasped hands. Jared seemed in his element, his head high and smile broad. Perhaps he was happier at arm's length from me. There was no evidence that he was holding my connection with the slayers against me. At the end of the song, Jared left me without a word and approached the singer. With a pleased smile, she nodded and said something to the band leader.

By the time Jared wove back through the crowd, grinning, the singer had begun. I knew those 'Ba da das' – the band were playing 'Kiss from a Rose'. The woman's voice soared through the notes, and the hairs on my arms stood on end.

Jared stepped up in front of me, and I stood on my tiptoes to talk into his ear. "You convinced them to play Seal?"

"For you."

We'd heard the song a few weeks ago when we watched *Batman Forever* in Della's car at my first ever drive-in movie. Jared twirled me from one hand and my skirt billowed out around me.

We soon found our rhythm, turning in slow circles. I made the most of our proximity, admiring Jared's costume.

"What?" he asked, smiling down at me.

"Nothing much," I said. "Just thinking what a hot Dracula you make."

His smile widened, turning wolfish. "Better than Lestat?"

"I didn't say that."

We passed the rest of the song in comfortable silence, and for once I had nothing on my mind but being with him.

"Thank you," I said at the end, kissing his cheek.

He looked pleased, but there was strain beneath the surface. We joined Della and Libby on some ridiculously comfortable chairs. "This party is somethin' else," Della said, "I could get used to dressin' like this."

"You should," Libby said. "You look beautiful."

"Thank y'all for comin'." The musicians stopped playing, and a rich, southern-accented voice quieted the background noise. A handsome white man around his mid-forties had stepped up to the microphone, and the singer moved aside. He wore a white suit and a smile just as bright. His light-brown hair was touched with grey, and his eyes were the palest blue, with smile lines fanning out around them.

"I've been rentin' out this gorgeous venue every Halloween for quite some time, and this has been the best party yet. I'm afraid the band will be stayin' for only one more song, but the DJ will be on later if y'all would like to stay for the Halloween festivities."

"Yes!" Libby whispered. "That's what I've been waiting for."

"I was once a singer of some renown, and it's customary for me to sing the last song to all you *strange* and wonderful people. Feel free to join me for drinks on the porch afterwards."

The crowd erupted in cheers as a banjo plucked out the

opening refrain of 'People Are Strange'. The man had a resonant, mesmerising voice that soon had the crowd swaying and singing along. He had charisma to spare, staring his guests down as he gripped the microphone. This was a faster country version than The Doors' original, and I was converted. When the singer held the note on the last 'strange', the captivated audience roared in appreciation. "Thank y'all very much!" he said, retreating to stand by the bar as we clapped and stamped our feet.

When the noise died down, Jared leaned in, "That's Claude Sejour. He owns a lot of property in New Orleans."

"Huh," Libby said. "Looks like I made the wrong friends when I moved here."

Afterwards, we followed other partygoers onto the porch. Some walked off down the dark driveway, red lights shining in the trees. Others were coming in the opposite direction. The refined ball must not have been their thing. Claude Sejour held court at the opposite end of the veranda. A female bodyguard towered over him, standing to one side but evidently there for protection. I found myself watching him while the others talked.

Soon the 'Monster Mash' blasted out from the mansion and stopped the conversation dead in its tracks. We all grinned as the horror movie soundtrack intro and bubbling kicked into a drumbeat. "Sounds like the party's back on," Jared said.

This party was a whole new creature. The room had darkened, and a host of black pumpkins had been placed around the room, their electric candles red. A ratty, black spider's web had been stretched across the high ceiling, jewelled spiders dangling down on long silver threads. Black-clad waiters in masks wove through the dancers. Their hidden faces reminded me of the masked killer that the victim's elderly neighbour had described. We were out on a remote estate, and for a while I'd put aside the risks the people of New Orleans were facing.

Everyone else was bouncing around and singing to the 'Monster Mash'. I slotted in between Libby and Della, and my sister wrapped me up in a sweaty hug. I forced myself to dance, and it lifted my spirits. I was with my friends in a public place – we were safe.

The song morphed into 'Thriller', and we dove into the dance routine with more enthusiasm than co-ordination. It only got worse the longer we danced.

When it finally ended, a woman's voice trilled, "Sisters! Won't you join me on stage a while?"

Three women who looked exactly like the Sanderson sisters from *Hocus Pocus* stepped onto the platform where the singer had stood. They were dressed in the witches' corset dresses, rags of lavish fabrics trailing down. Sarah Sanderson had curls of long blonde hair, Mary had her hair piled up in a precarious twist, and Winifred had puckered red lipstick and ginger hair in two oversized buns.

"We invite you to dance with us all night," Winifred said, matching Bette Midler's iconic voice, "or until the end of the song at least." Like the partygoers Winifred cursed in the movie, we were captivated.

She clapped once, and the opening of 'I Put a Spell on You'

sent us into a dancing frenzy. The sisters were amazing, fully embodying the characters while they sang.

We danced and laughed, hugging each other and getting breathless with the silly fun of it. Once the Sanderson sisters finished, I needed water and a trip to the toilet. "Bathroom break!" I shouted.

"Want me to come with?" Jared said into my ear.

"To the girls' bathroom? I think I can manage."

I squeezed through to the side of the room so I had a clear path to the door. Although I was having a blast, it felt good to get into the hallway and breathe air not exhaled by other people.

A waiter directed me down a corridor, and I ended up in a room that wasn't a bathroom. Either he or I had got it wrong, but I wasn't upset about it.

I was in an elegant room that probably wasn't meant for party guests. The walls were decorated in silky turquoise paper. A chandelier made of silver spirals and glass teardrops cast patterns of light on the walls. There was so much furniture: a teal velvet chaise longue, a writing desk made of the palest wood and Japanese screens etched with cherry blossoms. An enormous bookcase filled one wall. A quick look at the books, and I'd get back to the party.

The spines were all leather in shades of silver, beige, sky blue and grey, blending with the colour scheme of the room. I recognised some titles and authors, from Shakespeare to Dickens. Checking them out would definitely be pushing it.

The door slammed, and I spun around. The room appeared empty. I started towards the exit, instincts screaming even though nothing seemed out of place.

One of the Japanese screens moved in my peripheral vision –

a slight change of angle and scrape on the hardwood floor. My route to the door was clear, and I should've bolted. Instead, I looked at the screen. There was a blur of blonde hair and white clothing, and that was when the danger of my situation sank in. Veronica was in here.

Chapter 31

I took off towards the door, but she blocked my path before my eyes could catch up. She was so pale, from the milky shade of her skin to the ice-blonde of her hair. Even her dress was white – a lacy number that came high to her throat and fell to her feet in a straight shape that made her appear almost childlike. She wasn't carrying her trademark mallet, so that was something.

She ran an idle hand through her sheet of platinum hair. "I didn't expect to see you here."

"I have to get back to the party – my friends are waiting," I said.

"Right . . . You have a full set of those. I'm down one, as it happens." Veronica held out the hem of the skirt, swaying from side to side like a little girl.

"Two of my friends died," I said. Lucas brought it on himself, but Thandie had been innocent.

"True. But I only killed one of them."

"You killed Thandie?" I said. We'd found Veronica standing over Thandie as she lay there dying, blood flecked and gripping her mallet. But I'd always suspected it was John that ended Thandie's life.

Veronica stopped swaying, tilting her head on one side. "You didn't know? I am *so* sorry. We left you in one piece though, didn't we? Mostly." She reached for my hand, and I stepped out of reach. "I felt sure Jared would've drunk you dry by now."

"He's not like you," I said, checking my periphery for ways out. No other doors ... A window covered by elaborate blinds. Veronica was blocking my only exit. I had my stake, but I'd keep that until I needed it. She was likely to turn it on me before I got anywhere near her.

"You're so sure of him," she laughed prettily, the kind of overpowering sweetness that rots teeth. "Don't you know we usually take a page out of our sire's playbooks? Take mine, for example. Sadistic old bastard who treats me like a child and makes me attend stupid parties, so here I am." She curtsied, pulling out the sides of her dress. "It won't be long before Jared's evil comes oozing out of him. Hope you're nearby when it happens."

She'd confirmed Jared's every fear, but I wouldn't let him turn out like that. She glided closer, her tongue flicking out between her lips. "I am planning to let you go, you know. But I could just take one bite ..."

I snapped open my bag and drew out the stake, holding it loose at my side like I'd seen Rosario do. "I'm here with slayers," I said. If I took her off guard and ran, I wouldn't have to use the weapon. "Touch me and you'll never make it out of here."

Veronica sneered down at my stake. "Slayers . . . running around with their little sticks and big egos. I was just teasin' anyhow. You can go." Veronica stepped clear of the door.

I should have left, but I wouldn't get another opportunity like this. "You say you're teasing, but aren't you the one sending me notes?"

I had no proof that she was responsible, but I watched her reaction. Her brilliant, chilling smile told me nothing. "Notes were John's thing, remember? Are you sure you killed him? No . . . you got his *brother* to do your dirty work."

I was wasting my time, and every moment I spent with her was another that she could snap. She laughed when I eyeballed the space between her and the door. "Relax. I'm not going to kill you . . . tonight."

Terror and hatred boiled inside me as I passed her. I had to get so close that I smelled the coppery wrongness of her, overlaid with cloying perfume that reminded me of rotten fruit. I gripped the stake tight in my hand, preparing myself in case I had to use it.

"Enjoy the party!" she said.

As soon as I was clear, I broke into a run, stumbling on my high heels. I still needed the bathroom, but that would have to wait. I stuffed the stake down the side of my dress for easier access.

After encountering Veronica, the party room had turned menacing. Someone had switched on a strobe light that illuminated everything in flashes of red. The dance floor was packed and people were shouting out the lyrics of 'Bullet with

Butterfly Wings' by the Smashing Pumpkins. The chorus about being a rat in a cage was too apt.

I hovered in the doorway. I couldn't see Libby and the others, so I plunged onto the dance floor.

That was a mistake. People trod on my skirt even though I tried to lift it, and I got batted around by arms being flung in the air and people springing up and down. The costumes were creepier than earlier. Horror make-up mimicked flesh melting off the bone, and a spiked Pinhead face loomed in front of mine. Everyone was dressed as a killer or a monster.

Hot, sticky skin pressed against my arms over and over again, but worse were the brushes of cold. Vampires were all around me, and Veronica was here somewhere. Would she get to one of my friends before I did?

Jared appeared, eyes wild with worry. Relief washed over his features. "Come on!" he shouted, putting his arm around my back to usher me through the crowd. I kept my head down and let him lead me, hoping my sister and friends were on the other side.

The entrance hall was deserted, and I slowed down, breathing fast. "Did you see Veronica?"

"No – did she hurt you?" Jared took my hands, turning them palm up to check inside my wrist and elbows.

"I'm fine," I said. "She was trying to scare me, and she succeeded. What freaked you out if it wasn't her?"

"A bunch of vampires are prowling. We decided to split, but I couldn't find you." Reassured that we were both in one piece, we went out into the muggy night.

Libby, Della and Tessa were waiting. "What's going on?" Tessa asked. "Della said there were gang members causing trouble.

I didn't see anyone." She noticed everything – we'd be lucky to get this past her.

"Yeah, it was scary," I said. "Let's go."

The taxi driver had excellent taste in Britpop, even if I was too rattled to enjoy it. Blur, Oasis and Pulp songs played in a jumble, and the driver sang along in an accent close to French.

When the taxi pulled up at some traffic lights just off Bourbon Street, Tessa scrambled out first. "I'm staying out tonight, but I'll catch you guys tomorrow."

We followed, our costumes dishevelled and wigs crooked. She'd gone before we could respond.

"There she goes," Libby said. "Oh to be that innocent."

"I have to tell you something," I said, moving to one side of the busy street so they'd follow. "I saw Veronica. I'm so sorry Libby – she told me she killed Thandie."

Libby shrugged, her face hardening. "I guessed as much. It won't bring her back."

"Did she say anything else?" Della pressed.

"Nothing coherent. She said she didn't send me the notes, but I don't know if I believe her."

"Hold up – what notes?" Jared asked.

"I didn't get chance to explain . . . Someone sent me two notes about Fang Fest. I think they're trying to mess with me – it wasn't threatening or anything."

"Let's hope it stays that way," Jared said. I felt bad for not telling him sooner. With his days and nights flipping, he missed so much.

"I kinda hoped she'd gone off to be an evil psycho somewhere else," Libby said. "But I feel like she'd admit it if she did something shitty to us – she'd want the credit."

"I hope so," I said. There weren't many worse people to be taunting me.

"I know y'all won't like it," Della said, "but I'm going out with the slayers tonight. I'm sorry y'all aren't on board, but it's somethin' I have to do."

Jared ran his tongue along his teeth, distaste flashing across his features. "You can both do what you want. I'm not gonna stop you."

That was hardly a blessing, but I'd take it.

"Can I go on record to say I don't want you to do this?" Libby said, harder to take seriously when she was dressed as David Bowie. "But I know if I try to stop either of you, it'll make you resent me, and I don't want that."

"Thank you," Della said. "You comin', Mina? We can change at my place."

"Sure," I said. Libby and Jared both looked miserable as we walked away. Libby would forgive us. Her anger was ferocious, but it always burned out fast. For Jared, our actions were entangled with what he'd become.

As we hurried down the street, I found my perception was changing. Instead of concentrating on the city's striking locations, I was checking for threats in alleys and shadowed areas. A group of laughing people could have a vampire among them.

Della was doing the same thing, her gaze roving over the scene and lingering on passersby. Even though she looked like a Disney princess in her *Labyrinth* getup, she was fierce and sure of herself. I wanted to be like that.

Della's apartment was on the ground floor of a three-storey building on Esplanade Avenue. It was pale pink with grey shutters, and two balconies were surrounded by flowery iron railings.

Della led me into a cosy living room with a polished mahogany floor and so many patterns. The sofa was neutral and piled with cushions in various bright block colours. A rainbow rug lay under the coffee table and the curtains were covered in splashes of colour. "This place is great!" I said.

"Make yourself at home. My dad has a late shift at the hospital, so it's just us. Let me grab you some clothes. Bathroom's over there."

Once I'd scrubbed my face and scraped my hair back, I was free to wander. I'd always liked exploring other people's spaces, building lives for them in my head. I never went through their drawers or anything, but I learned a lot about people from looking at their video and book collections. Mum used to cringe when I did that. She was only interested in herself, so other people held little interest. Case in point: she'd gone silent since our failed meeting the other day. Hurt threatened to set in, so I moved on to Della's family photos on the mantelpiece.

The first picture was of Della being hugged by her parents. Her hair was in coiled bunches, and she was wearing a yellow sundress. She obviously got her joyful grin from her dad, but it was her mum she looked like: laughing eyes and dimples below high cheekbones. The photos weren't in chronological order, so baby Della was next to her high school graduation photograph. Her mum had passed away by then, so the photo was of Della and her proud dad. This was what a family looked like.

The next picture must have been from the wake after her

mum's funeral. Strained faces, everyone dressed in black . . . A younger Della curled up on the sofa with her head on her dad's lap. His expression was desolate and empty compared with the other images.

I'd almost moved on to the next photograph when I recognised someone. I picked up the frame, and there she was in a black shift dress: Emmeline.

Chapter 32

The photograph was old, and Emmeline was in the background. She wasn't even looking at the camera.

Della joined me. "Mom's wake," she said, touching the frame reverently.

"That must have been hard," I said.

"It was, but kinda nice too. Remembering her, bringing together the people from her life . . ."

"Do you recognise her?" I asked, pointing to Emmeline. "She's one of the few people I know in New Orleans."

She examined the photograph. "No . . . I've never noticed her before."

"She's called Emmeline – she owns a shop called Fanged Friends."

"I don't know many of Mom's friends. I'd love to meet her." Her hope was lovely and heartbreaking. I understood wanting to latch onto anything that would make your family feel closer.

"I can introduce you," I said.

Della leaned a head on my shoulder. Having her close felt so comfortable, like someone who had been there all along. "Thank you. Now let's get dressed and go hunt vampires."

"I think you might have left out a few details about this location," I said to Della. We were lurking in the shadows of a boarded-up doorway, which gave us too clear a view across the street.

"And if I'd said derelict clown museum you'd have come running?" Della asked, her eyes gleaming mischievously in the near darkness.

"In the opposite direction," I mumbled, patting the stake at my hip.

"Taz will be along any minute, then we can get in, check for vamps and get out," Della said.

"Wait . . . So we're on a *stake*out?" I tugged the stake out of my waistband, rolling it around between my hands.

Della groaned. "You spend too much time with Jared."

My laughter ran out as I took in the museum. The windows were boarded up and the wooden planks running along the outer wall were either broken or missing. One of the four pillars that had once supported the front of the roof had collapsed. The whole place sagged in the middle, forming a devilish smile. What kind of creature would choose to live there?

"It was pretty fun before the flood damage," Della said. "My mom took me one time. The newspapers said the owners left everything behind once the insurer paid out. The basement and first-floor exhibits were totalled, but the second floor survived. They had a café and theatre room up there. If a gang of vamps are hiding out, that's where they'll be."

A black Jeep Cherokee pulled up down the street. Taz got out, jogging right over to us, so we couldn't have been as inconspicuous as I'd thought. "Sorry y'all – I got held up." She was dressed all in black, a knit cap snug over her shaved head. "So I heard you kicked some ass last night. Ready to do the same tonight if we have to?"

That was the part I was struggling with. "I think so – my aim definitely needs some work though." I'd hardly had time to process my staking attempt last night, and I was here again with two slayers, ready to walk into another unknown.

"We should do a quick pass and go. I watch horror movies – none of that splitting up crap, especially in this creep fest," Taz said.

"Let's try round the back," Della said.

The light optimism from our chat fizzled out. This was it. We were about to walk into a sagging, possibly vampire-infested clown museum. By choice.

We stayed low and quick as we crossed the empty road, traipsing through thick weeds down the side of the building. I copied Della and Taz, keeping below the bottom of the windows with the stake in my hand. Adjusting and readjusting my grip, I finally found a way of holding it that felt right: the hilt resting against my wrist and the point coming through my clenched fingers.

The wooden porch at the back bowed and creaked underfoot as we approached the back door of the museum. It was ajar, and I couldn't figure out if that was a good thing or not.

"Stay undetected and if we come face to face with any vampires, we read the room. If they'll answer some questions then great, but otherwise we split. Got it?" Della ordered.

"Sounds like a plan," I answered. Della pushed the door open. The creak shuddered through my whole body. We froze, listened and waited.

Nobody came, so we entered one by one. The back room was full of swollen, water-damaged boxes of museum brochures and guides. Everything smelled of damp and rot, the stench invading my nostrils and crawling all over my skin. Taz eyed a fire escape map. "Found a route to the second floor. Looks like we gotta get through some exhibition rooms first."

Taz led the way, while I was mired in a complicated mix of emotions. I wanted to prove myself at the same time as being scared out of my mind. It must have been worse for Della, if she last came here with her mum.

The hallway carpet was stained and peeling. Every step felt spongy, like moisture from the flood had seeped into the building and never escaped.

The first exhibit showed the history of circuses in the USA, with blown-up pictures of circus tents and advertisement banners through the decades. Mould had bloomed across most of them, obscuring the faces of smiling ring masters and clowns.

"Watch out!" Taz pointed down at the missing floorboard extending across the width of the room. Glass-eyed wax mannequins stared up at us from a tangle of circus tenting and poles. If we'd fallen down into the basement with them, our broken bodies would've been lost and forgotten too.

Hopping over the hole, we came up in front of a door with two signs beside it. One read 'A History of Clowns'. The other was a warning – anyone with a heart condition or fear of clowns should stay away. Libby fit squarely in the latter group, but she'd never walk into a clown museum. It wasn't the clowns I was afraid of. Last night, we'd ventured into a seemingly abandoned crypt and had to fight our way out.

With no windows, the second exhibit was darker than the first. We couldn't risk turning on the lights and alerting anyone. The room was long and narrow with a closed door at the far end. The only light was coming from our door, so with each step the room got darker. Della turned on a pocket torch that lit up a circular patch in front of her.

A dozen pairs of clown eyes stared at us, illuminated by the torchlight as we crept past. None of the clowns looked quite right. The floodwater had infected their waxy faces, leaving them bloated and misshapen.

First came a distorted version of Jack Nicholson's Joker, his broad smile melting and eyebrows quirked even more than usual. Bozo the Clown was a lot scarier than he was meant to be, with thick white makeup, oversized eyebrows and mouth that almost entirely erased his humanity. He was too realistic, like he could step off the pedestal and lurch towards us. The Killer Klowns from Outer Space were as awful as intended, their faces contorted and hungry.

We shuffled past them in near blackness, only protected by the patch of light ahead from Della's torch. The clowns were so consuming that I'd temporarily forgotten about vampires. When I bumped into the child, I smothered a yelp.

Della and Taz leapt to my defence, but the rotten floorboard under Della's foot gave way. Her leg plunged down and she fell forward, taking the torchlight down to the ground with her.

She was pushing herself to standing as Taz and I moved on the small figure. If we were dealing with a tiny vampire, someone had a cruel sense of humour. I couldn't kill a vampire whose human life had barely begun.

I didn't have to. Taz picked it up, holding the clown doll in the beam of Della's torchlight. This one had survived the floodwater with little damage. "Are you all right?" I asked Della.

"I'll live," she said.

Taz glowered down at the clown. "I don't recognise this one," she said. "And I don't like it."

"It's from *Poltergeist*," I said. Its round, rosy-cheeked face was distorted by eyes and a mouth that were much too large. "In the movie, the ghost possessed the clown doll and grabbed the kid."

"I really didn't need to know that," Taz said, tossing it at the wall. It lay limp on the ground, face turned upwards.

"Let's move," Della said. "Watch your step."

We proceeded cautiously, following Taz's lead along the wall at the back of the exhibition. Even though she was testing our route, each step was a gamble. Krusty the Clown lifted my spirits from across the exhibition, his completely not-scary face smiling and one hand raised in a wave.

The final clown was by the exit, and his was the real face of evil. His eyes were circled in blue and mouth was painted red, and his red and white outfit made him no scarier than any others. But the sign on the wall read 'John Wayne Gacy'. That meant he wasn't a movie serial killer – he was the real thing. He'd put on his clown costume to perform at parties and hospitals but also murdered people and collected their bodies in the crawl space under his house.

"Let's get out of this shit show and check for vampires," Taz murmured, opening the door.

We followed Taz up a musty flight of stairs. The air was dry and suffocating, and every step groaned. Circus memorabilia adorned the walls, including clown horns, hoops, unicycles and juggling balls. As we progressed, sounds drifted down to us: the blare of a movie playing and voices competing. I clutched my stake, my chest tight at the stuffy air and heartbeat pulsing loudly in my ears.

Taz paused at the top. The door across the hallway was ajar, and a lively conversation was going on. Listening, Taz held up four fingers. Humans or vampires? Either way, we were outnumbered.

Through the gap in the doorway, I could see a huge screen showing *Dazed and Confused* with a few chairs set up around it at angles. Each was occupied, and I knew we were dealing with vampires when I recognised one of them.

Chapter 33

"**D**oesn't he work at the movie theatre?" Della whispered. I winced, expecting the four vampires to rush towards us.

Their conversation never faltered, so I felt safe to whisper, "Yeah. We'll fill you in later," I added to Taz, and she nodded.

They were drinking beer and smoking. Three vampires were seated, all looking like young guys though there was no guessing their real ages. A woman sidled into view. She looked older and carried herself like she was in charge. While the guys were dressed in shades of grunge, she was wearing a smart blouse and jeans with full make-up and her hair blow dried and sprayed into smooth, honey-coloured waves.

"They don't look like the crack team heading up the surge," Taz whispered, "but she has potential. Let's give it a minute."

"I hope you idiots didn't lead the gang to our hideout," the female said, wafting their smoke away from her face.

The cinema guy spoke up, gesturing with his cigarette. "Nah, we lost 'em. That leader dude was trying to get us to join with this big plan to attack on Halloween."

"Yeah, it's his sire's thing. Whoever that is sounds scary as shit," another guy chipped in, letting ash fall all over his Black Sabbath T-shirt. "Sorry Mom. But that blonde dude was bad enough – his mullet was terrifying." Mom? Were they a vampire family?

"I'd tell you to lay low," she said dryly, "but that's all you do anyway. We have willing donors at Crescent Screens, and I don't want any of you to screw it up."

I went over what they'd said. Some big plan was being carried out on Halloween, and we had only two days to figure it out.

Taz was about to speak when she steadied herself on the wall of circus memorabilia. *Honk-onk!* A clown horn blared, and I jumped right along with the vampires. There was no time for debate. Della took off downstairs, and I ran after her.

The woman's voice rang out. "Go see who that is, boys."

Vampires were usually fast, but their heavy, loping footsteps gave me some hope. As we ran down the stairs, a groan rippled through the building and the whole thing shifted. If it didn't collapse around us, we might make it out with our information. Anxiety zinged through my muscles as we skidded into the clown exhibit. John Wayne Gacy's figurine leered from the doorway, as the slacker vamps were gaining on us. Their stumbling steps and grunts of exertion were drawing nearer, and Taz was my only shield from three pissed-off vamps.

"Jump!" Della yelled as she leaped over the hole she'd almost disappeared down earlier. I did what she told me, and the floor let out an ominous cracking sound as I landed. When Taz's feet hit seconds after mine, the board bowed under her feet and I yanked her onto solid ground. A loud creak vibrated through the house.

Wax faces loomed around us as we ran, and we'd reached the other end of the exhibit when there was a crash. Checking backwards, I saw cinema vamp peering down a new hole, "You OK, dude?"

"I bruised my butt!"

That was the last thing I heard as we pelted out into the night, ditching the stealth mode we'd used on our way in.

"My car!" Taz called, not at all out of breath, even though my breathing was coming hard and fast. Della and I piled into the back of the Jeep, and Taz set off before I'd even rolled into a seat. A U2 song blasted out of her speakers as she floored it: *Hold Me, Thrill Me, Kiss Me, Kill Me.*

Taz's eyes were bright in the mirror. "I thought that place was coming down around us! You did good for your second patrol. Just shows not all vamps are the kind you have to stick with the pointy end."

Our victory was buzzing through her, but I couldn't get too excited. "Did you hear what they said? Something big is going down on Halloween."

"Yeah – we finally got a solid lead, and we have two days to figure it out. Let me know where you guys need dropping off and then I'll update Rosario. We'll send someone to the movie theatre tomorrow to question that kid too in case he knows more."

"That was a close one," Della said, sinking down in the back seat.

"We got some good information though," I said, feeling safer in the confines of Taz's car.

"It's a start," Della agreed. "But it don't make our job any easier."

Back at home, Della pushed Libby's door open. Libby was lying on her front, face close to the TV. *Blossom* was on – it must've been one she'd recorded at this hour. She and Jared had both changed out of their costumes. Libby was wearing *Care Bear* pyjamas, and Jared had dug up an *Eerie, Indiana* T-shirt from somewhere.

"Not my choice," Jared said, pointing at the TV. "I voted for *My So Called Life*." He had his back against the wall at the other end of the bed, but it was good to see them together.

"What are you talking about? Blossom's a style icon!" Libby said. "How did it go?"

Della fielded that one. "We got some good intel."

Jared stood up, already closed off. "I should go. I'll catch you after dusk tomorrow at Armand's new restaurant."

Della eyed him warily as she sank down on the bed with Libby. "Night."

"Hey," Libby said sleepily. "You're not completely horrible for a vampire, by the way." Her face was half buried in the quilt, but she turned her head to show her grin.

"And you're a decent human, I guess," he shot back, some affection creeping into his smile. "Night."

I followed Jared into the hallway. "So you made it back alive," he said. "Any vampires who can't say the same?"

"Nope," I said. "Tonight was reconnaissance."

Jared nodded curtly. "I want to understand – I really do."

"I appreciate that," I said.

I was so physically and emotionally drained that I craved contact. Having his arms around me would've given me the peace I needed, but I couldn't make the first move. The ball at Orchard Estate had given us a break from our issues, until Veronica's appearance, but the friction was back. There was a hallway between us, but so much more than that in reality.

Pain tightened his features. "I should go. Have a good day with Cafferty tomorrow. Night, Mina." Neither of us attempted to bridge the gap before he closed the door.

I got washed quickly, scrubbing off the grime of the night and then crashed down on my pillow. I'd survived another outing with the slayers, but the spectre of Veronica hung over me. She hadn't seemed especially interested in us, but knowing she was around was bad enough. After the encounter with her and my conflict with Jared, exhaustion pulled me into a fretful sleep.

The next morning, I felt refreshed despite the blur of events from the previous day and another late night. Cafferty had learned vampires were real, but with the sunlight streaming in, all the vampires were tucked up inside. They were future Mina's problem.

Libby was hunched over a cup of black coffee at the kitchen table, bleary eyed. "It's possible," she croaked, "that I drank too much last night."

"Did you?" I said with no sympathy, pouring a bowl of cereal.

We didn't have Reese's Puffs in England, and the chocolate peanut butter goodness was an instant mood lifter.

"I'll walk you to the police station." Della breezed in, definitely talking louder than usual.

She bit into an apple, and Libby grimaced at the crunch. "I'm going back to bed." Libby shuffled out of the room, blowing a half-hearted kiss at Della and touching my arm on the way out.

"You ready?" Della asked when I was washing out my bowl.

"Give me five minutes."

The day was chilly and autumnal, and the air smelled unusually fresh. I was getting used to New Orleans's distinctive smell, and today the faint swampiness was lacking. This changeable weather, warm one day and cold the next, was more like what I was used to in England.

"You OK this mornin'?" Della asked, as we passed a house where a woman was standing miniature tombstones along her windowsill. She smiled and wished us a good morning.

"I'm still getting used to the late nights, but otherwise fine," I said, probing at the things that were bothering me. Days had gone by since I'd received any notes, and I couldn't do anything about the vampires in my life during daylight hours. The encounter with the slayers had given me a confidence boost that I wasn't making a huge mistake. "How about you?"

"I'm good," she said, "though I'm kinda freaked about what those vamps said. Halloween's tomorrow, and somethin's goin' down. Do you think they've planned it for the Halloween Mask Parade?"

That was the end of my optimistic mood. "It could be. There are probably loads of things happening on Halloween."

"Hopefully we'll figure it out before then," she said. "But I could actually use your help. Do you mind if we stop by Fanged Friends to meet that woman . . . Emmeline?"

"Sure," I said, checking my watch. I could spare a few minutes. Della had waited long enough to find people who knew her mum.

Fanged Friends wasn't open, but Emmeline was behind the counter. I tapped on the glass, and she waved us in.

"Mornin', *cher*," Emmeline said.

"Morning. Thanks so much for Thandie's letters. It was nice to read things Thandie had written about herself and the mansion."

"It was my pleasure. You brought me a new customer? I should start payin' you commission."

"I won't say no to that," I said. "This is my friend, Della."

I'd expected some recognition, but there was nothing. The wake had been a long time ago.

Della came to the rescue. "I think you knew my mom – Mahala Abellard. You were in a picture from her wake."

Recognition alighted on Emmeline's face. "Mahala, of course. I'm so sorry, *cher*. You lost her so young. Based on the bump at your hip, I guess you have the same extracurricular activities."

Della touched the place where she kept her stake, even during the day. "I do. How did you know her?"

"We were friends, but we drifted apart," she said haltingly. "We met through another friend who's also passed."

"I'm sorry," Della said, her lips curving downwards in disappointment. She'd wanted more, but I was glad Emmeline had been honest. It would've been cruel to spin out a story because

Della wanted to hear it. "What do you remember about her?" Della asked, her desperation so keen that it was painful to witness.

"Your mom was kind but strong. She fought for what she believed in – I'm guessin' you're like that too. I'm sure she'd be very proud."

"Thanks," Della said.

"I wish I had more for you," Emmeline said. "Do you know how she died?"

"Sort of – a female vampire got to her."

"In that case, I do know more, though I'd rather not be the one to tell you."

"I can take it – believe me," Della said.

"All right," Emmeline said, regret putting lines across her smooth forehead. "I'm really sorry to say it, but I know who killed your mother."

Chapter 34

"Who?" Della asked, her need becoming intense.

"I'll get to that, if you're sure," Emmeline said.

"All right . . . How did you find out?" Della's frustration was threatening to break through.

"I pride myself on knowing other people's business. It's important to stay ahead in this city. I heard chatter about your mom's murder. A witness was too scared to go to the police, but she confided in me."

"Why are you only tellin' me this now?" Della asked.

"I told no one when I found out. Your father wasn't aware of your mother's calling as a slayer. He never would've believed me if

I'd told him her killer was a vampire. Even if he'd somehow found them, he would've died trying to avenge your mother."

"So who was it?" Della asked, her desperation undisguised.

"If you're sure you want to know. You seem like a good kid – I don't want to get you killed."

"I'm sure," Della said. "Tell me."

Emmeline didn't flinch. "It was a vampire who's known to be very vicious and unfortunately is part of the landscape of this city. She's called Veronica."

Cold fear shivered over me, whereas anger coursed through Della's tight muscles. "Thank you," she said. "I have to get Mina to work, but I appreciate your time."

"I hope I've done the right thing tellin' you," Emmeline said. "She's not one to trifle with. I told you to give you peace. I hope it doesn't bring further anguish."

"It won't," Della said.

"In that case, perhaps you and your slayer friends can bring her to justice for all of us."

We said our goodbyes, and Emmeline watched us leave with a grave look. My nerves were raw and exposed after seeing Veronica last night. Had Emmeline done the right thing in telling Della about her mum?

Della set off so fast that I could barely keep up. "What are you going to do?" I asked.

"I'll call Auntie Jackie when I get to work. But for now, I'm gonna help the slayers get this surge under control and keep up my training," she said, full of a feverish intensity. "When that's done, I'll ask them to help me find and kill Veronica."

By the time Della dropped me off at the station, I was seriously rattled. Emmeline had fired Della up and pointed her in Veronica's direction. At least she was letting the surge take priority and not rushing out to find Veronica.

I had to put that aside, because Cafferty was waiting outside the station. He'd had his own vampire revelations to handle.

"How's Carly?" I asked.

"She's doin' good," he said. "Hospital patched her up and sent her home. Thought I'd better wait here," he said. "We can't talk about . . . you know . . . inside."

"Have you recovered from finding out?" I asked.

"Did you ever recover?" he shot back.

"Surprisingly . . . yes. I had a pretty unconventional upbringing, so it wasn't too hard to wrap my head around."

"What I'm struggling with the most . . ." He paused to glance around. "There are cops risking their lives, and I'm guessin' none of them know."

"Apparently one does," I said, "and they've obviously never told you. This is how it's always been – should we decide for the whole world? If you tell people, they probably won't believe you, and it might wreck your career. Plus every vampire in town would want your neck if it got out that you spilled."

"I know," he said. "That's basically where I'm at. Can I ask . . . the scar on your arm . . . ?"

"Yeah – that was . . . one of them," I said, pulling back my sleeve to reveal the bite mark, still livid purple after months of healing.

"Jesus," he breathed. "OK, I think we'll have to leave it there. Last thing though . . . Do you think your slayer friends can get this surge under control, so the police can concentrate on our regular cases?"

"I'm sure they can," I said, "but vampires will exist even when the surge is over . . . and you'll have to live with it."

"Yeah . . . I can never unlearn that, can I? When this surge ends, I'll work on being at peace with it. Let's get back to the case. I'm afraid I've got bad news – there's been another stabbing that fits the pattern."

Four people were dead – presumably another not much older than me. I wanted to be brave enough to face this threat, but at what point would it become too much?

Cafferty led me to a room I'd not visited before. "I have some evidence to show you, if you're up for it?"

"Always," I said, hoping I had the stomach for whatever it was.

"OK," Cafferty rubbed his eyes as he let us into the room. "I spent a few hours at the crime scene last night. The victim was found not long after it happened – a girl."

"And we're no closer to catching the killer?" Someone had died almost every day since I'd started my work experience.

"Not yet," Cafferty said. "But hopefully we'll get an ID on that mask when the sketch artist goes out to the Broussards' neighbour."

The room looked like a laboratory. Glass cabinets full of equipment lined the walls and the surfaces were brushed steel.

One of the worktops had a silver tray on it covered in labelled objects. Cafferty explained the chain of custody: evidence had to be logged in and out and not tampered with or it could prove inadmissible in court.

"This is everything that was inside the victim's pockets or at the crime scene. We're looking for anything that ties her to the other victims or establishes a timeline of her movements over the past few days. Grab some gloves, but only handle evidence if absolutely necessary. Ask me if you're unsure. I've signed us in, so we're good to go."

"Got it," I pulled on the gloves. "What was her name?"

"Sami. She was a high school senior."

Like me. She could've been in one of my classes, making notes or laughing with her friends in the corridor afterwards.

We started at opposite ends of the tray, and I couldn't stop thinking about Sami. We were doing this for her. There'd be no bringing her back, but we could catch the person who murdered her.

I catalogued the objects, going over what Cafferty had taught me: we were looking for patterns or a timeline. I dismissed a lipstick in a gold tube, getting a glimpse of a girl smoothing it over her lips without realising she'd never do it again. I hovered over a broken necklace. A yin-yang symbol was connected to a long silver chain that had snapped on one side.

"Could someone have grabbed her and broken this?" I read the label. "It was found at the scene."

"I'll make a note of it," Cafferty said, jotting something in his notebook. "Could mean there was a struggle. That's good – keep going."

There were a couple of loyalty cards with stamps, though without dates they weren't helpful. Then I came to a gold-sequined coin purse. "Can I open this?"

"Of course," Cafferty said. "As long as you don't damage it."

Easier said than done. I pinched the snap opening. The catch resisted but gave in to light pressure.

The lining was gold satin, and a red object was nestled in the bottom. I guessed what it was before I squeezed the purse to reveal it. "Another Underground token," I said to Cafferty.

"Shit," he said. I'd never heard him swear before. "There's our connection between victims. Someone's targeting their clientele maybe? One of whom is my sister."

Jared was there every day on the other side of the biting relationship . . . and I'd been too. The case was moving uncomfortably close. "Maybe they are."

"Time to hit The Underground, but I'm afraid you'll have to stay in the car for this one. It's way beyond what I decided with Boudreaux, and you have a connection to the place."

"Agreed," I said reluctantly. They'd taken a risk letting me do this experience, and I couldn't ask them to break the rules. "I'll think over what I know about The Underground and see if I missed telling you anything."

In the car, I fleshed out what I'd told him about speaking to Elvira there with Jared and Della when we were trying to prove Libby's innocence, then going again with Armand when I ran into Carly.

"How come you went with him?" Cafferty asked the question I'd hoped he wouldn't.

"I wanted to understand how it works – because of Jared." Cafferty could live without knowing that I was trying to equip myself in case the right time came for Jared to feed on me.

"Right," Cafferty said. Even though his job involved

digging into people's business, I appreciated him not doing it to me. "That must be hard."

"Thank you," I said. "It is." No one had ever come out and said that, and the feelings I'd held back for months threatened to erupt. Eyes stinging, I looked out of the window.

I smelled the smoke before Cafferty did. I'd thought my pent-up emotions had made my eyes hurt and throat scratchy. But I'd always been sensitive to smoke, and soon I couldn't ignore the thick, burnt stench sitting heavy on my lungs. "Can you smell that?" I asked Cafferty.

"I was going to ask you the same thing," Cafferty said, reaching over to close the vents. I closed mine too.

Cafferty hit traffic as we pulled around the corner, so we approached the scene in slow motion. The Underground was on fire.

Chapter 35

The fire was so bright that the imprint of it was seared onto my retinas. My concerns darted to Jared, until I remembered that he couldn't be there in the day. It only opened at night, so with any luck the place was empty.

Fire fighters were spraying plumes of water into the blaze. Its blackened frame was exposed like a charred skeleton. The Underground was toast. Members of the public were scrambling for a look, so the police had their hands full.

Cafferty pulled the car away and parked a block over. "I need a word with the fire chief," he said, pushing an agitated hand back through his hair. His best lead was going up in smoke. "I'll be right back."

He gave no instructions about staying put, but I wanted to. The smoke had left a chemical taste in my mouth, and the flaming building had evoked a primal need to stay away.

Cafferty soon returned, his expression subdued. "Let's get back to the station."

He'd brought the smoke smell in with him, so I tried not to breathe it in as he turned the car around. In the rear-view mirror, The Underground's remains were black, and orange flames devoured what little was left.

"What did the fire chief say?" I asked.

"Suspected arson," he said. "They'll know more when the blaze is out."

The significance of the fire was sinking in. "You know it's not just human lifestylers who go to The Underground. Real vampires feed on people consensually. Now it's burned down they'll have nowhere to go. They could set up somewhere else, but that'll take time."

Cafferty pinched the bridge of his nose. "I didn't think of that. And it'd probably be less regulated."

"So what now?" I asked.

Cafferty took a long time to answer, running a hand down his jaw. "I'm not sure," he said. "But I do know one thing – someone is going to get stabbed by our masked killer in the next day or two if I don't figure it out."

The slayers were under similar time constraints. A vampire plan was due to unfold tomorrow – on Halloween. Every minute brought us closer to those deadlines.

The mood at the police station was sombre. We went over the case files, rereading notes and talking through everything. The Underground connection between victims had been Cafferty's best lead, and it was gone. We had a vague description of the killer's mask, but that wasn't a lot to go on.

As the afternoon went on, news filtered in about the fire. Some was gossip, but one thing seemed certain: it was arson.

Cafferty was about to drop me off at home when an officer called us over. "Detective – you have a fax coming in. The cover page says it's from the sketch artist."

That's all it took to lift the glum shadow from Cafferty's face. He'd just needed a new direction.

We waited by the bulky fax machine. It was printing painfully slow lines, gliding back and forth as an image gradually emerged. Neither of us spoke as we watched. The mask was like nothing I'd ever seen. If the witness had got it right, the killer was wearing a mask of an old, severe man's face. The main distinguishing features were a hooked nose and prominent chin. His mouth was a pursed, disapproving line.

The machine spat out the page, and we went back to Cafferty's desk to examine it. "I've played a lot of video games and seen some weird stuff on the streets, but nothing like this. Is it from any movies I should know about?" he asked.

"Not that I've seen," I said, rifling through my memory. Michael Myers, Leatherface, Hannibal Lecter and Jason all wore masks, but none of those fit. "I heard the *Halloween* movie mask is a Captain

Kirk mask that they moulded from William Shatner's face to use in his death scene. They modified it and sprayed it white. This mask kind of reminds me of it, but the features are wrong."

"Captain Kirk died?"

"That's what you're taking away from the story?" I teased. "It was a one-off episode."

"Phew," Cafferty said. "OK, so we don't know who this is, but it's a lead. If you're good to work on Halloween, we can look into it tomorrow. How do you feel about visiting every fancy dress store in New Orleans?"

"Pretty good," I said. "Are you going to the carnival tonight?"

"Probably not," he said, "but you should go and have a good time. We're putting extra officers on duty."

"I will," I said, excitement about the carnival threaded with misgivings. The slayers would be patrolling the carnival too, and it was my turn to do a sweep with Della near the end of the night. Apparently big public events often drew vampires out, and what was more enticing than a spooky carnival in New Orleans?

The house was empty when I got back. I tried to read while I waited for someone to come home or for night to fall. I thought about phoning Nat to take my mind off everything, but I was too jittery. She knew me so well that she'd notice something was up.

Jared arrived as soon as the sun had set. "Someone torched The Underground," he said when we got into my room. His expression was hopeless.

"I know," I said. "What are you going to do?"

"The owners are setting up a new location, but Armand will help me until then."

He looked awful, leaning against the wall as if he couldn't stay upright. The skin around his eyes was inflamed, and a harsh pallor had drained his colour.

"You look like you need to feed now," I said.

"I can wait until I've seen Armand," he said. Now we'd mentioned feeding, he couldn't drag his eyes from my body. They kept drifting between the best places to get blood: neck, wrist, inner elbow, thigh . . . He ran his tongue over his teeth, showing a flash of fangs before he pressed his lips together.

"You don't need him," I paused, preparing myself. This was a big step: one that could ruin or cement our relationship. "I'm right here."

"We've talked about that." He backed away, his expression pained.

"Things have changed," I said, "and your safe blood source has gone. Armand told me how it works. If I consent and you're careful, it won't hurt. I might even like it." The memory of his last bite burned as bright as the pain I'd felt, but I wanted to do this for him. A small part of me also wanted to know what it would feel like if I did it on my terms.

His tongue crept across his lower lip, fangs still bared. "You know what happened last time."

He moved closer, taking my scarred wrist in his hand. He traced a thumb over the raised purple mark, continuing the path over the blue thread of my veins. The skin there was so sensitive, intensified by the risk in what we were doing. His eyes glazed over, hypnotised by the blood so close to the surface.

"Jared," I said, heavy on the warning.

He snapped out of it and dropped my hand, looking at me with naked contrition.

"My scar isn't your fault," I said, aware of my quickening heart and the effect it would have on him. "John had just turned you against your will. Armand's been teaching you control. This is your chance to test it."

He swallowed hard, the swell of his Adam's apple rising and falling. "Where? If we do this . . . Where do you want me to . . .?"

He caressed my wrist with the steel of control. Pleasure rippled across my skin, making me feel soft and pliable.

"Where's somewhere discreet?" I asked.

Jared trailed a finger along the paler skin of my inner arm, every nerve waking up at his touch. He stopped in the crease of my elbow. "What about here?"

His yearning for my blood was almost painful, and I wanted him to take it. "That's fine."

"And you're sure? If I feed on you, we can't undo it."

"I'm sure." Only I could let my boyfriend bite me before we slept together.

Jared's smile was achingly beautiful, full of peril and expectation. He edged towards me, closer than we'd been for quite some time. I hadn't seen his face this close or had time to trail my fingertips down the rough of his stubble without him pulling away. I put a hand on his chest, the lack of a pulse more sad than frightening.

He leaned towards me, lips parted, and the need for him was almost unbearable. He pressed a lingering kiss against my mouth. The crush of his lips tasted of salt and metal.

"Let's sit down." He took my hand and led me to the bed. We sat closer than he'd been comfortable with for months, and he cupped my elbow in his hands. I'd never seen his face like this. When he'd bitten me last time, he'd been overtaken by ferocious hunger. This need was purer and more contained. He was waiting for my permission.

"Ready?" he asked, fixated on the faint blue lines in the crook of my elbow and the blood pulsing beneath the surface. What would it feel like when he sank his fangs into my skin, drawing out what he needed?

"I'm ready," I said, steady and certain. I needed to do this for him but also for myself.

Some people would have closed their eyes. I wanted to see everything. I watched his mouth lower slowly and the shift when hunger overcame him. The fine points of his fangs slid over his canines again. He gripped my arm harder, and I had a sneaking doubt that I was making the same mistake again.

His lips brushed the delicate skin inside my elbow. He was in control. Two memories blurred together: the first night I met him at the mansion, when he'd pretended to bite me as Lestat, and the time he'd bitten me when he'd first turned. That was when he lowered his mouth.

Chapter 36

The first sensation was a flare of pain when my skin broke, then a strange ebb and flow as he pulled blood from inside my elbow. I closed my eyes, and that was when I felt it. The pleasure was subtle at first, like being kissed or eating chocolate. Then it built to a rush that made everything light and dizzy. I was floating on a dream, connecting with him and all the time feeling that pull and release, pull and release. The press of his normal teeth on my skin. The light skim of his tongue and the heated pressure of his mouth.

His teeth made a pop as they came away from my skin. Smears of my blood had stained his lips. "I've taken enough," he said hoarsely, running a hand over his mouth. "Thank you."

"Are you sure you don't need more?" I was lost without the feeling. I needed longer with that sense of letting everything go.

"I'm fine, thank you." He was eying me strangely, like he wasn't sure whether to be amused or concerned.

I was there with him. How could being bitten feel so good? I looked at the twin holes inside my elbow that were practically closed. I'd need to cover them up, but it was hardly the torn flesh he'd left on my opposite wrist the first time.

He ran a thumb over the marks. "The wound's already closing. Are you OK?" he asked, while I drifted in the after buzz.

"I feel great."

"Good," he said. "Thank you . . . for letting me do that. It felt different with you. I don't usually feel as relaxed as this." He put an arm round me and kissed my head, his expression brightening. "The cravings have gone! Usually they go quiet but . . . I kind of feel like myself."

"Even though you're a vampire, you're still yourself." I moved forward, sitting in front of him on the bed.

He leaned in too, everything suggesting he was at ease. He threaded his hand through my hair, looking at me with those hazel-green eyes. It was too long since we'd done this – really seen each other and prolonged the moment.

He ran the back of his fingers down my cheek, and the light scratch of his nails left a shivering trail. Closing my eyes made the feeling more potent. When I opened them, his face was very close.

When he rested his thumb on my lower lip, I kissed it impulsively. He gave a low laugh as he leaned in and returned the favour.

Lately, our kisses had been quick brushes of lips before Jared retreated. There was no rushing as our mouths came together with all kinds of sweetness, our lips moving in time as we discovered each other all over again. He brought his hands up to my cheeks, deepening the kiss. I moved forward, forcing him to lean until he was almost on his back, my pillows under his head.

I'd never felt passion this intense. His hands grazed my shoulders and then ran down my sides to squeeze my hips. Everything was desire and sensation, and it was strongest where his hands touched me and our lips came together.

I took my time to explore him, kissing along the hard line of his stubbly jaw and letting my mouth fall on his throat. Impulsively, I nipped the skin between my teeth and he laughed, his body shaking under me.

In the end, we lay face to face with our legs entwined and chests pressed together. He stroked the lengths of my hair, playing with the curls. "I've missed this," he sighed.

"Tell me about it." I nestled my head into the crook of his neck, and everything felt right. "Guess we've figured out how to be close."

"Only if you're sure," Jared said, resting his forehead on mine so we couldn't get any closer.

"If we get back moments like this, it's worth it."

I heard the front door open and the thump of a dropped bag – Tessa.

"Let's not tell the others," I said. "I don't think they'll understand."

"Don't we have enough secrets? Tessa doesn't even know about me," he said, tilting his head towards the door where we could hear her moving around.

"Just for now then," I said. "There's so much going on."

"OK with me," Jared said, wrapping his arms around me. I relished the strength of his embrace and the feeling of being utterly connected to him. "If I'm going out to not eat dinner, I should shower."

"You do stink," I said conversationally.

"Thanks a lot."

He headed to the bathroom, and I sat cross legged on the bed to French plait my hair. The slayers' looming Halloween deadline and the spectre of Cafferty's killer were competing to freak me out the most, but the encounter with Jared had taken the edge off. As I ran my fingers through my wiry curls, I felt renewed trust in the slayers and the police. I was working with both sides because I believed in them, and I had to trust that we'd succeed. Tonight, I'd do my duties for the slayers but try to cut loose with Jared too. We'd earned it. I wasn't naïve enough to believe we'd solved all of our problems, but we'd made a start.

Tessa appeared in my doorway as I pulled the front of my plait round to secure the bobble. "That looks cute," she said.

"Thanks. Want me to do yours?"

"That would be awesome."

Tessa sat down on the bed, and I started brushing out her shiny black hair. "One plait or two?"

"Let's go with one," she said. "You look extra happy today."

Nothing got past her. "I am." I parted her hair before separating it into three sections. "How are you?"

"Tired, busy – the usual!" Her laugh came out hollow. I should've paid more attention. We were becoming friends, and I hadn't known she was struggling.

"Let me know if there's anything I can do," I said, weaving the strands into a simple French plait.

"Just offering is enough," she said. "OK, so this might come out super awkward – but I'm gonna say it anyway. I know I've been off around you. I wanted you to like me and didn't want the Jared thing to be an issue. So I think I tried too hard and made it worse?"

"You've been fine," I said. "To be honest, I've felt weird around you. You're kind of a hard act to follow, you know?"

Tessa let out a raucous laugh. I was used to her being so in control. It felt good that she was loosening up around me. "I doubt it."

Della and Libby arrived home as I finished Tessa's hair. Before I left my room, I put the stake down the waistband of my jeans, moving my leg around to check that it would stay in place.

We got ready fast and met Jared in the hallway. He'd put on fresh clothes and his hair had separated into damp curls. "You all look great!" he said, so relaxed when he sidled up to kiss my cheek. His stubble tickled my face, and I smiled up at him. I'd never take small intimacies for granted again.

"We will when we put the Halloween stuff on!" Libby said. Tonight was about quick costumes for dinner and the carnival. I was so ready for good food and thrill rides, though hopefully with a decent break between the two.

Libby handed me a black fluffy halo and angel wings with feathers that were already shedding. She picked the cat tail and ears, while Della went for Devil horns. "Satan would be very disappointed with this," she said, gesturing with the bendy plastic fork.

"You look hot anyway," Libby said, cupping Della's cheek in one hand.

"We have a unicorn horn and pirate bandana," Libby said, holding the bag open for Tessa.

"As much as I'd like to see Jared as a unicorn, I'll let him be a pirate." Tessa took the sparkly horn and tied it under her hair.

"I could be a unicorn," Jared said, but he accepted the bandana.

"How am I supposed to tie this?" he asked, as the other three left the house.

"Here," I said, folding it into a triangle. "Turn around and crouch down."

He bent his knees and I pulled one side of the triangle across his forehead, my thumbs brushing his cool skin and downy eyebrows. I tied the two points at the nape of his neck, letting my fingers sink into his thick hair. Curls escaped beneath the bandana, and I took my time tucking in the final point. It was so good to be able to touch Jared without knowing it was tormenting him. Only the question about how long it'd last took the shine off the moment.

He turned to face me. "I like the halo. Very appropriate."

"What are you trying to say?" I asked. I didn't feel all that innocent these days.

We set off, trailing behind the others with his arm around me. Even though his legs were long, we managed to match our gaits so I could snuggle into his side.

We were soon plunged into the sensory experience of the French Quarter. The lingering heat of the day clung to my skin, and from every side there were bursts of music and scents of delicious cuisines. But New Orleans felt different with Jared. He had a way of bringing the city alive for me, pointing out locations of interest and telling stories. On this occasion, it was a mansion with white pillars, balconies and a tower to one side.

"You'd think I'd have a story about this building, right? It's called the Cornstalk Hotel," he said. "But it's the fence people are interested in." Now that he mentioned it, the dark green iron fence with its golden cobs of corn and pointed leaves seemed noteworthy. "A wealthy man moved his new bride here, but she missed the cornfields back home in Iowa. So he had the cornstalk fence specially made to bring her a piece of the country."

"That's a more romantic story than you usually tell me," I said, leaning against him. Like the new bride, we'd made sacrifices for each other. We stayed as close as we could possibly get as we walked through the dark streets, the oversweet smell of pumpkin flesh in the air. We passed a bar where the *Ghostbusters* theme was playing, then a restaurant where everyone seemed to be eating a sticky meat dish with their fingers. My stomach grumbled.

Armand's new restaurant was on a corner. It had a balcony bar on the top floor and the restaurant on the ground floor, leading down into the basement. He'd had the building painted black with red balcony railings and red shutters that were nailed closed. The sign was shaped like flames and hand painted in yellow, orange and red. In the centre, it said 'Nine Steps to Hell'.

"He could've picked a cheerier name," Libby said as we joined them in the queue.

"It goes with 'Empire of the Dead' though, don't you think?" Della asked.

"I like it," Tessa said. "It's very New Orleans."

Jared stood on his tiptoes, trying to look inside. "I can't wait to see how Armand finished it off," he said, and I got instant creeps at the thought of the prior owner. John had started refurbishing the restaurant, and Armand had taken over when his brother died.

"Can we change the subject?" I asked.

"Sure – how's the case going?" Jared asked.

The others had moved ahead, and I didn't mind discussing it with Jared. I lowered my voice. "A sketch artist drew a mask based on a witness testimony, so we finally have a lead."

"Like a movie killer's mask?"

"We don't know yet – that's tomorrow's job. I'm not getting my hopes up too much. They had sketches of Jack the Ripper and never caught him."

"I dunno – they helped to track down Ted Bundy and HH Holmes."

I'd heard of Bundy – the vicious murderer of around 30 women in the 70s. "Who's HH Holmes?"

Jared gave a fiendish grin. "Our first serial killer. In England, you guys had Jack the Ripper, but around the same time we had HH Holmes over in the states. He built a hotel for tourists visiting Chicago during the World Fair. Unfortunately, most of them never left. He modified hotel rooms to kill people in different ways, from gas to trap doors. Now for the interesting part. HH Holmes and Jack the Ripper were operating on different continents at around the same time – two of the first serial killers on record. And there's some evidence they were the same person."

"No way!" I said. "I've never heard about this."

"I have a book I can lend you. It was the sketches composed from witness testimonies that made people wonder. The two men looked virtually identical."

"Great story," Tessa said over one shoulder. "I've never heard the Jack the Ripper part." I hoped that was the only element of the conversation she'd picked up on.

The concierge smiled as we entered the welcome area. Her suit and shirt were black, and a red bow tie was the only pop of colour. "Evenin' y'all. You got the bar upstairs to the left, the family-friendly restaurant right behind me or the themed room downstairs, along with a Dante Alighieri exhibition."

In red calligraphy above the stairs, it said 'Abandon hope all ye who enter here'.

"I think we're downstairs people," Jared said. "Who doesn't like a quote from Dante's *Inferno*?"

Chapter 37

As we advanced down nine steps, one for each circle of hell, I reeled at the disturbing beauty of the artwork all around us. Each level had a scroll beside it, the names varying from 'Limbo' to 'Treachery'. The nine circles of hell represented nine sins and how the people who committed them were punished. The tiny people in Treachery were frozen in a lake of ice, their skin blue and faces contorted. The people full of Anger were doomed to fight each other for all eternity. "This is incredible," I said to Jared.

His smile was sad. "As far as I know, the painting of his mom and this mural were the last things Lucas painted before he died."

Lucas had told me he didn't want his art to outlive him. His last work finished with the level of hell marked 'Treachery', the act that got him killed.

As we entered the restaurant, 'It's the End of the World as We Know It' by REM came on, a blur of fast lyrics over guitar until the catchy chorus.

The basement of Nine Steps to Hell was decorated to resemble a crypt a lot like the one I'd visited with the slayers. The walls looked like grey stone but turned out to be fibreglass. Wooden torches with electric flames lit the room.

"I'll be right back," I said, spotting a 'Restroom' sign that had letters made of bones.

"Don't be too long or we'll order for you," Libby said.

On the way back, I stopped in the Dante exhibit. It was a long, cramped space with dim red lights to read the notes by each display. Armand needed to brighten things up – I had to squint to make them out. Near the entrance was a huge replica of Dante's tomb. A lean, stern-faced man glared down from the top of the tomb. A statue of a woman gestured at him and another woman wept.

The end of the exhibit was shrouded in shadows, and something gleamed white. The gut punch of dread hit me hard. A shadowy figure was wearing the mask from Cafferty's fax.

I backed up, not wanting to take my eyes off them, and bumped into Dante's tomb. The figure watched me, unmoving, perhaps deciding on their plan of attack while I measured the distance to the door. Could I make it before they got to me?

I bolted, expecting running feet and panting breath behind me. I got to the door, clear and safe, but where was my attacker? When I turned, the figure hadn't moved – almost like a statue. Exactly like a statue.

Embarrassed, I advanced down the narrow room. The white mask was hung on a pillar. A sign said it was Dante's death mask and had been moulded from his body after he'd died. His face had been forever captured in a frown, the eyebrows drawn together and heavy-lidded eyes blank. This was the face the killer had chosen – I had to tell Cafferty.

"Mina?"

I jumped at Jared's voice. "Are you all right?" he asked, taking my face between his hands. I wasn't used to the returned intimacy, and the cool of his skin was a steadying influence where his fingers touched my cheeks. "I'm fine. I just figured out something about Cafferty's case."

"That's great," he said, though I could tell neither of us were thinking about Cafferty.

It would've been easy to rush the kiss, but we took our time. One of Jared's thumbs drew lazy, shivering circles on my cheek while the other hand came down to my chest. He pressed his palm over my heart, and I wondered if he felt my pulse quicken.

I gave in first, looping my hands around his waist. His eyes were bright in the gloom, and there was none of the tension tightening his face that he'd carried around these past months.

I stood on my tiptoes. My hands crept up his shirt, exploring the smooth skin of his lower back. He put his arms around me, bringing our bodies closer. Only our mouths had yet to meet, and we finally drew together. Before I'd met Jared, kissing had never felt like this: lust and connection and trust entangled. Our lips parted at the same time.

Once we got to our table, I was hot and flustered. "Can we please order?" Libby asked, looking around for a member of staff. So she'd missed my interlude with Jared. From Tessa's enormous grin, she hadn't. After our conversation earlier, I understood her better. It felt good to know she was rooting for me and Jared.

"Didn't you have a call to make?" Jared asked, his mouth closer to my ear than strictly necessary.

"Right!" I said, scanning the choices. "I'll have the three-course menu."

On the way to the bar, I passed a VIP area roped off by thick gold chains. Black curtains were drawn across it. Even though it reminded me of the curtained booths at The Underground and snooping never rewarded me there, I tried to peep inside. No luck.

Armand was stacking glasses at the end of the bar. "What now?" he asked dryly.

"Nice to see you too. Do you mind if I use the phone?"

He brought it over to the bar, pulling the wire taut. He looked deeply suspicious that this was all I was asking of him. The station put me through to Cafferty, and I explained how the Dante death mask matched the sketch of the killer's mask.

"Are you thinking what I am?" he asked when I'd finished. "Nine stab wounds – nine circles of hell in Dante's *Inferno*."

"You've read it?" I asked.

"I've been to the bar – Armand serves good buffalo wings. So either the killer read the book or went to Nine Steps to Hell."

"Hundreds of people must have been here since it opened," I said.

"It's not a lot to go on," Cafferty agreed. "But it's a start."

I hung up and handed the phone to Armand. I was about to go back to the others when I spotted Will at the other end of the bar, wearing the same long, black jacket with skinny black jeans and a white T-shirt.

"Drinking alone?" I asked, leaning on the bar.

"Just a quick one on the way home," Will said, grinning at me from under a loop of shiny brown hair. "Can I get you anything?"

"I'm here with everyone," I said. "Do you want to join us?"

"Nah, I should get back to Nat and Mom. It's been a rough day – it would've been Louisa's birthday."

"I'm so sorry! I didn't know. Nat doesn't talk about her much."

Will shrugged, jerking at the collar of his jacket so it stood up. "We all deal with our shit in different ways. I should get going, but thanks. It's refreshing to meet someone genuinely nice. Doesn't happen all that often."

"Wait," I said. "Why don't you two come to the carnival with us? Bring Sam too."

I expected him to say no, but he just looked at me. He was one of those people that felt like he really saw you, taking everything in. "Are you sure?"

"Don't you know me by now?" I teased. "I wouldn't ask if I wasn't."

"OK then," Will said, uncharacteristically awkward. It was endearing to see beneath the cool-guy act. "I mean, I can't speak for Nat and Sam, but I'll ask them. And I'll come. A distraction would do us good."

"We'll meet you outside," I said. "Give us an hour or so to eat?"

"Nat will need that long to get ready," he said. "See you." Then he was gone with a swish of his black coat.

"Did Will get dreamier?" Libby asked when I got back to the table. It was decorated with a skeleton's hand clutching a crystal ball. Static electricity sparked inside it.

"Same Christian Slater vibes as before. I invited him to bring Nat and Sam to the carnival – hope that's all right."

"Of course," Della said.

The waitress brought a platter of grilled-cheese sandwiches, giving me an especially friendly smile. I almost didn't recognise the vampire from the graveyard in the neat black uniform, her bouncy blonde hair pulled back into a sleek ponytail. She'd found her way to Armand like I'd suggested.

"Hi Fiona," I said, the employee badge reminding me of her name. "How are you?"

"I'm doing good. Thanks for helping me out with this. Armand's a great boss – he's letting me stay real cheap in one of his brother's apartments."

How much property had John Carter owned? I was glad the conversation was staying fang free, considering that Tessa was looking on with interest. "Happy to help," I said.

"Was that guy at the bar your boyfriend?" she asked, biting her lip. "He's cute."

"No, just a friend," I said, defensiveness towards Will rising up. Getting involved with a vampire would be disastrous without the full story. "But he's going back to college soon."

"Shame," she said, rushing to the next table with a last smile.

"Who was that?" Tessa asked right away.

"Just someone I know who needed a job." I grabbed one of the sandwiches. It'd been cut into the shape of a skull and skewered with a cocktail stick, ketchup blood leaking out of the hole. I bit into it reluctantly, mainly to stop Tessa's line of questioning.

Libby tucked in, showing no regard for the red sauce oozing

from the sandwich. Jared gazed at it, but I was drawn to movement by the curtained area across the room. A hulking, suited woman with a blonde buzz cut came out of it, pulling back the curtain.

The man who threw the Orchard Estate party, Claude Sejour, stepped into the entrance. He was wearing an immaculate grey suit with a green cravat, his body language communicating absolute confidence and entitlement. He crooked a finger in the direction of the bar, and Armand swept across the room towards Sejour, his chin high and defiant. The stiff way he was carrying himself didn't line up with the appearance of self-assurance.

Their conversation looked intense, and my desire to know what they were talking about put down deep roots. Jared's attention had been stolen from the blood-like ketchup, and he was staring too. Della, Libby and Tessa carried on eating and chatting while we watched Armand and Claude Sejour.

Then Armand beckoned in our direction.

Chapter 38

Armand mouthed words at us that I couldn't decipher, beckoning again.

"What's happening?" Libby asked, finally noticing the exchange.

"I'll be right back," Jared said.

He set off across the restaurant and I followed. "They could want me too," I said, not entirely sure that was the case.

Jared let out a harsh, annoyed breath lightened by a laugh. "Come on – they're waiting."

"Any idea why the Orchard Estate guy wants to meet you?" I asked.

"Guess we'll find out."

By the time we got over there, Sejour had sunk down into a high-backed velvet armchair that looked like a throne.

The bodyguard stationed herself to one side of Sejour, leaving Armand at his other side.

I presumed Armand was giving me that despairing look because I'd invited myself over. Claude Sejour's face was harder to read, though touched with something like amusement.

"I must be gettin' old," Sejour said to me in that slow, honeyed voice. "I don't remember callin' y'all over here."

"Sorry," I said, hoping to sound innocent. "I thought Armand was gesturing to me too."

Jared stood stiffly beside me, hands behind his back.

"She can go," Armand said. Everything about him was different, from the haughty way he carried himself to his distant demeanour. "This doesn't concern her."

Sejour's grin was chilling. "No, she should stay. I'm interested in how a little human got herself mixed up in our business."

There was only one reason he'd call me a human – he wasn't. My curiosity had landed me in a conversation between vampires.

"She's with me," Jared said, respect barely covering over his fierceness. He held my hand, turning it so the bitten wrist was visible.

"I can see that. The scent of her blood is all over you. Allow me to introduce myself. Apologies for the subterfuge at my event – I have to be cautious in public forums. The name's Jacques Saint Germain."

He seemed to expect a reaction, but I had nothing beyond a vague recollection. Jared looked concerned enough for both of us, and some of it leached into me.

"So you've heard of me," Sejour ... Saint Germain said to Jared. What was it about vampires shedding identities like last season's plaid shirts?

"Yeah, but I thought you were a myth," Jared said.

I went through the local legends Jared had told me, then I had it. He was the wealthy man that Jared had described on his tour, who claimed to have lived for centuries and got accused of being a vampire.

Saint Germain let out a bark of laughter. "I like him," he said, looking at Jared but addressing Armand. "You're not much of a mentor if you didn't tell him who I am. How would you describe me, Carter?"

It made my skin crawl to hear Armand referred to as Wayne Carter. I preferred to think of him as having left that life behind.

Armand ran his tongue along his teeth. "If Louisiana has a king of vampires, you're looking at him." And I'd put myself right in his crosshairs.

"That's very kind," Saint Germain said. "And as your king, I'd like to know what you're doing about our fledgling problem. Reckless vampires are risking exposure all over the city, and as far as I can tell you haven't lifted a finger to help. You know I'm in desperate need of someone with your ability on my payroll."

"I've told you before – I'm too busy running the businesses John stuck me with. Besides, I thought your employees were taking care of it," Armand said.

"You always were a loner. One day I'll change that. Veronica's lookin' into it for me, but they continue to grow their numbers and attract too much attention."

Horror flooded through me. First Veronica cornered me at

Orchard Estate, and now she was investigating the surge for the most powerful vampires in the city.

"I'll keep my ear to the ground," Armand said. "We should let these two return to their meal."

"I'm not through with them yet," Saint Germain said. "I got a question for you, boy. What ability do you have?"

He tried to sound casual, but his intensity set off a deep sense of wrongness. He was looking at Jared like an object he wanted to possess . . . very much like the vampire who wanted to use Thandie's ability. Saint Germain matched the description in her letter exactly. Decades after pursuing Thandie, he was still collecting vampires for their powers.

"Nothing," Jared said, the muscles along his jaw twitching.

"Pity," Saint Germain said. "Some of us never get a power, but I have a feeling yours will come. Let me know when it does. You two can go for now. Stay a while, Carter."

Saint Germain had held my life in his hands and deemed it worth sparing – this time.

The next course had come out when we got back – fish with a Cajun-spiced crust. The food was full of flavour, but the encounter with Saint Germain had stolen my appetite. Luckily we'd have the carnival for a few hours of escapism. I'd expected Libby or Della to ask what had happened, but perhaps they figured we couldn't say it in front of Tessa.

She was already suspicious about Jared not eating. "Since when don't you order food?" she asked. "When we were dating, you'd be eyeing my plate for leftovers by now."

"I ate before I left home," he said, slouching down in his chair. His eyebrows were scrunched low in thought.

When we left Nine Steps to Hell, Libby went off with Tessa, and Della got the questions in as we made our way down the busy street. "What was that all about? Who was behind the curtain?"

"Claude Sejour – the guy who threw the Orchard Estate party," Jared said grimly, "who is actually a badass centuries-old vampire called Jacques Saint Germain."

"From the legend?" Della asked.

"That's the one. He seems to be in charge of all the vampires in the city – including me, I guess."

"And he has Veronica investigating the vampire surge," I added. I hated saying her name, especially after what Emmeline told us she'd done to Della's mum. It was like the word could conjure her. The streets felt less safe knowing she was on them. A crowd separated us for a moment, and paranoia had me seeking out ice-blonde hair and white dresses.

Della's face hardened when I mentioned Veronica. "Rosario needs to know – she'll be at the carnival. If Veronica's looking into the surge, their paths might cross. We're supposed to do a sweep at the end, so we can catch up with her then."

Della went to join Libby and Tessa. "I hope I never get a power," Jared said, taking hold of my hand but seeming reluctant to make eye contact, "but if I do, Saint Germain is the last person I'll tell."

"Thandie mentioned an influential vampire in one of her letters, who liked having vampires around him with powers," I said. "It sounds like he's been doing this for years."

"Maybe he's got no powers of his own," Jared said, "or he's just one of those guys that thinks he deserves the best of everything – even if it means treating other people like possessions."

Libby slowed down to give us her most disapproving look.

"Can you two lighten up? We're about to go to a carnival . . . in New Orleans . . . and it's Halloween tomorrow. Do any of those things do it for you?"

"All of them," I said, anticipation stirring. The wrong kind of vampires wouldn't ruin this night for me. Slayers and police were patrolling the carnival. We could be on our guard and have fun at the same time.

On the outskirts of the carnival, two police officers surveyed the crowd. Their badges and stab vests marked them out. Nat, Will and Sam were waiting near the turnstiles by a continuous flow of people. Between Will's restlessness and Sam's tense posture, only Nat looked excited to be there. She wrapped me in a tight hug, and I pulled back to admire her clothes. Under a cropped denim jacket, she was wearing a black T-shirt dress covered in cartoon ghosts. "Love your outfit," I said.

"Thanks. Will told me it's too much. Like he's one to talk with that jacket surgically attached to him."

Will shrugged. "The understated makes more of an impression."

"Thanks so much for inviting us," Nat said. "Mom's doing a lot better – she's looking forward to a night to herself."

"That's great," I said.

"Yeah, thank you," Sam chipped in quietly, his cheeks pink from the effort. I used to be like that, and Libby had been more than happy to speak for me. Growing up with Nat and Will was probably similar for Sam.

The Wandering Witches Carnival was only in New Orleans for

a few days, but they'd set up a whole community. Trailers where the staff lived and equipment trucks were off to one side. A black and white circus tent sat in the middle of a sprawl of rides and food trucks. Music blasted, different songs coming from all sides. Neon signs flashed against the black sky. The blaring lights and sounds were strangely comforting. I could only concentrate on things outside my head. Occasional sightings of police patrolling the crowds helped too.

The rides had a serious witch theme. One that slowly raised thrill seekers and then let them drop was called 'Gallow Falls'. The haunted house was 'The Witches' Lair'. It had pointed turrets and green smoke pluming from the lopsided chimney. Children swooped and cheered on the 'Broomstick Battle' roller coaster.

We bought fizzy drinks in potion bottles and sipped them as we checked out the rides. My 'Eye of Newt' tasted of apple and had jelly eyeballs at the bottom that burst in my mouth. Sam sipped his while the others chatted, clamming up when I tried to draw him into a conversation.

We got the standard rides out of the way first, and Della kicked our asses at mini golf. None of us could match her accuracy, though Will came close. Sam tried too hard, and his irritation was obvious each time he missed. Nat and I were as bad as each other, but that only made it funnier.

A go-kart course was set up on an unused car park. Will and Jared were almost getting on too well, bumping and battling for first place while the rest of us cruised around. Sam won when they spun each other out. The two of them went ahead, quoting lines from *Days of Thunder* and arguing about which of them could play

Tom Cruise's character.

"This one next!" Nat declared, tossing her bottle in the recycling bin with a crash.

The 'Hell's Spells Carousel' had fantastical creatures that rose and fell as 'Where is my Mind?' by The Pixies played.

"I don't know," Libby said sceptically. "Aren't carousels for babies?"

"I'm with the big sister," Will said, looking at Jared as he pointed at the next ride. "Want to settle this once and for all on the bumper cars?"

"You're on," Jared said. "Whoever doles out the most hits wins."

"You coming, Sam?" Will asked.

Sam considered the options of riding a mythical creature or the bumper cars ramming into each other. "OK," he said, trailing after Jared and Will.

"Go easy on each other!" I called. Jared was bouncing and rolling his shoulders like a boxer. Will lit a cigarette, dark coat flapping around him. Sam dragged his feet, looking like he was regretting the whole decision to come.

"Come on Libby," Nat said. "Don't be a spoilsport like my brothers. Be the fun older sister."

"Yeah, live a little," Della said, kissing Libby's cheek. "Let's work our way up to the scary rides."

"Fine," she grumbled.

"I don't care what we ride," Tessa said.

We moved forward behind a rowdy group dressed in leather biker gear and sporting big 80s hair.

"Is everything OK?" I asked Tessa.

"Fine!" she said, extra bright and smiley. "Why wouldn't it be?"

It was our turn to climb aboard. I picked a unicorn, its silver horn twined with black. My friends took up mythical creatures around me: Tessa on a griffin, Nat on a purple dragon, Libby on a tentacled kraken and Della on a flaming phoenix.

The ride started, and it was more fun than I expected. I felt light and relaxed as it went round and round and up and down. The music shifted to 'Red Right Hand' by Nick Cave and the Bad Seeds, the distinctive medley of bells, percussion and guitar blasting out.

Only the other riders ruined the experience, yelling and weaving among the animals. They started on the opposite side of the carousel but soon took to leaping up by our creatures and whooping. Blood boiling, I willed the ride to end.

Then I saw the fangs – real ones.

Chapter 39

It was easy to tell real fangs from costume ones. No fake pair could slide out of slitted gums like that, settling over teeth that looked human.

Their outdated looks should've given me a clue. Our mythical beasts weren't the only creatures on the carousel.

I clutched the vertical bar in front of me, touching the stake at my waist. If they kept their behaviour in check, it wouldn't be an issue. What was I supposed to do if they made a move in public?

A vampire loomed beside me, and my unicorn glided down towards him. His shoulder-length black hair was pushed back so I could see the deathly pale face and gleaming fangs. The skin around his eyes was red and raw. He was hungry.

He reached for me and instinct kicked in. I swung off my unicorn at the same time that Della struck. She leapt off her phoenix and got in his face. "Back off," she snapped, "unless you want me to use this."

She lifted the front of her T-shirt, showing the butt of a stake. Of course Della knew what to say. She was born to be a slayer.

The vampire lurched towards her, and I grabbed his jacket collar. He spun around to me instead. Great.

Another vampire clapped hands on his back, this one with a bleached mullet that had to be modelled on 1980s Kiefer Sutherland. He wore a leather jacket with the collar turned up and a long earring. "She's a slayer," he said. "Leave it."

The ride slowed down and the vampires leapt off, cackling and yelling despite their brush with pointy-wooden death.

"What was that?" Nat asked, clambering off her dragon. "Was he hittin' on you?"

"Yeah – what a creep," I said.

"He was after her body," Della said, smirking at me. "We saw him off."

"Are you OK?" Libby asked.

"I'm fine. It's just my pride that took a knock." That part was true. I'd come face to face with a vampire and choked.

A cold hand closed around my arm. I jerked my elbow backwards and heard a satisfying "Oof!"

Not so satisfying when I came face to face with Jared bent over his stomach. "Sorry!"

"Don't be," he said, straightening up. "That was pretty impressive. Guess who won?" Jared raised his fists in Rocky-style victory.

"Look who we ran into on the bumper cars." Jason stepped into view, wearing torn jeans and a fitted T-shirt – a much better look than the Candyman costume. He must not have seen Tessa, or I doubt he would've come over based on what I'd heard about their breakup. Jared could've avoided this encounter, but he probably didn't think since he and Tessa had no baggage from when they'd broken up.

"More like they ran into me – over and over again," Will said, rubbing the back of his head with a bitter grin. "These two ganged up on me."

Sam had his arms wrapped around himself as he chipped in, "I was on your side." He looked like he'd taken a few good knocks too.

"Sorry, man," Jason said. "I might have got carried away."

Tessa stepped forward, her eyes bright and angry. "That sounds about right. I'll catch up with you guys later." She started walking off.

"Can we talk?" Jason pleaded, following her.

"We've talked plenty," Tessa said. "It won't do any good."

"Please . . ." Jason tried to steer her away from us.

Tessa batted his hand away. "I mean it."

Jared's concern was obvious, even though Tessa was handling herself. The rest of us stood there, trapped by the question of whether or not to intervene.

Will put a hand on Jason's shoulder. "Come on, man. Why don't we go get a beer?"

Nat called after them, "Only have one – we need a ride home!"

Will kept walking, turning to answer. "I'll be back in a half hour tops." That was a smart move on Will's part. The tension disappeared with Jason.

"Are you OK?" Libby asked Tessa.

"Fine," she said tersely. "Can we go on something scary?"

"How about Gallow Falls?" Nat asked. We all looked up at the vertical drop.

"I think I'll sit this one out," Della said. "Why don't you two go on it?"

"We'll meet you at The Witches' Lair when you're done," I said.

"I could use a soda." Sam held a hand over his midriff, stumbling away. Poor guy – he must have taken too many bumps from Jason and Jared.

"What was that on the carousel?" Libby said as soon as the others were out of earshot.

"Vampires," Della said. "I nearly had to stake one to get it away from Mina."

Jared rubbed his chest just off to the left – a small, unconscious motion.

"What do we do?" Libby asked.

"They're gone," Della said. "Hopefully they've crawled back to whatever cave they came from. They didn't hurt us, so the code's not in play."

Jared kept quiet, though his smile had turned strained.

"The slayers are here somewhere, and Mina and I will do a quick pass later. Let's forget about the vamps and enjoy the rest of the night."

A few minutes later, we reconvened at the haunted house. Sam had regained some of his colour, sipping a Coke. Nat and Tessa were deep in conversation, so those two had obviously hit it off.

"Ready for some scares?" I asked.

Tessa hesitated. "I've had enough rides for now. I'll go grab a snack – anyone want one?"

We all shook our heads, and Tessa went off. Jared grabbed my hand, and we pushed through the black doors of the haunted house with the others trailing behind.

The first room was dark, and ragged fabric trailed down over us. Libby squealed, and I heard her batting it around behind us. "There'd better not be spiders in here!"

"Ow," Sam said. Libby must have swatted him.

We came out into a witches' spell room. The lighting was green, and a cauldron coughed out billows of dry ice. Every shelf and surface was crammed with the tools of a witch's trade, like a pestle and mortar, crystals and leather-bound spell books. The shelves were covered in neatly labelled bottles. It was sort of like the endless rows of jars and bottles at the Pharmacy Museum, only these contained delicacies like crows' feet and frogs' eyes.

"Eeeew, why?" Nat asked gleefully, reading the labels.

"Who said being a witch was glamorous?" Jared asked.

We advanced into the next room, and I had that giddy rush building like the mansion gave me on my first visit.

It was a realistic forest in near darkness. It made no sense – the building hadn't looked big enough. It must have been some kind of illusion. Skeletal trees created a winding path only wide enough for one person to pass.

After some nudging, Nat and Libby got me to the front. A breeze lifted my hair off my back and made me shiver.

Lights danced through the trees, and a distant chant began. I couldn't make out the words, but they sounded odd and guttural, full of ill feeling. The trees pressed closer and I had to turn sideways to get through them, branches snagging my hair.

I relaxed once we pushed through the curtains at the end of the room, facing a wall of mirrored panels that reached to the low ceiling. I could handle a puzzle.

I pushed one experimentally, and it swung open. Nat tried the other mirrors. "Not all of them open – I think there are three paths."

"Let's split up," Libby said, taking Della's hand.

"Says no one who survived a horror movie ever," Jared said.

"I'm with Sam," Nat said, throwing an arm around his neck. He looked deeply unhappy, either about his sister's proximity or our presence in a mirror maze.

"Come on," Jared said, grabbing my hand.

It was a clever set-up. Each door sprang back into place when you walked into the next section, sealing you inside a mirrored box. It'd be too easy to get lost, and claustrophobia wormed in.

"Are you OK?" Jared asked.

"Ish," I said. "Not a fan of enclosed spaces. Let's keep track of our route and get through as fast as we can."

That worked a few times, until we came to a box where the only door was the one we'd come through. "We must've gone wrong," Jared said. "Let's retrace our steps."

The blue-white light was making my head ache. It took a second to find the next door, and that's when I spotted Libby and Della.

One of the panels was transparent. I knocked on it, but they continued checking for doors, even pushing the window I was looking through without seeing me. It had to be mirrored from their side. They vanished through another door.

"What was that?" Jared asked.

"I saw Della and Libby," I said. "Not all of the walls are mirrors."

"How about we try and race . . ." Jared stopped. A shadow appeared through the glass. The figure glanced towards us before disappearing into the next compartment. It was the blonde-mulletted vampire from the carousel, and he'd taken the same path as Libby and Della.

"We have to warn them," Jared said. We got into a rhythm of moving fast through the boxes, pushing a door and holding it open until the other person passed through.

I went through the next door first, but the light bulb was out. The door sprang shut behind me, swallowing me in pitch darkness. "Jared?" I said. No answer.

After frantically pushing against panels, I got back into the compartment I thought we were in last. It was empty. "No, no, no," I muttered. This wasn't happening. Jared was gone, and he wasn't the only vampire in the maze with us.

All I had to do was track which doors I'd tested and keep moving, one door at a time. Trying to control my breathing, I pushed through a door and entered the next box. Easy. Don't think about coffins or suffocation. Just breath and move, breathe and move.

I kept that up for a few boxes, growing in confidence. Then I spotted Jared in the next compartment. He was taking a more measured approach than I was, looking through each door before trying the next one.

Someone pushed the door behind him – the blonde vampire. Jared was testing another panel and didn't turn around. I banged my fist on the glass, shouting Jared's name, but he gave no response. He pushed against the glass where I was hammering, completely unaware while the vampire advanced on him.

I fumbled for the next door, pushing through one after the other until I tripped and landed hard on my knees.

A strong, cold hand grabbed my arm. I thought it was Jared until I was yanked to my feet.

The blonde vampire grinned at me, his mouth too full of teeth even before the fangs slid into position. He stank of sweat and decay. "Where's your slayer now?"

Jared was in the next compartment and seemed unscathed. Panic widened his eyes as he started trying panels, but I knew he'd reach me too late.

I whipped out the stake, lifting it to shoulder height with the point towards the vampire. He laughed. "Now what are you planning to do with that?"

He leaped towards my neck, pinning my stake hand against a mirror. I struggled against him, pushing his chest with my free hand to keep those fangs at bay. He snapped at my throat, rancid saliva flecking my skin. If I survived, I'd scour my skin with the hottest shower on record.

He was much stronger, and eventually my body gave way. Instead of clamping onto my neck, his momentum propelled us into a heap. I fell across his chest, and he smelled so much worse from this close: rotten, dead things and spoiled blood. I scrambled to my feet, but I wasn't fast enough. He sprang up, latching his mouth onto my arm.

Chapter 40

Jared burst through the mirrored door, using both hands to prise open the vampire's mouth. The vampire let me go and bolted the way Jared had come, the mirrored door closing on him.

"Here – let me look," Jared said, the consummate nurse even though the sight of my blood must have awakened all kind of urges. The wound was leaking blood, but I'd been lucky. Jared held a hand over it, and the contact stung.

"I'll keep the pressure on for now," Jared said, gritting his teeth when he wasn't speaking. His gaze was locked on the hand covering my bleeding arm, but he was coping. "The wound seems shallow – you're going to be fine."

"OK," I said, taking in breath too fast. I'd had a lot of near misses lately.

When my breathing had quieted, Jared removed his hand from my arm. "The bleeding's stopped – you sure you're not a vampire?" he teased. "I'll need to clean and dress it, but we should get out of here first."

We moved into the next compartment, and the opposite door opened. Jared snarled, fangs bared.

Libby clutched Della, before pushing into the tiny space. "Are you hurt? What the hell happened?"

"A vampire bit me, but Jared stopped him."

"Not in time," Della murmured, unzipping a bag at her waist. I wanted to leap to Jared's defence, but this wasn't the time. She wiped the blood away in one stinging sweep of an antiseptic wipe. "I don't think you need stitches – I'll cover it for you." She pressed a compress onto my lower arm, and I tugged my sleeve down over it.

"That's just a scratch," Libby scoffed, leaning her head against me. "Way to scare me half to death."

"Wait here." Jared darted into the next compartment and then out of sight. We waited in tense silence, listening for the spring of an opening door that would announce Jared or the other vampire.

"Did he come after us on purpose?" Libby whispered, her reflection frightened. The mirrors showed our grimy faces over and over again.

"I don't think so," Della said, stake raised and ready. "He didn't seem to know who we are. I probably presented him with a challenge on the carousel that he couldn't resist. He seems kinda familiar – doesn't he fit the description those guys gave at the clown museum?"

"The leader with a mullet and his gang . . ." I said. "There can't be too many people who fit that description. So those guys are linked to the surge?"

"We have to get out of here and find Rosario," Della said.

The door burst open. Della leapt forward, relaxing when she saw Jared. "I found the exit – let's go."

"Way to go, Lassie," Libby joked as Jared led us out into the neon-lit night. "Good boy."

"Where are Nat and Sam?" I asked, scanning the crowd, relieved to be breathing reasonably fresh air again.

"I'll go back in," Jared said. His hand was on the exit when it opened outwards, and he backed up.

"A little help here!" Nat had her arm around Sam. He was staggering, his throat and the front of his T-shirt soaked in blood.

"I'll call an ambulance," Della said, unhooking the medical kit from her waist. She tossed it towards Jared, and he snatched it from the air. "If you can handle it," she muttered.

We sank down to the muddy ground, and Jared's teeth were clenched as he examined Sam's wound. It looked deeper than mine, and Jared pressed a thick wad of bandages over the damage. Sam was pale and listless, and my memory cast me back to all the death I'd witnessed: Lucas bleeding from a knife to the chest, Heather chained in the attic and covered in blood, Elvira lying limp and bloody in the basement . . . Both girls would have been alive if our mum hadn't gotten us entangled with John. Just like Sam wouldn't have been here if I hadn't invited him. What made me think I could guarantee a safe night for my friends?

"Some guy with wicked sharp fake fangs jumped us," Nat said.

"You've lost a lot of blood," Jared said, his hand locked to Sam's neck. Jared's skin was almost as ghostly as Sam's. His nostrils were flaring, and his gaze lingered on his blood-smeared hands.

"Let me," I said, before he fell off the wagon. "Why don't you see how Della is getting on with the ambulance?"

Gratefully, Jared jogged to Della and Libby in the ride operator's booth. I took up the pressure on Sam's throat.

"How did you get away?" I asked Nat.

"Kicked him in the balls," Nat said cheerfully. "Simple but effective." She put on a good front, but I saw through it. She'd already lost her sister. Losing a brother too would be more than anyone could bear, especially on Louisa's birthday. Will had missed everything and still was nowhere in sight.

An ambulance had been waiting nearby, so medics arrived in minutes. I kept my injury quiet. It wasn't too bad, and I preferred to skip the explanation about why someone had bitten me as well.

They got Sam into the ambulance, and Nat hopped in as Will finally came jogging up. The colour drained from his face at the sight of Sam. "What happened?" he asked.

"He's hurt – luckily one of us is looking out for him!" Nat said, too angry to reason with.

"He was attacked, but he's stable," Jared added.

"OK," Will said shakily, calling to Nat, "I'll meet you at the hospital."

She nodded, tears falling, as the door closed.

Will wrenched a hand through his hair, and the five of us watched the ambulance speed away. "I've seen worse," Della said.

"He'll be all right. Nat's just scared – don't take it personally. You OK to drive?"

"I'll be fine." She gave him the address of the hospital and he took off.

Tessa crossed paths with him, a potion bottle in her hand. "I couldn't find any decent snacks, but this is pretty good!" she said, assessing our faces. "What happened?"

"Sam got attacked," Jared said again. "Nat's gone in the ambulance with him."

"No way!" Tessa said. "I hope he's all right."

"Anyone else want to go home?" Libby asked.

"You guys should go," Della said. "There's someone I need to find, and I'll be right behind you. Mina – you comin'?"

"I am too," Jared said at the same time that I agreed. "No arguments," he added, giving me his most serious face.

"Fine," Della said, scowling.

We convinced Libby and Tessa to get a taxi straight home. Tessa looked utterly confused about why we were staying behind, but Libby was smoothing things over as they got into the taxi.

"You really wanna hunt vampires with us?" Della asked, harsh and sceptical.

"It doesn't mean I agree with what the slayers do. I want to keep Mina safe," he said.

"Can't argue with that," Della said. "Now let's find that vampire."

"I think I still have his scent," Jared said. "No more Lassie jokes." He strode ahead, and between him and Della I was practically running to keep up.

We were halfway down a row of carnival games with cuddly

toys for prizes when the vampire slipped between two game stands ahead of us. Three members of his gang from the carousel were with him. "Let's see what they're up to," Della said.

We fought through the crowd. I kept my focus on that space between the stands, but the vampires didn't resurface. People flowed past the opening, and a woman dropped her handbag. She crouched to retrieve it, and two arms grabbed her around the waist. They snatched her away so fast it would've been impossible to spot if you weren't watching.

Della broke into a run, pushing through the crowd. Jared stayed back with me, and we were knocked around in the ebb and flow of people before we made it to the other side.

We joined Della a few steps from the opening, just as Rosario and Taz followed the vampires into it.

The woman tumbled out, clutching her throat. "Are you all right?" Della asked.

She looked at the smeared blood on her fingers. Her throat was only scratched – the slayers had got there in time. "He attacked me . . ."

"Did you come here with someone?" I asked.

"Oh my God!" A group of women swarmed us. We escaped as they fussed over their friend, ducking into the tight, shadowed space.

Rosario was grappling with the blonde vamp, and Taz was trying to fend off the other three. Blonde mullet snapped towards Rosario's neck, holding on tightly to her arms. She was trying to jab him with the stake, but the gap was too narrow and she couldn't wriggle free.

Della advanced, stake out. I took mine out and followed her, trying to size up the situation and convince myself that I could do this. Jared didn't have the same reservations. He grabbed a vampire on either side of its jaw, snapping its neck with a quick jerk. The vampire slithered to the ground, and Della staked him.

Della and Taz rounded on the second vampire, Taz making the kill with a clean swipe. Jared grabbed the third vampire's throat and pulled. Skin and flesh tore, and his fingers burrowed into sludgy blood. Jared's face was expressionless, and the blankness behind his eyes resembled John Carter.

Sam's attacker and Rosario were fighting. She kicked him hard, and Jared caught him from behind in a choke hold. With the vampires subdued, Taz moved towards the noise and fun of the carnival, taking the role of lookout.

The vampire tugged at Jared's arm, but he hung on. "That hurts, man! Why are you attackin' your own kind?"

"I'm nothing like you, 'man'," Jared said. "I don't attack people to feed."

"Don't kill him," Rosario said to Jared, then addressing his captive. "He's right. Someone's failed you along the way – either your sire or yourself. Who turned you?" Rosario trailed her stake across his chest and pressed the point against his heart.

"Like I'd tell you," the vampire scoffed.

"A vamp matching his description keeps turning up in our interrogations – in the graveyard and at the clown museum," Della said.

"Guess we'll need to keep goin' 'til he talks," Rosario said.

Jared tightened the grip on his throat, yanking one of the vampire's arms behind his back. I heard the crack as his shoulder came out of the socket.

His mouth opened in a scream, though nothing came out because Jared's arm was crushing his throat. "I'll loosen up if you talk," Jared promised, giving a last squeeze before he relaxed his grip. His ease with violence was hard to see.

"OK!" the vampire wheezed. "It was John Carter."

Chapter 41

The name 'John Carter' conjured all the things he did to us.

"When?" Jared asked, giving another emphatic squeeze on the vampire's throat.

"A few months ago . . . It was all for Veronica . . . She's planning something."

"What's she plannin'?" Rosario asked, pressing harder with the stake. "We've heard it might happen tomorrow on Halloween."

"She told me to bring willing recruits to the French Quarter docks at 7pm tomorrow. She's bringing her army and giving the final details of the plan. It's been a huge secret, even from me, and I was one of the first."

"What was your part in this?" Rosario asked.

"She left me out in the field to turn more people, but most of them have bailed," he snarled. "Even when I've applied some pressure."

"So Veronica didn't send you here tonight?" I asked.

The vampire barked out a laugh. "You make it sound like she has a handle on us. She's in over her head."

"Do you know who *she* is?" Della cut in, pointing her stake towards me.

"Why would I?" he spat, squinting at me with no recognition. "First time I saw her was on the carousel." Some of my fear eased – it wasn't about us.

"So you don't know how to find or contact Veronica?" Rosario asked, and the vampire shook his head.

"No, so you might as well kill me," he spat. "I'm dead anyway for betraying her."

"Fine," Rosario said and rammed the stake in deep and hard.

Jared released the vampire, and he collapsed. I'd been gripping my stake tight and holding on to so much tension. Some of it eased when he fell.

"Thanks for your help," Rosario said, all breezy despite the existence she'd ended. He wasn't one of the good ones, but it shouldn't have been so easy. She crouched down, retrieving her stake.

Jared stepped back, ready to react if needed. Rosario wiped the stake on the grass before tucking it down the side of her jeans. "You can relax. I'm Rosario." She extended her hand towards him. "Who'd have thought a vampire was the missing ingredient to get a confession?"

"Jared," he said, shaking her hand. "Suppose I can get close enough to them without worrying about getting bitten."

"You were awesome! I always said we needed a vampire vampire hunter. I'm Taz." She grinned and waved at Jared.

"So Veronica not only killed my mom – she's behind the surge too," Della said. She steadied herself, then explained to Rosario and Taz that Saint Germain thought Veronica was investigating the surge for him.

"Turns out nobody can trust her," Rosario said.

"How about we move these guys before they get all gross?" Taz asked.

We lugged the vampires into the empty storage space behind one of the stalls. I dragged a slim male vampire under his arms, trying not to look at his face. The rotten meat smell had to be the start of decomposition. Rosario must have seen something in my body language, because she responded to my misgivings. "I don't like leaving bodies, but we don't have many options in a public place. We'll dump them properly tomorrow, unless someone finds them first. Let's move."

We rejoined the crowd. There was no screaming, so nobody must have seen what we'd done.

"You go on home," Rosario said. "We need you rested up by 7pm tomorrow. We know the who and the where, so we can be ready. I'll do some digging to see if we can locate her sooner. I'd rather take her out during the day while she's stuck inside than tackle her whole army in public."

"I wanna help," Della said fiercely.

Rosario shook her head. "You've been pushing yourself too hard. Rest. Worst case we fight them tomorrow night at the docks.

Whatever happens, we can finally end this."

We parted ways with them at the entrance to the carnival. Too worn out to walk, we grabbed another taxi. Della sat in the front, and I held Jared's hand across the back seat. "Thank you for helping us," I said, conscious of the driver and my disapproving slayer friend in the front seat.

"I understand why you want to do it," he said, tightening his hold on my hand. "And that Rosario is impressive."

We dropped Jared off at his apartment and continued home. Della paused on the doorstep, key in hand. "I'm proud of you," she said.

"I didn't do much," I pointed out.

"You will."

I managed to shower and get ready for bed before crashing out, shifting between vague, disturbed dreams all night.

I woke way too early the next morning, even though I could've done with the extra sleep. It was Halloween – the day Veronica would execute her plot. I got out of bed before I could dwell on that for too long. The house was quiet, so I put on some exercise gear and grabbed my stake. I practised jabbing it from different angles: underarm and thrusting forward, driving it down from over my shoulder. I repeated each motion over and over again until my arms ached, wondering how long it would take to sink into my muscle memory. Mr Miyagi had Daniel waxing cars all day, but this would have to do.

I was sweating by the time I went out into the hallway. I should probably force myself to go for a run – I'd hardly been this week. I decided to ring Nat first. I dialled her number, keeping quiet so I wouldn't wake the others. "Hello?" She sounded distant and strained.

"It's me," I said. "How's Sam?"

"Still in the hospital," she said. "You just caught me – I'm grabbing a few things for him. He was real weak, but he picked up after they gave him a blood transfusion and a boatload of painkillers. They kept him in overnight for observations, but they should let him out any time now. He was reading some old book when I left, so he must be feelin' better."

"That's great," I said. "How's your mom?"

"Freaking out," Nat said. There was no wonder. Sam had got hurt on his sister's birthday – she could've lost another child. "I should go – thanks for callin'."

"Any time."

I hung up, heading towards the door. That was when I caught an unpleasant smell. I was passing Libby's room, so it was likely she'd left some food out.

I almost set off for my jog when I noticed the second strange thing. Tessa's keys were on the doormat inside the house.

I swept them up, the metal cold in my hand, and turned to the kitchen to put them on the key hook. Tessa's door was ajar. Maybe I wasn't the only one whose body clock had woken me at dawn.

I pushed the door open. Tessa was in bed. I gripped the keys so they wouldn't jangle and reached out to put them on top of her drawers.

I hesitated, still holding the keys. The first hint of daylight had touched her room, and I made out a dark stain on the wooden floor. Tessa wasn't moving – no shifting position or even the rise and fall of breath.

I'd been in this situation before. I thought back to the mansion's attic . . . Heather in a chair, chained and surrounded by blood . . . It couldn't be happening again. Tessa had to be asleep. The things we'd suffered were making me see death everywhere.

I took a step towards her. No movement. I forced myself onwards, trying to dismiss the rising dread. The mark by the bed was congealing blood. If she was alive, any delay on my part would put this on me.

Hurrying to her side, I saw her face. It was blank, eyes flat and unseeing, lips parted. All of my shock and pain came out in an incoherent shout.

Chapter 42

Della appeared at my side. Even though there was no point, she thrust two fingers into the pulse point under Tessa's jaw. She shook her head, lips pressed together. "Libby – call an ambulance."

I sat there looking at Tessa: the sallow skin shrunken on her skull, showing her teeth in a final grimace. "How did she . . .?" I asked Della, swallowing hard.

"Some kind of wound – probably hidden by the bedding," Della said. "Don't touch anything. In fact, go wait in the kitchen. I'll be right behind you."

I was distantly aware of Libby talking in the hallway, though as I passed her I couldn't make out the words. We'd survived a vampire attack last night. Was that what had happened to Tessa? Whether human or vampire, it made no difference. A murderer had crept into our home while we were sleeping, and Tessa was dead.

I sat at the kitchen table, feeling hollowed out. Bad things had gravitated towards us again. Did we attract the someone or something that killed Tessa?

"Hey." Della put a cup of tea in front of me and sat across the table. I clung to the mug, heat searing my skin through the thin ceramic. Della put her hands on my wrists, and I let go.

"The ambulance is on the way, and the police will come," Della said.

I needed to keep moving. If I stayed here, I'd keep picturing Tessa how she was when I found her. "I should call Cafferty . . ."

"I'll do it," Della said.

"What about Jared . . .?"

"He's asleep at his place," Della said firmly. "He couldn't come out in the sun anyway, and it's better if he's not here." It was good to see her on his side. As much as I needed comfort from him, he was best kept away. He couldn't walk out in the daylight to go to the police station if they needed us to answer questions.

Libby pulled up a chair, her face drained of colour. "Someone came in while we were asleep."

When she put her head on my shoulder, the soothing familiarity split me open. We sobbed together, our bodies shaking out of time.

So many people got involved when someone died. Soon, Tessa's bedroom was abuzz with activity, as if making up for the fact that she'd never move again. People came in and out in an endless stream, and all the while she lay there. Someone had called her family, and they were coming from LA.

Cafferty and Boudreaux walked in. Although she had small stature, Boudreaux's authoritative presence filled the room, and it was such a comfort. Her hair was scraped into a bun, and her normally smooth dark brown skin had a fretful line across her forehead. "It's good to see you three again," she said brusquely. "I wish the circumstances were better."

"So do we," Della said for all of us.

"You found her?" Cafferty asked me, suited and sombre.

His sympathy almost shattered me again. "Yeah," I said, throat dry. I sipped my cold tea, and it churned in my stomach.

"I'm sorry to do this now, but we have some questions," Cafferty said.

"We'll wait outside," Della said. Libby went to object, and Della cut her off. "Whoever did this needs to be brought to justice. I'm not having them get away with it because we ruined procedure."

"Thank you," Boudreaux said.

Libby ran a hand over the back of my head, and I held on to her reassurance even when she'd gone.

Boudreaux went on, "Detective Cafferty mentioned you've been a big help on his case. I'm headin' up the new taskforce."

"So you think the same person . . . killed Tessa?" It hadn't fully hit me that she was gone.

"We'll get to that," Boudreaux said. "Do you mind if we record the interview?" When I shook my head, she pressed record and ran through the introduction. "Talk us through what happened."

Cafferty had a pen poised over his notebook, and I focused on his sympathetic expression. I felt very separate from myself as I recounted what had happened, from finding Tessa's keys on the doormat to Della and Libby following the sound of my shout. I explained it like a scene from a movie, not one I'd lived through.

"Thank you, Mina," Boudreaux said. "That was very thorough. Can you describe your movements last night, particularly the time you spent with Tessa?"

I told them about the carnival, minus what had happened to Sam. I wasn't about to reveal the existence of vampires to Detective Boudreaux.

She became more thoughtful as I went on. "Did Tessa's behaviour seem normal to you in the time leading up to her death?"

"She's been quiet and tired lately," I said. "I'm not sure if that's relevant."

"Always worth mentioning if you're not sure," Boudreaux said. "Just one last thing. Can you think of anyone who'd want to hurt her? Anyone with grievances or that she's argued with lately?"

Jason popped into my head. I'd thought he was one of the gentlest people I'd ever met until last night. "Just one. She broke up with her boyfriend recently. We ran into him last night, and they argued. He tried to grab her arm."

Boudreaux's relaxed composure took on a new intensity. "Thank you for that, Mina."

"Detective Boudreaux?" a high voice called from the hallway.

"I'll be right back," she said to us.

The moment she left, Cafferty moved his chair closer to me. "How are you doin'? I'm sorry you had to talk about this so soon after losin' your friend."

I ignored the twinge of emotion. "Talking is better than thinking about it."

"I really shouldn't . . ." Cafferty said, checking the door, "but I'd appreciate your insight. You've been a big help this week. Let's forget you found her. You're just doing work experience with me and talking about the case."

I nodded, preparing myself. I was holding the mug so tightly that the handle dug into the root of my thumb, but I couldn't stop.

"OK, so you found Tessa's keys on the doormat, and she was in bed. Who do you think put the keys on the mat?"

"Tessa could've dropped them on the way in . . . or someone pushed the key through the letterbox once they'd left."

"My thoughts exactly," Cafferty said, flicking back through his notebook.

I steadied myself before asking, "What were her wounds like?"

"Nine wounds like the others, so it's likely the same perpetrator, but the location has obviously changed – she was in her bed, not outside the front door." Cafferty lowered his voice. "And while you're here . . . Any news about the surge?"

"We know who's responsible, and the slayers are tracking her as we speak."

"Let me know if they find her," Cafferty said. "I meant it when I said I want to help."

We heard footsteps in the hallway, and both of us went quiet. Boudreaux returned from Tessa's room with gloves on and a plastic evidence bag containing a single sheet of paper covered with red writing. Even though I felt sick at the sight of it, I stood up. "Can I get something from my room?"

"Detective Cafferty will walk you," Boudreaux said.

I followed him into the hallway, keeping my eyes low. Tessa's door was open, and I hurried to my room. As far as I knew, she was still in there. I couldn't see her like that again. I grabbed the notes with Cafferty hovering in the doorway and went straight back to Boudreaux.

She put the notes on the table and read them with Cafferty at her side. The muscles along his cheeks tightened as he read.

"You received these? When?" Boudreaux asked.

"A few days ago. One was left in my backpack in the changing rooms at the mansion and one came through the door. I'm sorry I didn't tell you sooner . . ." Could I have saved Tessa's life?

Cafferty cut me off. "It's OK . . . You couldn't have known it was relevant – we didn't even know 'til now. We're lucky neither of you tossed them in the trash."

"The note came through your door, so it could've been meant for Tessa, but that doesn't explain the one in your bag at the mansion," Boudreaux said. "We'll interview Elizabeth and Della, then talk strategy."

The detectives got through Libby and Della's interviews quickly, then we got on to the next steps. "The notes you've received mean you can no longer work on the case," Boudreaux said.

"I guessed that." I'd wanted to see this case through, but we were in too deep. Too many threads tied me to the murders. The anxiety that I'd been keeping at bay was gathering potency. Why was this happening to us again?

"Is there somewhere secure where y'all can stay? I'll have an officer check in on you periodically and put one outside overnight, since the other attacks took place around midnight. It's possible you're not at risk, but I'd rather be sure," Boudreaux said.

"The mansion is as secure as it gets. We can stay at Thandie's . . .

in the apartment there." Libby paled as she mentioned Thandie's name.

"I'll set everythin' up," Boudreaux said.

"Detectives?" A CSI wearing glasses stuck her head through the door. "Can you come in here please? You'll want to see this."

I waited with my sister and Della, trying not to think about Tessa lying there and the next awful piece of evidence they might have found.

Cafferty came back with a black leather-bound notebook. He parted the pages, understanding dawning.

"What is it?" I asked.

"Looks like a client book. Apparently Tessa used to cut and feed on people at The Underground."

Chapter 43

"I'm not sure that's something her friends need to hear, detective," Boudreaux said without any real sternness. She leaned against the kitchen counter, one hand rested on the badge at her waist.

"We had no idea," Della said, her distaste evident.

Tessa's time at The Underground made sense of her tiredness and the strange hours she kept, but I couldn't reconcile it with the girl I knew ... that I'd known. She'd been a lifestyler, acting out the role of a vampire with scalpels or her teeth.

"I think we're about done here," Cafferty said. "I'm sorry to have been the one to tell you about Tessa. We'll get you a ride to the mansion."

We hastily packed bags of clothes and other essentials. Officer Dupres arrived minutes later. He chatted about his daughter on the way, distracting us with talk about books and funny things she got up to with her friends. He helped us to carry our bags up to Thandie's apartment, and his big, friendly personality filled the space while we were feeling so lost. "Is there anything else I can do for y'all?" he asked kindly.

"We're fine – thank you, officer," Della said.

We settled into the apartment, a cosy place with cushy brown leather sofas, fluffy rugs layered over the floor and piles of blankets and cushions everywhere. Artefacts cluttered every surface: a gilded Egyptian statue of a goddess, a green bronze urn and tiny terracotta warriors among others. Thandie hadn't travelled much as a vampire, but she'd brought artefacts from all over the world to her.

I unpacked in the spare room, while Libby and Della set up in Thandie's old room. Della ran downstairs to phone Rosario and came back with the news I'd expected. The slayers had found no trace of Veronica last night or where she might be hiding an army. Taz had gone to hassle the cinema vampire, but he was clueless. Halloween night was creeping closer. Unless we took Veronica out in a surprise attack, we'd be fighting her and countless other vampires on the docks at 7pm.

I sat on the purple flowery bedding, almost overwhelmed by frustration. The police were struggling to track down the killer, and the slayers had no way of locating Veronica. But I knew someone who might be able to help with the second problem.

I went down to the hallway and phoned Armand at home. No answer. I tried Empire, and he answered on the first ring.

"Hello Mina. Before you ask, I didn't see you in a vision. You're the only person who calls me."

"I need a favour. Do you mind if I come to the bar?"

"As long as you bring someone with you. I don't want you wandering the city alone." If Armand was showing concern, I must have been in trouble.

"We'll be right there."

As soon as I put the phone down, I dialled the police station and asked to be patched through to Cafferty. He might still have been at our house . . . trying to uncover what happened to Tessa.

"Mina? Everything OK?"

"Sorry to bother you," I said. "I know you're working on . . . I know you're busy. I can't help with the . . . murder case, but you said you wanted in if anything went down with . . . the Lestats and Louies of the world," I said, playing it safe in case this was being recorded. "We finally have a potential lead on the location." I felt guilty for tearing him away from Tessa's case, but Boudreaux was on it and the slayers' time was running out.

"I can take off to follow a lead."

"Thank you. We'll meet you outside the mansion."

Della took no convincing to come along. She seemed as restless as I was. Libby was more reluctant to let us go, but eventually she caved. Poor Jared had no idea what was going on. When he woke at sunset, we'd have a lot to tell him.

Cafferty drove us to Empire of the Dead. On the way, Della and I filled him in. "So you think this Veronica is responsible for the rise in vampire activity and that she's planning somethin' for tonight?"

"Yeah, and we're hopin' Armand can help track her down before then," Della said.

"With his mind powers. Just when I think I have a handle on everythin', you throw me that curve ball."

Armand hadn't bothered to decorate the bar for Halloween, but it was macabre enough without adornments. Inspired by the Paris Catacombs and its maze of bones, cages of animal skeletons peered down at us: birds with bone wings extended, coiled snakes and rodents of every size. Their creepiness was heightened by the terrible things John Carter had done to us right beneath where we were standing. Della had carried on working here without it seeming to bother her, but everything came back to me each time I was here.

Empire was quiet, so we spotted Armand behind the bar immediately. 'Mmm Mmm Mmm Mmm' by the Crash Test Dummies was playing. The singer's deep voice and underdog stories had always resonated with me.

Armand took in the sight of Della and Cafferty with zero surprise. "Police and slayers," he said idly. "Am I in trouble?"

"Not yet," Cafferty said, "but it's still early."

"A funny cop. I thought they ranked among unicorns and Bigfoot. Can we skip the pleasantries? I'm quite busy."

"I can see that," I said, looking pointedly around the empty bar. "It turns out Veronica is the one making a load of new vampires."

"I see." Armand hardly looked blown away by the revelation. "And you believe I can do something about that?"

"Do you know where she is?" Della asked.

"Fortunately not," Armand said. "I prefer to be as far from her as possible . . . but I may be able to help you."

Armand led us into the staff room. Somehow, it smelled of worn socks and deodorant at the same time. "Veronica stopped showing up for work after John died, so some of her possessions must be in here. I might be able to use one to see her, but it's a long shot."

Armand snapped the padlock at the end of the row of lockers as easily as tearing through a sheet of paper. He pocketed it and opened the locker. "Let me see . . ."

Inside was a jumble of hair brushes, make-up and clothes. A long, sheathed knife was wedged at the back.

Armand drew a white denim jacket from the hook. Unlike the rest of the locker, it was pristine. Black and red glittery writing on the back said 'Devil in the Pale Moonlight': the Joker's words repurposed to describe a murderous vampire.

Della and I stood back while Armand sat on the bench. He closed his eyes, squeezing the fabric of the jacket in both hands. "I see water and fire . . . That part's unclear . . . A blonde girl playing on the top level of a steamboat. A man calls, 'Veronica! Stay away from the railing.' There's more . . . words on the side: *The Belle of New Orleans.*

His face screwed up. "That's all – an image that appears to be a century old."

"Thanks for trying," I said, turning to Cafferty. "Sorry we dragged you here."

"Don't be sorry – I think we're gettin' somewhere," Cafferty said, looking nowhere near as dejected as Della. "It can't be a coincidence that you saw a boat, when Veronica's meeting point is a dock. You're sayin' this is a vision from her childhood. Can you recall her mentionin' anything about a boat more recently?"

Armand hung the jacket back in the locker, closing the door on the disarray. "There is something . . . Her father was the captain of a steamboat on the Mississippi in the early nineteenth century. He died in a boiler explosion, which was all too common back then. She was very young. She took exception to the new man her mother married and ran away.

Saint Germain found her. He'd suffered his own tragedy . . . losing a daughter to a fever when he was alive in the 1600s. He took Veronica under his protection, turning her into a vampire when she turned 20 – the age his daughter was when she died. She said he suffocated her with affection, but she finally threatened to fillet him in his sleep if he didn't ease his hold on her. He relented, keeping her in his employ but allowing some freedoms."

Saint Germain was Veronica's sire – that explained a lot. "She told you all of that?"

"Not exactly," Armand said. "Over time, I've pieced it together from her and Saint Germain."

Was that what he did to all of us – building a picture from the secrets we'd never tell another soul?

"So the last time Veronica was human and happy was on a boat with her father? If your vision held clues about her current location, couldn't she be on a boat now?" Della asked.

Armand looked stunned. "I don't usually need someone to make sense of my visions. As ever there are no guarantees, but . . . I believe you're right. I feel it. Find the right boat and you'll find Veronica."

That sounded like hunting for a needle along a really long river, but Cafferty did it with one phone call to the Mississippi River Coast Guard. Della and I listened impatiently to Cafferty's side of the conversation from across the bar.

He hung up, writing something in his notebook. "There are a handful of decommissioned steamboats in Louisiana large enough to meet Veronica's needs, and only one of those is in New Orleans. It was decommissioned after being damaged in a hurricane and the name was changed to *The Belle of New Orleans* this year."

He held up the address but didn't hand it over. Della extended her hand, but I guessed what Cafferty was planning before he said it. "I'm coming with you. I swore to defend this city . . . and I have a crossbow."

"I don't think Rosario will say no to that," Della said. "Does Veronica have a power we should be aware of?"

"Fortunately not – nor will anyone she's turned," Armand said. "Only a vampire with a power can pass one on. Even then it isn't certain, or likely to be the same as their sire's. Saint Germain doesn't have one, though don't underestimate the two of them because of it. Knowing Veronica as I do, I almost hope you don't find her."

Chapter 44

afferty went off to 'suit up' as he put it, and we went to the slayer cave to update Rosario. She took the news that we'd invited a detective along with good grace. "Suppose he took down that pool hall vamp. He's in." She was more reluctant about me. "I'd expected y'all to come on some recon, not head straight into battle with us."

"So don't you need me more than ever?" The promise of a battle was swelling in my mind, painting pictures of blood and carnage. But I couldn't opt in and out of this. Veronica had killed Della's mother, Thandie and countless others, and we needed to take her down before her plan unfolded tonight.

"If stubbornness will keep you alive, then you'll be fine," Rosario said. "Della and Cafferty are responsible for you though."

The slayers mobilised at impressive speed, the deadline looming. Jared would be sorry to miss this, but he'd be no help during daylight hours.

Soon, we were all wearing lightweight gear that was apparently densely woven to deter a glancing strike of fangs. I hoped that would be enough. We were also armed to the teeth, strapped with as many stakes as our bodies could hold. I had one holstered to each calf under my black leggings and one at my waist. I was constantly aware of their bulk and couldn't stop touching them through my clothes.

We piled into a few cars and drove to the Mississippi where we were meeting Cafferty. Taz drove her Jeep fast, and I bounced around in the back.

The water was as smooth and grey as the sky. Moving fast, we loaded up our 'borrowed' booze-cruise boat with weapons and first-aid kits. My tight outfit cut out most of the bitter breeze that came off the river. Keeping busy wasn't holding off my nerves. My vision was too bright and my mind was working fast, cycling through what we might encounter on Veronica's boat.

Every time I met Taz's eye, she grinned in encouragement. Della never left my side, and she was quiet and intense in her preparations. Her mother's killer was within our reach. Paige looked happier than I'd ever seen her, bouncing around and doing little to help us.

Cafferty roared up the dirt road in a car that said 'Impala' on the boot, Metallica blasting out of the windows. The car was as glossy black as it was loud. He got out, hair mussed and the collar quirked up on his black leather jacket.

I jogged over to him with Rosario, and she spoke first. "We've only ever had one cop who knows about vamps. Guess you're the second."

"Hope I can contribute something," Cafferty said, popping the boot of his car. He unzipped a bag full of stakes and unclipped a case that housed a compact metal crossbow loaded with wooden bolts. "I've put my evenings whittling to good use since I found out about vampires the other day – you're looking at handmade stakes and bolts right here." The thin bolts of wood would work like airborne stakes, fired with lethal force. He slung a quiver full of them across his back.

"I'm Rosario," she said, offering a hand. "I think you'll do just fine."

"Matt," he said, shaking it hard.

With introductions out of the way, we hurried on board. Fifteen of us sat there at the tables usually occupied by partying guests: eight guys I hadn't really got to know and seven girls, who ranged from the hostile Paige to friendly Taz.

We were heading into a treacherous unknown. If Veronica was there, we'd be fighting her to the death on a huge metal coffin floating on the water. And I'd chosen to do this rather than eating pumpkin-flavoured things and working my way through the *Halloween* movies. My conviction that I was doing the right thing was potent, but being ready was an entirely different thing.

A blur of building sites, flood defences, greenery and buildings passed by. Della pointed out a grey hotel with white columns and a spire to one side. A brick building had boarded up windows and graffiti along the top that said 'You are beautiful'. St. Louis

Cathedral appeared in the skyline, and I was struck again by the rare and varied qualities of this city.

"That's it." Rosario pointed over the railings, and we watched as the steamboat that may house a murderous vampire drew closer. It was draped in green moss and mildew like a monster that had lurched out of the depths of the Mississippi.

"According to the coastguard, the ship was decommissioned after a hurricane. The steering system and paddlewheel shaft are shot, so she's not going anywhere," Cafferty said.

"Looks like they blacked out the windows," Paige said, shifting a backpack around on her shoulders, "so they could be anywhere."

So this was likely to be the vampire ship and not a dead end. I touched the stake at my waist, trying to believe I could do this . . . that I wasn't willingly walking to my death.

"Damn," Rosario said. "I was hoping they'd be confined to the lower levels. Lights are on, so the generator must be running. We can use the noise to our advantage. With any luck, they'll be resting before their attack tonight. The plan is simple – take down Veronica and any vampires that strike to kill. Stick to the code." Rosario threw a meaningful look at Paige.

"Inexperienced slayers need to shadow someone more senior. If they get compromised, find me, Paige or Taz. We start at the top level and work down."

'Compromised' was a nice way of saying 'dead'. I'd wanted to be here – to have my chance to save people and make a difference. Now it had arrived, it felt unreal.

Our cruiser pulled up alongside the steamboat. We hopped over the metal railings, landing quietly on the wooden deck. We'd debated landing further down the coast and walking in, but Veronica could spot us either way. We had the advantage of ambushing them in the daylight. It had to be enough. Cafferty and Della flanked me on either side. His crossbow was raised, and Della was ready with her stake. I followed her example and removed the one from my waist, wishing I felt more comfortable with the smooth wooden weapon in my hand.

Even though the steamboat was moored, the moving water created a light sway as we walked. We entered through the control room, which was empty apart from the captain's wheel and lots of gauges caked in grime.

The top floor of tourist bench seating was deserted, so we traipsed down the metal stairs in one long line. With every thud of feet on metal, we were possibly getting closer to Veronica. We came down in a corridor with a row of closed doors on the right.

Rosario made some hand gestures, raising fingers and pointing. Della whispered, "We take a door per group."

Rosario held up three fingers. I recognised the gesture with a tight feeling of inevitability. She counted down to two. We were about to find out if we'd come all this way for nothing or the fight of our lives. Rosario put down the second finger, leaving only one.

We parted into our groups, one standing by each door. Cafferty and Della both looked determined and tensed for action.

When Rosario's last finger fell, we moved. Della opened our door, and I stayed close behind her and Cafferty. If there were vampires inside, they probably knew we were here.

It was a kitchen, with grubby white fixtures and wooden worktops. Empty – as you'd expect on a boat full of vampires.

Several rooms must have been occupied. We heard shuffling, followed by the thump and clash of scuffles. One pained yelp cut through the quiet confrontations. That was bad news for someone.

The three of us left the kitchen. Taz was crouched outside the room, wrapping duct tape around a muscular guy's upper arm. His face was clenched in pain. The tape was a smart move – sealing the wound and hopefully the scent of blood inside it.

We advanced down the corridor. A few slayers hung back to treat wounds and restock weapons. I made myself look in each room. We'd left a trail of dead vampires. Some hadn't made it far from their beds, and one had fallen in the doorway with her face frozen in a sneer. All had gaping holes in their chests, the stakes removed to kill again. Could I do that – look something living in the face and make it dead? If it was me or them, I thought so.

Rosario, Taz and a scared looking guy left the last room. A dead vampire lay on her back with a knife by her hand – a predator made even more deadly.

As a group, we approached a staircase that led downwards and was labelled 'Boiler Room'. "Change of plan," Rosario said. "We go down to the boiler room and work our way up. Everyone with us?" I did a quick count, and everyone had caught up. Each face was serious except for Paige, who still looked way too happy to be here.

We walked down to the depths of the boat, our feet loud on the metal stairs. The cloying smell of mildew and damp greeted us in the vast boiler room.

The boiler was to one side, with tanks and arms coming off it. The ship's interior was painted green and cream, though it looked like it had been done some time ago. Piping ran across some parts of the room with all kinds of wheels and knobs. The boiler was off, but the generator sounded as if it was nearby. The floor and walls hummed with a vibration that made my teeth ache.

Paige crouched down as we fanned out around the room. I stayed behind to see what she was up to, so I saw the explosives when she unzipped her backpack.

Chapter 45

"Where did you get *those*?" Rosario asked. The look on her face was all wrong, like she was assessing the possibilities instead of planning to stop Paige.

"You know my daddy's in demolition. This is our backup plan." She laid out blocks of beige putty with black writing on them that said 'C4 demolition block'. She also unpacked wiring and compact electrical boxes.

"I wish I'd not seen that," Cafferty murmured to me.

Della heard. "You can be Detective Cafferty again tomorrow," she said. "Just be Matt for today."

Rosario bent down and snatched up the remote control. She

secured it in the inside pocket of her fitted jacket. "Fine, but there's no way you're having the detonator. You have two minutes to install it."

Watching Paige wire explosives was intense. She laid the putty along the bottom of the old boiler, so at a glance it would blend in. I wouldn't trust anyone with explosives, least of all Paige. It was a whole extra layer of stress, guaranteeing I wouldn't relax until we were far from the boat.

"Why don't we leave and blow it all to hell now?" A young guy with a brown Mohawk stepped up, eying the explosives with dreamy speculation.

"We need to confirm Veronica is here. The explosives are a last resort if we have to take the boat down. We don't need that kind of attention," Rosario said.

Paige stood up, brushing off her hands on her black leggings. "All done."

"Good. Let's move," Rosario said.

We came out into the engine room, where a giant metal shaft was connected to three long piston arms. Numerous pipes and valves snaked off them. The electrical generator appeared to be the only thing operating, and up close the noise was almost unbearable, starting a dull pain deep in my ears. A metal balcony surrounded the upper level of the room, with several doors leading off it and ladders for access.

A group of vampires were chatting beyond the electrical generator. Between the noise and the obstruction of the engine, they hadn't reacted to us.

"Spread out around the room. Leave the vamps to us." Rosario gestured at Paige, Taz and Della. I guessed that included me by association. "Matt – you cover us from behind."

He nodded, readying his crossbow.

I copied the low stances of the other slayers, their stakes in hands, as they crept around the wall of the room. This was it. With panic pulsing in time with my heart, I was clinging on to my resolve. What had made me think I could do this?

No time for second guessing myself. Paige grabbed an axe from the wall under a sign that read 'In Case of Emergency'. "I think this qualifies," she whispered to me. With the fight ahead, we were finally on the same side.

Rosario and Taz staked two vampires from behind as Paige swung the axe at another. A stake would've been cleaner. Rosario and Taz's vampires fell, but Paige had removed a female vampire's arm. She cried out, the noise almost swallowed up by the generator. Blood sprayed Paige, lost against her black gear but showing red on her arms. Taz lunged to stake the vampire. Della had been pulled away from the group by a small but ferocious female vampire, and they were fighting fiercely.

That all passed in seconds, and the two remaining vampires turned on me and Cafferty. He backed up to take aim but the male vamp rushed at him, grabbing for the crossbow.

The female lashed out at my left arm so the stake spun out of my hand. As Cafferty wrestled with his vampire, trying to free the crossbow, I slid under a rack of metal cylinders, aiming for the open space and my lost stake at the other side.

I was almost there when a hand grabbed my leg. The vampire started dragging me back the way I'd come, and I scrabbled for purchase on the bumpy metal floor. Cafferty appeared in front of me, grabbing my arms. Pain ripped through my limbs as they pulled me from either side. I kicked out hard, but the vampire clung on.

All at once, I was free and shot forward. Cafferty and I hit the deck. "You OK?" he asked, checking me over as we clambered to our feet.

"Yeah. I always wanted to be taller."

I rescued my stake, and we rushed back to the vampires. Only one was left standing. The female who grabbed me now had Paige's arm around her neck in a headlock. I'd learned at the carnival that a slayer wouldn't usually get so close to a vampire's fangs, but Paige played by her own rules.

Taz rested the point of the stake against the vampire's chest. "Is Veronica here?" she yelled, making herself heard over the generator noise. "Where is she?"

"Just kill her already. She'll never give me up," Veronica shouted from the upper balcony, holding her trademark mallet. She was wearing a form-fitting white catsuit that looked like a superhero costume. Around 20 vampires fanned out behind her. "Will someone turn off that infernal generator?" Veronica yelled, resting her free hand on her temple. Taz's vampire broke free, scrambling up the ladders to join Veronica.

The roaring noise cut off, leaving a high whine in my ears.

"That's better. Now where was I . . .?" Veronica asked. A handful of vampires spilled through our exit, blocking the door on our level. They outnumbered us more than two to one.

Cafferty unleashed a bolt in Veronica's direction. It bounced off the high balcony railing, and she laughed as he reloaded. "Nice try, pretty boy. As I was saying, I'd like to thank y'all for comin'. My recruits need practice before tonight. And this isn't all of them."

"Why turn them all?" Rosario shouted.

Veronica dragged her mallet along the railing and the metallic chime rang out. "Let's stop delaying, shall we? Thanks for bringing Mina here as we discussed, Della."

Not Della. Of all the people I knew, she was solid. Wasn't she?

Veronica let out a harsh laugh. "Kidding . . . Don't worry – this isn't a friends betrayin' friends thing. It's a cold-blooded murder thing."

She signalled to a few vampires, and they started climbing down the ladders from the balcony. Veronica remained where she was, watching us like a queen sending gladiators into battle. Cafferty backed into a corner and started firing bolts at the descending vampires. He was a good shot and his first bolt stuck in a vampire's arm, but it took time to reload.

Rosario and Taz bolted back towards the boiler-room door. Della and I hesitated as the carnage began. Some slayers had run for the descending vampires, dragging them down and jabbing with stakes. They were soon overrun as more and more came down the ladders.

"We can't help them," Della said, pulling me after Rosario and Taz as hungry mouths clamped down on throats and arms. When had taking down Veronica turned into abandoning our friends?

Paige appeared at the door with us. She swung her axe and hit a vampire in the shoulder, allowing Rosario to finish her off with a stake.

Rosario and Paige pushed the body clear of the door. Cafferty hopped through, helping Taz and me shove the heavy door shut on the room full of vampires.

I had no time to appreciate the safety of the boiler room.

Someone yanked me backwards, and I staggered towards them, whipping round to face a vampire right before he bit me.

Chapter 46

I managed to pull away so his jaws closed on my shoulder instead of my neck, tearing through the mesh of my gear and hitting skin. I swung my stake without connecting, fear making me clumsy. The vampire's mouth came free with a tearing sensation, and I drew back the stake, pain raging in my shoulder. I drove the point downwards and it sank into the flesh above his collarbone.

Taz appeared, thrusting her stake into his chest. He fell backwards from her momentum, his mouth bloody and his last expression one of astonishment.

Taz freed our stakes from his body and handed mine back. "Sorry! I thought the room was clear."

"I'm fine," I gasped, checking out my shoulder. "It's not the first time I've been bitten." The ragged, circular wound was seeping blood, which had to be better than gushing.

Della appeared with an antiseptic wipe and adhesive compress. She swept the wipe over the gouged skin, which stung almost as badly as being bitten. Then she applied the compress. "It's not too deep – this should hold."

"Good," Rosario said. "Now we run."

"Not so fast!" Veronica called. She'd appeared on this room's balcony with vampires around her. If she could move so easily from one balcony to another, that put an end to our escape plan.

"Dammit," Rosario said. "There are more than I thought."

The five of us looked beaten up, bloody and defeated. But we had our stakes, each other and Cafferty's crossbow. I thought about Libby and Jared. I wouldn't give up.

Della had some fight left in her. "You killed my mother," she called out in a clear voice. "I know I can't bring her back, but you owe it to us to explain what we're all here dying for."

Veronica groaned. "It's a good thing every orphaned child doesn't track me down. I'd never get anything done. It's quite simple, really. I need an army to take out my suffocating sire – I believe some of y'all have met the great legend *Saint Germain*." She bared her teeth at the last part.

"Along with all those stuffy old vampires who have been in control way too long. I thought Halloween would be quite fitting – every year when the city celebrates, they'll be unknowingly celebrating my victory over him too. The vampire queen of Louisiana has a nice ring to it, don't you think?" She grinned, so certain that she'd defeat us and then him. "Every time I've tried to gather numbers, you slayers show up. I got real close in the 70s. John was supposed to be my lieutenant this time, but that didn't work out for him. Is that enough for you? Have we done with the explanation portion of the fight?" Not waiting for an answer, Veronica shouted orders to her vampires. They'd be down here and at our throats in moments.

"We have the explosives," Paige said to us. "If we're losing, we take them down with us."

"No one else is dying," Rosario said.

"You got that right!" Monique appeared at the other side of the room, flanked by the other veteran slayers.

An older man had a hefty wooden crossbow loaded with wooden bolts, while Monique, Jacklean and the others had stakes. The odds were evening up.

"Sorry we were late," Monique said. "It took forever to find this place."

"I had my own back-up plan," Rosario said to Paige. "No dying in a blaze of glory needed."

"Who let y'all out of the retirement home?" Veronica called down. "Go!" She gestured at the vampires, and they swarmed down the ladders. Veronica leapt over the bars, landing in a crouch on our level.

Taz and Rosario were closest, and they launched at her. Everyone else spread out to tackle the other vampires. Rosario sidestepped the swing of Veronica's mallet and approached her head on. Taz rushed forward, staking arm raised towards Veronica's back.

Veronica swung her mallet in a vicious lash behind her. It smashed into Taz's head and her body was limp as she crashed down.

Angry heat burned behind my eyes. I wanted to go to Taz, but she was gone – her eyes open but unseeing. The other vampires were coming. Della was shoving and fighting through them to reach her mother's killer. Jacklean was kicking ass alongside her.

Rosario got tangled up with them as Paige strode towards Veronica. "Looks like I'll be the one taking you down," she called.

They were equally arrogant, circling each other with Veronica wielding her mallet and Paige holding the axe.

The fight reached me, and I lost track of Veronica, staying on the defensive as a solidly built male vampire grabbed my shoulders, pain lancing through the recently bitten one. I ducked out of his grip and lunged with the stake, but he veered away.

"Stand down, Paige!" the older slayer armed with the heavy crossbow yelled.

I risked a glance at him as the vampire strafed around me, my stake keeping him at bay. The point of the veteran slayer's bolt was trained on Paige and Veronica.

Paige ignored his command, her axe clashing against Veronica's mallet.

The vampire stopped dancing around and lunged at me, so I went for it. I replayed all the times I'd seen the slayers staking a vampire like the weapon was an extension of them. I stabbed his chest with all of my strength, forcing the stake in deep. Flesh buckled and bone crunched as the point sank in. It was right on target. His face lost its animation, and he was gone. I pulled out the stake, and he hit the floor.

I'd killed a vampire. Horror threatened to freeze me in place, but I blocked it out, the bloody stake shaking in my hand. I had to make it out of here first, and then I could work on living with my actions.

Della was fighting across the room, and Jacklean was curled up behind her. Did Della know? Della's eyes were unfocused and blood smeared her face. The vampire she was fighting dropped, and Cafferty stepped up to tape Della's throat.

Paige and Veronica were battling on, and Paige was losing. Veronica had her on the ground, arm raised to deal the killing blow. I set off in that direction when a bolt sliced through the air and lodged in Veronica's upper arm. Cafferty was crouched beside Della, crossbow raised.

Veronica rolled her eyes, yanking the bolt free like removing a splinter. She caught me looking and ran towards me, mallet raised.

All patched up, Della appeared in front of me, so Veronica swung at her. Della dodged and Veronica's mallet smashed into a metal pipe that ran along the floor.

The mallet jammed, and Monique appeared as Veronica tugged on it. She plunged her stake into Veronica's chest. "That's for all of us slayers," Monique said.

Veronica laughed – Monique must have missed the heart. That wasn't how it was supposed to go. Where were the oblivion and just deserts for her?

Veronica grasped the stake and yanked it out, examining the blood on the pointed tip. "Ow. My turn."

She turned the stake towards Monique, and I realised what was going to happen the second before she sank it deep into Monique's chest. The colour drained from Monique's face, and her fingers pawed at the stake.

"How embarrassing – you've been doing it all wrong. You need to aim higher . . . like this." Veronica forced the stake in deeper, until the full length was buried in Monique's chest.

Monique was dead when she fell, the spirit that had kept her alive through two waves of vampires extinguished.

Veronica looked from me to Della, and I was only vaguely aware of the fighting around us. "Sorry for the interruption," Veronica said. She drew a knife from a sheath at her waist, throwing it at Della like a dart.

Unable to dodge, Della flung her hand up. The blade sliced through her palm and came through the back of her hand, spraying blood and only stopping at the hilt. The tip of the knife almost touched her nose. Della gasped, cradling her skewered palm.

Rosario appeared behind Veronica with a length of piping in both hands. She swung it like a baseball bat at the back of her knees, knocking her off her feet.

"Quick, pull the knife out," Della said, her face clenched against the pain as she thrust her hand at me.

"What about the bleeding?" I said. It looked so unnatural – the hilt protruding through her palm. How much damage would that have done?

"We can bind it."

I gripped the knife handle in one hand and gently held Della's injured hand with the other. Then I pulled. The knife came free with little resistance.

Della looped bandages around her hand and secured them with the last of the duct tape, her teeth gritted.

Veronica leaped up. She batted Rosario aside, beckoning me. "Come on, Mina. Are you ever going to fight me, or are you just playing at being a slayer?"

I could never defeat her hand to hand. She strolled towards

me, grinning her feline smile, and I played my only card. Copying what Veronica did to Della, I threw the knife.

Miracle of miracles, it sailed on a wobbling path towards Veronica's chest, turning in the air. What would happen if a vampire took a knife to the heart?

Veronica slapped her hands together, catching the blade.

"So close . . ." she cooed. "Watch this."

We didn't get to see what Veronica had planned. Della ran at Veronica, raising her leg in a flying kick. Her heel slammed into the tip of the handle, driving the knife Veronica was holding into her chest.

Veronica flew backwards with the force of Della's kick, flopping onto her back. The knife was lodged in her chest, but she was alive, her expression stunned.

Paige raised her axe. "Knives don't work on vampires," she said matter-of-factly. "So this is my kill." She slammed the axe down on Veronica's neck.

Within seconds, the room went quiet. Whether Veronica's death had distracted her vampires or it was one of those rare moments of timing, the fight was over. Cafferty and the other crossbow fighter picked off two vampires who tried to flee, drenched in slayers' blood. Rosario stalked over the bodies, staking any that hadn't been pierced through the heart. We were past deliberating every death against the code – these vampires had fought to kill.

I sank back against the wall, trying to take in the damage while what I'd done caught up with me. I'd killed someone, but I was only alive because I'd done it.

Utterly drained, I forced myself onto my feet. Monique was gone . . . Taz was gone . . . So many vampires were dead. My shoulder felt like it had its own pulse, and every beat came with more pain.

Paige had severed Veronica's head from her body, and the two pieces lay there in a pool of blackish blood. Her long, blonde hair snaked away from her body, dyed black and red. Veronica had caused so much misery, and Paige had cut the head off the monster that was plaguing the city.

Paige dropped the bloody axe by Veronica's body and picked up the mallet. "Mine now."

A slithery, unpleasant feeling trickled over my skin. Not all monsters had fangs.

The older slayers huddled around Jacklean, and the sickening realisation struck me that Della's aunt could be dead too, when they'd only recently reconnected.

Then Jacklean sat up. "Why are y'all crowdin' me?" she said, one hand to the back of her head. "Did we win?"

"We did, and we need to get out of here," Rosario said.

We limped after her, a sorry group of aches, bruises, blood and bandages, much lower in number than when we started. But we'd beaten Veronica. I had a last look at our fallen friends, knowing the sight of Taz's broken face would never leave me. We were too badly hurt and few in number to take them with us.

We reached the floor where tourists would've hung out, and my heart sank. Two vampires barred our exit.

Our crossbow-wielding slayer and police detective fired at the same vampire. One of them got him in the heart and he fell, but the other vampire wasn't going down so easily.

He surged towards us, a bloodthirsty lone wolf against our worn-out group. Paige swung at him with the mallet, stumbling as it overbalanced her. The mallet fell. Leaving Jacklean's side,

Della scooped it up. She swung with both hands and smacked the vampire in the side of the head.

He went down with his head at an awful angle, his neck appearing boneless. Add that to the list of ways to kill a vampire.

Rosario chuckled as Paige swore, still on her knees. "I think the mallet's found a new owner."

We agreed to meet at the Halloween Masked Parade later, a sliver of elation breaking through the exhaustion. We'd lost a lot but achieved something together that would help the whole city.

Paige and the uninjured slayers hopped back into our borrowed boat to sail into the French Quarter docks. They were going to hang around until 7pm and deal with any vampires who turned up, not knowing Veronica was dead.

Me, Cafferty, Della and Jacklean climbed into the open bed of the pickup truck that the veteran slayers had arrived in. Rosario got into the driver's seat. "I know a vet who'll stitch y'all up without getting the hospital in our business," she called through the open window.

As we drove off, a blast of heat washed over us. The steamboat disintegrated in a ball of fire and shrapnel.

"Goddammit Paige!" Rosario yelled from the front of the truck. She must have swiped the detonator from Rosario's pocket during the fight.

Some vampires bobbed on the surface of the water before sinking into the river. If any had survived, the sun and the heat of the wreckage would get them.

Despite their bumps and bruises, Cafferty and Jacklean were chatting with the animation of two people who had been through hell together.

Della was staring at the wreck, her neck taped up and expression bleak. "You OK?" I asked loudly, the engine noise and bumping of the vehicle forcing me to raise my voice.

"I don't know," she said. "I swallowed some vampire blood."

Chapter 47

"What happened?" Jacklean shouted.

The truck came to a halt as she was talking, so it came out too loud.

"I swallowed some blood," Della said, flat and emotionless. "I was trapped under a bleeding vampire, and I couldn't breathe. The blood ran down my throat."

"How much?" Jacklean asked, her voice trembling.

"It doesn't take a lot." Rosario had appeared at the opening of the truck bed. The hardness in her voice was troubling, like she'd written Della off. "Let's get you seen to, then you need to go home and wait it out. The first symptoms would show within a few hours."

"OK." All of Della's usual confidence and certainty had evaporated. She was withdrawn as the kind vet cleaned and dressed her wound.

I watched her constantly. The vampire who killed Della's mum was dead, but Della could become like her. She'd rather die than let that happen. My shoulder burned as the vet put tiny pieces of tape across it to close the deepest gash, but I was more concerned for Della.

We stood outside the vet's surgery afterwards: the slayers, the cop and whatever I was.

Jacklean took one of Della's hands. "I know I've not been there for you in the past, but I'm here now. Here's how it's gonna go. If you lost too much blood and ingested enough of theirs, the vampire blood will move through your system like a virus and you'll turn."

Panic flared in Della's eyes. She tried to jerk her hand away from Jacklean, but her aunt held on. Cafferty had backed off, leaving us space, while Rosario stood there, stony faced and not helping.

"It might not happen – if you've not bled or ingested much," Jacklean said, "but I wanted you to know how it is. Like Rosario said, the change would start within a few hours. I'll wait with you."

"So will I," I said, taking Della's other hand.

"I have to get to work," Cafferty said regretfully.

"Thanks for your help," Rosario said. "We could use someone like you."

"I'm not sure I'm cut out for it full-time," Cafferty said, "but I'm here if you need me."

The two of them left, and we walked back to the mansion to tell Libby.

I'd seen her get bad news. Usually, she raged or swore, throwing anything within reach and wallowing in the destruction. She sat entirely still on the sofa, Della beside her and me and Jacklean on the floor. "It's not going to happen," Libby said simply. "You won't change – you can't." I'd been here with Libby and my mum before. They often thought denial could get them through – that things couldn't catch you if you ran far enough.

Della put her fingernails under the edges of the tape on her neck. We'd known Jared had turned when his bite had healed too easily. What would Della do if her wound was gone? "Well?" she asked, peeling back the tape.

A clotting red bite mark was livid against her dark brown skin. "Still human," Libby said, kissing her on the cheek. She pressed the tape back over Della's wound. "You can do this – just a bit longer." I knew Libby was experiencing an awful thing – I'd been through the same with Jared. But she might not be able to outrun our fears for much longer.

Libby grabbed a stack of videos for Della to pick from. "It must be serious," Della joked. She grabbed *The Mask*, and Jacklean put it on. Even though it was Halloween, there were enough scares in real life.

I tried to watch the movie, but I was more interested in the clock. How long had it been? Not long enough. I remembered the signs from Jared: sweating, sickness, a wound that healed too easily. Della was showing none of those, but it was too soon.

The doorbell rang. It seemed wrong that the outside world could encroach on such a private, painful moment.

"I'll go," I said. I wanted to stay with Della, but I couldn't expect her aunt or girlfriend to leave her.

I ran down and checked through the peephole. It was Nat.

It felt like my life as a schoolgirl was waiting outside, but the dark reality was in here. Nat had enough on her plate – she didn't need to be on this side of the door.

Reluctantly, I opened it, knowing I couldn't invite her in. Della had a bite on her neck just like Sam's. How would I explain that?

"Sorry I haven't been round to see Sam. We've had a rough day. Tessa was found dead this morning."

Nat brought up one hand to her mouth. "I'm so sorry! I didn't know. Are you OK?"

"We will be," I said, hand still on the door.

"This is probably not the best time, but I have to talk to you about a few things . . . like how your wrist has a bite mark on it just like my brother's neck."

She was so close to something she didn't need to know. "I'm so sorry, but I'm not ready to talk about that."

"Even to your best friend? You never share. I'm sorry you're going through something, but so am I. What's the point of being friends if you can't trust me? I thought coming over here would give me the answers I needed, but you can't even do that." She thrust a Radio Shack bag at me. "Here's your Dictaphone. Will's colleague fixed it. Apparently it works now but some buttons still stick down. Guess we'll talk if you ever decide to open up."

She was walking away before I could decide what to say. She was right. What kind of friend couldn't open up about the big things in their life? The one thing she had wrong was that I wasn't being selfish. I was trying to protect her.

I could've run after her, but the pull of checking on Della was too strong. Either Nat would forgive me or she wouldn't, but Della was family. I went inside and put the Dictaphone on the living room drawers for later.

After *The Mask*, we kept the Jim Carrey marathon going with *Dumb and Dumber*. The vampire blood in Della's system was a constant in my thoughts. After what happened to her mum, she couldn't live with being a vampire. Jared had been one of her best friends, and even tolerating him was a struggle.

Two hours bled into three, and then four. "How are you feeling?" Libby asked, her voice wobbling.

"Like myself," Della said, closing her eyes. "You do it – please. I don't wanna look."

Libby nodded even though Della couldn't see, one thumb jammed in her mouth to bite a ragged cuticle. With the other hand, Libby reached for the bandage taped onto Della's throat.

Libby was shaking, her fingers scrabbling to latch on to the tape. She finally pinched it between her thumb and forefinger, taking a deep breath before she pulled it back.

The wound was just as bloody and angry as it had been hours ago. "Give it one more hour," Jacklean said.

We gave up on the pretence of watching movies. We'd passed 7pm, so Jacklean phoned Rosario to see how it'd gone at the docks. Without Veronica, there was no war. The stragglers who showed up got a harsh warning that death would come to those who broke the code.

With that victory confirmed, the four of us sat on the sofa together. We all leaned into each other, and waited, and hoped.

Jacklean finally said, "OK girl, time's up. You feel any different?"

A grin spread across Della's face. In a tangle of long legs, she clambered off the sofa and across to Thandie's gilded-framed mirror. She ripped off the plaster as the three of us joined her. The bandage was bloody, and Della's neck was still marked.

The worry and tiredness vanished. Libby wrapped her arms around Della, swaying her from side to side. "I'm so happy for you!" she squealed, happy for herself too.

We jumped up and down, hugging and celebrating until the chime of the doorbell jerked us apart. Had Nat come back for round two?

We jogged down together and opened the door onto the street. Night had fallen while we willed away the hours. The unlikely duo of Jared and Cafferty were there: Jared in a hoodie over a checked shirt and Cafferty back in his suit. "Cafferty caught me up," Jared said. "I slept for one day . . . We lost Tessa, you got Veronica. And I'm guessing from the way you're dancin' around . . ."

"Della didn't turn!" I hoped he understood what this meant for Della – that the last thing I wanted was for my excitement to hurt him.

A strange look had fallen over his features. "There's somethin' else."

Jared looked to Cafferty, who tugged uncomfortably on the collar of his suit jacket. "They arrested a suspect in connection with Tessa's murder . . . your friend Jason."

Chapter 48

They thought Jason had killed Tessa and all of the others?

Libby managed to speak first. "Can we not trust anybody? First Lucas and now him?"

"What evidence did they find?" I asked, latching on to an angle I could work with. I'd believed without question that Jason was a decent person. But Lucas had fooled us too.

Cafferty hesitated. He would usually shut that question down for civilians, but we'd been through so much together. We knew Jason, or thought we did. "It doesn't look good for him. Tessa used her appointment book for The Underground as a diary, and she described their whole break-up. He found out she'd been going there and saw it as cheating. He even caused a scene at The Underground, but the bouncers kicked him out. They broke up in June and she went home to LA. When she got back, the persona of Elvira had opened up, and she leapt at the distraction. She got real busy with her existing clients and Elvira's."

The bouncer at The Underground had said the Elvira I'd met had been replaced after her death. Tessa had been the new Elvira. No wonder she'd always looked shattered.

"It gets worse, I'm afraid," Cafferty continued. "Tessa had regular feeding appointments with all of the other victims, which gives us the connection between murders."

"That's awful," I said.

"He's not talkin' yet, but we're workin' with the motive that he wanted revenge on the people he thought she cheated with . . . maybe trying to scare her into quittin' by killing her clients but movin' onto her when she didn't comply."

"I can't believe it," Libby breathed. "They had a fight at the carnival last night . . ." The night Tessa was murdered. "He hated people who went to The Underground that much?"

"Mina mentioned the fight," Cafferty said, turning to me. "You obviously weren't on Tessa's client list, so we don't know why he sent notes to you yet. Could be it's The Underground connection or you accidentally intercepted notes meant for Tessa. There's one more thing. We found a hunting knife in his possession – we're testin' it for trace evidence as we speak. We have plenty to hold him for 72 hours. Detective Boudreaux is confident we'll get the confession by then."

I pictured Jason's dark brown eyes behind the Dante mask as his knife drove into flesh. Those evil actions were so far removed from the person I'd thought he was. But he had been at the mansion when I got the first note, and he'd worn serial killer masks at work in the past.

"I for one am glad they got him. The slayers and police are on a winning streak." Jacklean said, reaching for Della's hand. "I have to get goin', but I swear I won't disappear again."

"Thank you for being here," Della said, looking at where her hand and her aunt's were joined.

"I'm done with work for today," Cafferty said when we'd closed the door on Jacklean. "All of the victims were clients of Tessa's and we've got the guy, so technically there's no need for the protective detail tonight. But I can hang around if you want."

"We should go to the Mask Parade like we planned," Libby said decisively. "All the bad guys are dead or arrested – don't we deserve some fun? Tessa would want that for us. You too, Detective Do-Gooder. You helped to keep Della and Mina safe." I had to admit, I'd be glad to have Cafferty there.

"I wish I'd been there for you today," Jared said, looping an arm around me and drawing me close. The hazards of daylight excluded him from so much.

Della's gaze flicked to his arm around me, probably wondering why we could get close all of a sudden. I'd have to tell her and Libby about him feeding on me – just not yet.

"OK, so we shower and go. I have enough masks for all of us. It is the Mask Parade, after all," Libby said. She scowled at Cafferty, gesturing up and down at his suit. "I'm not sure what to do about *that* though. Want me to find you one of the mansion's costumes?"

"I have a change of clothes in the car," Cafferty said quickly.

Jared was lying on my bed when I got out of the shower, towel wrapped around me. After the time by myself, everything hadn't sunk in. So much had happened today that it was hard to believe Tessa had died too. I kept forgetting, and it rubbed the wound raw every time it came back to me.

I'd got used to separation from Jared, and consistently assessing what small movements I could make towards him. Standing there, hair damp and only a towel covering me, I realised we didn't need to stay away from each other.

Jared sat up quickly. "Sorry! I thought you'd be dressed."

"It's OK," I said. He turned his back as I went to my drawers to choose an outfit.

I dressed with my back to Jared, hyper-aware of him as I pulled on every item of clothing, the fabric skimming my sensitised skin. We were looking away from each other, but his presence was a constant pull on me.

"All done," I said, flustered by the time I was wearing black dungarees and a grey polo neck. After the losses we'd suffered, it felt respectful to go subdued. I wasn't sure I wanted to be out in the tumult of New Orleans at Halloween, but I understood Libby's drive for activity.

Jared turned back, opening his arms. With no hesitation, I sank down into them. My head slotted under his chin, cheek against his chest. I wrapped my arms around his waist, and he closed his arms around my back. "Are you OK?" he asked, his mouth against the top of my head so the words tickled.

"Not really," I replied. So many things had happened that I'd gone numb. When everything hit me later, it would hurt. "How about you?"

Jared held me tighter, and I shifted so I was sitting between his legs. They formed a protective frame around me. "Jason was my friend – I thought he was a good guy. But now Cafferty's filled us in, it makes sense."

"I know," I said. "As much as I want to know more, the police have the reins."

"And Libby's going to make us leave any minute," Jared said.

"You need to feed," I said, rolling up the sleeve on my unbitten arm. His gaze strayed to my exposed flesh, but his conflict was obvious. "I'm fine," I said. An expectant feeling of nerves rose up.

Jared held my hand in both of his. Instead of leaning down for a bite, he kissed me. The gentle motion of his lips on mine came with unexpected sweetness. Blissful warmth spread through me, kindling heat low in my stomach. I held his rough cheeks, the muscles of his jaw shifting beneath my palms.

He pulled back, only leaving inches between us. "I love you," he said, his voice cracking with emotion.

Tears blurred my vision, and my response was easy. "I love you too."

We hugged so tightly that I could only take shallow breaths, but I hung onto him. "We should do this before Libby bursts in," I said, my voice muffled against him.

"Right," he said, releasing me and holding me at arm's length to get a good look. "Are you ready?"

Elated at the words we'd exchanged, I offered my arm and he bit down. There was that nip, followed by the steady pull and release on my arm. It came with a pleasant, sleepy feeling rather than the dizzying intensity of the first time. Everything felt clearer once he was done.

"Thank you," he said, lightly kissing the two neat holes in my arm. I ran my finger over them as he leaned back, feeling the twinge of tight, sore skin.

There was a knock on the door, and I yanked down my sleeve as it opened.

"I'd say get a room but you're in it," Libby said, covering her eyes and looking through her parted fingers. "Anyway, we're leaving! Cafferty looks thrilled about the mask I've picked out for him."

Minutes later, we were masked and ready. Libby wore a sparkly brown mouse mask that covered the top part of her face, complementing Della's black cat. Jared's Wesley mask was a black bandana that knotted at the back of his head and obscured the top half of his face, apart from the vivid hazel-green of his eyes. Continuing the *Princess Bride* theme, I had a yellow mask covered with silk buttercups to represent the love of Wesley's life.

Cafferty had a bandana tied across the bottom of his face like a bank robber from the Wild West. "Don't," he warned, spotting the look on my face.

"I didn't say anything!"

On the way out, I spotted a new feature on the coffee table. Veronica's mallet had been scrubbed clean, but it carried the menace of its previous owner. "What are you going to do with that?" I asked Della.

She shrugged. "Put it in the museum. She's just another dead vampire for people to tell stories about."

I hoped killing Veronica had given her some peace like Emmeline had said.

I tried to set aside the things we'd been through today – I couldn't do anything about them. We'd come out tonight as a break from real life. When we hit the crowds, New Orleans slowly worked its usual magic. The city pulsed with life more than anywhere else I'd visited, and the Halloween atmosphere was wild. People were crammed into every space along Bourbon Street. Everyone was dancing and smiling as a riot of jazz music blasted from an invisible sound system, and Mardi Gras beads in orange and purple were slung around every throat and snaked around arms. Nat should've been there with us, but I doubted she'd feel like celebrating with me today after I'd pushed her away. I hoped she'd forgive me. With Sam hurt, I was probably the last thing on her mind.

The masks were a troubling note as we blended into the crowd. We were surrounded by monsters, animals and movie serial killers. Everyone had hidden their identities for the parade, and it rested uneasily on me with Jason so recently doing just that.

Della and Libby were dancing, and a smiling guy draped beads over their heads. Cafferty made no attempt to dance, checking the packed area around us with definite cop vibes. He'd said he wasn't into partying.

Jared took my hand and led me closer to my sister, but the masks stopped me from fully letting go. Each glimpse of white had me seeing the flash of a blade. Every blonde had my heart pounding, even though I'd witnessed Veronica's bloody death.

Tonight was letting Della and Libby cut loose, but I couldn't do it so easily.

Then Jared's mouth grazed my neck, and he began to dance behind me. The drumbeat thrummed through our bodies, and the knot of tension around me slackened ever so slightly. I moved with him, leaning my body into him as he wrapped his arms around my waist.

Then he ripped his arms away from me so fast that I stumbled backwards. "What are you doing?"

The noise and music carried my voice away. I spun round but couldn't see Jared or the others. All around me was a sea of masks. The most efficient serial killers hid their faces until the big reveal.

All of a sudden, I was whisked off my feet and rushing through the crowd.

Chapter 49

The darkness, dancers and music were disorienting, so I couldn't see who'd grabbed me. There had to be one person holding my arms and another at my feet.

I was surrounded by strangers and no one answered my screams, but why would they? I was gone in seconds, swallowed up by the crowd as if I'd never been there. I twisted and kicked, knowing I could plunge to the ground but that the alternative would be worse.

The clamour of the parade quieted, and the press of bodies eased. I could finally see that the person at my feet was dressed as a police officer: a woman with her hair scraped back into a bun.

Arching my neck, I saw another at my head too. No wonder nobody had helped me. Their uniforms were too cheap and plasticky to be real, but good enough to pass a quick inspection. I couldn't tell if they were humans or vampires, and I was feeling sick from getting shaken around.

Before I could orient myself, they dropped me onto my feet. One of them held my arms from behind while I kicked and yelled. There was no one on the empty street, but it was worth a try.

The woman came into view long enough for me to see her holding a small sack. "No . . ." I pleaded as she rammed it over my head. As I struggled, someone held my hands behind my back, wrapping rough rope around them. My skin burned when I tried to tug at the binds.

They picked me up and flung me onto a hard surface. The bag was full of my hot breath, and claustrophobia was eating into me. I didn't want to die at all, but feeling my air slowly running out was my nightmare.

We started moving, so I was inside a van – like when John Carter had taken Jared. He'd come back as a vampire. Was I going to come back at all? Unable to see, hearing and feeling the hum of the van and nothing else, it felt like I was disappearing.

I knocked into something solid but soft. "Is someone there?" I shouted, my voice thickened by the sack.

"Mina!" Libby said, and a clumsy arm started slapping me across my face and upper body.

Laughing and crying at the same time, I turned my face away from her swatting. Either they'd left Libby's hands free or she'd got out of the rope.

"I'm here too." Jared and Della said some variation of the same thing.

"Me too," Cafferty added.

Someone had taken all of us. That couldn't have been a coincidence. Having a mystery to solve was good. If I was working through what had happened, I wasn't thinking about being wrapped up and delivered somewhere or the bag robbing me of oxygen.

The van stopped, throwing us forward in a jumble of bodies. We were about to find out who had done this to us.

I heard the doors at the back of the van open, and someone yanked me out. One assailant lifted me with ease – probably a vampire. They set me down on my feet, dragging me by the arm. I decided not to fight yet. Running off with my hands tied and head covered would be a great way to concuss myself. If I kept a handle on my fear, we could beat this. The five of us were together. We had an assortment of skills, and we'd got through our share of scrapes. I knew those things, but terror was slowly stealing my logic.

The vampire shoved me into a seat and then yanked off the bag, ripping off my Princess Buttercup mask and taking some hair with it.

I clamped my eyes shut at the dazzling light, letting them adjust in increments before I opened them fully.

We were sitting in the pews of a cathedral, facing the altar. Even though my hands were bound, I could tell the stake at my waist was gone. Cafferty and Jared were on either side of me, while Della and Libby were in front. Her hands had been secured again. Candles lined a sculpture of angels, and columns were topped with more religious figurines. Large black and white tiles covered the floor and everything was light, bright and at odds with being dragged here against our will. A sixth person had joined us: Rosario.

Her hands were also tied behind her back, and even from across the aisle her fury was obvious. "They got you too," she said. "They grabbed me outside the slayer cave."

"Who are *they*?" I asked, but no one answered.

Eight vampires, including the fake police officers, were positioned around the room, all looking at the altar. We were waiting for someone.

Saint Germain walked slowly in front of the altar, standing at the top of the steps. His palms were upturned and hands extended in front of him like a performer waiting for applause. He was wearing a pristine ivory suit with a matching waistcoat. Confidence and power rolled off him, although he had no abilities of his own. We'd been kidnapped by the self-proclaimed vampire king of Louisiana.

"Welcome, y'all," he said smoothly. "Apologies for the *the-a-trics*," he drew out the last word, like we had all the time in the world. Technically, *he* did. "I wanted to bring y'all here to talk about a grievance that I'm afraid I hold against you."

"I mean this with the utmost respect," Libby said, her voice defiant but too loud for genuine confidence, "but what the hell did we do? I'm tired of vampires giving us ultimatums. No offence, Jared. You don't suck as much as the rest of them."

"None taken," Jared said. He leaned against me, and the solid familiarity of him grounded me.

"I appreciate that y'all wanna get to the point. Some of you killed my lieutenant, but I believe you all knew her – a brilliantly sadistic vampire by the name of Veronica."

Della spoke up. "That was me – you don't need the others."

"How self-sacrificin' of you. I admire that." Saint Germain pointed a finger at Della, cocking it like a gun. "This is what I get for rushin' – I didn't tell y'all the full story. I brought you here to kill you for what you'd done to her, but I just learned from one of your friends that Veronica has been puttin' together a little band of vampires. I believe her final desire was to knock me from my position of power tonight. She was previously workin' with another vampire y'all knew – John Carter. I assume they wanted to kill me, though I don't like to speculate."

So he was planning to kill us for killing her? I tried to steady my jittery urge to do something. The wrong move would get us killed.

"I wanted revenge, but I'm flexible given how y'all prevented a war today. However, it seems you've robbed me of the opportunity to take Veronica out myself, as a lesson to the other would-be usurpers of New Orleans. So what to do about that?" He tapped his chin, letting the question hang over us.

"Lucky I have a contingency plan. I picked up one other person who was there when Veronica passed, and we came up with a suitable arrangement. Darlin', would y'all come on out here?" Saint Germain called off to one side towards an alcove. "Bring your guest."

Chapter 50

"With pleasure!" Paige stepped into view, closely followed by Armand. Shock pressed down on me. Turning on us to save herself was in character for Paige. But if Armand was betraying us after everything we'd been through together . . . We'd trusted him.

"Vampires like you give the rest of us a bad name," Saint Germain said, and I relaxed. "How come you didn't foresee all of this? It shouldn't have taken a *human* to inform me."

"I've told you before that my power doesn't work that way," Armand said, every muscle clenched. "Visions come to me sometimes, but I can't control them."

"So what you're saying is that you serve no purpose. Fortunately, Paige here gave me a brilliant idea, if I do say so myself. If I bring the slayers onto my payroll, something like this won't occur again. They can take out as many reckless vampires as they like, but under my control."

"The slayers under your control? That will never happen," Rosario said.

"I thought that might be the case." Saint Germain gestured, and two lean, hungry-looking female vampires strode across and yanked Rosario to her feet.

"No!" Della yelled, leaping up.

"Sit down unless you'd like to join her." He turned to the vampires struggling to keep their grip on Rosario. "Deal with her outside the cathedral. I'm not a heathen."

Rosario fought the whole way out. There wasn't much she could do with her hands fastened behind her back. Once outside, she let out an anguished scream that cut off abruptly. Another life snuffed out with a few casual words from a vampire, and we'd had to sit back while it happened.

Della's shoulders were shaking, and angry tension ran down her arms and across her shoulders as she sat down. Which one of us would be next? Rosario, who'd been so full of spirit and ambition, was gone. We'd lost too many people, and it wasn't over.

Cafferty's hand brushed against mine. I let my gaze fall without changing position. He had a pocket knife slotted into the layers of rope and was slowly, painstakingly sawing through them. His wrists were bloody where the rope had chafed through the skin. Would he be next to die if he got free – his reward for trying to save us?

"Now that unsavoury business is out of the way – meet the new leader of the slayers." Paige's grin was pure smugness. "If y'all don't like that," Saint Germain added, mainly directed at Della, "you can always join your prior leader. Though it might be hard to find her – she's prob'ly in pieces at the bottom of the Mississippi by now."

"You've got the slayers under your thumb," Armand said from the other side of Paige. He'd adopted the cold voice that disguised a multitude of feelings. "They're more than a worthy replacement for Veronica. Let the children go. You've always wanted me to work for you, and here I am."

"We're not even close to done here, Carter," Saint Germain said, for the first time losing some of that Southern-gentlemanly veneer. Beneath was a ruthless predator that didn't need to show fangs to be terrifying.

Cafferty made his move. He leapt over the pew in front of us, skirting around Saint Germain to hold the knife against his throat. It might not kill a vampire, but a slashed throat would hurt. I got the first cautious hope that we might escape this, although Saint Germain looked decidedly unafraid.

"Release the kids," Cafferty said, "Armand too. Then when they're clear . . ."

His eyes glazed over and the tight V of his arm went loose. He was staring at a vampire with a shiny shaved head and eyes of an eerily pale grey. Armand wasn't the only vampire with a power.

Saint Germain stepped away. Cafferty's arms fell to his side, though his eyes remained locked on the vampire.

"Well that was quite a thing," Saint Germain said, straightening out his cuffs. "Your body is frozen, boy, but you should be able to hear me. I could kill you for that move, and it would be so easy."

Jared was shifting about beside me, and when I risked a glance at him, his fury was plain. I hoped he wasn't planning anything stupid. We'd seen how that'd worked out for Cafferty.

"I've wanted a detective on the payroll for quite some time. Armand's gonna need someone like you on his first assignment. Here's the deal: you and Armand take a road trip to New Mexico where I'll utilise both of your skill sets. If you both agree, the rest can go free."

Saint Germain waved a hand and the grey-eyed vampire turned away, rubbing his eyes. Cafferty staggered, quickly straightening up. "You think you can do that and give me orders? I can't go off and abandon my job."

"Let me put this in terms you understand. You two – the nosy human and her sister. Get up."

Getting closer to Saint Germain and his icy ferocity was the last thing I wanted to do. Thinking of Rosario, it felt like Libby and I were walking to our deaths when we stood in front of him. Libby's face was white and pinched. "Face the crowd, girls," he said.

We did what he told us, my fear crystallising into something primal and knowing.

"You do what I say, detective," Saint Germain said, coming up behind me. "Or I have my way with these two. I think I'll drink this one dry." He flipped my hair over one shoulder, a shudder running through me at his touch. Jared and Cafferty's faces were livid, and Della looked about ready to leap over the pews.

Still behind me, Saint Germain brought his face up next to mine. His breath reeked of whiskey and old blood. He ran an icy hand down my cheek and throat, letting it close around my neck. His skin felt dry and thin as paper. My pulse must have been hammering against his hand, the reminder of my life that he could extinguish so easily. He put pressure on my windpipe, and I gasped.

"Leave her alone!" Libby said.

"That's enough!" Cafferty said. "I'll take a leave of absence . . . I'll make it work."

"That's what I thought." Saint Germain removed his hand from my throat and stepped away from me, hands raised. Even though he'd released me, fear kept me in a tight hold. We weren't safe yet.

"Come on!" Libby said to me. We stumbled away, made clumsy by the hands tied behind our backs.

"Thank you for helpin' with my little demonstration, girls. You and Armand had better skedaddle before sunrise, detective. I took the liberty of havin' your keys removed and your Impala brought around." He'd been so confident that tonight would go his way.

Saint Germain took a set of keys from inside his jacket. Cafferty patted the pocket of his jeans in disbelief, holding up a hand to catch the keys when Saint Germain tossed them.

"I need to speak to Jared before we go," Armand said.

He was usually the one to melt away into the shadows. He and Jared went to one side, though when Armand spoke, the church's acoustics carried his confession. "It wasn't John's blood that changed you. It was mine."

Chapter 51

"It was you?" Cautious hope alighted on Jared's face. Would he no longer be burdened by the expectation that he'd turn into John?

"My brother was Lucas's sire," Armand explained quietly. "He was the protégé who John wanted to mould to be like him. You were . . . part of his plan. I bled into a bottle, and he forced you to drink."

"Why didn't you tell me?" Jared asked.

"You'd assumed it was John and blamed him for what you'd become. I wanted to help you, not for you to shut me out for causing you such anguish. Besides, I wasn't convinced you'd be any happier to learn that my blood made you what you are. But

I've seen you struggling, and I wanted you to know that a vampire's sire has no control over who they become. You care for people – in time you'll have the ability to become a nurse."

"That is a lovely sentiment," Saint Germain said loudly, "but I'd prefer you to leave for New Mexico before the sun comes up and reduces you to a pile of smouldering ash in Cafferty's car. Off you go, Carter. The rest of you can leave – I'm true to my word."

Cafferty and Armand murmured their goodbyes before hurrying out of the back door of the church. I took a last look at Paige as Jared, Libby, Della and I went the other way. Her smugness hadn't worn off, but she'd had to align herself with the bad guys to get the power she'd craved. She'd never liked the way Rosario ran the slayers. How would they feel once they found out how she got the gig?

A vampire let us out of the wooden doors at the front of St. Louis Cathedral, slicing through our binds with a small blade. Jackson Square was alive with colour and sound, the leaves turning and artists selling their wares along the iron railings. Tourists wove around us despite the late hour and oblivious to what had passed behind closed doors. We'd lost Rosario, and two of us had become indebted to a powerful, sadistic vampire. That he could hold us captive in such a prominent, special location was further testament to his power.

New Orleans was still partying, but Halloween was over for the four of us. We slumped down on the sofa back at the mansion.

"Is it over?" Libby asked. "Because I don't know how much more we can take."

"We're done," Della said. "Now we grieve and take time to make sense of what happened. And you got some good news," Della said to Jared. She rarely directed positivity at him, and I was grateful for whatever had changed.

"Yeah," he said. "Knowing I don't have John's blood running through my veins . . . It feels like I have a chance. I know Armand said it doesn't matter who turned a vampire, but it does to me."

"I'm more bothered about the slayers," Della said. "What are we gonna do with Paige in charge?"

"We'll keep her in check, or we could branch off on our own. Jared was pretty handy at the carnival," I said. While we were talking about him, I realised there was another drama to air. "Jared doesn't have an issue being close to me anymore . . . because he's started drinking my blood."

"We figured," Della said sleepily. "Since The Underground burned down, right?"

"Worse reveal ever," Libby said. "Behave if you're staying over."

"Thanks, I guess," Jared said, putting an arm around me and looking pleased with himself.

"We should get some sleep," I said to Jared.

After we got ready, we climbed into bed and lay face to face, legs and bodies slotting together as if we'd been sleeping like this all along. While his skin once felt almost too hot for sleeping, it was now cool against mine.

My eyes were heavy, but I fought sleep for as long as I could. Jared leaned down to kiss my wounded shoulder, the brush of his lips leaving my skin tingling. He moved on to the bite from the carnival vampire, bringing my arm to his mouth for another kiss. Having him feed on me had given us back so many parts of our relationship.

It hadn't fixed everything, but we had the chance to move forward.

I'd wanted this closeness for so long, but I was so comfortable and happy that I fell asleep.

I woke with my back to Jared. I snuggled into him, getting as close as I could. I'd never get tired of how the contours of his body felt against my back: the firm pressure of his chest and the comforting weight of his arms around me.

Deciding to let him keep to his nocturnal habits, I snuck out of bed. I got dressed quietly and went into the living room. I checked my wounds in Thandie's ornate mirror. The one on my arm had healed to a faint imprint of teeth. My shoulder was messier, but the wound had closed quickly. I'd been lucky, but I'd possibly have some new scars.

I'd left the bag with the Dictaphone in here after Nat dropped it off yesterday. Earlier in the week, I'd read Thandie's letters, but hearing her voice would hit much harder. The Dictaphone was sealed in a plastic wrapper, so hopefully Nat hadn't heard anything about vampires that could complicate our relationship further. I hoped we had a relationship to complicate.

I pressed the play button and the record button stuck down with it. "No!" I gasped, hammering the stop button and praying I hadn't recorded over Thandie's voice.

"What's the matter?" Jared slouched into the living room. His hair was stuck up in a truly magnificent bed head.

"Sorry . . . Did I wake you?"

"It's not you – stupid vampire hearing." He paused, wincing as he brought a hand up to one temple. "Well this sucks. I'd forgotten what happened to Thandie when John left the city."

So had I. When a vampire was too far from their sire early on, they suffered the most awful headaches. "Hopefully Armand will be back soon."

"Yeah. So whose Dictaphone is that?" Jared already looked more alert as he sat on the sofa beside me.

"It's Thandie's. It's dated the day she died, but I don't know what's on it yet," I said.

"Let's find out."

I pressed play and was greeted with high-pitched static. Then Thandie spoke, her familiar voice low and rasping. It didn't feel like three months since I'd heard it.

"I've not recorded myself for years, but there are things I need to get off my chest."

She paused to inhale and exhale deeply. I imagined her sitting behind her desk, cigarette smoke curling up over her head.

"I haven't been to church for even longer than that, so saying my confessions aloud will have to do." She coughed, letting out a bitter laugh. "I'll probably delete the thing once I'm done, but maybe I'll feel better for it."

I pressed stop, too overcome with emotion to hear more.

"It's weird to hear her voice." Jared ran a hand down his stubbly face. "Shouldn't Libby be here for this?"

"I think so," I said.

I knocked on Libby's half-open door. She and Della were curled up in bed, but they both lifted their heads. "I found a tape that Thandie recorded . . . It starts by saying she wants to get something off her chest."

I'd expected Libby to pull the quilt over her head and come up with some excuse. Instead, she was out of bed before Della. "Let's hear it then."

Della looked as surprised as I felt, but we followed Libby out of the room. The four of us had barely sat down when Libby put the Dictaphone on the coffee table and hit play.

Chapter 52

"Rewind it first," I said, "but be careful – the buttons stick so I almost recorded over it."

Grumbling to herself, she did what I said and pressed play. Of course the buttons behaved for her.

Thandie's introduction played again before she went on. "The girls got me thinking about subjects I'd rather ignore when they came in here talking about vampires, but it seems I can't any longer. They told me the Carter brothers are back. I tried to hide how deeply they frighten me, but I can scarcely think through it. I've retained enough presence of mind to update my will to ensure my wealth passes to those who deserve it, but I'm afraid my time is coming. This prolonged life should never have been mine anyway.

Seeing Della today was hard, like always. That poor girl. I never got over the guilt of killing her mother, and I don't deserve to. My dear Emmeline went to the funeral for me, but it wasn't the same as paying my respects for myself."

Thandie paused, her voice trembling. "I want to apologise for what I did, but how do you say sorry for something like that? I don't deserve forgiveness. The one time I was careless, feeding in public, and she found me. Only one of us could live, and I chose myself. I regret that dearly. When I realised who Della was years later, that I'd murdered her mother, I knew I was being punished by having her put into my path. It wasn't enough for what I'd done, but it was something."

She sniffed, and her shaking voice steadied. "I've bottled that up for too long, but no one can hear this tape. I'll dispose of it when I'm done in case something happens to me. Time to put on a brave face. We're holding the finale to Fang Fest at the mansion tonight, so this is the police's best chance to catch John Carter once and for all."

There were clicking sounds and then Thandie muttered, "Why won't the tape stop? Stupid button . . . How do I . . .? Ahh, I'll just pull—"

Her voice cut out. From the date written on the tape and the events she'd described, Thandie must have recorded it within hours of her death. She'd never got to destroy the tape like she'd planned.

Static replaced Thandie's voice, so I jabbed the stop button over and over again until it worked. The three of us faced Della. She was utterly rigid, hands clasping the fabric of her flannel pyjama bottoms. "We killed Veronica . . ." she said, her voice uneven.

"And she deserved it," I said quickly. "Don't be mad at yourself. You only acted on the information Emmeline gave us."

"It's a pretty big mistake," Libby asked. "Do you think she was lying?"

"I don't know what to think – either she lied to us or someone lied to her," Della said, her voice all kinds of broken.

"What are you going to do?" Jared asked.

"I need to let it rest a while. I don't want to do something I'll regret."

We'd decided to run a mansion event to mark the end of Halloween. It was a movie murder mystery night, where each tour group would move through the house solving puzzles and analysing fake crime scenes to figure out which movie murderer was causing mayhem in the real world. After Armand's vision of me as Freddy Krueger earlier this week, I'd asked Libby if I could play him, but she insisted that I stick with Claudia.

Della went off to confront Emmeline and then cover Empire for Armand. You wouldn't have known she had a hole in her hand and wounds on her neck – she kept going like normal.

Jared joined us when the sun went down, going out to collect much-needed fried chicken even though he couldn't eat any. We had a final walk-through of the mystery before the other employees arrived.

The evening went off without a hitch, although the lack of a Candyman left a sombre feel that none of us mentioned. Our mystery was just tricky enough, and half of the groups figured out that Michael Myers was the one leaving a trail of bodies through the mansion. We'd planned it all out before recent events, but I managed to immerse myself in the show and not think about it too much. Jared rushed off to check on the Nine Steps to Hell restaurant for Armand before doing his tour, leaving me and Libby to clean up.

Soon we had the mansion to ourselves. It started raining as we settled down on the sofa in the apartment upstairs. For a few minutes we sat there, Libby's head on my shoulder.

"I think I've earned a ridiculously long shower," Libby said, lifting her head and sloping out of the room.

Lightning lit up the night and rain lashed against the windows, but I left the curtains open. Since I'd hardly read this week, I picked up *The Forbidden Game*. Then I was plunged into darkness, along with my book.

I shuffled through the room, reaching my hands out to catch furniture before I crashed into it. Thunder boomed. Shadows stretched out as my vision adjusted, and dark corners gave the room a formless appearance. Everything was scarier in the dark.

My shins were stinging by the time I got to the bathroom door and banged on it. "Mina?" Libby yelled, the shower running. "What the hell?"

"I didn't do it! The fuse must have blown."

"I just put shampoo on," she called over the pounding water. "There's some light coming in from the streetlight for me to rinse."

"I'll go. Where's the torch?" I asked.

"Can't hear you!"

I was pretty certain the torch was in the kitchen drawer – further away than the fuse box under the stairs.

Thandie had thought of everything, so faint emergency lights guided my way when I got into the hallway. The lights meant I was less likely to tumble down the stairs, but they also created monsters in the shadows. Another boom of thunder, so loud that it vibrated in my chest. Pressure built in my ears.

I made it to the top of the stairs, the bear-trap chandelier glinting murderously in the moonlight, its teeth partially cloaked in shadow.

Rain hammered and the wind whined as I took the first few steps. The plaintive ring of the phone cut through the storm noise. I'd forgotten that it didn't need power. I jogged the rest of the way down, hoping I'd get there before it stopped ringing.

"Hello?" I said, breathless.

"Mina? Detective Boudreaux here."

"Hi! How are you? It's good to hear your voice," I said.

"I'm good, thank you. I'm not sure you'll be saying that when you hear what I have to say. We released Jason."

The news split me right down the middle. I was relieved that he could be innocent, but that meant the killer was on the loose.

"Mina?" Boudreaux asked.

"I'm here. How come you released him?"

"His knife doesn't match the wounds, and his alibis finally came forward. We still think the killer is targeting people connected to Tessa's clientele at The Underground, but it's hard to confirm since it burned down."

My hand hurt from gripping the phone so tightly. "What happens now?"

"I've sent an officer over. We have no reason to believe you're in immediate danger, but if those notes were meant for you, it's reason enough to err on the side of caution."

A loud, insistent knock rang out. "I think the officer is here."

"Wait! Don't open the door unless you're certain it's Officer Dupres. If you have any doubts, call 911."

"Got it. Thank you."

"Take care, Mina." The phone went dead. A lifeline had been cut off.

I hurried to the door and peered through the peephole. Officer Dupres was shivering and smiling even though the rain had plastered his black hair down against his head.

I flung the door open. "Thank you for coming."

"Not a problem. I'll be waitin' in the car, so you holler if there's any bother." His large, amiable presence put me at ease. "Before I go . . . Looks like the storm's taken out the power – can I check that for you?"

"Thank you – the fuse box is in the cupboard under the stairs," I said. "I'll make you a coffee to take to the car."

"That would be real kind. My daughter asked me to thank you for those RL Stine books by the way – she says they're great."

"I'm glad she likes them. I'll grab more books for her and let Libby know that you're here. Then I'll make you that drink."

I set off upstairs as Officer Dupres closed the front door, shutting out the worst of the storm noise.

"I'll have the power back on in no time," he called.

I jogged to the top of the stairs, looking forward to Officer Dupres illuminating the shadowy house. I heard the front door open again and the pattering of rain, following by a wet gargling sound.

As I turned around, a strike of lightning lit up the hallway. Officer Dupres was standing in front of the open door, rainwater lashing down behind him. In the shadows, his features looked off. He put a hand over his chest and crumpled. A figure stepped into view behind him. It wasn't too dark to make out the Dante mask and bloody knife.

Chapter 53

The killer gave a jaunty wave with the blade they'd sunk into Officer Dupres, robbing him of his life and his children of a father.

With the mask in place, I couldn't see any distinguishing features beyond baggy overalls. I was upstairs – one of the cardinal horror movie sins. The killer was blocking the front door, and I was unarmed. I'd not expected to need my stake inside the mansion.

Thunder followed the lightning strike, and the boom set me in motion. When Officer Dupres's murderer took off up the stairs, I was already running. I shouted Libby, realising it was no use. The walls were insulated to keep screams inside each tour room.

I had few options. I couldn't get down to the phone, and Libby was tucked away in Thandie's apartment. I wouldn't lead the killer to her and corner us both.

I ran towards the start of the tour: the one-way path through this place. I could try to lose them and loop back down to the phone.

Diving into the *Candyman* bathroom, I tried to ram the door shut when an arm wedged it open, frantically slashing towards me. The blade nicked my arm before I could pull back – a brutal sting that quickly faded to a nagging pulse. I yelped, kicking the door as hard as I could. The killer grunted, whipping their arm and the knife back. I slammed the door, thumbing the lock.

Unbuttoning my shirt, I winced as the fabric rubbed where I'd been slashed. I squinted down at the wound in the greenish light. Blood was oozing from it, though not too fast.

"Come on, Mina – open the door." I knew that voice, though not the cruelty in it.

"Sam?" I said, voice trembling as I whipped off my shirt and wrapped it around my upper arm. "Why are you doing this?" While he was talking and not trying to get in, I had time to finish dressing my arm and get some answers.

"Isn't that obvious? I'm here to kill you. My knife had a taste, but it's not enough."

"Does your family know?" I secured the shirt, and blood stuck the fabric to my arm.

"It's just me and my blade. You're the last one on Elvira's list, and then we're done."

It was time to go, but I couldn't wrap my head around this. Kind, gentle Sam was outside the door and he wanted to kill me.

"What does Tessa's list have to do with this?"

"Are you really that stupid? My sister was the original Elvira – not that imposter. You met Louisa – remember?"

"I'm so sorry Sam – I didn't know." Nat had shown me a picture of Louisa once, her skin tanned and hair brown like Nat's. As Elvira, she'd had her face painted white and must have worn a black wig, and I'd not made the connection. I'd already felt awful for bringing Elvira to John Carter's attention. Knowing who she was and the family that had been torn apart made it worse. I couldn't save Sam's sister, but I could save myself and Libby.

"Sorry isn't good enough! Louisa's clients switched to Tessa like my sister's death meant nothing. They didn't care about her death then, but I made sure they knew their mistake in the end."

"Killing her clients won't bring Louisa back! Her killer's dead. You don't have to do this."

He gave no reply. Had I got through to him? He let out an inhuman roar and slammed against the door.

I bolted through the tunnel behind the mirror. Sam murdered all of those people, and I was next on the list. I had to be ready when he reached me.

I burst out through the mural of Candyman's mouth, bathed with eerie green emergency lighting. I grabbed Candyman's metal hook from over his gravestone headboard. It was a satisfying weight in my hand. Libby always made sure the thing was wickedly sharp to gut a mannequin every night.

I yanked open the door to Freddy Krueger's boiler room, turning the lock once I was inside. Terror made me clumsy, but I could do this. I knew this place better than anyone, except Libby.

Setting off the dry ice worked better than I'd hoped. Against the emergency lighting, the smoke became a writhing, solid thing. With my shirt covering my slashed arm, I was cold in my thin vest. I grabbed Freddy's sweater, yanking it on over my makeshift bandage with a jolt of pain. As I pulled down the jumper, I thought back to Armand's vision of me wearing it.

The *Candyman* door to the previous room gave up with a crash, and I ducked into the darkness beneath the metal walkway. Maybe it was the Freddy costume giving me confidence, but I felt the glimmer of a chance.

A bang echoed through the room, and I flinched. Sam was outside my door. "Don't you want to know how I picked my victims?" he called.

I kept silent. If he was trying to pin down my location, I wouldn't give it to him.

"So quiet! That isn't like you. I'm sure you're hanging on my every word. I found Louisa's diary in Nat's room and learned all the disgusting things they asked her to do – feeding on them like a monster. My sister was good, and they ruined her! She saw five of them the night she died, including you."

Tears pricked my eyes. I wished every day that my mum hadn't met John Carter and dragged us, and Louisa, into this. But John and Veronica had been the murderers, not me. They didn't have to kill to reach their goals.

"Still not willing to speak? I wonder if this will loosen your tongue. Louisa's clients were so eager to bleed for her, so I made sure they died bleeding for me. Nine wounds each, punishing sinners like in the nine circles of hell. I do like a literary reference. Imagine how much that's going to hurt when I get to you!"

He yelled the last part, ramming the door over and over again. It must have been painful, but he kept going. The door was groaning and splinters appeared on this side, almost obscured by the fog. I clutched the hook. What if the darkness and fog failed to shield me, and I was crouching in plain sight when Sam got inside? The door was giving way, along with my resolve. I had to hold on. If Sam was here, he wasn't going after Libby.

The wood buckled and Sam's face appeared in the hole. It was like a scene from *The Shining*, but I wasn't running away. It was him or me. His hand snaked through and thumbed the lock, then he was in.

Chapter 54

made myself small as Sam strolled into the room. He wafted the knife through the fog. "Mina . . ." he called. "Are you in here?"

He ran the blade along the fibreglass wall, and it sliced through with little resistance. He'd cut me once, and the dark stain of blood had seeped into the Freddy costume. If I made it through tonight, Libby would kill me.

I took a deep breath, releasing it slowly. A cough or fidget could end my life. Reaching out with my uninjured arm, I let the hook touch the walkway over my head. A metallic twang rang out. Sam jogged towards the sound, fog swirling around him

I'd have to time this right. My arm trembled, still raised. Instead of jabbing tourists through the grate like Freddy with his rubber claws, my plan was to go full-on Cobra Kai.

The suspense built to painful proportions as the metal grid shook above my head with every heavy step. Sam was hunting me, ready to run me through with a knife. I was hopefully one step ahead.

When he was directly over me, I reached up and swept the hook across his leg. He screamed, dropping on to the leg I'd sliced open.

I took the bloody hook and ran back the way he'd come. Splinters from the trashed door tore at my skin and snagged on my clothes.

I ran downstairs, listening out with dread. No sound of Sam or Libby. The door of the mansion was closed. Only a smear of blood marked where Officer Dupres had died. Sam must have left him outside like his other victims.

The 911 operator picked up immediately. I raced through the address and explanation, ending on the crucial point. "The killer's in the house with me – please hurry. His name is Sam Sullivan."

"Thank you for calling," he said. "The police are on their way, so I need you to get clear of the house and to a safe location."

I hung up, conscious of how much time had drained away. I wasn't leaving without Libby.

I had the bloody hook, but I needed a weapon with more oomph. The kitchen had possibilities, but instead I hit Thandie's museum. The newest item was propped up by the door – no one had found a home for it in the glass cases.

I grabbed Veronica's mallet, all kinds of emotions rearing up. We'd killed her in part for killing Della's mum, a crime she didn't commit, but she'd done plenty of other things to deserve it.

The mallet was heavy, and the wooden handle slipped as I adjusted my grip.

Clutching the weapon in both hands, I stumbled back into the hallway. Libby was at the top of the stairs, pyjamas on and hair wrapped in a towel. "Why are the lights not on yet? And what was all that noise?"

"Get downstairs! Sam's the killer – he's here!"

"What?" Libby's eyes widened as she processed what I'd said.

The split second of thought was too long.

She turned as Sam appeared, maskless and leaning heavily on the leg I'd taken a hook to. It didn't slow him down enough. He thrust the knife into her stomach so hard that it pierced the middle of her back with a burst of blood. She clawed and kicked at Sam as he yanked the knife out. His awkwardness was gone, replaced by cruelty and dead eyes. Libby slumped down at the top of the stairs.

He stepped over my sister where she'd fallen like he hadn't ripped a hole in my world. "Your time's run out – you can't escape this. I'll keep on coming."

The knife stained with Libby's blood was in his hand, and Veronica's mallet was in mine. I could smash him in the head with it. He'd never kill again after that. Never leave someone else without a sibling. Before my vision blurred too much, I swung for the wall.

The mallet's metal tip bit through the chandelier's chain and the links shattered. I felt dark satisfaction that Sam looked up and saw what was coming before the tangle of bear traps and lighting landed.

I'd watched enough horror movies to know you have to check

the killer is dead, but Sam was never coming back from that. I veered around the pieces of him, his blood soaking the carpet. I'd have to deal with what I'd done to him later. For now, I prayed that my sister was alive.

She was the toughest person I knew, because she was still breathing, hands pressed over the wound in her stomach.

"That . . . little . . . bastard," she gasped, blood bubbling between her lips. I knew what that meant. I'd seen it with Thandie at the end.

"Don't talk," I said, unravelling the wadded shirt from my arm and pressing it onto her stomach. "Just hold on – help is coming."

"Holy shit." I hadn't heard the door open, but I knew Jared's voice.

He joined us at the top of the stairs impossibly fast. Ignoring the pile of Sam bits below us, he honed in on Libby. "You're alive. I saw that dead cop outside and I thought . . ."

Jared spoke while he checked the wound under Libby's shirt, then he reapplied pressure. "I'm going to give it to you straight because we don't have time," he said, too controlled for the pain passing across his face. "If I don't give you my blood and turn you right now, you're going to die."

Chapter 55

ibby shook her head, coughing. Her own blood was choking her. "No . . . I can't be a vampire. Della . . ."

"She'll understand," I said, losing what little control I'd held onto. "Please Libs."

"No, I won't. I'd rather . . ."

She turned her head away, blood pooling at the corner of her mouth and mixing with tears.

"I won't force her," Jared said. "I never had the choice, but she does."

All three of us were crying. Jared pressed hard over her wound, and we waited. "Come on Libby. Just a bit longer," he said. Either an ambulance would come first or Libby would die. Either they'd save her, or I'd be lost too.

Libby started convulsing, and I held her fever-hot hand. Was this it – the last time I'd see my sister alive? Jared was deathly still and quiet. Perhaps he felt it too.

Grief set in as I thought about life without Libby . . . a world without her in it. Then she sat up. Jared jerked back from her, his back hitting the wall.

"I don't feel dead," she said, wiping her lips with one hand. "I was bleeding out of my mouth? Mina, you could've told me!"

"What's happening?" I asked, almost laughing through sheer hysteria.

"I don't get it," Jared murmured, still leaning against the wall. "I didn't turn you."

"I feel great," Libby said, pulling up the hem of her T-shirt. "Shit Jared, what did you do? If you turned me, I swear I'll stake us both." Her stomach was smeared in blood, but the wound was closed.

"I don't know!" Jared said. "That wasn't me."

"I think it was," I said. "When you fed from me the other day, I healed really fast. You kissed my shoulder and arm, and they're healing better than they should be. Is that your power? If so, it's . . . awesome."

Libby looked down the stairs. "I think it's too late for him."

Jared's eyebrows scrunched down low. "Holy crap . . . The first time I met Armand, he told me he saw death and healing in my future when he did that tarot reading. I thought he was talking about being a nurse. This is too much . . ."

One realisation stopped me cold. We'd need to make sure that

Saint Germain never found out what Jared could do, or he'd want to add him to his collection. The sound of sirens cut in, getting louder and louder.

"We're out of time," I said, confused and relieved and completely freaked out about what I'd done to Sam and what he'd told me about Louisa. "We need to get our stories straight."

Jared was weak after healing Libby, and he struggled to stay upright when the police questioned us in the kitchen of the mansion. The police kept Sam's remains out of sight, but they were never out of mind. When I tried to probe what I'd done, I hit emptiness. All I could focus on was what Nat would think when she found out about Sam – what he'd done and what I did to him.

Boudreaux kept the questions short. My wound had stopped bleeding, but it needed medical eyes over it. With no vampires involved except Jared, I gave it to her straight, only leaving out what Jared had done to save Libby.

Jared left, drained by his new power. Libby was standing to one side of the kitchen, not willing to let me out of sight. She was wearing a baggy T-shirt from the mansion's lost property to avoid questions about why her shirt was drenched with her blood.

"Do Sam's siblings know about . . . what he did? And what happened to him?" What I did to him.

Boudreaux was uncharacteristically silent, lacking her straightforward answers.

"Please tell me," I said. "I know they must hate me."

Boudreaux slowly turned her wedding ring, her usual composure faltering. "I'm sorry to be the one to tell you this . . . We have Nat under arrest as an accessory to murder."

"She can't have . . . She helped him?"

"We don't know everything yet," Boudreaux said, steady as ever. "She's not been particularly co-operative. But we know she was aware of her brother's actions and failed to report him."

Nat had known. How many people had died because she hadn't spoken up? I'd thought I knew Nat, but there was so much we hadn't told each other. If she was capable of protecting Sam, I hadn't known her at all.

"I'm afraid there's more. She's refusing to answer my questions until she talks to you."

That one was straight out of the horror movie handbook, but I wanted to talk to her too. I needed to see her face and work out what happened. "Fine," I said.

"Thank you. I know it'll be tough, but the case could hinge on this. Get some sleep if you can. Tomorrow, we'll record your conversation and get her to agree that everything she says will be admissible in court."

That felt like a lot of responsibility, but I agreed to it.

Libby came to hospital with me to get my arm stitched up. Jared could've tried to heal me, but we weren't sure if he could replicate what he'd done for Libby.

It was 2am by the time we got back to the mansion. I dropped straight to bed in my clothes, not needing any time to wind down before sleep pulled me under.

The next morning, a lot of crashing and stamping feet woke me. Libby had hired a range of contractors to rip out carpets and tear down doors, erasing what Sam had done to the place. It'd be impossible to come here without seeing the carnage, but I'd have to come to terms with it.

After washing the previous day off in a scorching shower and putting on fresh clothes, I packed the Dictaphone and Thandie's letters in my backpack. I had another person to confront before Nat. Della had visited Emmeline to say her piece last night, but I wanted to see her myself. I'd thought she was my friend, and I took Della to her. Della had only told me one thing about the encounter: Emmeline admitted to lying about Veronica killing her mum.

By the time I got to Fanged Friends, I was all worked up. I'd trusted Emmeline and Nat, and neither had deserved it.

Emmeline showed no remorse when I walked through the door. "Turn the open sign around." I did what she told me. "I expected you'd come at some point. Della already stopped by."

"You lied to us," I said, taking the Dictaphone out of my bag. "Thandie recorded herself confessing to murdering Della's mum."

"I did," Emmeline said coldly, "and I'd do it again. You brought me an opportunity, and I took it."

"Della's a person, not an opportunity. And she has to live with what she's done! We all do."

"Are any of you sorry that Veronica's gone?" Emmeline asked. Some kindness warmed her expression. "I'm sorry I had to lie to you. I don't think Thandie would've liked that, but she'd appreciate that John and Veronica are finally gone."

I wanted to feel straightforward anger, but it was muddled by understanding. "I know why you did it. If something happened to Libby . . ." Sam had tried to kill Libby, and I'd killed him. I'd done it to save myself, but revenge for what he did to Libby had played a part. Veronica had killed Thandie, and I'd brought Emmeline the ideal weapon to take down a vampire: a slayer.

"I don't expect for y'all to trust me again overnight, but I'm prepared to try. How 'bout we start with that jacket you love?"

Emmeline went across to the rack of very beautiful, very expensive black leather jackets that I'd admired with Nat at the start of fall break. "Here." She took one off in my size.

My arms slid into it like it was made for me. The leather was so pliable that my arms bent easily. "Thank you," I said. "You know this doesn't change anything, but I'm not going to turn it down."

"I know that won't cut it, but clothes are always a good start. I'm always here if you need me. My best friend's killer is dead, and I know I didn't achieve it by the most honourable of means. I owe you."

Chapter 56

I thought about the jacket on the walk to the police station. Wearing it made me feel like Kristy Swanson in *Buffy the Vampire Slayer* – I finally looked like one of the slayers if nothing else. I loved it, but it would always remind me of this Halloween. We'd lost so many friends. Clever, astute Tessa was gone. She'd always moved so fast and had so much going on, and all of that had been cut short. I'd miss Rosario and Taz too – the two slayers who'd given me a chance and stood up for their convictions until the end. Then there was Sam. I'd liked him and seen a lot of myself in him, but his sweet shyness had disappeared when he'd put on that mask.

I reached the police station and was glad not to dwell on Sam. As I approached the cells, it brought back memories of that frantic few days when Libby had been locked up here and we'd tried to prove her innocence. Jason had suffered the same fate recently. I felt guilty that the evidence had appeared to point at him, and we'd been too deep in grief and trouble to question it.

A young female officer searched my backpack while I walked through the metal detector. She inspected the Dictaphone and flicked through Thandie's letters, fortunately not reading them. "You're all good," she said, repacking my bag. "Go on through."

I'd expected to feel differently about Nat. Instead, I saw my friend in a prison jumpsuit, her hair flat and dull.

"I know," she said as I sat across the table. "Orange isn't my colour."

"It's not so bad," I said, reassured by the chains secured to her wrists and threaded through loops on the table. "At least they didn't make you wear the Hannibal Lecter mask." We were alone in a brightly lit white room. The table and chairs were the only furniture. A police voice recorder whirred to one side of the table, reminding me to think about what I revealed.

"Sam told me about Louisa," I said. "I'm so sorry about what happened to her."

"Sorry doesn't bring her back," she sniped, but quickly reined it in. "I've promised that detective I'll tell you what I know, but on one condition. Your sister was accused of the Fang Fest Fiend's murders, and they think Louisa was one of the victims. If you know anything about how she got dragged into it, you have to tell me."

"Fine," I said. "But you have to talk first."

She pushed her hair off her face. Despite the lack of her usual pristine make-up and killer wardrobe, she carried herself with her usual confidence. "Whatever. I'm not sure how much Sam told you about Louisa, but she was . . ." She took in a long breath and let it out slowly. "She was stabbed a lot of times, and the police said the Fang Fest Fiend did it. I couldn't sleep not knowing what had happened. After the killer supposedly split, the police stopped looking. So I went through her stuff. She'd written diaries about calling herself Elvira and going to this place where people bit each other and let people bite them – The Underground. I tried to go there to snoop around, but they wouldn't let me in – some bullshit about needing to be screened. Then I found her client log. She listed five people she saw the night she died – including you. And she wrote something cryptic on the page: 'I said something I shouldn't have. It's going to end badly – I know it.' That was the last thing she wrote."

Nat flexed her hands against the chains, her eyes filling with tears. "So I decided to start with the client names she wrote down. The police thought it wasn't worth pursuing, and I gave up too. But I got tired of doing nothing, so a couple weeks back I started looking up addresses and sending notes. I figured if I dropped off a note to each person and watched to see how they reacted, I might narrow it down to someone who knew what happened to my sister. I sent you two because I didn't get to see your reaction to the first one. I saw you through the window after the second, and it seemed like maybe you knew something. But I was never going to hurt you or Louisa's other clients – I swear. I wanted the truth, but then Sam found the diaries. And he wanted everyone involved to suffer, especially your friend Tessa, for taking over from Louisa."

"I was with Jared and Della at The Underground the night we spoke to Louisa, and they didn't get notes."

"You were? There was only space for one name per visit – I guess Louisa picked yours." That was probably because she only fed on one client at a time, though I kept that to myself. "Your address wasn't in the book and I couldn't track it down, so I thought your name was a dead end. Then you walked into class, and I struck up a conversation with you. It was easy."

"I get why you sent the notes," I said. "If something happened to Libby, I wouldn't stop until I found out everything."

"I'm sure you wouldn't," she said harshly. "Is it my turn yet?"

I thought over what Boudreaux would want to know, dreading telling Nat my part of the story. "So Sam killed all of those people? Not you?"

"Yeah, that was all him. Your taste in friends doesn't suck quite that badly." She allowed herself a small smile. I wished we could go back to a time before Nat set off down this path. "Sam found out what I was doing and said he wanted to help. The notes weren't working, and I thought he was just going to make people talk. I didn't figure it out until the people in Louisa's book were dying and he burned down The Underground. How did he put it? He wanted to see that disgusting place go up in smoke."

"So why didn't you tell someone?" I asked, stunned by the number of lives Sam had ruined: the people who'd died, their families, the vampires who had nowhere to feed . . .

"Louisa's gone. My mom's falling apart, and I didn't want my brother to get locked up," she said.

"Did you know he was coming after us?" I asked.

She hesitated. "Your name was last on the list, and I was hoping he'd find out why she died and stop before he got to you."

That wasn't a good answer. "Did Will know?"

"No! I swear. He had nothing to do with it. He didn't have the same bond that Sam and I shared with Louisa."

It was a small consolation that Will wasn't in on this. "And you know I killed Sam."

Her features twisted, transformed by hatred. "They told me."

"Is there anything else?" I asked, knowing it might be the last time I'd see her.

"I really was your friend," she said. "I liked you. In the end, I didn't want you to be the person Louisa talked to – the one she'd thought would get her killed. But you're the only one left so I'm hoping you have the answers."

The police tape recorder had captured everything Nat had known, and my friends had been through too much for me to drag them into another police investigation. There might already have been too much about me on there.

I could've lied to Nat and said I knew nothing, but I understood how the pursuit of truth could eat away at you. I reached over and paused the recorder. "Why didn't you ask me?" I said, speaking freely now my words were no longer being captured.

Nat laughed bitterly. "Like you would've told me. Any time I got close to bringing it up, you shut me down. When I dropped off your Dictaphone, I convinced Sam to give me one last try to get you to talk. But since you basically threw me out, he said he'd deal with you. That was enough for him to assume you were guilty."

I'd shut Nat down to protect her, and she'd left me to Sam. I told her what happened that night at Empire without any mention of vampires: how John Carter had taken us down to his cells and we'd found Elvira's body. That he blamed us for her death because we talked to her when we visited The Underground. "Someone called Veronica stabbed your sister for John Carter," I said at the end, "and she and John are dead now."

Nat's face had paled as I talked. "Sam was supposed to talk to you before . . . what he did – to make sure you were the one who talked to Louisa. Now I know my hunch was right and you got her killed, I'm glad he did it. I just wish you'd died and not him."

I had some responsibility for Louisa's death, and I'd had to live with it, but John didn't have to set Veronica on her. And Sam didn't need to murder innocent people over it. "Look, we both made massive mistakes and people got hurt, but neither of us killed anyone."

"That's not technically true," Nat said.

Chapter 57

The shock of what she'd said took a moment to sink in. "Who . . .?" I trailed off, eyeing the recorder that I'd paused to confess my involvement.

Nat followed my gaze. "So far, the recording only has me saying I should've ratted out my brother, and I'm good with going to court for that. The jury will eat up my grief – I might not even serve any time. If you press record, I'll stop talkin', and you'll never know what I did. What's it gonna be?"

Nat looked the same as she always had, apart from the prison uniform. No veil of evil had come over her. She knew me too well. I couldn't walk out of here until I knew what she'd done . . .

who she'd killed. "Tell me," I said.

"Sam was stuck in hospital after getting attacked by that vampire wannabe, so I had to kill Tessa. I didn't want to, but he talked me into it. I knew too much – he could turn on me as easily as I could go to the police. The first stab in her sleep did the trick, and the remaining eight got easier with each strike."

She sat back in her chair, smirking. Of course she was happy – she'd won. There was no record of this conversation. If I told anyone, it'd be my word against hers.

"We're done here," Nat said, waggling her fingers at me in a final wave.

I felt like I was outside my body as I left the room. Nat had only befriended me to sniff out whether I knew something about Louisa's death. She'd murdered Tessa and was going to get away with it. I'd paused the police tape at the crucial moment to protect my own secrets.

I waited outside Boudreaux's office for a while, and finally she took me inside. The room was as neat and organised as she was. Filing cabinets ran down one side and her desk was almost empty apart from a framed photograph and a mug. The wall was covered in certificates.

I wanted to tell Boudreaux about Nat's confession, but I was thinking through a haze. How was I supposed to explain turning off the tape? How would I convince Boudreaux to believe me? "What sort of sentence will Nat get?" I asked.

"I've listened to the tape. Obstructing justice is a crime, and we'll add further charges as needed." She paused, frowning. "What's that noise?"

I heard it too: clicking coming from my backpack. For an awful moment, I thought Nat might have put an explosive in there as I pulled it to the front of my body.

I unfastened the zip, and the Dictaphone was sitting there where the officer had placed it after searching my backpack. And the record button was stuck down.

"Part of our conversation didn't get recorded on the police tape, but the rest is hopefully on this one," I said, fully aware of what was riding on this as I hit rewind.

Boudreaux frowned down at the whirring Dictaphone. "I was going to ask you why our recorder stopped," she said.

"I'm hoping this will explain everything," I said.

I knew how much was riding on this as I pressed play. Instead of Thandie's rasping voice, Nat's voice came out. I'd got the whole thing. We listened to everything, eyes fixed on the Dictaphone, until the crucial moment: " . . . I had to kill Tessa. I didn't want to, but he talked me into it."

It took three attempts for me to get the stop button to work once we'd heard the rest of Nat's speech. "I don't know how you got her to confess that," Boudreaux said eventually, "but I need to get this tape to our tech expert to make a duplicate in case the Dictaphone malfunctions again."

"Good luck," I said. While I waited, my attention strayed to Boudreaux's Garfield mug. His grumpy face made me smile – Libby had always been a fan of the Monday-hating orange cat. I moved it to get a better look and accidentally knocked over the photograph. I picked it up and took a proper look. The picture was of Boudreaux and another woman I recognised: Monique. What was Boudreaux doing with one of the previous leaders of the slayers?

Boudreaux had snuck back in, and I almost dropped the picture. I set it back on the desk as she went to sit opposite me.

"She was my older sister. I usually keep the picture in my drawer – sometimes I have people in here that I don't wanna know about my personal life. It doesn't make much difference now . . . She passed yesterday." Boudreaux paused, composing herself with a deep breath. "I shouldn't be in today, but with Cafferty out I had no choice." He and Armand would be in New Mexico by now. I shuddered at the thought of what Saint Germain would have them doing.

"I'm so sorry for your loss. I knew her a little."

Boudreaux leaned back in her chair, smiling sadly. "Thank you. Does that mean you're one of them? That explains why you're always getting into trouble."

"You know?" I asked, filling in the gaps. She must have been the detective Monique had mentioned who knew about vampires.

"I do. Mostly the slayers and I stay out of each other's way. They have their role, and I have mine."

"Cafferty knows now, so it isn't all on you," I said.

Boudreaux smiled. "He was bound to figure it out some time. He's way too smart and inquisitive not to – kinda like you."

"Thanks," I said. "And just so you know . . ." I began, hoping that a small piece of Monique's story would be helpful. "Monique died a hero."

"I guessed as much," Boudreaux said, her full smile reminding me of Monique. "I really should go and talk to Nat. Stay safe now, Mina."

"You too."

I walked out of the station, relieved that I hadn't ruined the police's case against Nat. She was going to be held accountable for her crimes, so if there was anything on the tape that I was going to be questioned about, I'd deal with the consequences.

I was ready to curl up on the sofa of the mansion, done with my confrontations for the day, when I found Will smoking on the front step.

Chapter 58

There was a deep line between his eyes as he pulled on the cigarette, blowing the last plume of smoke away as he stubbed it out. His black jacket was absent, and he was wearing a black Meatloaf 'Bat out of Hell' tour T-shirt.

Will eased himself onto his feet. His eyes were bloodshot, and he couldn't look at me. "I can't believe . . ." he began. "Mina – I'm so sorry for what they did to you. I understand if y'all never want to see me again."

"It's not your fault!" I said. "You're not responsible for their actions."

He nodded gravely, touching his mouth with two fingers. He

seemed to be regretting putting out that cigarette. "I'm still sorry. I should've put it together. My stepmom's not doing too good, so I'm transferring colleges to stay with her. But I'll keep my distance from you if that's what you want."

He started to walk away. "Wait!" I called. His expression was cautious when he turned back.

"There's a stack of John Hughes films inside that are just begging to be watched. Are you in?"

I doubted he'd want to enter the place where his brother died . . . where I killed him. "As long as we can watch them in chronological order."

"You're such a movie geek."

Will looked so tired and broken that I opened my arms to offer a hug. He stepped into them, but stood there stiffly until his arms eased around me. He held on tight, his face buried in the crook of my neck. Soon, he disentangled himself. "Thanks."

Neither of us said anything about Sam as we jogged up the stairs, the new grey carpet erasing every trace of what had happened to him beyond what we conjured up in our minds. The absence of the bear-trap chandelier left my chest aching with remorse. Was there anything I could've done that would have left Sam alive, serving time in prison?

We put *Sixteen Candles* on and sank down low on the sofa. "You kinda look like Jake Ryan . . . the guy who plays Molly Ringwald's love interest," I said to him.

"Nah," he replied. "He's got way better hair."

We were halfway through the movie when Libby and Della came home. Libby paused in the doorway to the living room so Della bumped into her. "Hi," Libby said, hesitating. Finally her brain kicked into gear. "Mina, did you not offer him snacks?"

She whipped out of the room, soon returning with huge bags of crisps. "Scoot over, you two," Libby said.

I ended up sandwiched between Will and Libby. We ordered a pizza at the end of *Sixteen Candles*, and he stayed for the whole of *The Breakfast Club*.

Libby crawled over to turn off the video. "You know, you kinda look like that fist-pump guy at the end."

"Judd Nelson – another Molly Ringwald love interest," Will said, arching his eyebrows. "Did you put her up to that?"

"No, I swear!" I said. "You're obviously a John Hughes lead. Don't fight it."

"On that note, I should get going," Will said.

"I'll walk you out."

We hovered in the hallway by the open door. The evening had turned chilly, but Will stayed put. "I talked to Jason before coming here," he said.

"How is he?" I asked.

"He's taking the whole murder accusation thing in his stride," he said.

"He really is a nice guy. The police had that one wrong." And so did we. They'd figured out the connection to Elvira and her list of clients, but they'd linked the murders to the wrong Elvira.

"Hey guys." Jared was standing in the open doorway.

"Hey," Will said, weaving around him. "Thanks for today."

As Will walked down the street, he looked over his shoulder with a grin and did a Judd-Nelson style fist pump in the air.

"Looks like I missed a new in-joke." Jared wrapped his arms around me. "How are you doin'?"

"I'll get there," I said. "You still don't look right after healing Libby."

We walked back upstairs, and Jared was obviously using his last reserves of will power to keep going.

Della and Libby had put *Weird Science* on, but Jared made no move to join them. "Do you mind if I . . .?" He mimed biting his wrist.

Della slid off the sofa. "Let me. You shouldn't have to lose more blood."

Jared followed her into my room, looking astounded but not questioning it. Before the door closed, Della said, "Don't get carried away. This is a one-time deal for saving my girl."

Libby snuggled down to watch the movie, but I saw the significance in what Della had done. She'd finally accepted what Jared was.

Della's wrist was covered with a huge plaster when they came back. She and Jared sat on opposite ends of the sofa, sisters in the middle. "Let me get this straight, since I've missed all the action – not that I'm complaining," Libby said, counting the names off on her fingers. "Sam and Nat are way evil . . . Well, he *was*. Emmeline conned you guys to go after Veronica, but she was guilty of a million other things anyway. The vampire boss guy thought Veronica was investigating the surge for him, but she was actually responsible for it because she wanted to be the new vampire boss. Did I get it all? Is anyone we know not a master manipulator?"

"I think that's all of it," Jared said. "Will seems like a decent guy, but let's not make any more new friends."

Jared went home to clear his apartment, so I ended up sleeping alone. We'd decided to all move into the mansion, although Della would go back and forth to her apartment when her dad needed her. Jared was going to move into the attic, despite the grisly murder that had previously happened there. It was pointless to pay two lots of rent when Libby owned a home.

The next morning, I woke alone and shattered. One decent night's sleep wasn't enough to recuperate after what we'd been through.

A pile of post was on the mat in the hallway, and I carried it through to the kitchen. A New Mexico postcard stood out amidst the bills and flyers. Cartoon aliens and flying saucers were dotted all over a desert background.

Heavy footsteps stomped down the stairs. "Libby?" I yelled. "Who do we know in New Mexico?"

She came into the kitchen with her hands over her ears. "You could've waited until I got into the room. Dad's parents lived on a ranch near Roswell, I think. Why?" Cafferty and Armand were somewhere in New Mexico. So far, it'd been radio silence from them, but sending a cheesy postcard wasn't their style. The grandparents we'd never met also seemed unlikely to reach out. I turned the card over, recognising the scrawl. Mum's handwriting was as chaotic as she was . . .

Hey girls,

I've found your dad and figured out how to make us one big, happy family again.

Come to visit us?

Mum x

Acknowledgements

always wanted Mina and the Undead to be the start of a series, and I'm so grateful that I've been able to keep telling this story. I wouldn't have been able to write this book without the support of so many people.

To the hardworking staff at UCLan, who have continued to believe in my books and offered so much support, especially Hazel Holmes, Charlotte Rothwell and Graeme Williams. Thank you to Lauren James for helping me to whip my manuscript into shape.

To Becky Chilcott and Fred Gambino for creating a distinctive, striking cover that captures exactly what I saw in my head.

To my agent Sandra Sawicka for tirelessly supporting me and my books.

To the booksellers and members of the online book community who championed *Mina and the Undead*, getting it on shelves and in readers' hands. Special thanks to Jodie from Vanilla Moon for all the support during lockdown and since then.

To former detective David Quinn for explaining 90s US police procedure and work experience, so Mina's time with the police could be as realistic as possible.

To Hannah Kates – I don't even know where to start. You've helped me to bring New Orleans to life and to avoid missteps when writing about America. You've given feedback that has shaped Mina's story and made it so much better. Your stories about police ride alongs were amazing and terrifying in equal measure. I'm eternally grateful to Write Mentor for bringing us together – I just wish we lived on the same continent!

To Chelly Pike for answering my questions about New Orleans and for sharing her stories and photographs with me.

To Rachel Faturoti for giving such a thorough sensitivity read and for sharing the writing journey with me.

To Chelley Toy for her endless support, enthusiasm and friendship. I'm so glad we got talking about Point Horrors online and became friends in real life!

To Mia Kuzniar for being there to share the ups and downs of publishing and life with me. I'm very grateful that we found each other!

To Laura Poole and Jezebel Mansell for lending your keen eyes to give my book a very thorough check.

For Team Mina, who have shared the journey of these books with me and helped to get my book out there. I wouldn't have been able to write book two without you: Lauren Holder, Amanda Garrison, Claire Eastaugh, Kirsty Stanley, Kate Lovatt, Nicola Chard, Chantelle at Oh, the Stories, Emma Finlayson-Palmer, Noelle Kelly-Trindles, Lucinda Tomlinson, Lauren Watkins, Laura Jackson, Emma Perry, Chelley Toy, Lucas Maxwell, Andrew Hall, Rachael Mills, Emily Weston, Sabrina Accalai, Chantelle

Hazelden, Camp YA, Kelly at FromBelgiumWithBookLove, Cora Linn, Erika Davies-Budgen, Amber Griffiths, Carla Pérez Fernández, India McLeod Kay, Rosie Talbot, Harpies in the Trees, Violet Prynne, Rick Martin, Sam Ackerman, Bianca Smith, Brittany Roos, Amy Macdonald, Cherry Whittaker, Magdalena Morris, Lisa Chandler, Jess Law, Lauren Rachel Berman, Steffi Shott, Meg Malloy, Timothy Jenkins, Erin Talamantes, Ellie Clark, Vicky Martin, Ahlissa Eichhorn, Amy Rehbein, Kirstie Myers, Tasmin Keats Lewis

For the Good Ship, Swaggers and Fem 2.0 groups – you make me smile every day, and it's so good to know you're there in the DMs!

To my parents, brothers and sisters in law for your constant support and excitement about my books.

To my husband Kev for being a sounding board, tech support and all around amazing partner and dad.

To Nathan for being patient while Mummy is writing. I can't wait to read your stories one day!

Finally, thank you to the readers of *Mina and the Undead*. I wasn't sure if anyone but me would get my quirky 90s story, but it's been amazing to see all of the love and support for Mina in real life and online. I appreciate everyone who is following me on this journey, and I can't wait for you to read what I write next!

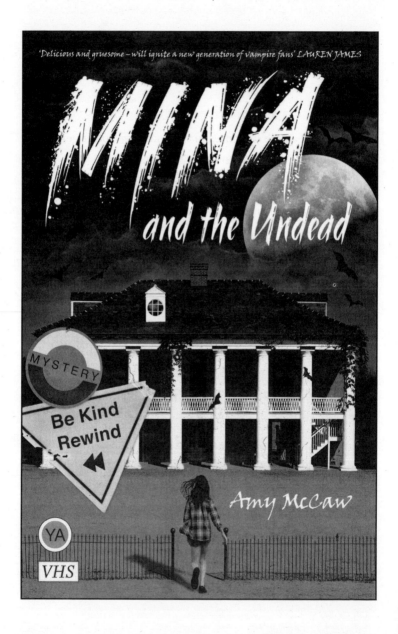

'A fun romp through nineties pop culture – vampires, *Buffy*, *The Crow* . . . need I say more?'
DAWN KURTAGICH

'90s + vamps + New Orleans, *Mina and the Undead* ticks off all the fun boxes in the Southern Gothic genre.'
GOLDY MOLDAVSKY

'A book of blood-thirsty fun, from the New Orleans setting to the strong *Buffy* vibes. Amy McCaw brings vampires back from the dead in style. I loved it!'
KATHRYN FOXFIELD

'Smouldering vampires, a New Orleans setting and a generous dash of bloodshed. A fun YA horror read!'
ALEX BELL

'A gorgeously rich setting, coupled with a fast-paced plot and characters to root for! I loved every page.'
NAOMI GIBSON

'The spooky, pulpy 90s book of my dreams.'
LORIEN LAWRENCE

HAVE YOU EVER WONDERED HOW BOOKS ARE MADE?

UCLan Publishing is an award winning independent publisher specialising in Children's and Young Adult books. Based at The University of Central Lancashire, this Preston-based publisher teaches MA Publishing students how to become industry professionals using the content and resources from its business; students are included at every stage of the publishing process and credited for the work that they contribute.

The business doesn't just help publishing students though. UCLan Publishing has supported the employability and real-life work skills for the University's Illustration, Acting, Translation, Animation, Photography, Film & TV students and many more. This is the beauty of books and stories; they fuel many other creative industries! The MA Publishing students are able to get involved from day one with the business and they acquire a behind the scenes experience of what it is like to work for a such a reputable independent.

The MA course was awarded a Times Higher Award (2018) for Innovation in the Arts and the business, UCLan Publishing, was awarded Best Newcomer at the Independent Publishing Guild (2019) for the ethos of teaching publishing using a commercial publishing house. As the business continues to grow, so too does the student experience upon entering this dynamic Masters course.

www.uclanpublishing.com
www.uclanpublishing.com/courses/
uclanpublishing@uclan.ac.uk